To

Kay

Congratulations ...

DIRTY LITTLE SECRETS

by

Antonia K. Lewis

... and enjoy !

Antonia K. Lewis

Southport - 1995

She knew this wasn't real life – knocking back champagne that probably cost more than her weekly wage, rolling around in a king-size bed between three hundred thread count Egyptian cotton sheets and watching the sun rise as the waves lapped against the shore. But for a few hours at least, she tried to pretend it was. It truly was bliss, but she knew in her heart that even if all the ancillaries were stripped away and she was left in an empty room with only Ritchie by her side, she would still be deliriously happy. He could promise her the earth, but all she would ever want was him – just him, and no more.

PART ONE

FAN

(1987)

Chapter 1

Kim was barely thirteen years old when Ritchie Joe Clarke entered her life and changed it forever.

A well-behaved and smiley child, she loved to gossip and giggle with her best friend Nicky and together they danced around Kim's tiny pink bedroom to the strains of the latest chart tunes on the radio.

She was also an avid viewer of Top of the Pops and envied each and every performer who clearly led a far more glamorous and interesting life than her own in the pretty - but dull - northern village of Tupperton, located less than an hour from the shopping mecca that is Manchester City Centre.

Occasionally, she or Nicky took a fancy to one of the popstars who graced the screen.

But Ritchie Joe Clark was something else.

He wasn't a solo performer, but one fifth of an awesome band. There were two handsome guys on guitars, another looker on the keyboards and an enthusiastic drummer peeping out from behind his kit at the rear of the stage. All good-looking, youthful and bursting with accumulated energy.

But this beautiful, bold boy with his shiny, jet black hair, sweeping over the most dazzling pair of emerald green eyes – this angel catapulted from heaven for the pleasure of every female in the land (and possibly a significant percentage of the male population too) was the magnificent lead singer - the frontman who demanded that you look only at him, forbidding you from averting your eyes for even one nanosecond. Not that Kim would ever want to.

She had only waved goodbye to her twelfth year three months previously, closely followed by the painful and frankly terrifying arrival of energy-zapping periods - bluntly announcing that she was now on her way to becoming a fully-fledged woman of the world. And now this.

As she gazed at Ritchie Joe Clark miming to an upbeat pop-rock number, his words warning of the danger of playing with fire, while his bandmates strummed and bashed and plonked along for all they were worth, Kim experienced a strange fluttering from the farthest point within her; an unusual sensation that resonated somewhere deep inside the pit of her

4

stomach and travelled on, further south, to a part of her she never knew could tingle in such a manner.

She had yet to recognise these unfamiliar sensations as disgustingly delicious spears of red-hot lust.

The band finished on a high with a yelp, a pout and a flick of the hair from the main man whilst the manic, mad-haired drummer launched his sticks into the air and Kim strained above the audience noise to hear the middle-aged, balding presenter say, 'And that, boys and girls, was a brand new up-and-coming band from the back streets of Birmingham who, I predict, are going to do very well for themselves indeed. Let's hear it once more for *Show Me Yours*! Great performance guys. Thanks very much.'

Show Me Yours. Slightly unusual and suggestive name choice but one she would be watching out for. And that *boy* - the singer. He was HOT. Kim couldn't wait to catch up with Nicky to find out if she'd been watching and drooling too. Maybe they could purchase that record from Terry's Top Tunes on Saturday instead of splashing out on crappy fruit-shaped erasers, miniature gonk pencil-toppers and their standard raspberry, brain-freezing slush puppies. Kim decided she would pinch one of her dad's blank videos to record any further television appearances so she and Nicky could replay the tape each day after school, until they knew every last song lyric and piece of choreography off by heart.

For once in her life, Kim was happy to head upstairs for an early night. She longed to hibernate and be snug and warm underneath her ancient Strawberry Shortcake duvet, dreaming about that band and the boy at the forefront of it (because he was surely only a few years older than herself and therefore still more boy than man) whilst cuddling up to her favourite knackered old teddy and wishing it was HIM she was kissing instead.

5

Chapter 2

'You'll wear that tape out,' Kim's mum repeated, for about the billionth time as she hoovered around her daughter and best friend, humming along to the latest cracker by *Show Me Yours*.

'He's a bit of alright, that Ritchie, with those piercing green eyes and that sexy wiggle...isn't he Nicky love?'

'He's *gorgeous*, Mrs Summers! I've pinned his poster on my wall, right above my bed, so he's the last thing I see before I fall asleep at night and the first thing I clap eyes on when I wake up in the morning.'

In the twelve months since *Show Me Yours* had first captured their attention, the girls had become rather obsessed. The band were again hovering right outside of the Top 40 with their latest number – *Dance Like Your Dad* - but their star was definitely on the rise and they were in all of the teen mags, baring their chests and looking mean, moody and macho for the camera lens. Shaking off the last vestiges of boyhood, all five of them were maturing into the most handsome of men in the glare of the public eye.

Kim and Nicky were, of course, completely clued up on all band members. From basic details such as full names and dates of birth to family, pets and places of education, like sponges they had absorbed any information they could glean from any source they could lay their hands on.

Richie Joe Clarke: Lead singer. Aged 22. Sex on Legs. Black hair, green eyes. Likes: clubbing and lager. Dislikes: idiots and cruelty to animals.

Todd Hargreaves: Guitarist. Aged 19 - but had the baby-face of a school boy. Golden, tufty hair and tawny eyes. Likes: his family and friends. Dislikes: sarcastic people and beefburgers.

Marty Johnson: Bass guitar. Aged 26 – the oldest of the band. Black with a tidy afro and huge chocolate button eyes. Likes: jamming with his mates, sleeping and his mum's cooking. Dislikes: fake friends and liars.

Ady Wheeler: Keyboards. Aged 22. Strawberry blond hair (short back and sides) with the darkest of blue eyes. Likes: playing tennis and strong tea. Dislikes: judgemental people and football.

Bren O'Sullivan: Drums. Aged 23, although he could easily pass for 30. Fudge-brown, wavy hair with blond highlights and mad, glaring blue eyes. Likes: pulling all-nighters, eating pizza and watching the sun rise. Dislikes: boring people and know-it-alls.

The girls were delighted to hear that all the band members were apparently single - no wives, live-in lovers, fiancés, kids - not even one gorgeous girlfriend between them. All apparently concentrating on their promising futures within the music industry rather than shackling themselves to commitment and family responsibilities.

They'd purchased all three singles and were waiting in anticipation for the release of the debut album – imaginatively entitled *Show Me Yours!* - due out at the end of November, cannily timed for Christmas. The band was also scheduled to embark upon a mini promotion tour, appearing in nightclubs and small venues across the country. Kim and Nicky were gutted that they wouldn't be able to attend. Sometimes life was so unfair!

Show Me Yours still hadn't achieved the bucket-loads of success they deserved, but Kim knew without a shadow of a doubt that worldwide fame and chart-topping hits were merely parked up around the corner. Their first three singles had done well, but not well enough. Each member of the band was driven and hungry and ready to take on the world. It was rumoured that post-Christmas they were to take a short break to allow for a change in record labels, the new deal affording the boys the freedom to pen the majority of their own material, rather than churning out songs forced upon them and deemed to be suitable tracks for their target audience.

When they'd appeared on a favourite Saturday morning kids' entertainment show, Kim had repeatedly dialled the number floating across the screen in an attempt to speak to the guys, but to no avail. Oh my...Ritchie looked so beautiful on there in his stonewashed denim jeans and matching Wrangler jacket (he'd clearly forgotten to put on a shirt underneath as he was completely bare-chested again). Spectacularly cheeky and witty, he had the female presenter eating out of his hand. She was embarrassingly giggly and playful, casually stroking his arm and complimenting him on his striking good looks. Kim desperately wanted to punch her in the face.

To make matters worse, presenter-girl was undeniably stunning with her mane of russet curls and kohl-rimmed huge hazel eyes and, of course, the obligatory model-like figure.

'How dare she maul My Ritchie!' Kim glared.

She wasn't naive enough to believe that he would ever really be Her Ritchie or even give her a second glance, but still.

For her fourteenth birthday she had been allowed to have her ears pierced and also received a fine-looking black leather jacket from her parents, but she was still hardly up there with the likes of Christie Brinkley. Although she had finally started to develop a figure, it wasn't exactly the one she'd been hoping for. Hips far too wide, thighs far too chunky and boobs that seemed to be self-inflating every day. Nicky declared this to be a bonus, claiming boys liked them big and bouncy, but they were two cup sizes bigger than all the other girls in their class and Kim didn't particularly like the way they bobbed about whenever she ran, even when they were uncomfortably squashed into an unflattering sports bra. Measuring a mere five foot two inches, she feared her she was almost as wide as she was tall and her top heavy figure surely meant she was in grave danger of toppling over at any moment in time.

She cursed the fact that she hadn't been born blonde and consequently often wore her chestnut brown, bum-length locks scraped back into a minimum fuss ponytail or French plait. She hated much about her appearance including her almond eyes that were also 'boring old brown', but at least her lashes were naturally long, meaning mascara was always surplus to requirements.

Her mum still accompanied her on shopping trips but Kim had become more fashion aware and image conscious. Out went the scruffy jeans and baggy t-shirts of the pre-teen era, and in came the tight trousers and off-the-shoulder tops, even though they made her boobs look humungous and the whole get-up did nothing to disguise the sheer enormity of her wobbly thighs and airbag arse.

Nicky insisted that Kim was the far more attractive one of the two of them, although Kim begged to differ as she adored Nicky's naturally curly fair hair and stunning, perfectly oval eyes which were an unusual shade of turquoise with amber flecks. Kim thought they made Nicky look far more alluring and exotic but her friend despised them of course, almost as much as she despised the curls, which she'd had lobbed short, boyishly, in defiance. She also moaned and groaned about her acne and weight because she was an inch shorter than Kim, hated any kind of sporting activity and had a penchant for chips. Nicky's mum tutted that it was nothing a well-balanced diet and regular exercise wouldn't sort out.

At least Nicky stood out from the crowd, whereas Kim feared that *she* merely blended in with her bland looks and dull-as-dirty-dishwater personality. If – no, WHEN - they ever met the God who was Ritchie Joe Clarke, it would be Nicky Taylor he remembered, not Kimberley Helen Summers – Little Miss Average from Averageville.

'Please god, let me unexpectedly blossom,' Kim silently begged in the dead of night. 'Please let my personality catch up with my boobs and my spots miraculously vanish overnight. I need to mature into a confident, attractive woman sooner rather than later or else I'm doomed.'

Because as things stood, she reckoned no sane boy or man would ever look at her twice, and especially not the likes of Ritchie Clarke, who could take his pick from the most desirable women on the planet.

*

The album did not disappoint. Besides the relatively successful singles, it contained a variety of ballads and belters – not a filler in sight – and the girls played it non-stop, studiously learning all the lyrics and choreographing complicated dance routines in the bedroom Nicky shared with her younger sister, Darcy.

Show Me Yours had smashed the mini-tour and their fan base was expanding daily. As a special treat for a passable school report, Kim's mum and dad had enrolled her in the fan club and she was the proud owner of a keyring, badge and, most precious of all, a signed photograph of the band!

AN ACTUAL SIGNED PHOTOGRAPH that Ritchie had autographed with his own fair hand. He'd breathed on it, looked at it, his beautiful fingers had touched this glossy image...and now it was in her possession. She gently kissed the photograph, taking care not to damage it in any way, as her older brother, Freddie, shook his head and muttered that she seriously needed to get a life.

After a short hiatus during which the band secured a more lucrative record deal and changed management, they exploded back on to the scene with a mighty fine tune that was to become a massive summer anthem – *Kissing in the Bay.* It quickly shot up to number 3 in the charts, meaning they had finally hit the big time and Kim was ecstatic! Unfortunately Nicky was now officially in love with Jason Donovan instead but almost all of the girls in their year were crushing hard on Ritchie - except those drawn to the daft-as-a-brush drummer Bren, who looked wild and angry now his hair was gelled into short, sharp spikes – but hey, everyone loves a bad boy.

9

The video to *Kissing in the Bay* showcased a far more mature Ritchie cavorting in the surf alongside a skinny girl in a fraying bikini and Kim almost lost her head, until she reminded herself that they were only acting - this wasn't real. And he *did* look hot to trot on that beach, dressed in only a pair of cut-off denim shorts, his tanned and toned body glistening in the Mediterranean sun, his tousled hair slicked back with sea water from his handsome, kissable face.

By the end of the summer the single had slid into the number 1 spot, easily beating off other stiff competition and huge new releases. The band celebrated with the party of all parties at the record company HQ in London and Kim celebrated by purchasing both the twelve inch single and the picture disc.

The publicity was endless and life was sweet for their fans. Kim's bedroom walls were plastered with their pictures and posters, Richie naturally taking pride of place, firmly sellotaped to the side of the wardrobe so he was directly facing her when she slipped under her duvet at night and fantasised about another life where, despite the eight year age gap, her idol would fall head over heels in love with her and they would never, ever be parted again.

Her fixation with *Show Me Yours* was threatening to take over her whole life, although she still saw her best friend whenever possible. Holidaying in Devon with Nicky and her family, they divided their time between beaches, amusement arcades and the rough-and-ready campsite disco, where they met two cute boys of their own age and they all hung around together for the duration of their stay. Nicky had already kissed numerous lads at school discos, but with the exception of an unpleasant, sloppy snog with a berk named Lewis, Kim had bugger-all experience, hormones were rampant and she was eager to indulge in some much-needed necking practice for when she encountered a real man.

Jonathan was quiet, nervous and equally inexperienced, but by the end of the fortnight they'd really quite got the hang of it, sloping off for a grope and a saliva swapping session behind the sand dunes at every available opportunity. He was dark haired, slim, and reasonably tall, and consequently when she closed her eyes she could almost imagine she was in Ritchie's arms instead – that it was Mr Clarke's sensuous, full mouth covering her own and fast-tracking her to heaven.

It was a wonderful break from the norm for the girls who returned home tanned and full of slightly embellished tales to relay to their classmates, despite genuine sadness at kissing goodbye to their holiday flings. They'd all cried like babies and promised faithfully to write to each other. Nicky and Marcus never did, but Jonathan and Kim put pen to paper for a few months afterwards, until it all eventually petered out and their short-lived romance became a distant fond memory, stored in the recesses of her mind.

Responding to a magazine request for *Show Me Yours* pen pals, Kim began corresponding with a Scottish fan, Sally-Anne Benton, who was also fifteen, funny and obsessed with Ritchie. Both girls were equally determined to procure tickets for at least one of the planned Christmas gigs – although Kim wondered how on earth she would persuade her mum and dad that it would be safe for her to go 'gallivanting down to that London', embarking on an adventure with a girl they hadn't even met.

'Muuuuuum...you know how *Show Me Yours* are playing those gigs before Christmas and each and every fan would practically sell their soul to the devil to be there...well...tickets are due to go on sale next week and...'

'No way, Kimberley. I'll stop you right there. You're fifteen years old and you are NOT going gallivanting down to that London on your own. And don't expect one of us to be chauffeuring you there either! Have you even the slightest idea of the cost involved? At Christmas too, when I haven't the time to clip my bloody toenails, let alone escort you to an overpriced gig where we would probably end up seated up in the gods!'

It was hardly a positive response.

'But mum...this Glaswegian girl I've been writing to...well, her mum has definitely said she's allowed to go, so we could travel down together and share a hotel room to cut costs. And failing that, she's positive one of the other SMY fans will put us up at their house. I'll be home safely before you know it...'

A simple solution. Kim thought she'd presented her case well.

'Are you out of your bloody mind, Kimberley? Do you know how many rapists and murderers there are lurking in the shadows, waiting to pounce on an innocent young girl like yourself? Don't you understand the dangers that are out there? As if I'm going to let my fifteen year old daughter swan off to the bright lights and dangerous streets of our capital city to attend a bloody gig! It's not safe and it's not happening. Got that?'

Well that was a reasonable discussion. NOT.

Undeterred by the negativity of Kim's parents, the two long-distance friends pooled their ideas, hatching a clever and cunning plan.

THE PLAN

1. Sally-Anne would buy gig tickets with her birthday cash whilst train fares would be purchased with weekly pocket monies and railcards once all other arrangements were firmly in place.

2. Sal would stay with Kim for a weekend to give Kim's parents the opportunity to see for themselves what a lovely and trustworthy girl their daughter had befriended. The generous invitation would of course be reciprocated - on the weekend of the London gig. Kim would travel up to Glasgow and be reunited with Sal, then they would both board the express train headed south, for old London town. It would in fact take them back the same way Kim had just come, almost passing the village where she lived en route!

3. On arrival at their destination they would freshen up in public toilets before hotfooting it across London to store Kim's overnight bag in the car of someone named Geraldine - a fan who Sally-Anne vaguely knew.

4. They would attend the gig and – oh my lord – it would be the best night of their lives.

5. After retrieving Kim's bag from Geraldine's car, they would find an affordable hotel room or a fellow fan to take pity on them before returning to Glasgow the following day, where Kim would finally meet her friend's mum and stay overnight.

6. Kim would travel home on the Sunday afternoon and all would be well. No one would be any the wiser.

Foolproof.

Chapter 3

The lead-up to the momentous evening when the girls were due to see their heroes in the flesh was a particularly tense one and every time Kim dwelled on their subterfuge, she broke out into a cold sweat. Despite her desperation to see this magnificent band in all their glory, fibbing to her parents - as uncool and embarrassing as they were – did not sit well with her.

As Gig Day approached, she was all over the place, terrified that her intricate web of lies and 'bombproof' plot would be unpicked and blasted wide open. Cover was almost blown when Kim's mum insisted she speak to Sally-Anne's mum, prior to her daughter's 'Scottish jaunt'.

Her parents had already met Sally-Anne of course, when she'd stayed with them in Cheshire. Her fairly strait-laced mother had commented that Sal's tight, ribbed skirts were rather short for a girl of her tender age.

Kim protested that it was impossible to wear a skirt too short or too tight, even though she'd secretly cringed every time Sal bent over and exposed the cheeks of her bottom to anyone unfortunate enough to be in the vicinity. She envied the girl's confidence though – she was never short of an opinion on anything and by all accounts had tons of boys queuing up to ask her out. And whilst she was no stunner, she had tried to make the best of her appearance by dyeing her sandy bobbed hair a very yellow shade of blonde and underscoring her hazel-grey eyes with thick lines of black kohl pencil. Her fingernails were always painted vampishly crimson, no matter the colour of her outfit.

What Sally-Anne lacked in fashion sense she more than made up for in scheming and lying. She'd arranged for the two mums to converse at lunchtime – knowing full well that her own mother would be dashing around, grabbing a quick sandwich in between her two cleaning jobs. A pleasant but rushed conversation took place between the two women, whilst a clock-watching Mrs Benton had her mouth rammed with tuna mayonnaise. She assured Alison Summers that *of course* Kim was welcome to stay at their house and *of course* she would see her safely back onto that train again on Sunday. No problem.

Kim had dodged a bullet. But it had been a close call.

It appeared that her mum had forgotten all about the *Show Me Yours* gigs in the pre-Christmas panic as she hadn't even mentioned them and was frantically running around cleaning, organising and purchasing mountains of festive food, drink and gifts for every man and his dog.

Meaning she was, quite literally, all wrapped up in the Christmas chaos.

She had taken her eye off the bauble and failed to notice that Kim was wide-eyed and almost hyperventilating when she hopped on that train to Glasgow – a service that departed so early in the morning it was practically the middle of the night.

Whereas it took Kim a full hour for the palpitations and hand sweating to subside.

She'd done it! She'd actually managed to fool the gullible oldies with the assistance of sneaky sod Sally-Anne and it was game on.

Watch out Ritchie Joe Clarke, your number one fans are on their way!

*

The carriage was heaving but Kim managed to elbow her way past a pack of gobby young lads to nab a seat, where she sat bolt upright for the entire journey, not even paying a visit to the stinking toilet for fear of losing said seat or having her bag stolen.

By the time she reached Glasgow, her head was lolling as she tried to fend off the urge to snooze and it was a relief to disembark. She quickly spotted Sally-Anne impatiently waiting near the ticket barriers and the two friends leapt on each other, whooping and screaming (a little practice for later in the evening), before racing off to board the London Euston service.

Once they were comfortably installed in their seats and the West Coast Main Line's finest was easing out of the extraordinarily busy station, they could finally breathe a sigh of relief.

'Look at this!' Sally-Anne unzipped her rust-coloured canvas bag and proudly produced and unrolled a huge, crinkly piece of cream cotton material, on which she'd painted in post-box red 'SHOW ME YOURS RITCHIE AND I'LL SHOW YOU MINE!!'

'*Sally-Anne!*' Kim giggled, wondering if the old age pensioners sitting opposite even had the faintest idea who 'Ritchie' was and quite why this girl, whose mini skirt was shorter than Madonna's, had defaced one of her mother's best sheets.

'I know, I'm so talented that I may have a future career as an artist. Hey, just think, Ritchie might see it and mention it on stage and then he'll always remember me and you...and one of us will go on to marry him and the other he'll take as his mistress!'

'You're terrible, you are! I hope we have a decent view though and we're reasonably close to him. Imagine a tiny droplet of sweat leaves his beautiful face, flies through the air and lands on one of us - I'd never wash again!'

By the time they arrived at their destination, Kim had hurtled through the exhaustion barrier and was running on adrenaline. After a quick titivation session in the toilets, they tackled the mad dash across the capital by tube and went on the hunt for Geraldine who had arrived much earlier in the day, determined to meet the band, but had missed them by ten minutes and decamped to Burger King, drowning her sorrows in a gallon of Diet Coke, whilst munching her way through a cheeseburger and large fries.

Sally-Anne eventually persuaded the very odd Geraldine to up and leave, whereupon they spent the next thirty minutes searching for her car, as she'd forgotten where she'd parked it. Christ. As Kim deposited her heavy bag in the crap-filled boot of the scratched and dented blue Ford Escort she silently prayed that it wouldn't be the last time she laid eyes on it.

Arriving at the venue a full hour before the doors were even opened to the public, even in sub-zero temperatures Kim found it heart-warming indeed to see a veritable army of fans milling around and they soon found themselves in conversation with three attractive Irish girls who were even louder than Sally-Anne, along with two extremely camp lads from Germany who had flown over purely for the gigs.

Kim hoped they'd catch a glimpse of their idols, but the fans were only rewarded with members of the crew zipping in and out of the stage door, although on one occasion a big beefy guy brought back sweets for Bren, which sent a ripple of excitement through the crowd. Callie, an attractive twenty year old with legs up to her armpits, insisted she'd spotted Ady's face peering out of an upper window. Everyone began screaming and chanting his name, hopefully reminding all of the band that there was a mass of teenagers camped outside on a bitterly cold evening, gloveless hands turning blue, runny noses glowing like beacons.

When the theatre doors finally opened, the crowds flooded into the warmth but Sally-Anne had another sneaky plan up her batwing sleeve.

'If we hang back we may catch one of the band nipping out for a crafty fag while the fans are heading in...you never know.'

Sadly, the band remained hidden inside, although Kim and Sally-Anne did manage to say hello to the tour manager, Barry - a short, stout, no-nonsense guy dressed very badly in a black, silky bomber jacket and skin-tight, slate-grey jeans. He was a tad brisk but assured everyone he would pass on any messages to the band. A likely story.

Eventually Kim and Sally-Anne surrendered their posts by the stage door before hypothermia set in and made their way into the crowded theatre, pausing only to purchase programmes from the busy merchandise stand in the lobby.

Their seats were excellent – only seven rows back from the stage – and the atmosphere was intense, thanks to a full house of mainly female, mostly screaming, hysterical teenagers, desperate to see their idols. The fans endured Mackenzie, the skinny young support act with the big voice and suggestive dance moves, until eventually it was time for the main event. When the house lights dimmed and smoke from the dry ice machines billowed out and filled every inch of the theatre, young voices were already hoarse from repeatedly shrieking out their heroes' names.

The next hour and a half were the best ninety minutes of Kim's life.

When the band emerged on individual platforms from beneath the stage, the whole place erupted and the volume was on max until beyond the end of the show. There was no denying that all five of them looked breathtakingly gorgeous in their shiny silver suits, but Ritchie almost sent Kim into cardiac arrest, with his hair so black that it was almost blue and his smile illuminating the stage, even when the lights dipped down. His extraordinary voice was like melted chocolate – warm, soothing and intoxicating. While the enraptured audience lapped it all up, the band belted out their hits and album tracks, chucking in a couple of vamped-up cover versions, bantering their way through the protracted introductions. They were awesome.

When a large proportion of the audience decided to rush to the stage immediately prior to the opening bars of 'Pulse' – the band's second single which had been remixed and was being hammered in the nightclubs around the UK – Kim was up and sprinting towards the stage with Sal as if her pants were on fire. Result! Luckily for them, they were that vital second ahead of the pack in the race for the finish, which achieved pole position, smack bang in front of Ritchie's microphone stand. Unfortunately, it also meant that they were squashed so hard against the wooden stage that Kim felt her rib cage was being crushed to pieces.

It was *so* worth it. To be in such close proximity to this vision of a man, now dressed all in black, with his leather jeans hugging his bum and his sparkly shirt completely open to his navel, it was worth enduring the worst pain imaginable. To be virtually inhaling the air that he was expelling was more than Kim could ever have wished for.

The final song was their latest hit – a touching ballad narrating the story of a family man almost working himself to death but desperately wanting to return to his beloved at Christmas – and Kim was reduced to tears as she glanced around and witnessed a sea of fans waving lighters from side to side, swaying to the music and warbling along to every last word of the emotionally charged lyrics. The rousing sound of the whole audience coming together and accompanying Ritchie and the boys as they hauntingly sang, 'I'm far away, with only the stars for company, and there you are, dreaming a Christmas dream about me…' made the hairs on Kim's arms stand to attention, a warm glow surrounding her that didn't emanate from the heat of the lighting or the sweaty bodies packed in like sardines at the stage.

Never shy and retiring at the best of times, Sally-Anne persisted on screaming out Ritchie's name until The Man Himself glanced down and squinted at her – which she immediately interpreted as a proclamation of his undying love – and then, to Kim's utter shock and disbelief, for a split-second Ritchie's eyes fixed upon her own and he smiled. She probably would have keeled over if there hadn't been a few hundred people holding her up.

All too soon the band triumphantly bid them goodnight and exited the stage, leaving the audience pleading for more. There were, of course, two encores, the second of which, *Kissing in the Bay,* became *Kissing on Christmas Day*, featuring a good dose of jingle bells and accompanied by fake snow drifting down from above the stage. A choked-up

Kim knew this unforgettable night was unfortunately almost over and, although she would be left with memories that would last forever, she knew nothing in her life would ever compare.

'STAGE DOOR!' screeched Sally-Anne, grabbing Kim's clammy hand in an attempt to drag her through the surrounding ocean of fans. Of course, they were hemmed in next to the stage, and by the time they escaped the theatre and raced round to the back exit, there was already a massive crowd waiting for the band to emerge.

Kim and Sal picked 'snowflakes' out of each other's hair, popping them into their purses to keep as souvenirs. They chattered, sang and shivered along with the other fans but it still seemed like an eternity before the boys actually made a brief appearance as they were bundled onto their tour bus, to the ear-piercing screams and desperate cries of the teenagers trying franticly to break through the wall of security. The girls had been hoping for autographs and a moment in which to tell Ritchie how much they adored him, but instead had to satisfy themselves with a wave and a thumbs up through the coach window. All too soon, the crowds had been shoved back and the bus sped off down the street, a few brave girls attempting the chase before it disappeared around the corner and out of sight.

'Oh Sally-Anne, that was amazing...it was off the scale of brilliance! I can't believe we finally saw them live and were *so* close to them at the end. I almost managed to touch Ady's hand when he danced over and knelt down in front of us!'

'I know, I know...and did you see Ritchie look at me? Isn't he gorgeous? He's even hotter and more kissable in the flesh! And you – you jammy cow – I saw him smiling at you, whilst you were gaping back at him, mouth wide open like a bewildered goldfish!'

'God, I nearly fainted when he caught my eye! He looked directly at me and his face seemed to light up! Wait till I tell Nicky on Monday - she won't half be jealous. Jason Donovan's alright but not a patch on Ritchie Clarke!'

'I wonder if he knows how hot he is. I reckon he must look in the mirror every day and sexily growl, 'My god, Ritchie, you are one handsome fella! Oh god, I *love* that man!'

BEEEEP! BEEEEP! BEEEEEEPPPP...

Their conversation was rudely interrupted by the persistent blaring of a horn. When Kim looked up she was confronted with the sight of the peculiar Geraldine furiously winding her window down, ranting that Kim had better get her bloody bag out of her bloody boot because she had to hit the road and couldn't wait around for her while she mucked about all night.

'Shit! My bag!' She'd nearly forgotten it in all the excitement. How on earth would she have explained missing belongings to her parents once she arrived home? That would have been an interesting conversation.

They quickly jogged over to Geraldine's rust bucket of a car and Sally-Anne prattled on whilst Kim grabbed her bag from the boot, and then this weirdest of women sped off into the night without so much as a goodbye. It dawned on them for the first time that they were now very much alone, in deepest, darkest London – where apparently all the world's serial killers, sex pests and sickos roamed the streets, according to Kim's mum. They had nowhere to stay, no money, and no bloody clue what to do.

'Oh my god Kim, we should have asked Gerry to let us bunk down at her house. I don't fancy joining the homeless brigade on a freezing cold night like this. We'd better find someone who can offer us a bed for the night or else we really are up shit creek without a paddle. Where did those Irish girlies go? I'm sure they said they'd booked a family room and I bet they wouldn't mind if we crashed on their floor...'

For once, Sally-Anne seemed a little unsure of herself. Gone was the devil-may-care attitude and confident facade, revealing a young girl scared witless of spending a night out on the streets. Kim merely trailed behind as Sal scooted around the theatre boundaries – checking entrances and exits and even squashing her face up against the window of a nearby pizza restaurant to see if she recognised anyone inside.

No success.

In a matter of minutes, it seemed like every last theatregoer had vanished into thin air; every fan had been safely collected, driven away or rushed off to meet their public transport connections and any hope the girls had of being taken under a kindly wing had been completely obliterated.

Kim's exposed fingers were already stiffening up from the biting cold and her teeth were actually beginning to chatter. With all of her heavy heart she wished that the band's tour bus would suddenly make a reappearance. Ritchie and company would realise they had forgotten something of vital importance and swiftly return, only to discover these two lost and lonely souls. Taking great pity on the girls, Ritchie would insist they board the bus, gazing adoringly into Kim's eyes, wondering who the hell *was* this young woman and why had they never been introduced before?

Reality check. They weren't coming back - no one was. The theatre was locked up for the evening and the only people on the mean streets were total strangers, any one of whom could have been a mad axe murderer with a fetish for silly, teenage girls who loitered in the heart of Theatreland after dark.

They stood, statue-still, as if waiting for some divine miracle to occur, before Sally-Anne eventually tutted and said, 'Well, we had better do *something*. Let's trot down the high street and see if we recognise anyone who was at the show. If all else fails, we'll have to make our way back to Euston, find a sympathetic guard and then persuade them to let us travel on an earlier train in the morning.'

It seemed like another very flimsy plan but Kim had nothing better to offer up to the table.

As she bent down to scoop up her flattened bag – which looked as if a really heavy person had been jumping up and down on top of it for several hours - she was sure she heard the faint sound of a voice calling out her name. The icy cold must have been playing tricks with her muddled mind and frostbitten ears because she was truly anonymous in this chaotic city where nobody knew her name.

'KIMBERLEY! *KIMBERLEEEEE!'*

There it was again.

'KIMBERLEY SUMMERS! KIMMMBERRLEEE...'

'Who the hell's making that racket at this time of night? I hope it's not someone being attacked and left for...shit a bloody brick! Isn't that your mum over there? Or is it her doppelganger? Oh jeez...it can't be her...can it?'

Oh good god. It was. Her mother. Pelting towards them. Looking angry. Exceedingly angry. She always folded her arms like that when she was apoplectic with rage. What the hell was she doing here? How did she even *know?* Lordy, Kim would be in for a world of pain after this.

Alison Summers came to a breathless stop in front of them. She'd never been a good runner at the best of times and hadn't managed anything more strenuous than walking briskly for approximately the last ten years.

Kim noticed the quick puffs of breath that burst out of her mum's mouth into the air, like little angry clouds, with every word she ferociously spat out.

'You! *YOU!* I've a good mind to leave you here and let some nutcase snatch you off the streets and murder you - it will save me the trouble later. Do you have any idea what you have put me and your father through? You lying, conniving little bugger. And YOU, Sally-Anne, your mum may have given this little unsupervised expedition her seal of approval but I made it perfectly clear that Kim wasn't allowed. I'm disgusted with you both, but especially YOU, Kimberley Helen Summers, when I expressly forbade you to make this trip to see this godforsaken band. Well, I hope the gig was a memorable one because you, my lady, are grounded for the foreseeable future. Right, we will attempt to find your father who has been trying to navigate the one-way system for the last half hour. He's probably been arrested for kerb crawling by now, which will be ALL YOUR FAULT, you selfish little sod! Kimberley, Sally-Anne – follow me and do NOT say a word because quite frankly I do NOT want to hear it!'

Despite her mother's furious threats, Kim only felt an overwhelming sense of relief to be out of immediate danger. They finally located her dad's car, complete with all hazards flashing, temporarily pulled up at a bus stop. The girls silently clambered into the back seat and not a word was uttered by Kim's father who stared straight ahead, eyes blazing, mouth set in a grim line, hands gripping the steering wheel as if holding on for dear life.

Kim and her dad eventually made eye contact in the rear view mirror and whilst Mick Summers noticed how small and scared his precious daughter looked, she in turn observed her dad's unusually haggard appearance, with unsightly saggy, bags under his exhausted, watery eyes. She experienced an instant flash of guilt as she realised he'd been slaving away, laying carpets all day, before making a mad dash down to London to retrieve his only daughter, no doubt all kinds of horror-filled scenarios playing through his mind as he raced along unfamiliar motorways and drove erratically through alien streets. *Sorry dad*, she attempted to say, telepathically of course - too wary of actually voicing any apology for fear of having her head bitten off, chewed up and spat out.

Despite her mother's huffing and puffing and the sound of her father's grinding teeth, Kim's anxiety soon began to evaporate. As she heard Sally-Anne start to softly snore beside her, she closed her own eyes, remembering how it felt to be a tiny part of that massive gig, to have dipped her toe into the wild waters that surrounded Ritchie's world – at least for that brief hour and a half. And the way that he had focused on her. Whatever happened, it had all been worth it – for that one look, that single smile that had made her whole body tingle and her heart ache. But when would she ever see him again?

*

The following morning, Sally-Anne was collected by her uncle, who was obviously none too pleased to have been landed with the job. Julie Benton had apparently been content for her daughter to simply return to Scotland by train but Kim's dad had insisted she be picked up, due to her being a minor and completely untrustworthy. So Uncle Bob was dispatched in the early hours and arrived with a face like thunder and breath that smelled of a thousand fags.

Kim was then treated to a full reading of her favourite book - the bloody Riot Act - and as punishment for her sins was grounded for two whole months. End of.

Thankfully, her parents relented because of the Christmas celebrations and normal service was resumed on 23rd December. They all piled into Mick's precious Ford Sierra to head over the moors to collect Kim's gran, who bounced into the car with a huge bag of gifts and a grin from ear to ear. How Kim adored her. With her cackling laugh and addiction to mint imperials, she always brought oodles of joy to the Summers household, along with a bottle of sherry and a homemade booze-injected fruit cake.

They enjoyed a wonderful Christmas together and Kim was ecstatic to finally receive the camera she'd been begging for, along with a whole host of goodies including an enormous poster of the band, their official calendar and the 12 inch of their latest single. They were relaxed and restful days spent in the bosom of her family and Kim laughed a lot, ate even more and threw herself enthusiastically into every game of charades and silly singalong.

All too soon the celebrations were over and her gran was delivered home safely for New Year's Eve, so she could attend her neighbour's annual mulled wine and mince pie get-together. Her parents met up with friends at their local pub and Kim popped out to see Nicky, who had been annoyed that Kim hadn't confided in her about London. Kim explained that she had merely been trying to minimise the risk of exposure (she was fairly sure that Nicky would have caved under interrogation) and that her friend's loyalty and integrity had never been in doubt.

After minimal investigation, Kim discovered that good old Freddie had deliberately dobbed her in. He'd actually heard Kim whispering and plotting over the telephone but it wasn't until he realised she'd pinched his personal stereo for the journey that he'd happily turned whistle-blower.

When she'd blasted him and asked why he was such a sneaky little prat he'd sneered and replied, 'And what if something awful had happened to you? God knows why but mum and dad seem to like you and would be devastated if you came to a murky end. You know, it's not always about you, Kim.' Her conscience was pricked and she'd softened a little until he'd rounded it off with, 'And take my stereo again, fatty, and I'll wipe the floor with you.' Charming.

None of her family had been particularly interested in hearing about the gig so Kim was thrilled to have a captive audience in Nicky, who didn't seem to mind her droning on about Ritchie's sexy little arse and the band's magnificent stage presence.

Kim was made up to be with her best mate again after an enforced week's absence. It was all well and good to do the *Show Me Yours* thing with Sally-Anne, whose craziness and zest for life truly boosted Kim up. But it wasn't the same as spending time with her best friend, slurping hot chocolate whilst they munched their way through the last of the shortbreads from the tin, gossiping about classmates and giggling about fit lads at school. Nicky was the one person who was on her wavelength - who she could truly be herself with.

Kim couldn't imagine that anything or anyone could ever come between the two of them.

Chapter 4

Eventually forgiven for her pre-Christmas misdemeanours, Kim had still been lectured sternly and at length and warned there would be no more gigs until she turned sweet sixteen on 8th of June. From then on she would be able to travel to any gig within the UK as long as she had the money to pay for it and she left accommodation and travel details with her parents.

As the group were still riding high in the spring, and their latest single *Much Ado About Something* was enjoying its third consecutive week at number 1 (and Kim was panicking about sitting the dreaded GCSEs after almost zero preparation or revision), a late summer tour was announced, to coincide with the release of their second album. Kim managed to secure an advance on her birthday money and the girls were able to book for six shows, including the all-important last night of the tour at Croydon.

On the evening of her birthday, after being spoiled rotten throughout the day, Kim was whisked away to a posh restaurant for a three course meal. She had carefully applied her most expensive make-up, liberally sprayed herself with her favourite Dior scent and slipped into her slinky new black dress before pausing to check out her appearance in the full-length mirror. She was pleasantly surprised to see the image of a completely transformed Kimberley Helen Summers looking back at her. During the last few months the girl she'd once been had quietly developed into a young woman and she actually *felt* different. Her face had thinned out, the thighs weren't quite so chunky and those pesky boobs had finally stopped growing - and anyway, she kind of liked them now. The hair that she'd previously scraped back and tied up had now been permed and hung loosely down her back in a far more flattering style. She had to concede, she was almost unrecognisable from the Kim of old, and although she could never claim to be the most confident of souls, she was a great deal happier in her own skin.

'Wow! Get you! I *love* that dress. You'd better let me borrow it for my holidays or else me and you will be exchanging strong words!'

Nicky had arrived and looked equally fine. Having cut out the chips and chocolate bars, she'd dropped several dress sizes and was proud of her newly discovered waistline. She'd also allowed her hair to grow past her shoulders and the highlighted curls were softer than the tight little spirals she'd hated so much. She was regularly being asked out at school, although she turned most of them down as they were all 'complete dorks'.

To Kim's amazement, *she'd* also been asked out a couple of times but hadn't been too impressed by either of the interested parties so she'd muttered an embarrassed 'No thanks' and continued to dream about Ritchie Joe Clarke. Her gran always said she'd get her head stuck up in those clouds one day - it was there that much.

'Course you can borrow it, after I've donned it for the Southport gig first. It'll do you a treat for your holidays, especially when you're as brown as a berry.'

Kim still felt dreadful that she couldn't jet off to Spain with Nicky and family because the holiday dates clashed with the tour. To her credit, Nicky hadn't banged on about it but she knew her friend was seriously disappointed, even though a cousin was to take Kim's place. They were, however, going to the opening night of the tour together so hopefully Nicky would be able to see for herself quite how fabulous the band were live and understand exactly why Kim couldn't possibly miss any of the gigs for the sake of a fortnight in the sun.

*

There was further excitement in store for Kim who actually acquired a real, live boyfriend when they struck up a conversation in the newsagents near the trendy boutique where she was earning a pittance as resident Saturday Girl. His name was Lee, he was a trainee mechanic, and although he was a little cocky, he was incredibly good-looking with tousled fair hair and blue-grey, sparky eyes. Kim was shocked that he'd shown any interest in her, but interested he was, and he not only coughed up for the cinema tickets and cheeseburgers but also drove her home in his nippy red mini. Bursting with pride – none of her friends had ever been out with anyone who owned a car – she prayed they would pass at least one person she knew. They didn't, of course.

When Lee dropped her off home, he risked a gentle, lingering kiss, despite the twitching curtains and the threat of her dad hauling him out of the car and growling, 'Now, son, come on...we'll be having none of that.' It had been a thoroughly enjoyable evening and Kim practically skipped up the path to her front door.

He was no Ritchie Clarke, but he was none too shabby in the looks department...and he had a CAR!

Sadly, it only lasted a few weeks. Lee had never been allowed upstairs and into her bedroom, which meant he hadn't seen the true extent of her madness. When she finally revealed the identity of her favourite band and confessed that she was smitten with Ritchie, Lee had monumentally taken the piss and worst of all, he'd said Ritchie was a wazzock with girly hair.

Furthermore, when she informed Lee that she'd need a fortnight's break but refused to elaborate, he presumed she was trying to dump him and a huge argument ensued. Rather that divulge that she was off to a string of SMY gigs, Kim said she thought it best they cool things for a while. Lee's eyes shone with tears, but he was too hard to actually cry in front of a girl.

She felt terrible for hurting him but concluded that it was for the best. After all, Ritchie was a sexy, stylish miracle of a man who oozed confidence and charisma. How the hell could a seventeen year old local likely lad in his dirty, skanky overalls ever hope to compare?

Although the odds were unfairly stacked against her, there was always the slimmest of chances that Kim would be lucky enough to meet Ritchie and she swore to god and everything that was great and mighty that she would never even glance at another male again if her dream came true. Never mind the hordes of screaming fans, the secret sound checks and the heightened security, Kim was determined she would somehow breach the defences and make herself stand out from the crowd.

Goodbye Lee Bradshaw…hello Ritchie Clarke!

Chapter 5

Of course, nothing went to plan on the opening night of the *Dad Dancing* tour.

They were late leaving, held up in traffic and then Nicky's dad, Colin, parked up approximately two miles away from the theatre in Southport. They raced down there, as fast as they could in high heels, only to discover they'd missed the band's arrival by hours. Colin then insisted they drink tea in a dingy backstreet café, where Nicky excitedly chirped on about jetting off to Sunny Spain the following day and Kim fidgeted, itching to be back amongst the crowds of like-minded fans milling about at the stage door, hoping to catch sight of one of the band or be tossed a crumb of gossip from one of the theatre staff.

To make matters worse, when they did return to the venue, Sally-Anne had arrived and gleefully informed them that Bren and Todd *had* been out, flanked by their burly security guys, for a short stroll along the beach. This had, of course, been curtailed by the presence of around two thousand panting girls, forcing the guys to make a hasty retreat. Kim was gutted she'd missed all the action but relieved it hadn't been her Ritchie.

As the lights went down, the screaming started and the drumbeat thudded through her chest, Kim shivered involuntarily, despite the stifling heat inside the theatre. This feeling, if it could be bottled – well, someone could make a fortune from it.

The gig was nothing short of sensational and the guys were on top form, but Nicky, Sally-Anne and Kim were almost trampled to death by a pack of determined scousers on the run-up to the stage, so they were further back in the pack than they'd have liked. Kim was still on cloud nine as she was reasonably up close to Ritchie again and she adored singing along with all of the other fans surrounding her. It felt good to be back amongst those who shared her passion and the goosebumps returned as she glanced around the darkened theatre, witnessing bodies, scarves and lighter flames swaying to the music, almost deafened by the fans belting out the old familiar song lyrics.

'*Quick*!' screamed Sally-Anne at the end of the show, as she shoved everybody out of her way and made a determined run for the stage door. Kim started to chase after her but felt a firm tug on the sleeve of her leather jacket. She turned to see Nicky beside her, almost forgotten in her desperation to meet the band.

'Kim, we can't stay! Dad's been waiting hours and I promised him we'd be off as soon as the gig was over.'

'What? Are you kidding? Of course we have to stay or there'll be no autographs…'

'Kim, we're boarding a plane in a few hours' time. Dad has to pick Charmaine up at five-thirty a.m. and then drive us all to the airport. It's hardly fair to keep him waiting while we hang about for a band that might dash past and not even acknowledge our presence!'

'But Sally-Anne's waiting…and loads of others are too! Can't we just stay another twenty minutes and see what happens…?'

'No, we can't, you dipstick! I've still got stuff to pack, and my dad's been good enough to drive us here tonight on the eve of his holiday!'

It was on the tip of Kim's tongue to blurt out that if she'd known he would drag them off the minute the gig had finished she'd have hitched a lift with someone else or bloody walked it if necessary, but the decent streak that ran through her acknowledged that would be an ungrateful, not-very-nice thing to do. So, with disappointment rushing through her veins alongside the adrenaline, she reluctantly said her goodbyes and returned to Colin's car.

'Cheer up, sulky chops!' Nicky nudged her, as they were clambering in. 'We've had a BOSS night and, yes, Ritchie, is sex on legs! And you, you lucky devil, will be doing it all again in a few days' time. Come on Kim, realistically, we were never likely to get near the band when there are masses of other fans at the stage door, all wanting a piece of them.'

Kim was forced to accept that her night was over. There was no point dwelling on missed opportunities or torturing herself with might-have-beens whilst they were zooming back down the motorway, speeding ever further away from the band. Only four more days until her next gig. Surely she could survive that long, no matter how bereft she felt at that precise moment in time!

*

As much as Kim loved her best friend, it was far easier without Nicky in tow. The other girl simply couldn't comprehend the level of devotion and the lengths they were prepared to go to, to creep within an inch of their idols.

Kim and Sal travelled for hours, arrived ridiculously early, kept their eyes peeled and hovered around stage doors until they couldn't feel their feet. And yet the nearest they came to rubbing shoulders with the boys was when they were dangling over barriers as the band were hurried past or when they found themselves on the receiving end of a sunny smile or a cheeky wink as Ritchie and co. worked the stage in front of them, belting out their hits and playing their hearts out.

The gigs were outstanding and the girls loved every minute but felt more of a sense of urgency than ever before to meet the band. Kim's dad said she'd lost the plot, wasting the end of her summer by dossing about, waiting for 'jumped-up celebrities' who were only interested in themselves. But he was wrong – Kim was convinced they cared about their fans and knew she wouldn't ever give up. It was frustrating though, making little or no progress and she longed for the day when Ritchie might acknowledge her existence.

And then just when they thought that all was lost, they had an unexpected stroke of luck on the last night of the tour.

Sally-Anne was experiencing serious camera trouble, which led to them hiking to the other side of Croydon, to a photographic shop recommended by Saffy, the landlady in the above-average bed and breakfast they'd booked for the night. The guy behind the counter was kind of punky and pretty cool and when they mentioned that they were off to see *Show Me Yours* later, he casually informed them that one of the roadies had popped in earlier to buy tapes for a video camera so he could capture the best bits of the end-of-tour-party at *The Happy Horse* – a trendy pub that backed on to the park over the road!

Unfortunately Sally-Anne's camera was only fit for the bin, so they bought an extra film for Kim's and she promised she would order a duplicate set of prints. They said 'See Ya' to Punky Cool Guy and sauntered out of the shop, all nonchalant, and swaggered down the street. As soon as they were out of earshot they let rip, diving on each other, screaming 'Oh my god, oh my god!' much to the bemusement of two elderly gentleman standing in the doorway of the betting shop.

They weren't daft enough to think they could worm their way into the party, but at least they could stake out the pub and wait for the band to show up. Hopefully they might catch them on the way out too. They would be right there, on the periphery of the action, listening out for any gossip, arguments or scandal.

Hugging their secret to themselves, they remained tight-lipped, in a 'I know something you don't know' fashion and had a blast throughout the show, which was definitely the loudest and silliest of the tour. Afterwards, it seemed the whole audience had emptied out into the car park to await the band's exit, as the girls tried to sneak past, covered in lengths of silly string.

'Oy, Sally-Anne! Where are *you* slinking off to?'

So much for slipping away quietly.

'Geraldine! Ssshh! We're just having a wander into town, because it'll be ages before the lads come out…'

'Bullshit! There's no way you're wandering off anywhere unless it's in the direction of the party! Where's the big bash then? Come on, divulge the details, you sly little dogs. And remember all the favours I've done for you in the past...'

Storing her bag in Geraldine's messy boot was the only favour she'd ever done for Kim, but Sally-Anne sighed and caved like a badly baked soufflé, disclosing everything they knew – the bloody idiot!

'Keeley! Get your bum over here quick and bring the others!'

Oh crap, she was involving the Irish girls too. Stupid, gobby woman!

Before they knew it, they had Geraldine, Keeley, Shannon and Caroline tagging along behind them. Kim was seriously peeved off, figuring the more fans outside the pub, the less chance they had of making any real connection with the band. She was disappointed to discover there were about twenty others also hanging around outside The Hungry Horse - but at least the odds were far more favourable than if they'd waited back at the theatre.

After only thirty minutes, a convoy of vehicles approached the pub, sending a tidal wave of excitement through the gathering, each and every fan hoping for a smile or an acknowledgement from their heroes. Naively, Kim had expected the boys to arrive on their tour bus but they'd apparently all transferred to a couple of waiting cars on the outskirts of the town, in an attempt to throw any followers off the scent, and in the main it had worked.

Kim was beside herself at the prospect of being in such close proximity to the band. However, she was NOT prepared for practically coming face to face with Ritchie Joe Clarke. When a black rover pulled up directly in front of her, out jumped Bobbo, their head security guy…and then suddenly there was Ritchie, within touching distance, until Bobbo roughly shoved her aside and she almost tumbled into the road.

'Hey...you okay there?' Her idol swiftly grabbed hold of her arm to save her, which meant she narrowly avoided landing in a heap on her arse at his feet. The heat from his hand burned a permanent imprint on her forearm, before she was quickly released and he was shunted forward in the small crowd. However, he still managed to turn around ever so slightly, presumably to check she was still standing.

'Be careful now,' he added with a grin, before Bobbo whisked him indoors and she stared after him in total disbelief.

'Be still my beating heart. The man. The god. He actually looked at me. He spoke to me. He smiled at me. He TOUCHED me. He was concerned for my welfare!'

Before she'd even had chance to process the incident, the other four were out of their cars and heading into the pub, but they all slowed down to say a brief hello on their way past. As the reinforced door to the private function room slammed shut and a man-mountain bouncer stepped out to guard it with his life, Kim finally had time to digest it all. Sally-Anne's mouth was hanging wide open in shock and Kim felt a sudden urge to sit down but the only available benches in the vicinity were already occupied.

They were further taken aback by the sudden arrival of Callie, the beautiful but often rather aloof leggy blonde who they'd met at the London gig. She showed up all by her stunning self in a private hire car, paid the driver and darted past, not daring to look any one of them in the eye. Kim thought she heard her utter Bren's name followed by her own, before the bouncer stepped aside and quietly let her in. Well, *that* was a turn up for the books! Assuming she wasn't Bren's long lost sister or his therapist, how *did* an essentially normal girl from a quiet little backwater get it together with a madcap drummer from a hugely successful, chart-storming group?

Kim silently seethed and loathed Callie for being so bloody attractive and effortlessly integrating herself with the band. Sally-Anne – not so silently. She roared that Callie was an ignorant cow who needed taking down a peg or two.

Two hours later, there'd been no further sightings of the boys and the temperature had dropped considerably, the chill seeping through lightweight jackets and flimsy summer dresses and shorts. But it *was* one o'clock in the morning and by that stage teenage daughters had been dragged off and prised into parents' cars whilst other fans had been forced to leave the scene to reluctantly catch last trains home or be safely ensconced in bed and breakfasts before doors were locked and bolted for the night.

Luckily for Kim and Sally-Anne, Saffy hadn't imposed any kind of curfew and had in fact provided them with a Yale key for the outer door to the house - god bless her and her pencilled-on eyebrows!

The minutes crept by slowly and the remaining fans became even more subdued, looking forward to eventually crawling into comfortable beds hopefully before dawn.

At ten-past three they were finally and justly rewarded when the door was suddenly flung open and one after the other, the guys staggered out – members of their staff propping them up as they weaved their way to the awaiting vehicles. Poor Todd, who still didn't look old enough to legally drink alcohol, was the worst of the sorry bunch, his eyelids drooping and his whole body swaying dangerously from side to side. Bren was steadier on his feet and managed a smile and a slurred '*Gernight ladiesh*,' as he passed them by. Ritchie was the last to leave and actually seemed the most sober of the lot and - oh my god - he was heading their way!

'Hi girls, you've been waiting for hours haven't you? Now, that's dedication. Let's sign one item each and take a quick picture and then I'll have to bolt before Bobbo bares his teeth at me!'

Tour programmes were autographed and then Ritchie took a moment to pose for individual photographs. Sally-Anne was beaming from ear to ear as the flash went off and Kim noticed she'd slid her arm around Ritchie's trim waist – my god, the thought of feeling the flesh of this divine man who was unbelievably sexy, even when bleary-eyed and dishevelled.

It was quickly Kim's turn but she didn't have the guts to even touch him. However, Ritchie's arm snaked out and curled around her shoulders and he gave her a little squeeze as Sally-Anne took the photograph. Bloody hell, if she were to die tomorrow then she would depart this earth a happy woman with a huge grin on her face.

'Thanks Ritchie, we've been to a few shows and they've all been wonderful.' she'd finally found her voice, but up popped Barry, leaning over to drag her man away by his distressed leather jacket. 'I'll never forget tonight, as long as I live!'

'Ah no, it was our pleasure. We love what we do and have the best fans any band could wish for. And rest assured, I won't forget YOU in a hurry!'

And then he was gone, lost in what remained of the crowd, only pausing briefly to sign the odd album sleeve or programme, not stopping to have any further pictures taken. All that Kim could see was his beautiful back and the studs on his jacket twinkling in the moonlight. Before the girls could even think about pushing their way to the front, he was in his car and away. Merely a blur in the distance.

Sally-Anne slumped down on the pavement, leaning against a manky old bin. Kim remained upright, not wishing to stink like a tramp's vest on this most memorable of nights.

'Did that actually just happen, Kim? It's a bummer that we missed out on introducing ourselves to the other boys, but did Ritchie actually just approach us, sign for us and pose for photographs with us – and *only* us – or was I hallucinating?'

'No. It was real alright, although I don't think anyone will ever believe us – at least not until we have photographic evidence, so I'd better make sure I take care of that camera! Sal, I think I'm still in shock. Obviously I'd hoped for an autograph or a handshake but never in my wildest dreams did I think we'd have photos taken with Ritchie. I can't stop trembling. He probably wondered what the hell was wrong with me!'

'Er, excuse me, but at one point I thought he was going to take you and smuggle you into the car with him! The two of you getting all close and chummy like that!'

'Oh I know...and he smelled heavenly too! Not of stale beer and cigs, but expensive aftershave and *manliness*. If I close my eyes I can imagine he's still beside me. I can still smell that aftershave and feel his touch. Does that sound stupid?'

It was true. As Ritchie had pulled her in close to him, their hips were in contact and she was intoxicated by his scent. It was still there, lingering, reminding her, clinging on to her clothing. And when his hand had brushed against hers, his skin had was so soft and he'd acted and moved with confidence. The sacred denim jacket she was wearing was NEVER being washed again.

Floating back to the guesthouse, they chattered incessantly, desperate to recall every last significant detail. They sat up all night, too wired to sleep. Kim couldn't help but stroke the sleeve of her jacket, marvelling at the fact that it had actually been touched by the one and only Ritchie Clarke. She never wanted to lose the scent that lingered on it and vowed she would save up to buy herself a small bottle of the aftershave so she could spray it on to her SMY pillow and bury her face in it whenever she was missing him – which would probably be all of the time.

Thankfully Sally-Anne understood completely as she was besotted too. Anyone else would have struggled to get on board with it and probably concluded that Kim was insane. But Sal shared the same feelings, thought the same thoughts, dreamed the same dreams and Kim didn't feel an ounce of embarrassment when she declared that she loved Ritchie Clarke and always would.

Chapter 6

From that night onwards, Kim wholly immersed herself in the world of *Show Me Yours* and when she wasn't glued to the television, mesmerised by their latest appearance on Top of the Pops or giggling along as they created havoc on otherwise dreary chat shows, her bedroom was constantly filled with the sound of their music. She was talking about them, thinking about them, fantasising about them and she couldn't remember what her life had been like before.

She was regularly corresponding with Sally-Anne and they'd also individually composed letters to Ritchie, which they sent to the management company, fan club and anywhere else remotely connected with the band. They begged to be allowed to meet him, particularly as they really were his Number One Fans. No replies were ever received but the girls never stopped hoping or believing.

Various other SMY pen-friends had been collected along the way, meaning Kim was forever nipping out to buy stationery and stamps. She moaned about the drain on her already pitiful finances but it cheered her up no end to witness those brightly coloured envelopes drop onto the mat and she enjoyed seeing photographs of bedroom walls plastered with *Show Me Yours* posters and hearing of other fans' devotion and exploits.

Sally-Anne had attempted to add Callie to her pen pal list by mailing her a sickly sweet letter, hoping to garner a little insider knowledge, but Callie was having none of it and had now taken to ignoring everyone's communications. Sod her then, snotty cow. She was too pretty for her own good.

Nicky was still, of course, Kim's best and oldest friend, although it was becoming increasingly difficult for them to maintain the same level of contact as Nicky attended college and then picked and packed at a local factory most evenings to subsidise her social life.

However, there were still occasional riotously joyous days spent together, like the sunny Saturday when the fair came to town and they rode the waltzers continuously until they were both sick behind the candyfloss wagon, before ploughing straight on to scoff a full bag of warm sugary doughnuts and scream their way through the haunted house.

There was also a disastrous double date with the twin brothers whose dad owned the local pet shop. Both lads were cocky and loud, but also fit, muscular and usually up for a laugh.

They insisted on paying for all of the cinema tickets and the Wimpy meal, but unfortunately the whiff of animal poop was real and had obviously clung to their hair and clothes long after they'd shut up shop for the day. The girls thought it would be amusing to see how many rabbit references they could drop into their conversation and poor Phil and Des never really understood that the joke was on them, assuming instead that the girls were quite bonkers. Kim's manic nose twitching and Bugs Bunny impressions resulted in Nicky laughing and snorting so manically that a whole load of popcorn catapulted across three rows of cinemagoers. Neither lad requested a second date but the girls returned home with aching jaws and shared memories of an hysterical evening.

But those occasions were few and far between and lately they didn't seem to have so much in common. Kim loved her best mate and she would always be her most treasured friend, but she'd noticed Nicky's eyes glaze over whenever Ritchie's name was mentioned and it infuriated Nicky that Kim could rarely afford to socialise because she'd frittered away what little money she had on records, videos and merchandise.

Kim's mum and dad were constantly on her back because she'd packed college in after a mere fortnight. They insisted she find a full-time job before she turned into a complete bona fide layabout, but Kim soon realised all by herself that she needed to earn a decent wage to fund life on the road with her men. To that end, she bagged a job working at a local Late Shop and actually enjoyed the interaction with the customers, apart from the junior delinquents and local smackheads intent on robbing them blind.

Her colleagues were friendly and fun and she was occasionally persuaded to join them for a quick drink after work. Janice was cuddly and mumsy but had a surprisingly naughty sense of humour, whilst sweet young Bryony, who was really quite pretty with her heart-shaped face and cutesy blonde pigtails, absolutely fancied the pants off the adorable Adam, the real joker of their pack. He was also incredibly handsome with his sun-streaked fair hair and laughing chocolate brown eyes and it was easy to see why Bryony was so enamoured. Kim teased her younger colleague mercilessly about all of her mooning around and gazing at Adam when she thought no one was looking, but then found herself blushing like a berry whenever anyone asked if there was a Mr Kimberley on the scene.

She'd produced the treasured photo she'd posed for with Ritchie at Croydon and Janice had incorrectly assumed he was Kim's boyfriend and swooned 'My, you're a lucky devil to have *that* to go home to each night!' Kim reluctantly had to explain that he wasn't actually her significant other – although she still dreamed that somehow he would be one day and wondered exactly what it *would* feel like to be able to tell everyone that she was his girl.

The next single, *Get Down and Dirty,* was released in the autumn and was their biggest hit to date, taking root at the number one spot for what seemed like forever. On the back of its success and their new album shooting straight in at the top of the charts, came the announcement of another tour to take place the following spring - even more dates at even bigger venues with a gruelling schedule that must have been planned out by someone who didn't particularly like them very much, as they were due to crisscross the country several times each week. It would be an almighty pain in the arse for Kim and Sally-Anne to reach some of the far flung places by public transport too.

However, they immersed themselves into the serious business of researching train times and accommodation, accepted they would be experiencing a period of financial hardship for, say, the next decade, and fizzed with excitement as they counted the days off on their *Show Me Yours* calendars, wishing their young lives away.

After sweet-talking the shop manager and persuading her workmates to cover her shifts for three whole weeks, Kim was able to book tickets for all but two of the gigs. She was only sorry they wouldn't be able to follow the band around Europe as they were due to perform in several other countries after their last UK date.

It really was such a joyful time and the promise of what was to come rendered Kim incapable of entering into any kind of normal life.

Then a fortnight before the boys were due to head out on the road, the entire tour was cancelled.

Kim was devastated.

The band's press officer released a statement to the effect that the lads were burnt out due to their heavy workload. The interviews, the television appearances, the photo sessions, the rehearsals, the jumping on and off aeroplanes for months on end had all put great stress on the individual band members, taking a toll on both their physical and mental health.

Kim cried, on and off, for two whole days. Of course, she was worried about Ritchie - and the other boys - and she couldn't bear the thought of him being ill and stressed to the max. She was also gutted she might not be able to re-arrange her annual leave and that even if she received a complete refund on all of the gig tickets, she would still lose deposits for a few of the bed and breakfasts.

But all that paled into insignificance when compared with the disappointment. It was gut-wrenching, knowing that she wouldn't be seeing the band, especially Ritchie, when she'd been looking forward to this tour so much. She'd hoped and prayed she would somehow get to meet him again and that he'd remember her. Well, that would never happen now. By the time the boys were rested and well enough to go out on tour again, it may be another year...or possibly even longer. And he would have forgotten all about her – the girl who'd almost fallen at his feet.

*

The band virtually disappeared over the next eight months. After the initial burst of headlines regarding the shock cancellation of the tour, they'd all but dropped out of the public eye, and there was only the odd snippet here and there in the press. The dedicated fan base waited, impatiently, for something positive to appear in the pipeline, still clinging to the fact that the five of them hadn't disbanded and all hope was not yet lost.

Finally, as bonfire celebrations were dying down and Christmas was rapidly approaching, the news came that they had all been waiting for – Ritchie, Todd, Bren, Ady and Marty were rested, recuperated and fighting fit, with an album full of spiffing new material ready for release. They'd thanked their army of fans profusely for their ongoing support and there was a copious amount of sobbing down telephone lines across the country as their most ardent supporters simultaneously received fan club newsletters and collectively heaved a huge sigh of relief. Kim was beside herself at the prospect of a new single too, particularly as it was rumoured to be another upbeat number, sampling an old 1970s disco anthem. It was sure to go down a storm at Christmas parties.

But there was a problem.

Eight months was a long time in pop and there were other bands emerging onto the scene. The single came up against the new releases of the other big groups of the time, all vying for that elusive Christmas number one and it certainly lost out in the battle for airplay. It was also panned by the critics and Kim was outraged. For goodness sake, it was one of the best songs they'd ever produced – what was wrong with people? She and Sally-Anne convinced themselves it would be a grower; a slow burner that would eventually work its way up to the top.

It didn't.

After two weeks hovering around outside of the Top Twenty, it slipped down and out of the charts, to the shock and bewilderment of the fans. However, the boys played down their lack of chart success, insisting their next release was a sure-fire hit – a pull-on-the-heart-strings ballad to be released in time for Valentine's Day.

Despite it being the most honest, cleverly written piece of music that had ever graced the airwaves (in Kim's opinion), and despite every single fan proclaiming that *this* was the best thing they'd ever done, *Unsaid* still didn't crack the Top Ten. Kim just didn't get it. Every time she listened to that masterpiece, the poignant lyrics and raw emotion in Ritchie's voice instantly moved her to tears. Why did the rest of the world not hear what she was hearing?

The famous five may have dipped out on chart victory but it didn't stop them planning to head out on the road again for the *Still Dirty* Tour. Kim was relieved to hear that there would only be ten dates, fifteen months on from when the original *Dirty* tour had been scheduled to take place – thankfully arranged in a more logical order this time around and in slightly smaller venues. Not only was there less risk of cancellation due to stress overload or – perish the thought – poor ticket sales, but the odds of her properly meeting the band were surely increased?

How right she was.

Although there was always a huge gathering of fans clamouring around the stage door, there certainly weren't the thousands that had turned out previously. However, many of these fervent band-worshippers were to become recognisable faces, who Kim and Sal bumped into at almost every gig and added to their collection of penfriends.

Geraldine was nearly always there – with her mousy tight granny perm and unflattering knitted cardigans. The Irish girls had lost one of their crew – Caroline had recently celebrated her engagement and was saving up for a house – hence the reason she only appeared at one of the shows, with a swarthy Latino lad glued to her side. Callie was another fan notable by her absence. She'd almost always been friendly towards Kim and Sally-Anne but they were undeniably glad to see the back of her, with her beautiful face and cracking figure – they agreed that they could well do without the competition she represented.

However, there were other pretty girls hanging around, notably The Witches of Wolverhampton - Rachell, Anika and Justine, who Kim often wished would bog off and find some other group to follow round the country. Between the three of them they practically fulfilled every man's fantasy.

Rachell was a petite blonde – with masses of curly hair almost down to her pert little bum, which was usually packed into the tightest jeans imaginable. She had dazzling blue eyes, and long lashes that seemed to flutter of their own accord whenever there was a band member in the vicinity.

Anika was dark skinned with dark eyes and shoulder-length, black sleek locks that she often tied up into a high ponytail, creating the impression of a cute, innocent little girl, although she was far from it. Her skirts were even shorter than Sally-Anne's but then minis seemed to be in fashion again and she certainly wore hers well.

Then there was Justine, with her flaming auburn bobbed hair, emerald eyes and fierce scowl, which miraculously disappeared, of course, when she was within spitting distance of a band member. Her skin was pale, with only a smattering of freckles dotted around her perfectly shaped nose and she was so tall and willowy that she could easily have passed for a model. However, she would never win prizes for nicest girl of the year. In fact, Kim would go as far as to say she was a total bitch – and she had real competition in that department from her two friends, who never had a good word to say about anyone. Kim hated her on sight.

Rod from Denmark, well he was a sweetie. Felicity and Claire - two red-headed young sisters from Newcastle - shy but pleasant, they were collected from every single gig by their jovial granddad Ginger George in his clapped-out van. Andy and Tania, a twenty-something couple from the West Country, who always brought sandwiches and a smile for everyone. Judy and her gorgeous boy Sonny who was wheelchair bound but never let anything hold him back. And God help anyone who tried to push in front of him - he would exact his revenge by accelerating over their foot (Sally-Anne swore he'd broken her little toe on one occasion).

There was also a dark-haired lady called Hannah who looked to be in her mid-thirties, and who usually had a little girl in tow. Hannah was nice but very much kept herself to herself. Whilst she was waiting for the band to emerge – usually dressed in her faded old Todd t-shirt – she lavished all her attention on her daughter, who Kim thought was an absolute angel to be fair, singing and clapping along throughout the shows and then waiting patiently, yawning, by her mum's side afterwards. Bless her.

Along with several other familiar faces, these were the regulars, who the band knew they could rely on to be present at almost every gig, to buy every single and album, to support them until their dying day.

The usual back stage crew and their trucks rumbled into Bournemouth for the first gig of the tour and unloaded all the gear, but not before Billy and Rob had paused to chat up any half-decent girls who batted their eyelashes. Sally-Anne was right in there, flirting and stroking Billy's tattooed hairy arm. Kim shuddered - he was a dead ringer for Meatloaf and always looked like he needed a bloody good wash. Yack.

It was obvious that security had been seriously scaled back on this tour, when the band arrived in their bus for the opening night, accompanied by only their tour manager Barry, their almost matronly wardrobe assistant Grace, and two peroxide blonde attractive backing singers, Zoe and Carmel (Kim and Sal took an instant dislike to them but later altered their opinions when they discovered that both women had steady boyfriends and were therefore deemed No Threat Whatsoever).

Todd, first off the bus, looked younger than ever, and he was such a honey that he made everyone want to squeeze and mother him – something that Hannah often did before his feet touched the ground.

Marty, who always looked deep in thought, paused briefly on his way in to sign and smile for the cameras but he maintained a distance, never giving much away or encouraging any of his admirers.

Bren, looking like he'd literally just woken up, with his hair stood up in tufts and his eyes slightly spaced out, stumbled off the bus but soon had everyone in fits of giggles with his weird antics. He was so loud and full of life.

A shy Ady, hiding behind Bazza, almost slipped backstage unnoticed until Geraldine caught up with him and strong-armed him into having his picture taken and giving her a peck on the cheek. He looked positively distressed as he eventually made a break for it and scooted into the building.

And last, but by no means least, was the man they'd all been waiting for. As he emerged from the bus, the crowd surged forward with their album covers and tour programmes all ready to be signed and Kim was dismayed to be almost swallowed up in the chaos. She squeezed in between The Witches of Wolverhampton, ignoring their looks of contempt as she thrust her precious photo right under Ritchie's perfectly shaped nose. He accepted it from her outstretched hand without comment, but one quick glance at the item in his grasp and his head was up, eyes darting about until they settled on the owner of the picture and the shaking hand.

It was a promising start.

'Hi,' Kim said coyly. 'We met you outside The Happy Horse after the end-of-tour-party in Croydon - when that photo was taken.'

'I remember you,' he replied in a raspy, throaty voice, causing her to swallow hard. She became very aware that her heart was pounding furiously against the walls of her chest, as if trying to break out of her body.

'The pretty girl who almost fell at my feet! How could I forget?'

Oh dear god, he *did* remember her. And did he just say she was pretty? Any minute now her legs would give way and he *would* find her spark out on the ground in front of him!

He stared then, as if waiting for something from her. She realised that he wasn't only scrawling *Ritchie Clarke* on the picture, as was the norm - he was writing *'To...'* and he needed to know her name; he was prompting her to say it.

'I'm Kim,' she said, in barely a whisper, flicking imaginary stray hairs out of her eyes and trying to act cool, calm and collected – although it may have been rather too late for that.

He wrote her name. HER NAME. And then scribbled something else - probably just *his* name, but still. He had addressed something to her personally. He knew who she was now. Result.

Returning the picture to Kim's shaky hand, he quickly moved on to sign memorabilia for other people, whilst Barry steered him in the direction of the door.

'He's heading inside for the soundcheck now folks,' Barry said, sweating slightly from the effort of pushing along a much younger and fitter man. 'They'll all pose for photos after the show, if there's time.'

'*Yeah, right*', thought Kim.

Ritchie turned back to wave at the fans as he was about to slide through the door being propped open for him. His eyes scanned the faces in the crowd until they rested on Kim's.

He smiled. She smiled. And then he was gone.

'What the fudge is going on with you and Ritchie, you brazen little hussy?' Sally-Anne was smiling but the glint in her eyes warned Kim that her friend was royally pissed off - presumably because Ritchie had never asked *her* name and had merely signed the usual barely legible *Ritchie Clarke* on her photograph.

'I can't believe he remembered me and thinks I'm pretty. He actually knows my name now too!' Kim did wonder if she should play it down to spare her friend's feelings, but knew if roles had been reversed, Sal would have been shouting it from the rooftops. 'It's the stuff dreams are made of - him looking at me in that sexy, smouldering way, and me – oh lord! I was a hot, gibbering mess! My cheeks are still burning, even now...'

Kim realised that no one was listening to her. Sal had swiftly turned away to wander off and tag onto Shannon's little group, clearly bitten by the green-eyed monster and deciding she'd heard enough. Sod her then!

There may have been no one to discuss it with but it didn't prevent Kim's mind working overtime, thinking about her encounter with Ritchie. Every time she recalled the way he'd said her name and looked at her in an almost provocative way, she had to remind herself to breathe.

For a moment, she remained rooted to the spot, alone and still reeling with shock.

It seemed impossible that she'd been singled out by Ritchie in such a manner. She wanted to relive every second, every gesture and every word and somehow preserve it before it was diluted in any way.

Was it conceivable that it had all been a trick of her mind and she'd imagined the look, the flirty comments, the compliment?

She'd been so busy admiring his smooth, flawless skin and inhaling his aftershave that maybe she hadn't noticed him being as friendly and over-familiar with other girls. She was certain he hadn't but hoped she wasn't reading too much into it and making a fool of herself.

And then she remembered the precious photograph he'd signed and she delved in and retrieved it from her bag, wanting to examine the way he'd written *Kim*; how he'd joined the three letters together and somehow elevated it from being a nothing name to something of importance and value.

But that day was full of surprises and there was one more.

Trembling, she gazed at the scribbled words he'd added to the bottom of the sacred picture and she couldn't help but whisper them aloud.

'*To Kim, Pretty Lady. When you fall, I'll catch you. Much love, Ritch xx*'

That was their beginning.

PART TWO

FRIEND

(1992)

Chapter 7

The entirety of that tour was a dramatic series of highs, each one elevating Kim ever further up to a position she'd never dared to dream she could occupy.

From the opening gig in Bournemouth to the closing night in Birmingham – back in the boys' home town where they almost raised the roof of the grand old-fashioned theatre – it was almost as if she was ticking off items on an invisible wish list:

1. Autographs from and photographs with all band members - check.
2. Surprise shout out from Ritchie on stage ('A big Hello to Kimberley who's celebrating her eighteenth birthday today!') – check.
3. Ritchie's arm around her waist and unexpected hugs – check.
4. Pecking Ritchie on the cheek and an actual kiss ON THE MOUTH! – check.
5. Ritchie serenading her from the stage – check.
6. INVITATION TO END-OF-TOUR BACKSTAGE PARTY TO HOBNOB WITH FAMILIES, FRIENDS AND MINOR CELEBRITIES – CHECK, CHECK, CHECK!

Ritchie had continued with the charm offensive at Bournemouth, repeatedly smiling down at Kim in the audience, reaching out to clasp hold of her hand as she was crushed against the stage and then later throwing his arm around her when he posed for photos post-gig. Sally-Anne had alternated between sarcasm and sulking, then was unusually quiet for the remainder of the evening. The following day, she suddenly decided she had a thing for Bren, claiming Ritchie was a little too clean cut for her liking. Apparently she preferred a bad boy with attitude – and Bren certainly fitted the bill. The switch of allegiances suited Kim just fine. It certainly made her life a whole lot easier.

Kim was still envious of Rachell, Anika and Justine (Witches 1, 2 and 3) who seemed to have it all going on, and who weren't exactly short of attention from the band although, surprisingly, Ritchie generally didn't go overboard. But there were occasions, when they were flirting with him - fluttering their perfectly mascaraed eyelashes, hanging on to his every word and using any conceivable excuse to lay their hands on him - when she couldn't help but wonder why he treated her differently.

'*Kimberley...*' He'd taken to using her full name, rather than the abbreviated version and with only a hint of a Brummie accent, the way he said it rendered her breathless. The only other person to call her Kimberley was her mother, usually when Kim was in deepest shit. When Ritchie was the one addressing her...she wanted him to be the one *undressing her...*

It seemed he never missed an opportunity to pull her in closer when they were posing for yet more pictures together. By the end of the first week, she was convinced she wasn't imagining it. He was definitely *pressed* against her and she was sure his hand rested a little longer on her hip bone than was absolutely necessary.

Ady and Marty tried to dodge any physical contact whatsoever with fans but Bren and Todd were game for a laugh, hugging and puckering up to anyone who asked. Many amorous fans requested a kiss from Ritchie but only a chosen few were actually allowed a fleeting peck on the lips – and they were usually the more attractive ones like the Witches and the Irish girlies. To Kim's surprise, she had also been included in the 'A' list. It certainly raised eyebrows that Ritchie often sought her out and when he kissed her he seemed almost reluctant to tear himself away.

When he took to serenading her from the stage – the same chorus of the same song in every single show - it really did seem that Ritchie had taken a shine to her. Kim felt that she was sinking ever deeper with this man, more that even she dared to admit.

'I see you stumble and I'm there waiting,

No ulterior motives, no time to think,

But a taste of love, a world of anticipation

And suddenly I catch you,

I'm powerless to resist.

Seizing the moment...stealing the kiss.

I'm falling...falling...'

Every evening she glanced around, checking that he wasn't actually singing to another person – fully expecting there to be a more attractive woman behind her. She had to be certain she wasn't making a fool of herself and that he wasn't directing the lyrics to someone else.

But he wasn't, and she wasn't, and those moments were theirs, and belonged to nobody else.

Barry the Beast was still pretty strict when it came to segregating band members and fans - presumably Callie had slipped through the net. However, on arrival at the theatre on the last night of the tour, without any prior warning, Ritchie reached out and gripped Kim's hand, leading her up the staircase and along the cluttered corridor to the tiny dressing room he was to share with Ady.

Struck dumb with shock and almost drowning in a lake of nerves, Kim quaked in her court shoes not only at the prospect of spending time alone with Ritchie, but also at the thought of mixing with other band members in a private setting, rather than on the outside, where they were more or less public property.

She was on friendlier terms with them all now and they always addressed her by name and made general chit-chat. Todd was brilliant – so much fun, kind and sweet to everyone. Bren was still a mad bastard. Rumours were rife that he was inhaling and injecting illegal substances and there were times when he seemed completely off his trolley, bouncing around the place, blurting out random stuff and occasionally tugging on her ponytail if her hair was tied back. She liked him though. He was exceptionally loud but spectacularly entertaining, particularly when he was in his element, up on stage, smashing the life out of his drums.

Marty and Ady were quieter. Initially she'd thought Marty rather standoffish but soon realised that wasn't the case. He was actually far more mature and worldly wise than the other four and it was clear he believed it appropriate and sensible that there were boundaries between the band and their fans. To be fair, he was always smiley and fairly obliging but there was definitely a reluctance to allow anyone to overstep the mark.

Ady was the shy one. He spoke quietly and carefully and although professionally polite, his responses could often be brief. He was happy to take a backseat during interviews and blend into the background. Kim hoped he wouldn't mind her entering into his personal space.

He didn't actually seem too surprised to see her. A bright smile and then he carried on leafing through his daily newspaper, occasionally dunking a digestive biscuit into a steaming mug of tea. If he preferred solitude and peace before taking to the stage, he was too polite to say so.

To Kim's horror, she suddenly regressed into a giggly, silly little girl and for the life of her couldn't seem to string an intelligent sentence together whereas Ritchie's words flowed and he spoke confidently and with the air of someone used to taking the floor.

'So, last night of the tour tonight and it's been an amazing run. It's what it's all about, you know, performing for the fans and feeding off their reaction. And meeting so many, particularly those who travel for hours, showing up night after night, hanging around the stage doors in all weather. I must confess, Kimberley…seeing you almost every day for the last fortnight has definitely been one of my highlights and - please don't tell anyone I said this - you're absolutely my favourite fan, without a shadow of a doubt.'

Yes! Eat that, Three Witches!

'It's been fantastic, Ritchie. We've had the time of our lives and we're gutted that it's all over, for now at least. It doesn't seem real that I'll be back home, sleeping in my own bed tomorrow night - no more shows, no more seeing you until…well whenever the next time that is.'

'Your own bed...mmm. And where is it, this bed of yours? Tell me, where are you living when you're not existing out of a suitcase, like the rest of us?'

Was he actually flirting with her? Because from where she was perched, on the edge of a wobbly glass-topped table, it certainly sounded like he was flirting. Oh, dear god!

'I...I live in Cheshire...not far from Manchester…on the outskirts…in the suburbs.'

Oh my, was that the best she could do? The wicked glint in his eyes suggested he was teasing – that he was well aware of the effect he was having on her and it gave him a thrill.

'And tell me about your life back home - what do you get up to when you're back in Cheshire?'

Well Ritchie, I like to listen to your music, watch you on the TV and bang on about you incessantly, whilst constantly imagining the pair of us writhing around in a king-size bed, butt naked and slathered in…

'Erm…actually nothing too exciting. I work, of course - only in a local convenience shop but the money's decent and the staff there are a lively bunch. I enjoy the occasional night out with friends and spend the following day nursing the hangover from hell, but otherwise,

I'm just hanging about at home. There's no boyfriend on the scene at the moment. I'm well and truly single.'

For goodness sake, why had she said that? She may as well have grabbed herself a great big plate, sat on it, and offered herself up to him. Christ she was a bloody gibbering idiot sometimes.

'Now, I don't believe that for one minute! I bet all the boys are scratching at your door, clamouring for a date with such a beautiful girl.'

Beautiful! As if!

'You've got to be kidding! And even if that was the case – and it most certainly isn't – I haven't yet found a man worth getting serious about...'

The conclusion of that sentence was of course, '...apart from the lead singer of my favourite band...and I'm hoping that he might suddenly have an epiphany and realise he feels exactly the same way about me.'

'Ahem...' Ritchie cleared his throat and turned to face Ady, who glanced up, took the hint and stood up to leave.

'Just nipping to the bog,' he muttered, awkwardly. 'Be back in five.'

There was an uncomfortable moment as they waited for Ady to slip his shoes back on and exit the room. Once the door had shut firmly behind him, the tense silence was broken by the low, seductive tone of Ritchie's voice.

'Come here,' he instructed, seizing hold of Kim's hand and drawing her in to his body. As Ritchie's capable hands encircled her waist and her own shaking hands tentatively reached around his form, feeling the contours of his back beneath the fine cotton shirt, Kim bravely dared to rest her head on his strong shoulder. They shared a few blissful moments locked in that position before he shifted away, only a fraction, to tenderly cup her face in his hand and plant a gentle kiss on her forehead.

Kim was desperate for him to do away with the pleasantries; to stick his tongue down her throat and stick his hands anywhere he liked, but he merely continued to delicately hold her chin, as he softly said, 'We're having a party here tonight, backstage – there's a bar area on site and enough room to cram everyone in. Seeing as me and you are friends now, would you like to join us? You and that loopy mate of yours, of course.'

Would she? Try and stop her!

'Wait by the stage after the gig and I'll send Bobbo down to fetch you. Make sure no one else follows behind.'

'Of course...we'll be there. Thanks for the invitation Ritchie and for letting us celebrate the end of the tour with you.'

'All my pleasure,' he whispered into Kim's ear and the heat of his breath made hers catch in her throat whilst her insides melted into pure liquid desire.

Thank the lord she had donned her best Little Black Dress for the occasion. It looked slightly out of place during daylight hours – like she'd deviated from the Red Light District – but would be just the ticket for a good old knees-up later. And Ritchie's eyes seemed to be roving up and down appreciatively. In fact, he was gazing at her mouth now, and edging ever nearer, closing the space between them as his luscious lips sought out hers...

Those divine lips, so soft but firm, had no sooner connected with her own when the door was noisily flung open and in burst Barry. They immediately sprang apart but he quickly registered the scene and the guilty faces, whereupon Kim was unceremoniously ejected with a 'Come on Ritchie lad, time to do that soundcheck. He'll see you later love.'

Unsteadily descending the stairs and floating out into the car park, it felt like Kim was leaving one planet and landing on another. The fresh air smacked her in the face and was sucked into her lungs. She took several huge gulps and tried to make sense of what had just occurred.

Ritchie. Ritchie Joe Clarke. He had held her, kissed her and invited her to the famously wild end-of-tour party where the other guests would be his bandmates, the crew and anyone and everyone who worked with them. And possibly a few family members. And maybe the odd celebrity they hung out with.

Oh my days!

There was hardly anyone around outside now, but Kim spotted Sally-Anne perched on a low wall behind the tour bus, swinging her legs and scuffing the backs of her black patent heels as they scraped the bricks on impact. She wore a scowl that would sour the freshest of milk, but Kim knew exactly how to win her round.

'Oh, thanks for disappearing backstage without me,' Sally-Anne whinged, her bottom lip jutting out as she let her friend know in no uncertain terms that she was seriously pissed off.

'Come on, Sal – *I* didn't even know I was going backstage! One minute I was chatting to Ritchie and then suddenly my hand was in his and he was leading me away. There wasn't time to turn back to keep you informed!'

'And what exactly DID happen back there, or shouldn't I ask? Did you shag him? Come on, spill the beans!'

'*SALLY-ANNE*! Of course I didn't. It wasn't like that. We were only chatting for a matter of minutes but guess what? He's only gone and invited us both to the backstage party here later on! How good is that?'

'What the....you're kidding me, right?'

'No, of course not! We have the golden tickets...we're in!'

Discharging an ear piercing scream that Kim felt sure could be heard on the other side of town, Sally-Anne's mood flipped in an instant. Squealing, whooping and almost jumping for joy, her previously miserable face was now glowing at the prospect of partying with the band while all other fans waited enviously outside. All beef with Kim was temporarily suspended as she dived on her, squeezing her tightly and bouncing up and down like Tigger on a trampoline.

'Calm down woman!' Kim laughed, attempting to smooth down her best dress before the whole of the clientele in the bar opposite was treated to a full view of her lady parts.

'Calm down? Are you joking? I'll never be calm for the rest of my life if we make it into this party tonight. You're a little star, you are! Are you sure you didn't shag him? Or perform anything else in return for tonight's invitation?'

'Stop it! We're only friends and I'm truly not that kind of girl. He honestly didn't take advantage of me, so there's zilch to disclose. We did have a lovely cuddle and he gently kissed me on the forehead before moving on to my lips. It was mind-blowing and I think we would have snogged good and proper if bloody Bazza hadn't burst in like the grumpy old tornado he is!'

'*OH MY GAWD*! You lucky little cow! It's just as well we're wearing our best clobber. Now, give me your honest opinion. Shall I tug my dress down a bit to treat Bren to an eyeful of my best assets or shall I opt for a classier look and keep them tucked in for the night?'

Despite the end-of-tour mayhem, mishaps and mixing pot of emotions, Kim couldn't remember much of the gig once it was over. Naturally, it was funny and frantic and the perfect end to the perfect tour. Goodness knows how many encores the rowdy audience had demanded. But the finer details later escaped her.

She did, however, remember everything about the after-show party.

As promised, the girls were whisked through the hospitality door by Bobbo (who was a pretty nifty mover for a tank) and up the steep staircase that led to the inner workings of the theatre, where they heard cheesy music belting out, glasses chinking and bursts of raucous laughter. In contrast, the two of them remained usually quiet and Kim wondered if Sal felt as nervous as she did, unsure as to how they would be expected to behave. Just what was the etiquette when one was in this position? They clearly weren't family, crew, or even close friends and yet they were about to slip through the door that had previously been closed and barred to the likes of them; allowed access to a zone where they were more than fans but not quite enough of anything else. Yet.

Kim had fully expected to witness all of the band members singing and swaying together in a tight little huddle, affectionately rehashing the highlights of the tour and toasting its undeniable success. She was surprised to discover that they were dotted around the room in completely separate camps. As the girls cautiously entered the room and were immediately abandoned by Bobbo, the first person of interest Kim spotted was Bren, because her eyes were literally drawn to him - the loudest of the lot. His pint was sloshing around, spilling over on to the carpeted floor, as he gesticulated and performed for his captive audience, consisting of several dodgy-looking mates, a bruiser of a crew member who should have been back out front dismantling the set, and a couple of pale, Morticia-like girls who were pretending to laugh in all of the right places. Not a Callie in sight.

Todd was propped up against the far wall, almost shielded by his family. Jovial but relaxed, every person in his close-knit group was smiling. He looked simply content to be in their company, his arm draped around the shoulders of his proud mum. He was just the cutest.

Ady's parents weren't present but Kim recognised his younger sister right away as she was incredibly pretty and just so like Ady, with her matching strawberry blond hair and intense darkest blue eyes. She appeared to have brought a selection of friends along and they were all making their way over to a table beside a make-shift dancefloor, closely followed by a tall, attractive guy of Scandinavian appearance, with immaculately styled white-blond hair and almost translucent, flawless skin. He'd clearly been lumbered with getting the round in from the free bar as he was carrying an overloaded tray of glasses and bottles. As he approached the gang a chair was pulled out for him beside Ady's sister - presumably he was her latest squeeze. They certainly made a striking couple.

Unsurprisingly, Marty was tucked away in a corner, behind the two backing singers and their partners. He was virtually hidden amongst a huge assortment of friends and family, who all seemed to be thoroughly enjoying themselves but were far more sedate than the other partygoers.

So where was Ritchie?

Ah. The door on the opposite side of the packed room opened to reveal him in all his splendour, flanked by a couple of friends Kim recognised from old fan club pictures. On those snaps the three boys had been almost identical - mucky little lads with tatty clothes and scabby knees. They were worlds apart now. Whilst Ritchie had matured and transitioned from boy to man, reeking of money and good taste, the other two seemed like kids in comparison, with their tracksuits and scruffy, badly cut hair. At least Ritchie didn't have any siblings and his parents weren't around to distract him. Hopefully his mates would be more interested in sinking the free alcohol rather than hanging on to their childhood friend's every word.

'Come on - let's nab a little drinky.' Sally-Anne dragged Kim towards the bar by the strap of her handbag, leaving her with no option other than to follow. As they weaved through the mass of bodies and tried to dodge falling cigarette ash, Kim continued to watch Ritchie, willing him to glance over in her direction, but he never even looked up as Clive, the eccentric little sound man, badgered him about something clearly of vital importance. Piss off Clive.

Perilously carrying vodkas, Britvic 55s and a selection of bottled beers – because Sally-Anne had decided to fill her boots at the bar – they managed to locate two vacant seats at a table occupied by a couple of solemn-faced older men who, they could only presume, were management or record company executives. The chaps looked none too thrilled to have company but the girls ignored their intimidating glares, dragging their chairs as far away as possible from the po-faced old gits. Kim really hoped they were hard of hearing because before she'd even had her first slug of beer, Sally-Anne was already describing exactly how she'd like to lick melted chocolate off Bren's naked body.

Despite the initial thrill of being allowed to party with their favourite band, Kim was slightly miffed that Ritchie hadn't come looking for her. Even if he hadn't spotted her amongst the crowd, surely he could have sought her out?

Ady and Todd dropped by to say hello and the girls were even treated to a lob-sided grin from Marty, but they'd been there for almost an hour before Bren and his gang stormed the dancefloor and Ritchie chose that moment to break away from his friends and wind his way across the room.

Kim didn't want to stare but found she couldn't help herself. Whilst most of the other younger males in the room were dressed in loose t-shirts and well-worn jeans, Ritchie was modelling a pair of tailored slate grey trousers with a white, almost transparent, linen shirt hanging out of the waistband. Only two shirt buttons were fastened up, revealing a tanned, taut chest with barely a smattering of body hair. All the flesh on display did nothing to calm her nerves or suppress the agonising ache she endured inside for him.

He caught her openly admiring him and winked – a teasing, playful gesture that also managed to be as suggestive and sexy as hell.

'Hey!' he said, approaching their table and holding out his hand for Kim to take. 'What are you two doing, floundering amongst the money men? We can't have those cute little party dresses going to waste now, can we? Time to have some fun!'

Abandoning their drinks without so much as a backwards glance, they obligingly followed his lead and found themselves in the middle of the 'dancefloor', being unintentionally bashed about by an over-excitable Bren, who was clearly high on life or *something*. Ritchie was as sexy a dancer offstage as he was on, and although they couldn't compete with his fluid body moves and fantastic arse wiggling, they were determined to have a bloody good go.

Bren misjudged another twirl and landed in a heap on a completely taken-unawares Sally-Anne, but before she'd even started to voice her outrage, he'd scooped her up and was raising her in the air as if she was weightless. Thank the lord she wasn't knickerless because everyone in the vicinity was treated to an eyeful as her skirt wrinkled up around her waist. If she hadn't been so pissed, and it hadn't been Bren hoisting her up and spinning her around, she might have had an awful lot more to say on the subject.

Ritchie took the opportunity to wrap his arm around Kim's waist and they were soon grinding to the music, bodies locked together, Kim's heart beating furiously. Even in her inebriated state, she thought to herself, 'I can't believe this is happening to me. I can't believe I'm at a backstage end-of-tour party for this famous, popular, *magnificent* band and this man – this POP IDOL...this ROCK STAR...this human being who literally makes my heart turn over – is holding me and looking at me in *that* way, leaving me in no doubt as to what he has in mind for later...'

'Shall we take a breather in the dressing room while everyone else is busy?' Ritchie's low voice in her ear, barely audible over the volume of the disco beat, interrupted her musings and Kim saw that he was gesturing towards Bren and Sally-Anne, who were gyrating so low down that they were practically grazing the floor and all of the beer slop on it. Yes, they were definitely busy.

With alcohol-induced bravado, she tried to raise her eyebrows in what she hoped was a sultry manner rather than one which made her look simple and said 'Sure.' They quietly slipped out of the room and he led her through the maze of corridors, banging through countless fire doors before they arrived in an area signed PRIVATE: ONLY PERFORMERS BEYOND THIS POINT and they stumbled through the next door and into his cluttered dressing room.

There was no Ady on this occasion. And no doubt where this was headed when Ritchie sank down on the two-seater sofa, growled 'Come here', and patted the cushion next to him. Before Kim could even respond he suddenly caught hold of her weak little arms with his far stronger ones, dragging her on top of him and she ended up in a kneeling position, his legs sandwiched between hers. Their eyes locked and Kim gasped, as fireworks exploded down below.

Reaching up to brush errant curls away from her face with his thumbs, as her heart thundered in her chest and the Little Black Dress rode up so high that the hem dug into her waist, Ritchie sighed and whispered 'My god, you're so beautiful. Kiss me, Kimberley...'

His lips bore down on hers before she had chance to oblige and she was forced to clutch the lapels of his shirt to steady herself. He pushed his tongue into her mouth and she had never known pleasure like it, instinctively mirroring his actions. He tasted of red wine and ever so slightly of cigarettes (Ah ha! The rumours were true – he clearly did enjoy the odd cheeky smoke) but it was delicious and moreish and neither of them apparently wanted to come up for air.

His gold signet ring caught the fine hair at the nape of her neck as he slid his hand under her curls and twisted them around his fingers, tugging the tendrils sharply. Her head jerked backwards and he homed in quickly, his lips finding her neck, nibbling and sucking and eventually blazing a trail down to her chest and cleavage. Involuntary gasps escaped from Kim's mouth and her hands quickly found their way inside his shirt, her nails scraping his chest and her fingertips daring to touch and rub and explore.

She was shaking, terrified of what was to come, as much as she wanted it. Oh yes, she definitely wanted it. But he was older, girls literally worshipped at his feet and he'd no doubt bedded hundreds of them. She couldn't allow herself to become merely another notch on his bedpost. She was still a virgin and worried that any sexual relations between them might turn out to be an unsatisfactory experience for him due to her inexperience and nervous disposition.

His hands were cupping her backside now...and she sensed he was about to take it to the next level. She wanted to stop him...but she didn't want him to stop.

And then he stopped.

Kim blinked in surprise as he drew away slightly and caught his breath for a moment.

Oh, don't stop!

'You're shaking darling? Are you okay?'

Silently nodding her head, she allowed her hands to reach lower down inside of his shirt - previously unexplored territory.

Ritchie tipped his head back, moaned and then sighed dramatically.

'I like you a lot Kimberley – you know that. But that's the problem. I treasure our friendship and respect you too much to treat you like a groupie. So we can't do this – not here and now. Not in these circumstances. For a start, you're younger than me and it would be wrong to take advantage when you're slightly inebriated, or use my celebrity status to try and have my wicked way with you. So let's take our time – there will be other occasions. Besides...Barry and Derek would go ballistic if they rumbled us!'

Derek was the band's actual manager who dealt with their day-to-day affairs when they weren't out on the road – a tall, wiry, stern looking man who she'd only seen on a few occasions. He said little, was highly intimidating and Kim totally understood where Ritchie was coming from – probably best to keep him on side. And the band had gone on record, time and time again, stating they were well and truly single, concentrating on their music careers. They couldn't afford to be distracted by relationships. It was totally their image – this clean-cut, wholesome, attractive, young band who were committed to nobody but each other. It was a huge part of what had attracted the fans in their thousands from the outset.

'Is it true you all had to sign to say you would remain single for the duration of your contracts?' she enquired, reluctantly hoicking up the straps of her dress which had somehow slid down over her shoulders to reveal much of her black lacy Wonderbra. She'd noticed Ritchie ogling her more than ample chest.

'More or less, yes. Apparently, we wouldn't be as sellable with girlfriends, wives and children in our lives. It's probably not even legal but I know we'd be toast if we crossed that line – Derek's made that perfectly clear.'

'Bloody hell, he's ruthless isn't he?'

'Worse than that. I hate him. But he knows what he's doing and it's worked thus far and, unfortunately, the music isn't enough. We've no problem getting bums on seats for gigs but record sales have slipped, so we have to comply. I'm not prepared to risk losing everything I've worked my arse off for and Derek says it's non-negotiable. But for heaven's sake, how am I supposed to comply when I have an irresistible young thing nestled in my lap, making me want to commit unspeakable acts? I must be a real life saint!'

'Saint Ritchie! Yes, I like that. You're a very naughty saint though,' she teased, leaning forward to nibble on his chest.'

'Mmmm...and you are a very naughty girl, Kimberley with the very kissy lips and the fabulous pair of tits...'

'Oy!' she swatted him playfully with her hand and he caught hold of it and tenderly kissed the inside of her wrist.

'We have to return to the party now darling, before Derek or one of the others comes looking for me. If they find us like this, I'm in a whole heap of trouble.'

Reluctantly, she slid off his knee and stood up, wiggling slightly to pull down her dress but before she could complete the job, Ritchie leant forward and gently licked the inside of her thighs and it was almost too much to bear. His tongue wetting that delicate skin was the most erotic experience of her life. She'd never known anything else that even came close.

'Okay, you go first and then hopefully no one will suspect anything. Turn left, through the fire door, up the stairs, through the next set of doors and you'll see the entrance to the bar a little further along. I'll be back in a minute. Apparently I need to do some networking and smarming with the suits so you'll have to excuse me for a while.'

His lips expertly homed in on hers again and she dissolved. When he eventually held the door open and murmured, 'See you later, Kimberley,' she smiled shyly, despite all that had just occurred, and slipped through, glancing furtively around to check there was no one else lurking around. Once the fire door had safely closed behind her, she paused to try and take stock.

'Oh my fucking god! Oh my fucking Christ!' Kim tried to calm down, pinching herself to confirm that she'd actually been awake and hadn't been dreaming. Difficult as it was to comprehend, Ritchie Joe Clarke was attracted to her. She had been kissed, stroked and *wanted* by one of the most lusted-after men in Britain.

With doddery legs, like an old aged pensioner on a damp day, she headed back in the direction of the party and tried to slither into the room without raising suspicion. Of course, all eyes seemed to be on her.

A knowing look from Todd. A concerned frown from Carmel. The hint of a smile on Ady's face as he shook his head.

She was beginning to wonder if she *had* remembered to pull her skirt down after all.

The one person who appeared to be oblivious that she'd gone AWOL was Sally-Anne. She had her back to Kim but was clearly snogging the face off Meatloaf Billy in a dark corner of the room. Eugh. *She'd* have hidden in a dark corner if she'd been forced to tongue *that* guy.

However, when Sal eventually came up for air and trotted off to the toilet, she looked pretty pleased with herself, so who was Kim to judge?

She ordered another vodka and retreated to a quiet spot, half-hidden behind a huge plastic yukka plant, where she recalled every word, every touch, every moment from the secret liaison in the dressing room.

It seemed like forever before Ritchie returned to the room. When he did, he was immediately ambushed by Barry and the money men, and she knew it was unlikely that she'd command his attention again that night. But it was okay. She could still taste him, still feel his touch on her skin, still hear him whispering her name – and she knew she meant something to him - that he wanted her.

That was enough. For now.

Chapter 8

Returning to normality once the tour was over proved to be a struggle for Kim. Her home life, work and relationships that existed outside of the *Show Me Yours* bubble were her reality. The life of fame and fortune she'd glimpsed was one that belonged to other people, not destined for the likes of her. She had to learn how to fit in again with family, friends and colleagues because, if truth be told, they'd been all but forgotten whilst she was off crisscrossing the country, allowing her heart to be stolen by the man she'd adored since she was thirteen years old.

After a few stern words from the Senior Summers' concerning lack of contact while she'd been away followed by an initially frosty reception from her exhausted colleagues who'd been covering her shifts, everything began to settle down and Kim slowly slipped back into her old life, tolerating the confines of her mundane existence. But she remained restless.

She couldn't, of course, reveal everything but she did confess to her mum that she'd been edging ever closer to this extraordinary man who'd been singling her out for attention throughout the tour, singing those special words to her as if she was the only girl in the world. The worried expression on her mother's face said it all and there was an uncomfortable moment when she cleared her throat and warned, 'Just be careful, Kimmy, and don't do anything silly. The likelihood is that this man has a girlfriend on every continent and he's probably a master at covering his tracks...'

Like an atomic bomb, Kim went off.

'Oh, thanks very much!' she shrieked. 'You couldn't simply be happy and congratulate me on meeting someone as drop-dead gorgeous as Ritchie. Nooooo...of course not, because Pessimism is your middle name! How very typical of you to take the shine off everything and put me firmly back in my place! *Stay in your lane, Kim! Don't reach for the stars! Someone like you should never dream big!* Good to know I have your unwavering support, as always *Alison*!'

Kim raged that she was done confiding in this suspicious, sceptical woman who clearly had no understanding of what made her daughter tick nor any clue as to what constituted real love.

Nicky at least was pleased for her: 'Bloody hell, I can't believe you got down and dirty with an actual real-life rock star!'

She did, however, raise a perfectly sculptured eyebrow when Kim reluctantly admitted that there were no plans for her and Ritchie to meet up privately.

Kim instantly knew what Nicky was thinking. If Ritchie was keen as mustard then why hadn't he given her his number or arranged to see her again? But this was a real-life popstar whose diary was full to bursting. Kim accepted how difficult it was for him. They hadn't even been able to say goodbye properly on the night of the party. He'd been stuck with the suits and nobodies who made money from his talent until Barry had decided it was finally time for them to leave, before someone picked a fight or disgraced themselves. A little too late for Bren, who'd thrown up over the nearest table, smashed approximately a thousand beer glasses and almost come to blows with Carmel's boyfriend.

A bright light was extinguished when Ritchie left the room and suddenly Kim had felt very alone. At least he'd blown her a kiss on his way out and she knew he wouldn't forget her. And there was always next time. Meatloaf Billy had also disappeared around the same time – to do some work, or take some drugs or go and get his head down (*where* didn't bear thinking about) – so she had Sally-Anne back again, complete with swollen lips, angry love bites emblazoned around her neck and shredded tights.

With all five band members gone, there was little reason for the girls to hang around, even taking into account the complimentary bar. Approximately fifteen minutes later, like Elvis, they had left the building, Sally-Anne cursing that they hadn't departed earlier, or preferably WITH the band, to enable all of the other fans to witness them fraternising with the boys.

So, no - there were no exchanged numbers or whispered promises and Kim would have to exist on the memory of those kisses until the next gig, whenever that was.

Reluctantly accepting that 'life goes on', Kim began socialising with her work mates again – after pay day of course. Everyone was eager to catch up on all of the tasty titbits from the tour, although she only provided her colleagues with a watered down version of events. Janice sighed and demanded to know if Ritchie had any single, older friends whilst Bryony kept asking if they'd set a date for the wedding, and Adam, bless him, told her he would duff 'that Clarke fella' up and he'd never sing again, if he ever hurt her or let her down.

She never expected them to completely understand. How could they imagine what it was like to dance in her shoes when they weren't a fan and they hadn't been there. Even to her own ears her situation appeared bizarre and she sounded incredibly naive whenever she tried to justify the reasons for keeping her new romance shrouded in secrecy

As time passed and there were very few updates on the band, Kim grew increasingly more frustrated and wondered if she had in fact dreamt what had occurred between herself and Ritchie. If only she had a number for him or some way of contacting him personally!

Eventually Sally-Anne decided to write to Bren via their management's Post Office Box number and Kim eventually caved in and mailed off a letter to Ritchie, begrudgingly including a stamped addressed envelope. She was careful with her words and the letter was heavily censored because she knew Ritchie wouldn't be the only one to read it. She wanted to pour her heart out to him but was forced to keep her tone light and frothy.

Every day she dived on the post, desperate for a response, but there was nothing.

The weeks dragged on. When she'd finally given up hope, she returned from work one afternoon to find a familiar looking envelope propped up on the fireplace. With a shaky hand, she tore open the envelope, anticipating a short letter or something that would let her know he was still thinking of her – that he missed her as much as she missed him.

A signed photo of Ritchie dropped out. Granted, it was one she hadn't seen before and it was personally signed to her, but it was still only a photograph.

'IS THAT FUCKING IT?' she bellowed to an empty room. 'Is that all I'm worthy of after all your bullshit?'

And then she noticed. A tiny detail but it was of great significance. Ritchie only ever added one kiss after his name, even when he was writing a personal dedication, no matter who was the recipient.

There were three kisses on her picture. Three.

It was a sign, she was convinced. He clearly couldn't add a message when all and sundry would see it before it was dispatched to Kim. He was hardly likely to stick his telephone number on there or any terms of endearment. No, this was their little secret.

She hugged the picture to her chest. His signature. His kisses. Their secret.

*

With no gigs on the horizon, Kim agreed to venture out with her colleagues to celebrate Adam's birthday. Nicky tagged along and it was almost like old times as they glammed up and got tanked up in Kim's bedroom before taking a taxi into town, giggly, giddy and raring to go.

Nicky was her usual assertive, vivacious self, somehow squeezing into a scrum of bevvied-up rugby players who, despite their huge, bulky exteriors, were incredibly sweet and entertaining. As soon as she clapped eyes on a blond, blue-eyed hunk with an endearing smile and, thankfully, all his own teeth, she was smitten and it appeared that the attraction was very much mutual. She and Connor spent the rest of the evening glued together and gazing into each other's eyes and Kim had a feeling this was the start of something spectacular. Good for Nicky.

They had a fantastic night but, without warning, Kim was clattered with a sudden bout of loneliness, as she contemplated the distance between herself and Ritchie, yearning to be back in his arms. Kim took advantage of Adam's genuine concern, by assigning him the role of designated Agony Uncle, complaining about her miserable predicament and the agony of coping with long distance relationships. Adam insisted she deserved someone who could devote ALL of their time to her rather than only a fraction of it – that someone as beautiful as her should be cherished, rather than neglected. Kim told him he was the kindest, loveliest man ever, but his arm draped around her shoulders and the warmth of his male form budging up next to hers in the stairwell only served to remind her how complete she had felt with Ritchie and how empty her life was without him.

She tried to contain her unhappiness – it was Adam's birthday after all - but the night ended with Kim crying into her pillow, wondering exactly where Ritchie was and what he was doing.

And if Kimberley Helen Summers was on his mind.

*

'He's done what?'

'He's given his notice in, that's what he's done!' Bryony's face was an unflattering shade of burgundy as she delivered her newsflash within thirty seconds of Kim's arrival at the shop.

'But WHY? He loves his job!' Kim was gobsmacked that Adam was leaving. There'd never been any indication that he was unhappy or on the hunt for another position. In fact, it was rumoured that he was up for promotion, likely to take over as manager when their current boss moved on to pastures new.

'Why? I tell you what - why don't YOU ask him *why* he's leaving. Just take a moment to go question the man himself and find out exactly WHY he can no longer abide working here.' Kim might have expected the besotted Bryony to be upset but the young girl was positively spitting venom at her for some unknown reason, in a reaction that was totally over the top.

Kim's heart sank because *she* was also gutted that Adam was going. He'd been a real friend to her and they'd formed an incredibly close bond. She couldn't imagine working in the late shop and not being on shift with him and the thought of not seeing him most days, or hardly ever at all, and losing his valued friendship was actually too sad to contemplate. She didn't understand how he could have made such a momentous decision all by himself, without consulting anyone else. He could have confided in her.

Seeking him out during her lunch break, after a fraught morning when he certainly appeared to be avoiding each and every one of his colleagues, she finally caught up with him out back, where he was breaking down cardboard boxes and looking particularly miserable, a frown most definitely turning his warm smile upside down. And the way he was thumping those boxes left her in no doubt as to his state of mind. But why?

'Hey you,' she said softly, approaching with caution. 'What gives? Bryony filled me in on your news and it completely knocked the wind out of my sails. Why on earth are you leaving? I can't believe you've handed in your notice without speaking to any of us first. Everyone's devastated and I, for one, am absolutely in pieces. Presumably you've found a better job where you will earn a shit-load of money and not have to wear these nasty polyester shirts that are covered in all manner of stains?'

Eventually he paused and made eye contact with Kim but said nothing. Pretending to punch him in the arm, Kim added, 'You must be mad! I can't believe you want to leave behind the temperamental toilet that only works on every fourth flush, the stupidly timed shifts designed to allow maximum waiting time at bus stops and, of course, our witty and intelligent banter!' She figured a joke might break the ice a little, however feeble it was.

Slamming down the crisp box he'd been ripping the hell out of, he took one step towards Kim and rewarded her with a weak smile which didn't quite meet his eyes. They shone brightly, but not in a good way.

'Okay, if you insist, I'll tell you the real reason I'm leaving, Kim. I'm jacking this job in not because I've suddenly developed a deep hatred of shelf-stacking, nor because I've become massively ambitious overnight. The reason why I can no longer work in this little shop that's been a second home to me for the last two years is because I need to get away from YOU. Because guess what, I'm in love with you. Yes, me. In love with you. There, I've said it.'

He kicked the dismantled crisp box and launched it across the car park. A shellshocked Kim tried to speak but couldn't get a word in edgeways as Adam continued with his rant.

'But you're in love with Ritchie frigging Clarke. I've tried to drop hints and show you how I feel but you've remained completely oblivious because of your infatuation with a man who I can never compete with. Let's face it, why would you be interested in me when you have a world famous pop star dribbling over you, seducing you in dressing rooms and keeping you dangling on a string?'

Stunned, like an armed robber who's just been tasered, Kim opened her mouth to say something in response, but this time no words came.

'I've had to listen to you whining on about him – how *gorgeous* he is, how much you *love* him and what a *fantastic kisser* he is – while all the while it's been slaying me. Every time you mention his bloody name, it chips away another piece of my heart, but not once have you ever noticed my misery. And you expect me to continue working alongside you, now things have stepped up a gear between you and this vain, arrogant gobshite? Well I'm sorry but I'm done. Seeing you all of the time whilst knowing I can never have you because you'll never, ever look at me *that* way, is only rubbing salt in my wounds. It's time I grew a pair, obliterated you from my life and moved on.'

He stamped on another box, venting a degree of his frustration and previously concealed anger...and Kim felt like someone had stamped all over her heart. How could she have done this to her compassionate, considerate friend? When did she turn into such an insular, insensitive bitch?

'Adam, listen to me – please!' She caught hold of his arm, but he shrugged her off and took a step backwards. 'I'm so sorry, Adam. You're right, I never knew but honestly, if I had, I would have behaved differently and I promise you, I would never, ever, have knowingly hurt you. Since the day I was lucky enough to bag this job, you've been an amazing friend to me – to all of us - and...and although I may not have considered you as boyfriend material, it's not only because of Ritchie – who I *do* love, and I'm sorry to say that if it hurts you but I really can't help how *I* feel. You and I have such a beautiful friendship and I could never risk losing it for the sake of a boyfriend-girlfriend relationship that may, or may not, work out. It's certainly not because I don't care about you, because I adore you. You're handsome and hilarious and so special to me...'

'But clearly not special enough.'

Adam threw Kim one last pained look, abandoned the torn piles of cardboard and returned to the shop, leaving her standing alone in the middle of the car park, with the first spots of rain beginning to fall, and a huge lump forming in her throat.

*

Bryony had organised an intimate leaving party for Adam – so intimate that Kim wasn't invited. When he finally hung up his staff fleece for the last time and said his goodbyes Kim cried like a baby and flung her arms around him. His eyes filled with tears as he gently extracted himself from her hold and then he walked out of the shop and out of her life.

He promised to keep in touch with everyone but Kim certainly didn't hear from him again. She missed him at work and the situation was exacerbated by the fact that (a) his replacement was a strange, middle-aged man named Bert who harped on incessantly about his pigeons and (b) Bryony behaved like an absolute cow – deliberately landing Kim in the shit a few times and refusing to speak to her, even when it made the job virtually impossible.

Bryony quit a few weeks later.

The job Kim had actually enjoyed, despite all of her protests to the contrary, had suddenly deteriorated into a slog she hated with a vengeance, but she needed the money so she had to stay put.

And then suddenly there was light at the end of a very long tunnel when it was announced that there was new SMY music in the pipeline and several television appearances in the offing – one of which was on a weekly entertainment programme produced in Manchester! And the beauty of it was, that most fans were unaware of the actual date of recording – it was widely understood to be at the end of the month – but, thanks to a contact Kim had acquired at the television studios (she'd sweet-talked an old guy over the telephone who she suspected felt sorry for her), she knew better.

On a quiet Thursday morning, after Kim had pulled a sickie from work, they found themselves loitering outside an old grey stone building that housed not only various television studios but also the local radio station.

Sally-Anne had arrived by coach the previous evening and the girls had whispered long into the night about Ritchie and Bren. The next morning, they spent hours styling hair and applying copious layers of make-up to try and ensure they looked their very best - hoping Ritchie and Bren would instantly sit up and take notice.

Sal had backcombed her recently bleached blonde bob and slapped on a hot pink lipstick to match her even hotter pink micro mini skirt. Her fitted black polo neck sweater, which she'd deliberately shrunk in the washer, left nothing to the imagination.

Kim was aiming for a rather more sophisticated and elegant look, with her relatively expensive, well cut trouser suit (but low cut blouse of course, revealing a cleavage Pamela Anderson would have been proud of), high heels and simple gold jewellery. But waiting in a force ten gale for over an hour soon put paid to that plan.

By the time the two black cabs pulled up an hour later than scheduled and the boys spilled out onto the pavement, both girls were weary and weather-beaten but Bren, Todd, Marty and Ady looked delighted to see them. There was an immediate chorus of 'Kim! How good to see you again. Sally-Anne! Hello you. How have you both been?' and each girl basked in the attention and familiarity.

Ritchie, however, seemed in no rush to leave the back seat of his cab and Kim was peeved. He must have seen her by now. God forbid that he should leap out and make a fuss of her.

Finally, a long, slim pair of legs, encased in gun-metal grey, torn jeans, slid out of the vehicle and Kim saw for the first time that he was sporting a ripped, crew neck, Rolling Stones t-shirt and fringed, jaded black leather jacket, looking for all the world like he was about to straddle a Harley Davidson and take off into the sunset (hopefully with her riding pillion). His hair remained as shiny and styled as ever and she felt an overwhelming urge to run her fingers through it whilst checking if those lips were as ripe and kissable as she remembered...

'Kimberley!' he exclaimed, enveloping her in a tight, affectionate hug, his warm breath on her hair, his scent rocketing up her lust levels. They stayed together in that position, probably a moment longer than any pop star and fan should, before he released her - reluctantly it seemed. Clamping both of her shaking hands in his warm ones he said, 'Good god, you're freezing! You must have been waiting a while. Come on, let's get you up into that canteen where we can grab a coffee and do some serious catching up.'

And just like that, they were in. Sally-Anne was impersonating a goldfish again, as they followed Ritchie through security and onwards into the lift, along with Marty and a young Chinese girl with the most beautiful name, 'Ah Lam'. The tiny little thing sported long plaits, huge gold-rimmed glasses and was apparently employed by the record company. It was to be hoped that she was also discreet.

Marty was humming some funky tune he'd apparently been working on that morning, and Ah Lam chattered incessantly about tight schedules and reclaiming expenses, as Sally-Anne remained freakishly quiet and in awe. Ritchie repeatedly squeezed Kim's hand and, as the doors opened and they exited the lift, she felt a gentle pat on her bum. She hoped to god it was Ritchie and no one else.

Again, she was surprised at the lack of banter and contact between the band members off stage. Todd, Marty and Ady retired to a quiet corner with freshly brewed coffees and daily newspapers, whilst Bren held court amongst the catering staff who giggled and shrieked as he juggled first doughnuts and then cigarette lighters for their entertainment.

Ah Lam had wandered off, complete with her clipboard and pager, and Ritchie treated Kim and Sally-Anne to hot chocolates topped with huge dollops of whipped cream. They sat down at a freshly wiped table, exchanging pleasantries, but it wasn't long before Ritchie stood again and abruptly hauled Kim to her feet, instructing her to follow him whilst shouting over to Bren that he should 'Keep Sally-Anne company,' as there was something he needed to show Kim.

Her mouth was suddenly as dry as the time she'd sunk eight Black Russians at a friend's eighteenth birthday party and thought she was actually dying from dehydration the following morning. She complied with his instructions, studiously avoiding making eye contact with Sally-Anne in case her composure slipped and she blurted out something ridiculously inane that would make her sound like a first class chump.

As the door swung closed behind them, Ritchie reached for Kim's hand and she positively glowed from head to foot with the heat of his touch. Anticipating that they were heading for his dressing room, she expected it to be a lengthier journey before they reached their final destination, but within thirty seconds of leaving the canteen, she was literally yanked into what could only be described as a broom cupboard, and her last thought before he covered her mouth with his own, was, 'Oh Jeez, I'm going to be doing it next to the mop.'

His kisses were long and loving and there wasn't a millimetre of the inside of her mouth that he didn't reach with his ever-probing tongue. She was putty in his hands, and their fumblings in the tiniest of spaces in the pitch black, with staff and visitors shuffling up and down the corridor outside of the very firmly closed door, somehow made the whole experience more erotic. She was the hottest and horniest she'd ever been as he pinged open the buttons of her shirt and delved inside, with a huge sigh and a 'God, I've missed these.'

Kim's hands were up inside his designer ripped t-shirt and she couldn't resist a tweak of his nipples. Ritchie released a strangled moan and then she was pushed even harder against the wall as his hands urgently roamed under the soft fabric of her shirt. Presumably she was about to get a taste of her own medicine.

Ideally there would have been a king-size, four poster bed with the gentle sound of rhythmic music in the background – and if champagne, rose petals and satin sheets had been involved then that would have been stupendous. She'd never planned a quickie in a smelly cupboard with a brush handle digging into her back.

And it would seem, neither had he.

Despite the fact that she was arching and aching for him and quite prepared to get down and dirty amongst the cleaning products, Ritchie again halted the proceedings mid-action.

'No, Kimberley. No. As wonderful as this is, it's not right. Not here. Not now. You deserve better than this – and you're going to get it. When the time *is* right and we're not sneaking around like a couple of school kids hiding from parents, I'll take you somewhere special and show you how it should be done...'

Oh god, take me now! Show me now!

'Ohhhh...' She couldn't hide the disappointed moan that escaped from her throat. She knew that waiting was the sensible option, but her body was betraying her head and she was willing him to change his mind. Still, she couldn't doubt the integrity of the man. If he'd just wanted a no-strings, quick shag he could have had it – and afterwards dropped her like a hot potato. But instead he was prepared to exert a degree of self-control and treat her with care and respect. There was no denying he had feelings for her - that this wasn't simply an opportunist fling for him. When the man who can have anyone is prepared to wait for you, then that really is something.

'Oh Ritchie, you're one of a kind! Very few men would have the decency or willpower to say no in these circumstances.' She buried her head in his chest in the dark, drinking in the scent of his aftershave and the smell of pure, undiluted *him*.

He held her as she nestled in and they remained that way, clamped together, until Kim had to pull away to voice her frustrations.

'But I don't understand why you guys can't go public with girlfriends. Surely your fans would expect at least one of you to have found love by now. It's pushing the boundaries of believability to claim that NONE of you are romantically involved or have an active sex life...'

'We're still under contract darling, and although living like a monk isn't in the small print, we've been told in no uncertain terms that it's all over if we start parading any women around. Apparently it would drive away the fans in droves. I've told the Big Boss and all his flunkies that I truly don't think it would make much difference now and, I'm guessing, fans probably *are* wondering why we've all been single for so long. But Derek doesn't mind us having our fun as long as we're discreet and keep it under wraps. Actually, I can let you into a little secret if you promise to keep it to yourself?'

'Ooh yes please...and I promise faithfully it won't go any further than this room.' The thought flitted through Kim's mind that Sally-Anne had a weird talent for worming out the most deeply buried secrets. She'd have to be careful she didn't crumble under interrogation.

'Well you mustn't breathe a word of it, but Marty's had a girlfriend for years and they've recently got engaged.'

'What? Oh my god, how *has* he kept that from everyone, especially the press? I can't believe no one knows! Surely that paves the way for the rest of you to have a partner?'

'You would think! But no, apparently. Marty's older and his fan base is significantly less, particularly when you compare it to mine or Todd's. Ebony – his good lady – has also stayed completely out of the limelight rather than strutting down the red carpet or accompanying him on trips abroad. But what kind of relationship is that? You're right, you know – it *is* ridiculous in today's day and age! It's time I spoke up and stopped falling in line. The trouble is, our fan base is still relatively young. If we were appealing to a more mature or mixed market then there would be no issue, as the majority of those fans would be happy to see us firmly ensconced in a relationship, married or even on the cusp of starting a family.'

'But you're *all* growing up now. You can't stay single forever – surely the management must realise that?'

'Yes, but they're hellbent on milking the teenage market for as long as they can - it's a limited shelf-life, you see. Later they'll have to consider an alternative strategy. Watch this space...' He whispered into her ear and Kim shivered as his fingertip trailed lightly down between her breasts. Oh my, this man was good!

There was no way round it - she would simply have to take what she could get at this stage. But Ritchie seemed hopeful that change was on the horizon, so who knew what the future held. Maybe the day would come when she could be by Ritchie's side for the whole world to see and no one would bat an eyelid.

Maybe.

*

They exited the broom cupboard at precisely the same time as a cleaner entered - but the sight of them fastening up buttons and tugging down tops didn't even raise one of her caterpillar eyebrows. Clearly she'd seen far worse in this building. Their return to the canteen was met with a chorus of wolf whistles but before Kim had even recovered from her blushes, Ritchie and the other band members were whisked away to hair and make-up, leaving Kim to be grilled by Sally-Anne.

'Dirty bastard!' she practically shouted, causing several heads to swivel round, as people sought to identify the lowlife in question. 'Fancy forcing you into a scummy cupboard to have his wicked way with you! I thought the man had class!'

'Sally-Anne, will you keep your voice down and – just for the record – he didn't *force* me in anywhere. It was merely a convenient quiet place – probably the first unlocked room we stumbled across – and, believe me, I went in there willingly. And he did *not* have his wicked way with me! There was some kissing and a degree of fondling but that was it. He was adamant that he didn't want to take advantage and promised we would go somewhere much nicer to...well...become intimate when the time is right. He's so considerate and caring...'

'Fondling? Become intimate? Are you actually ninety-eight years old? And I'm not being funny, but he's had multiple opportunities now to roger the living daylights out of you and he hasn't. My guess is either (a) he doesn't actually *want* to do it with you or (b) he's absolutely 100% gay.'

'Please lower your volume,' Kim begged. Discreet Sal was not. And if Kim wasn't careful, she could really screw things up between her and Ritchie.

'Honestly, it's not a case of that. His sexuality is certainly not an issue – believe me – and he definitely wants me and bloody hell, I want him. But he's desperate for the setting to be perfect and the time to be right, to make it as special and memorable as possible rather than risk turning it into something seedy...'

From the scornful expression on Sally-Anne's face, it was clear she wasn't exactly convinced but let it go as she was desperate to talk about Bren. He'd apparently hinted at the possibility of Sal joining him in his hotel suite one night for some fun and games, although she'd been shocked when he'd added that she might like to bring an adventurous friend along too. Kim hoped *she* wasn't that 'friend'. Anyway, Sal was happy because she'd had a very touchy-feely Bren all to herself, so all was well for the time being.

The recording of the show went fairly smoothly, although Kim was seriously tempted to remove her shoe and launch it at the ditzy presenter if she fluffed her lines one more time. To the girls' dismay, they weren't allowed to leave the studio as soon as the band had finished recording their segment and had to endure another hour of inane chat about the scanty outfits of the latest top model and how make-up on men was all the rage again.

When they were finally able to make a break for freedom, shoving their way through dawdling audience members, the boys were nowhere to be found. The security guard at the exit confirmed that yes, he had seen where the band had gone – out of the doors and back into their awaiting cabs.

Sally-Anne spat out a variety of expletives and Kim actually cried. What had been such a magnificent morning that had held so much promise had suddenly gone up in smoke and *Show Me Yours* had disappeared as fast as they had arrived. Ritchie hadn't even said goodbye, let alone made plans for the future. There would be no night of passion in a five star hotel to look forward to.

'I don't suppose the lead singer of the band left a message for me?' she asked – even though she already knew the answer. The guard looked at her as if she was an idiot, and she certainly felt like one.

Yet again she'd been short-changed. She'd expected to take away something tangible, something real, something *for her*…but all she had was another memory to add to the album, of a day when she'd thought Ritchie was hers – but he really and truly wasn't.

Chapter 9

'Lend us a bit of your lippy, Kim. This frosted pink gloss of mine is practically invisible...and I can't have Bren thinking I've let standards slip.'

Trying not to think about cold sores or exactly where that mouth of Sal's had been, Kim tossed her the expensive plum coloured everlasting lipstick she'd treated herself to in Boots the previous week, wincing as Sal applied such pressure that it was likely to snap in two, as she painted her lips and also a couple of her front teeth.

Kim couldn't believe they were finally about to see the boys again after an interminable wait. Unfortunately, despite everything she'd shared with Ritchie, they would still have to hang around outside with all of the other followers, not yet promoted to Higher Fan Level and able to rock up at the venue with the band. That was a difficult pill to swallow. It was as if time had stood still since she'd last hooked up with Ritchie. She'd no real means of contacting him and no real way of knowing if the words he'd said were truly heartfelt or if he'd only been messing with her head.

The months had dragged on as they'd anxiously waited for gigs to be announced but when that time came, they were all in the Midlands or 'down south', clashing with every other significant event in Kim's diary.

Nicky's birthday night out, a theatre trip with Janice, Spa Day with her former school friends, *her parents' Silver Wedding anniversary party, for goodness sake...* she had to bail on it all, leaving a trail of at best, disgruntled, at worst, downright furious family and friends to voice their opinions.

Worst of all, she would be at the last of the gigs – a huge deal for both band and fans – in the heart of London on the night of her grandmother's eightieth birthday. Her gran was super-excited about the planned celebrations and, of course, Kim had always been aware of the significance of the date. She really had no acceptable excuse which would wash with any of her family.

Her mum had stormed out of the room leaving Kim alone with her dad, who shook his head sadly and sighed, 'It's your gran's big birthday, Kim. An important night for the lady who worships you and who would move heaven and earth for you...and for all of this family. If you can't make a decent judgement call on this then god help you. If you can't see, without any prompting, that the right thing to do is to be there for this woman who has adored you since the day you were born, then I'm beginning to wonder what we've raised. Now, I'll give you a night to sleep on it and I'll ask you again tomorrow what your intentions are. But if you miss this party, for the sake of *that* band and *that* man, then I'm warning you, your mother will never forgive you.'

With a heavy heart, the following morning Kim rang her gran and quietly explained that unfortunately she wouldn't be around for the party – that the gig in question was the most significant, unmissable one of the bunch. Her gran insisted that she understood – apparently she'd stalked a glam rock band in her youth, which meant she totally empathised with her granddaughter's dilemma. She said not to worry but Kim's guilt was suffocating and compounded by Freddie, who bounced unannounced into her room, yelling that she was a 'Selfish Bitch', adding that if she didn't start considering someone other than herself and that 'jumped-up wanker' any time soon, then she risked alienating everyone who cared about her.

Even though she hated herself for it, she still couldn't, and wouldn't reverse her decision. What was the point in attending the party anyway, miserable as sin, knowing what she was missing? She would also be running the risk that someone else would take the opportunity to sidle up to Ritchie in her absence. Sally-Anne assured her she'd done the right thing.

Ah well, there was no point dwelling on what couldn't be altered.

Kim was a nervous wreck at the prospect of seeing Ritchie again but couldn't wait to sink into his chest, with his protective arms wrapped around her. She felt safe there – like nothing could hurt her. If only she could capture that feeling and douse herself in it when they were apart.

Except this time, something appeared to be wrong.

When the boys arrived, for once Ritchie was first off the bus, but even though she was practically standing in front of him, eagerly awaiting a smile or a nod or *anything*, he looked right through her, as if she wasn't there at all. He lowered his head and dashed straight past, making a beeline for the open stage door.

Kim was crushed.

Hadn't he noticed her? Of course he had - she was almost blocking his path.

Was his mind completely elsewhere? So much so, that although he'd seen her, he hadn't actually *seen* her? It was a possibility, but she was sure she'd spotted an initial flicker of recognition in those stunning green eyes of his before they'd glazed over and he'd disappeared faster than a magician's assistant.

Had she done something to offend him or upset him? Not that she was aware of. Dear god, she hadn't seen him in an age and that was hardly her fault. If he'd clicked his fingers, she would have been there.

'For fuck's sake, cheer up, will you. Bren's just hugged us, Ady said you looked lovely, and even Marty stopped to say hi and thank us for our commitment to the band.' Sally-Anne was her usual sympathetic self.

Had they? Kim had been vaguely aware of their interaction with the various band members and had gone through the motions with a smile on her face because she did, of course, love each and every one of them. However, there was an overbearing, angry voice in her head shouting 'HE IGNORED YOU! HE DIDN'T EVEN SAY HELLO!'

'Sorry,' she mumbled, swallowing what felt like a solid lump of hurt and wondering how she could rectify the situation.

'I suppose you're stressed after Ritchie zipped past and didn't even look your way. Listen, Kim, you have to face facts - he can't always have his happy face on and, at the end of the day, you *are* just a fan. We're lucky to have got so far with Ritchie and the others - most fans would *kill* for all the achievements we've racked up. Oh, and here comes Todd at last! Looks like he's driven here today. Todd! TODD! Over here! It's us!'

She was waving frantically as Todd, flanked by his mum and her sister, headed for the rear entrance to the theatre, weighed down by a huge sports holdall and a navy-blue clothes carrier. The two ladies looked like they meant business, evidently protective of their son and nephew, but it didn't stop him pausing to greet fans, accepting gifts of teddy bears and flowers whilst posing for as many photos as he dared before he was pushed inside.

'Hi Kim,' he called out as he passed by. 'Great to see you. Love the hair.'

She'd had bronze streaks added to it recently and everyone agreed that it really suited her, but to hear it from Todd, shed a little light on her dark day. What a shame that Ritchie hadn't even noticed.

'Can we have a picture please, Todd,' Sally-Anne butted in. Ever the obliging pop star, Todd passed his belongings to his aunt, placed himself in the middle of the girls, arms around both, and said 'Cheese!' as his mother snapped the three of them together. Kim hoped the pain in her eyes wasn't visible for all to see when the film was developed.

For the first time ever, she struggled to enjoy the show. It was difficult to exude enthusiasm when her mind was rattling through a variety of reasons why she'd possibly been blanked, so her heart wasn't really in it. As usual, the band gave it their all and went down a storm, but the girls were shoved further back when everyone pelted down to the front, so Kim couldn't even try to catch Ritchie's eye. Thankfully, *Falling* wasn't included in the set list so at least she wouldn't have to worry about whether he would still sing those deeply personal words to her – when he couldn't even acknowledge her presence. She couldn't imagine what the hell she was supposed to have done wrong.

After a prolonged wait outside of the theatre in the pouring rain after the gig – lord only knows what the lads were doing in there – the fans were finally rewarded with a fleeting glance of their idols as they burst out of the stage door and were bundled onto their bus and away. They wore beaming smiles and were waving furiously but, nevertheless, they opted to make a run for it rather than spare some of their precious time to sign autographs and make the day of the tired, wet troupe of devotees, who surely deserved more.

Kim felt that *she* deserved more?

Sally-Anne didn't help matters by harping on about how Ritchie had winked at Shannon earlier, adding that he'd always enjoyed cosying up to the beautiful Irish girl. She wasn't sure if Sally-Anne was deliberately trying to wind her up or if she was merely oblivious to the pain she was inflicting. In the circumstances, it didn't take much to set Kim wondering if Ritchie and Shannon were now going to be 'a thing' - if she'd been chewed up and spat out and replaced by someone far more attractive and exotic (with Shannon's porcelain complexion, shiny black hair and dainty physique, they would surely make beautiful children together). By the time she fell into a fitful sleep during the early hours, she had convinced herself that he would be marrying the bloody woman once the band's romances and relationships were allowed to be thrown out into the public domain.

Bright, alert and beautiful she was not the following day. With a muzzy head and bags under her eyes that the Tetley Tea Folk would have been proud of, one look in the mirror confirmed what she already suspected. She was pale and miserable. Luckily it was a relatively short train journey on to Brighton, where they quickly checked into their new B & B and Sally-Anne purchased a humungous cross-eyed teddy for Bren from a nearby toy shop. She apparently wanted him to have something to always remember her by. Privately, Kim thought she'd be lucky if Bren didn't eat it for breakfast. Rumours were rife about his substance abuse and erratic lifestyle, although all were strenuously denied in interviews and statements to the press.

He was first off the bus, laughing like a drain when Sally-Anne handed him the monstrosity of a bear, treating her to a big sloppy kiss in return.

Waiting in nervous anticipation for Ritchie to emerge, Kim felt slightly sick, yet again pondering on what exactly had gone wrong. Perhaps it was because she'd put on a few pounds since he'd seen her at the television studios. Maybe he'd taken one look at her and thought, 'Bloody hell, I'll be giving that chubber a wide berth in future.'

A pair of long, slim legs clad in cream (designer) jeans appeared and even though at that point the upper half of his body was obscured from her view, she knew it was him. Even though she was fairly short-sighted – but far too vain to wear glasses - she could still spot any part of his body, anywhere. He might be way in the distance but she would recognise his confident swagger. One of his tanned, toned arms could be hanging loosely out of the partially opened window of a blacked out vehicle and she would know that limb in an instant.

Steeling herself for the dreaded cold shoulder again - or perhaps a look of indifference – she was amazed when he jumped to the ground, yawned, stretched his shapely arms over his head (his shirt lifting slightly to reveal that navel and belly button she remembered so well), and cried, 'Kimberley! We were so busy that I didn't get to speak to you yesterday. The theatre manager didn't want us hanging about after the show either because of concerns raised about health and safety issues in that awful car park. It's good to see you babe. Let me sign a few things and then we'll catch up!' His hand briefly rested on Kim's lower back and she sizzled inside as if she'd been electrocuted.

She was still his Kimberley and had been fretting all over nothing! What a plonker she'd been! All worries and heartache from the previous day were immediately binned as she waited patiently by his side, occasionally joining in as he joked with other fans surrounding him. Out of the corner of her eye, she could see Shannon and the other contenders for Ritchie's affection glowering at her, but it didn't matter; nothing mattered but him.

For a brief moment, she wondered if he would even remember about their long overdue catch-up, but as he was adding his signature to one last item, his roving eye sought her out and he reached behind his back to clasp hold of her hand, guiding her through the stage door and into the world where she was no longer *just a fan*, but someone of significance in his life.

*

The minute they were alone - in a dressing room rather than a broom cupboard – their lips locked together and their hands were all over each other, desperately wanting to cover every inch of skin; to explore every curve and cavity. Thank heavens her longer length skirt was slashed up to the thigh, for easy access, and her fitted jersey top was practically begging to have its buttons pinged open. She'd never known anyone to be so appreciative of her body, and the fact it was Ritchie doing the kneading, squeezing and sucking, was altogether mind-blowing. Murmuring her name as he took a detour from Boob Central, he gathered up a fistful of her hair in his hand, tugging on it playfully and erotically, all the while gazing into her eyes. His stare wasn't unnerving – if anything, it heightened her pleasure as he conveyed without words exactly what he wanted to do to her. Eventually, he broke into a grin, grazed his lips over her neck and whispered into her ear, 'My Kimberley.'

'Always,' she purred, boldly dipping her right hand inside the waistline of his jeans and feeling the delicate smooth skin of his taut stomach beneath. She strained to reach further, deep down inside, which resulted in a 'Christ!' from Ritchie, as he shuddered and closed his eyes.

Kim liked it. She liked pleasuring this man, who consumed her.

Footsteps and voices emanating from the corridor pre-warned them that they could be interrupted by another band member or irate manager at any moment. With this is mind, they reluctantly pulled apart but he indicated she should sit with him on the old-fashioned floral settee and she slid down beside him, as close as was physically possible, lust and longing raging throughout her body as he rested his hand on her exposed thigh.

They settled in for a talk and Kim imagined for a moment that that they were just an ordinary couple lounging on the sofa in front of the television, easy in each other's company. After chatting about home towns, strange fans and favourite songs, she fully expected the conversation to turn to the usual band-related topics but was surprised when Ritchie began to open up a little. It was the first time he'd really let down his guard.

'We worked so hard to get where we are today and sometimes it feels like it's all balancing on a knife edge. Singing, writing - there's never been anything else for me. What would I do if it was all snatched away? I've never had a 'proper job' and my cousin, Jed, says that's because I'm a lazy bastard but he has no idea how it really is. Flying in and out of countries but only seeing the inside of hotel rooms and television stations – no time for sightseeing or holidays. There's been occasions where we've literally stepped off one plane and then made a mad dash to hop on another. When the hits are coming, the schedule is relentless. Interviews, photo sessions, rehearsing, writing, recording, gigging – and that's without all of the other time-consuming crap. We've had months – no, YEARS of that. Don't get me wrong, I'm not complaining. We're so lucky to have achieved our success, but we know there's always another band around the corner waiting to steal the limelight...'

Stroking his arm, Kim nodded and tutted and made other appropriate noises in all the right places, encouraging him to put his trust in her. In her book, communication was equally as important as all the physical malarky.

'But what's much, *much* worse is poor chart positions and pitiful sales figures which leave us in real fear of being dropped by the record company and management. I truly believe the music we're releasing now is a vast improvement on our earlier stuff which, let's face it, was cheesy pop – although we'll always love those songs because it's thanks to them that we hit the Big Time. But sales are plummeting, targets aren't being met and budgets are being slashed. Some days it truly feels like the axe is waiting to drop. I won't let that happen, Kim. This is my whole life and I have to fight for it.'

Now she knew why he was so focused on his music and career rather than relationships – why they all were in fact. The passionate way he spoke and the earnest look on his face made Kim's heart turn over, as he confided in her his worries about losing it all.

Hoicking up her skirt so that it didn't completely split open to the waist, she slipped on to his lap, face to face with this man who she loved, a squeal of delight escaping as she felt his hands pinch her bum cheeks. They laughed together and she kissed him tenderly on the lips. The urge to taste him and be skin-on-skin was ever-present.

He quizzed her about her family and she questioned him about his. She was thrilled when he revealed minor details about his parents and grandparents and where he'd grown up – private information she would be keeping to herself. Loose lips sink ships and all that. She couldn't bear it if this vessel carrying the precious cargo of their relationship – such as it was – hit the rocks and disappeared without a trace under a sea of disloyalty.

A knock at the door and in came Todd - he was so polite, a real credit to his parents.

Acutely aware that her backside was partially on display, Kim decided she had better brazen it out and made no attempt to hastily cover up. Ritchie didn't seem at all concerned as he cupped those peaches in full view of his bandmate.

'Sorry, Kim, but this reprobate needs to actually do some work. Everyone else is waiting to soundcheck.'

Todd's tone towards Kim was apologetic but he glared at Ritchie. 'And if *you* could kindly concentrate on the job in hand rather than trying to cop a *hand job* then that would be just grand.'

'Fuck off,' came Ritchie's curt reply. They both laughed, but it seemed to Kim that there was an awkward tension in the air and she hadn't thought Todd possessed that level of sarcasm in him.

He left the room and they were alone again. She accepted he had a job to do but was already aching at the thought of being separated from Ritchie.

'We've got five minutes yet,' he noted, glancing at his watch. 'And they can't start without me, so let's make them wait.'

Closing her hands around the nape of his neck, she nuzzled into him and let out a slow 'Mmmm...'

'So what can we do in the next five minutes?' she asked provocatively.

'I know damn well what I'd like to do with you in the next five minutes but I'd be hauled over the coals if I were to be caught with my trousers down!' Kim's cheeks burned at the thought of Ritchie with his pants around his ankles, unsure if it was due to embarrassment or desire. She had to get a grip.

'Tell me more about yourself then – you know, not the party line that we read in the papers and the standard fodder that appears in all of the gossip mags. Let me have all the nitty gritty - everything that makes you tick.'

'Well, what do you want to know?'

'Well now...let me think...' She pretended to be mulling it over but knew exactly what she wanted to ask.

'Okay...firstly, have you ever been in love?' Waiting with baited breath, she licked her lips nervously.

'Do I look like someone who's ever had *time* for love? I've lived and breathed this band for the past decade and it's all that's occupied my mind from dawn till dusk. Sadly, love and relationships have been way down my list of priorities but I'm now faced with a dilemma. You see, there's this sexy, young siren who's recently come into my life and this woman is seriously distracting me from my work. She's all I can think about, which is pretty scary for me as I'm in previously unchartered territory...'

'Oh right...so I'm guessing you've hooked up with a sophisticated businesswoman at one of your personal appearances? Or maybe there's been an exotic model who you've ravished on the set of a recent photo shoot? Or perhaps you've taken a shine to a pretty young secretary within the record company..?' Kim was teasing him, all the while knowing that *she* was the distraction, of course, and an apparently sexy one to boot!

'No, no! This girl is in a different class. I could travel to the far corners of the world and never find anyone remotely like her, although she is in fact pretty close to me right now - so close I can hear her breathing and can even reach out and touch her...like this...and this...'

'Ah Ritchie...you're so naughty...'

'Naughty but nice?'

'Nice is too inferior of a word. I prefer to use 'amazing' when I describe you, because you really are.'

'You know what? You're pretty amazing too, Kim.'

His lips found hers again. Still insistent, still delicious - until he reluctantly peeled himself off and sighed, 'I really do have to go now, before it kicks off in the auditorium.'

Clambering off somewhat ungainly, Kim sighed too, straightened her clothes and then examined herself in the mirror, ensuring she had wiped away all the tell-tale smudges of Perfect Plum lipstick. Turning around, she saw Ritchie was attempting to do the same.

'Here – let me do that,' she insisted, rubbing his lips with her finger, aware that he was watching her intently.

Taking a step back, she hesitated, unsure whether the words she were about to say should stay in her mouth for the time being, but before she could think it through properly they were out in the open.

'You make me so happy, Ritchie. I've never known anyone like you and I'm truly bowled over that you want me when you can literally have your pick of the girls here, or anywhere you go. I love you Ritchie Clarke…and I feel like the luckiest girl on earth.'

Reaching for Kim's right hand, Ritchie gently lifted it up to his lips and dropped the sweetest of kisses on to her skin. His gaze never left hers for a second.

'You're the best thing that's ever happened to me Kim and, believe me, *I'm* the lucky one here. You're so beautiful and special – in fact I'd go as far as to say that you're every red-blooded man's dream. God knows, I've erected enough barriers and tried to hold back but you've stolen my heart and it absolutely frightens the hell out of me...'

'RITCHIE JOE CLARKE! Get your skinny ass out here now and do the ruddy job you're being paid for - before this band recruits a new lead singer and you're signing on at the benefits office!' Barry's dulcet tones boomed through the building and the fact that the volume was cranked up suggested he was fast approaching and he was blazing. Ritchie grabbed Kim's hand firmly this time and tugged her towards the door.

'Shit! He doesn't sound too happy, does he? Come on babe, come watch us do the soundcheck...if you want to.'

'Want to? Are you kidding?' she replied incredulously. Of course she wanted to! Could this day get any better?

'I just need to grab Sally-Anne though, if that's ok? She'll kill me if she finds out I'm in on the soundcheck and she's out in the cold!'

'Oh god, do you have to? She's alright in small doses that girl but any more and she seriously does my head in. Okay, okay,' he laughed. 'You grab your mate while I grab a microphone. Just pop your head out of the door and call her in. Make sure you don't wander outside or you won't get back inside again...and I need my gorgeous girl watching me from the stalls now, don't I?'

They separated briefly in the corridor while she pelted off to collect Sally-Anne and he made a dash for the stage.

It was only as she was descending the last of the stairs, still in a state of shock, that she became aware of something, and a nagging voice in her brain refused to let it drop.

She'd opened her heart and exposed her true feelings to Ritchie; she'd actually told him she loved him.

But he'd never said it back.

Chapter 10

They had a ball, zipping around the country to the various shows. Kim and Ritchie had been edging ever closer with every passing day, sharing anecdotes and saliva as they entertained and devoured each other in equal measures in the confines of his dressing room.

All too soon, the last of the gigs came around but Kim tried not to think about their impending separation. Instead, she hugged the memory of the previous evening to herself. After another awesome performance by the band, the backstage manager had sought her out with a message that she was to nip up to Ritchie's dressing room - where she found him shirtless, breathless, covered in a sheen of sweat and horny as hell. The other guys were knackered and wanted to take flight as quickly as possible but Ritchie made no secret of his desire to hang around, treating Kim to a private show.

As she'd watched him towel himself dry ('God help us and save us') and then assisted him in dressing - very slowly - and packing up his bags, she'd hoped that this would be the night he would insist she return to the hotel with him. But apparently, he was sharing a room with Ady, so that was that.

Colour flooded her cheeks as she remembered gently but deliberately kissing each of his shoulders and snaking her index finger down his chest and further on to the promised land. It had been thrilling and sensuous and she never wanted to stop touching him.

Although the string of live appearances were coming to an end, she concluded that all the sacrifices she'd made had been worthwhile, to create the memories she had with Ritchie and the band. She worried though, about how she and Ritchie would part company. There'd been bucket-loads of pleasure and a plethora of promises made, but ultimately she dreaded another unsatisfactory close of chapter. She needed to know that they were headed somewhere.

The boys were due to immediately return home post-gig and, despite the fact that Ritchie still lived with his parents – it seemed pointless at this stage apparently to invest in a place of his own which would largely remain empty – Kim had high hopes that she would be asked to accompany him back to Birmingham and be introduced to his family. At the very least, surely they would exchange numbers or make plans to meet up away from the world of *Show Me Yours,* as fabulous as that was.

Palpable excitement amongst the fans, a flurry of activity at the stage door and the familiar rumbling of an approaching bus all pointed to the arrival of the band and Kim's heart soared at the prospect of being with Ritchie again.

The moment she saw him, Kim felt the familiar nerves and excitement bubble up inside. She suspected that even when she was an old aged pensioner, her tummy would still flutter every time she thought of him, remembering the crazy days of touring the country and the thrill of seeing the band live on stage. If she played her cards right, they might even be together in their twilight years, reminiscing over those heady days out on the road…

'Hi,' he said to Shannon, who smouldered and licked her lips.

'Howdy stranger!' he joked with Geraldine, who for reasons only known to her, was sporting a battered old cowboy hat, perched on top of her big old hair.

'Hey! Good to see you,' he drawled to the twins, who were panting like two sweaty Labradors on a hot summer's day, having run like the clappers down the full length of the busy high street after catching sight of the bus from way in the distance.

'Hello,' he said to Kim...and then walked on by.

'Ritchie,' she whispered, to his deaf ears, as he disappeared into the theatre as fast as his legs would take him and another piece of her heart was ripped out there and then.

*

'Jeez, Ritchie can't half be a moody git! Sometimes he's undressing you with his eyes...other times it's like he doesn't even recognise you. Do you think he's been borrowing some of Bren's drugs? Speaking of Bren, he squeezed my bum and said something which sounded positively rude but I didn't quite catch it over bloody Geraldine's booming voice...'

Kim let her ramble on as the whooshing continued in her ears, the unshed tears filled her eyes, and nausea rose within and threatened to project itself all over Shannon's borderline pervy PVC jacket.

What was it with Ritchie? Why did he ignore her? What was his excuse this time? No self-respecting girl would allow a man to treat her like this – to be allowed access to her heart and body and then cast her aside like a dirty rag.

Todd made straight for Kim and Sally-Anne when he bounced off the bus, hugging them both as he posed for pictures, and signing everything Sally-Anne shoved in front of him. Kim didn't have the strength to start digging stuff out for him to add his name to, but she appreciated his people-pleasing, positive personality, especially when he gently asked if she was okay. It was all she could do not to break down and let the tears pour.

They had front stalls, front row tickets for the gig and Kim tried to mask her distress by plastering on her perpetual happy face, aware that other fans may be watching and one or two smirking and wallowing in her misery. And besides – she genuinely didn't want Ritchie to see how distraught she was, although it was hard to listen to him banging on about falling in love during most of the songs, when he clearly had no clue what love was. To add further insult to injury, they'd replaced one of the slower album tracks in the set with *Falling*. Kim waited with baited breath, hoping that Ritchie would seek her out to sing those familiar lines that singled her out, but he didn't even glance over in her direction. It cut her right to the bone.

In fact, she didn't see him look at her once throughout the whole of the gig, although Sally-Anne later implied that he did - but only when she had her eyes trained on another band member. What kind of game was he playing?

She knew without doubt that it would be the same old story when the lads emerged from the stage door, with Ritchie, Todd, Ady and Marty all fooling around as if they were the best of friends and a spaced-out Bren bouncing off invisible walls. The fans cheered and joined in with an improvised acapella number in the loading bay but it was difficult for Kim to partake in the banter and jolly sing-a-long when she was so hurt and confused.

When it was finally announced that the boys were to depart, they all waved goodbye and blew kisses as they reboarded the bus. Only Marty stopped by to tell the girls to 'take care' and surprisingly he gave Kim a lingering, warm embrace – the reassuring, calming sort usually delivered by your dad. She almost disintegrated in his arms, nuzzling into his thick woollen overcoat. Maybe he was aware that Ritchie's treatment of her fell short, or perhaps she basically looked like a girl in need of a hug. Kim sensed he was a good man, under the popstar-with-attitude façade. Ebony was a lucky woman, and Ritchie could learn a lot from this older, wiser colleague.

As the wheels of the bus set in motion, and the sullen driver edged his vehicle out of the car park, she watched many of the other fans make chase, calling after their favourite band member...reluctant to let them go. Kim hadn't the heart to join them – although Sally-Anne was off like a shot, despite her determination to remain cool in an attempt to portray herself as a proper 'friend of the band'.

A door had been closed in Kim's face again. Where once she'd been welcomed in with open arms, now she was being firmly pushed back on to the doorstep.

'No,' she was being told. 'You don't belong in here.'

Again, she asked herself exactly what she'd done wrong, even though previously it had been a big fat NOTHING. She berated herself for having dropped the 'L' word so early on in their relationship and wished she had a naturally sunny personality that Ritchie would always be drawn to. If only she was funnier, more interesting, prettier – anything that would hold his attention.

Sally-Anne was royally pissed off that there was no after-show party – although it hadn't officially been a tour, rather a bunch of gigs to showcase new music from their forthcoming album. Still chattering on ten to the dozen, if she noticed Kim's quiet disposition then she didn't say so. But then she didn't dwell on other people's problems unless it affected her personally. She truly was all heart.

Regrouping with a tribe of the regular fans at the nearby pub, Kim immediately excused herself to pop to the poorly decorated ladies room, where she locked herself in an unoccupied cubicle. She didn't need to use the toilet. She was desperate for time and space, if only for a few moments – even if that space did stink to high heaven and make her want to wretch.

Leaning against the wall of the cubicle, she closed her eyes and tried to squeeze in the tears but they escaped anyway, followed by an unavoidable bout of silent screaming. It didn't ease her tension any but felt completely and utterly necessary.

Was this it for her and Ritchie or was there anything to salvage? Had he tired of her already and possibly moved on to someone else, or was this merely another of his unpredictable, inexplicable moods? She envisioned Ritchie returning to his parents' home that evening, full of himself and the band's successful gigs and never giving Kim a second thought.

Sharing memories and funny anecdotes, describing people he'd met along the way without ever mentioning her name. Invalidating her existence.

It was hurtful, it was painful and it was reprehensible.

And yet she knew that it would only take one casual smile from him – one brief look in her direction - and he'd instantly be forgiven.

Chapter 11

Remember, remember, the 5th of November.

It was a day Kim wouldn't forget in a hurry.

Returning home with Ritchie's rejection fresh in her mind, Kim took to her bedroom, hoping to avoid any unnecessary conversation and interaction, unwilling to deal with life. Her mother was not impressed.

'You swan off, travelling around the country doing lord only knows what and then you waltz back in here, Kimberley and expect everyone to tiptoe around you because *you're* upset. All you're interested in is that band and *that man* and God help anyone who distracts you from your favourite topic. You're sarcastic, self-centred and self-obsessed and since you became one of these groupie girls you have no respect for anyone, least of all yourself. The Kimmy we used to know and love was a kind, considerate girl who loved life and enjoyed healthy relationships with family and friends. What happened to her?'

Kim wasn't sure herself, but her blood boiled when she was spoken to like a child. 'Maybe if just one of you showed a smidgeon of interest in my life it might help, mum! For goodness sake, you all roll your eyes whenever I mention anything remotely connected with Ritchie or the band - as if my life is just one big joke...'

'Oh, I'm not laughing, because this has got completely out of hand. You ignore your brother, treat me and your father with complete disdain and hardly ever see your best friend these days. I've lost count of the number of times you haven't returned that poor girl's calls, yet you're quick enough to ring back good old Sally-Anne, despite the fact she only bothers with you when she wants something or feels the need to gloat. And what about your gran? When was the last time you contacted her or bothered to accompany us when we've taken a trip over the Moors? You know she's not been well so you keep saying you'll ring her *tomorrow*, or you'll come with us *next week*, but it never happens. She's not getting any younger and it wouldn't hurt to show her you care. Honest to god, it's like anything and everything and *everybody* else is irrelevant now. You're obsessed Kim. Infatuated. This crush you have on Ritchie Clarke...'

'IT IS *NOT* A CRUSH!' Kim yelled, furious that her feelings for Ritchie were being labelled as a passing fancy. 'Me and Ritchie are crazy about each other and you're only jealous because no one like HIM ever showed any interest in someone like YOU! Just because you've lived a dull little life, devoid of all fun and excitement, it doesn't mean I have to…'

'Jealous of *what* for goodness sake? If he's crazy about you, then where is he now? Is he coming to collect you later to take you out for a nice meal? No! Will he be treating you to a day out or taking you home to introduce you to his parents? No! Has he splashed out on flowers or lavished gifts upon you or even sent you so much as a poxy birthday card? No! BECAUSE IT'S NOT BLOODY REAL! Whatever's been going on – and you'd better not have been up to anything stupid that you're going to regret, young lady – it's going nowhere because *he's* a flash, fly-by-night popstar off the telly and *you're* an ordinary girl with a regular job from 'Up North'. It's going nowhere Kim…open your eyes!'

'DON'T YOU DARE SAY IT'S NOT REAL!' Kim screamed, practically foaming at the mouth with rage. 'Ritchie's a real person with real feelings and he's entitled to have a girlfriend and fall in love! You have no idea how real *my* feelings are. I can't even begin to explain how he makes me feel inside - how I come alive when we're alone together and we talk and touch and I know I've never known anything AS real in all of my life...'

'Oh, Kimberley...I never said *your* feelings weren't real.' Kim winced at the look of pity on her mum's face.

'But I know you're going to get hurt.'

Resisting the urge to tell her to piss off, Kim decided it was best to cut the conversation short before things were said that couldn't be unsaid.

'Well, I'll have to prove you wrong then, won't I? Because my relationship with Ritchie – not that it's anyone's business other than ours - is all that makes me happy.'

A fraction of the anger slipped from Alison Summers' face and she looked tearful, almost defeated.

'I haven't seen you truly happy for a long time, love,' she added softly, her eyes shining bright.

Christ. Kim wished people wouldn't pretend to care. She didn't need this.

'Mum,' she said, turning over to face the wall whilst yanking the duvet over her head. 'Close the door quietly on your way out.'

After the confrontation with her mother, Kim was already feeling wretched when she arrived at work and she dragged herself through the door without a minute to spare. She hadn't even reached the staffroom when she was accosted by her new manager, Val, who barked, 'Don't bother removing your coat, Kim. Janice, take over here. Kim, I'll see you in my office.'

Her 'office' was a crappy little space attached to the stock room – a glorified cupboard that smelled musty and was permanently heaving with crisp boxes and other surplus stock. There was only one single chair and she chose to occupy it while Kim was left standing there like a lemon, amidst the inferior brand bottles of lemonade.

'Miss Summers, this gives me no satisfaction but I'm afraid I am terminating your employment with immediate effect and I require the return of your keys and passes.'

WHAT? She'd only been off sick a few days – what on earth had happened?

'But...but...why...?' she managed to squeak, really wishing she had that chair now.

'Kim, I'm told you were once a hardworking, amiable, helpful member of staff. However, these days you're regularly late, you rarely treat us or the customers to a smile and I've had to deal with several complaints about your brusque manner. I was actually anticipating handing you a verbal warning today but when you claimed to be sick, yet again, immediately after taking the last of your annual leave, if truth be told, I was highly suspicious. My suspicions were confirmed when a customer casually mentioned that they'd seen you disembarking a train in Leicester – apparently they'd been travelling on the very same train, en route to visit their grandchildren – and they were most surprised to see a fairly familiar face from back home standing merely a few feet away on the platform.'

Kim's heart sank to her well-worn trainers. How on earth could she talk herself out of this mess?

'It wasn't me!' she responded, lamely. 'I was ill in bed, like I told you.'

'Yes, you did tell me, didn't you? Affording you the benefit of the doubt, I did assure Customer X that they must have been mistaken, but they were adamant it was most definitely you. Not only did they recognise your black leather jacket and the silver 'K' hanging from the chain around your neck but they heard you shout out to another young girl called 'Sally-Anne' – coincidentally the name of that cheeky young madam who's always ringing the shop. They said they'd know your voice anywhere.'

Bloody hell, the evidence was damning, but she couldn't afford to lose her job and her income. She had to give it one last shot.

'I swear, I was sick, in bed. Maybe it was my double they saw or perhaps this customer has a grudge against me. Because I wasn't there, honestly, I wasn't.'

'I thought you'd say that. So I did a little detective work myself with the assistance of my sixteen year old niece - who's a HUGE fan of *Show Me Yours* I might add – and she confirmed that the band had indeed appeared in Leicester on the day in question! Startling coincidence that, don't you think?'

Stick to your guns, Kim. It's Customer X's word against yours...and so what if the band were in Leicester that night? She's no solid proof that you were actually there too!

'At the risk of repeating myself, it wasn't me. Unfortunately I was stuck at home on my sick bed. I'd have been in work, not Leicester, if I hadn't been so poorly.'

'Mmm...you really don't know when to hold your hands up, do you? Call me psychic, but I had a feeling you would try and brazen it out until the end so I covered my back and checked which venue they were appearing at next. Back to London it was – they do get around, don't they? Anyhow, I rang the theatre and explained to the nice lady at the box office that I was trying to locate a Kimberley Helen Summers as a matter of great urgency and asked if by any chance she had a record of a booking under that name. She really was most helpful and confirmed that she did indeed have details on her computer system - two tickets for seats in the front stalls purchased by and mailed to a Miss K.H. Summers. I even confirmed the address with her – lovely woman.'

Oh god, why hadn't she let Sally-Anne book the tickets? Why had the gobby woman in the ticket office divulged her personal details? Why was it always her that was caught out? She didn't respond to Val's killer revelations because she couldn't. It was Game Over. Bye-bye job. Hello dole queue. Damn you – stupid bloody nosy customer! Damn you – tell-tale 'K' chain that Freddie had bought her for Christmas. Damn you – Miss Marple the Manageress who should be on the Serious Crime Squad rather than stuck behind a till selling baccy, beer and bread!

'I think you'll find the evidence is conclusive Kim and I am therefore left in no doubt that when you should have been at work – after you had telephoned to say that you had been vomiting for two days, had a dangerously high temperature and was seriously considering taking yourself off to A and E – you were actually travelling around our green and pleasant land, attending gigs and treating it like an extension to your annual leave. Now we need to attend to some formalities before you leave...'

'Don't bother!' Kim cried, as she fled the 'office', throwing keys, passes and company fleece on the counter, trying to ignore the tears swimming around in Janice's sympathetic eyes.

She fled from the building and dragged her feet as far as the rickety bench at the end of the road, collapsing on to it with her head in her hands, shoulders heaving, tears flowing.

She hadn't been there long when she heard familiar footsteps and then a gentle hand squeezed her shoulder. She glanced up to see Janice's concerned face looking down at her.

'I'm sorry, Kim, I really am. Despite the skiving and the moaning and everything else, I really will miss you and your cheeky quips. Me and you, we're the last remaining members of the old squad – the dream team. We used to have such fun and the camaraderie was second to none but all that's long gone. Your heart hasn't been in it for a hell of a long time and the rest of us can't continue to carry you. Soon I'll be off long-term sick recuperating from my operation and, between you and me, I'll not be returning to that bloody shop. I'm done with all the lifting and the extra hours I keep getting lumbered with. But I'm not having a dig. It won't seem like it now but I honestly believe this could be a positive thing for you. Have a think about what you really want love - at your age you could start afresh on a new career path and really make a go of it. You have the brains, the personality and charm still in there somewhere under the devil-may-care attitude and the head stuffed with anything and everything to do with *Show Me Yours*!'

Kim attempted the weakest of smiles as she was flooded with shame. Her absences had put strain on her colleagues and Janice in particular had suffered. Christ, she hadn't even realised that this darling woman was scheduled to have an operation. Her smiley, funny Janice with her heart of pure gold.

'Will you be okay love? Because I have to get back in there before the old boot sends out a search party. Get yourself off home - it's perishing out here and you don't want to be hanging around in the dark on your own. And think about what I said. Because you're better than this. Oh, and one more piece of advice – if you'll take it?'

'Sure,' Kim replied. 'I need all the help I can get.'

'This Ritchie guy – if he treats you well and you know for certain he's the one, then I couldn't be happier for you. But if you have any doubts, or he doesn't quite come up to the mark, then think about what you *could* have, in the future, with somebody else. You're a lovely, bonny girl and you deserve someone who will love you warts and all, respect you always, treat you like a queen and be proud that you're on his arm. That's all love. Just think about it.'

*

Kim's mum and dad hit the roof. Outraged at her duplicity - lying that she'd been granted the necessary leave for the gigs when in reality she'd only been able to cover half of it with her remaining holiday entitlement – they warned her that if she didn't get her act together, she'd be out on her ear.

Kim assured them she'd be out looking for employment the very next day – there was a lot of temporary work coming up in town for the festive season and she knew for a fact that not all of the employers required references and if you were halfway decent they'd more than likely keep you on after Christmas. Not that she would want to be, if she wasn't allowed the necessary time off for any *Show Me Yours* gigs. Best not mention that to the old folks though.

Accompanied by his attractive new girlfriend Rochelle, Freddie crawled home from the pub and called Kim a dickhead, which almost started World War III. Rochelle, who was well out of Freddie's league in Kim's opinion, instructed him to 'zip it' and dragged him off into the kitchen while her mum and dad continued to wipe the floor with their wayward daughter.

'You need to bloody grow up, Kimberley,' raged her mum. 'Try taking a leaf out of Nicky's book – I used to think she was a Dizzy Lizzy but that girl's really got her head screwed on. She has a raft of qualifications behind her and they've made her assistant manager of that smart salon in town already.'

Kim loved Nicky, but she was doing her no favours at the moment. Not only did Nicky have a proper job which paid well and was progressing into an actual *career*, but she and Connor were now a bona fide, seriously loved-up couple and they'd even booked a holiday to Portugal together. She'd also passed her driving test on first attempt and was now the proud owner of a shiny red Astra. Worst of all, she was projecting herself as the perfect daughter – running errands for her parents, dropping them off and picking them up like a taxi service, treating them to Early Bird dinners, bottles of whisky and the likes. She truly put Kim to shame.

Finally, her mum and dad ran out of steam and popped upstairs to watch the last of the fireworks from the landing window, but not before her dad delivered those dreaded words.

'Kimberley, we're very disappointed in you.'

*

Within a week she was working at a pop-up Christmas shop (not much likelihood of being kept on into the New Year then) and it threw mum and dad off her back, temporarily – although they were unhappy with her lack of ambition. Freddie said they were convinced she was wasting her skill set – whatever that was.

Much of her working day was actually spent outside of the shop, peddling bumper packs of cards of seriously inferior quality. It was bone-chillingly cold, her hands were often numb and she almost lost the will to live – a bit like waiting at the stage door for her favourite band to appear.

The end of her second week was topped off with a late-night telephone call from Nicky, who had returned from a romantic weekend away in the Lake District with her beloved and had an announcement to make.

'He proposed! Connor proposed! I thought he was taking me out to a swish restaurant to celebrate our six month anniversary but when the desserts arrived he suddenly went down on one knee and there in the middle of my chocolate fudge cake was the most beautiful diamond solitaire you've ever seen! Oh Kim, I love him so much and I can't tell you how happy I am. It sounds like a real cliché but I honestly knew from the very first moment we met that we would be together forever.'

Bit quick that, Kim silently sniffed. Half a year together and Nicky wanted to be tied down for the rest of her life. She was thrilled for her best bud but it only highlighted the fact that *she* was eons away from ever settling down. She'd dreamt of marrying Ritchie from the first moment she met him but hells bells, it hadn't quite panned out that way thus far.

'Congratulations, you lovely pair! I'm made up for you. When's the wedding then? I hope I've time to save up for my hat!'

'You won't need a hat sweetie because you'll be right behind me as I march up that aisle – as chief bridesmaid! I know we've had precious little time for each other lately but you're my best friend, the first person I wanted to tell and my only choice to head up that pack of bridesmaids. Imagine! Me – Mrs Connor James Flanagan...I still can't believe it myself!'

'Oh my lord, I've never been a bridesmaid before! You won't dress me in anything pink or ridiculously flowery, will you?'

'Course not, you numbty! But as soon as we've arranged a date, you best get planning a decent hen night...no way will we end up dining in a dive, watching Showaddywaddy like Stacey Miller's rabble did!'

Replacing the receiver at the end of the call, she returned to the living room to reluctantly share the news with her parents who were genuinely over the moon for Nicky. Kim couldn't help but wonder if they were secretly wishing their own daughter would settle for an ordinary lad like Connor rather than waiting around for someone of Ritchie's calibre.

When would she have an announcement of her own? She and Ritchie should be *that* couple, cementing their commitment to each other, but it seemed hell would freeze over before Ritchie told the world Kim was his girlfriend. In fact it all seemed to have gone horribly wrong again. Why wasn't she the sort of no-nonsense girl who could say, 'Look Ritchie, either sort your shit out or you won't see me for dust'?

She'd heard it said that 'Love Hurts', but this was absolutely taking the piss.

*

The band were booked to open an entertainment venue in Liverpool, the girls were delighted, and it had all started so well.

There was a carnival atmosphere - Kim was sure half the crowd had been on the booze since lunchtime. Apparently the band were to cut the ribbon and declare the huge nightclub 'open' before being rushed inside to perform a short set, autographs later.

The girls had foregone the band's appearance outside so they could be stage-side in the actual venue, but were rewarded when the boys exploded on to the raised dancefloor and immediately spotted them. Despite being full of trepidation that Ritchie may choose to ignore her again, Kim's heart soared when he waved, danced straight over and ruffled her hair, repeatedly returning to the same spot to sing to her, clasp her hand and give her that knowing look. The rather large lady to Kim's right who almost slapped Kim in the face every time she clapped her hands together gave her a sharp nudge, breathed beery breath in her face and slurred, 'Ooh you're so lucky…I wish *my* bloody fella was as handsome as your Ritchie!' Kim very nearly admitted that she wasn't actually his girlfriend but in the end allowed herself that moment, to imagine she was living that life.

Sally-Anne was also made up when Bren abandoned his drums, flew over and sank to his knees in front of her at the end of the set, planting a sloppy kiss on her lips and moaning into the microphone he'd snatched from Ritchie's hand, 'Oh, babyeee....'

After the show, the boys came straight out and whilst Kim waited to speak to Ritchie (who was always most in demand with the fans), Todd and Ady took turns to spin her round the car park and not only did she end up with a severe case of the giggles but also a prized memory that would stay with her forever. It quickly elicited a reaction from Ritchie too - she could have sworn she caught a hint of jealousy in his voice when he called out, 'Hey, you two reprobates…put my beautiful lady down and send her back this way.'

Kim was over there in a flash and Ritchie casually slipped his arm around her waist, whispering into her ear, 'Care to join us for a drink at the hotel?'

The first half hour in the private bar was a real buzz, mingling amongst the guys as if they'd been doing it all of their lives. Kim also noticed a marked change in Ritchie as he drank more and his stage mask slipped. He was more relaxed and the guard was down, as he sank into a leather armchair and beckoned her over to perch on his knee.

Within seconds he had homed in on her lips, his tongue easily sliding into her mouth and reacquainting itself with her tonsils. Christ, but he was a good kisser.

'Have you missed me, Kimberley?' he asked, breaking away and tenderly smoothing wayward wisps of hair back from her face.

'You know I have, Mr Clarke...you and your endearing smile and that lizard-like tongue of yours!'

He grinned and she adored the way his face positively lit up, but his eyes looked watery and tired and she wanted to rock him to sleep in her arms.

'I've missed you too,' he said, taking her face in his hands and staring at her almost hypnotically. Those eyes of his though - they shone in all of Kim's most precious memories and they brought both him and her alive.

Small talk. Kissing. Small talk. Kissing.

It was heaven and in hindsight Kim probably should have been happy with her lot. Unfortunately, her mouth sometimes ran away with her and led her into all kinds of trouble.

'Ritchie...I need to ask you about something that's been bugging me. I mean, *this* is amazing and I have your undivided attention now, but there are days when you completely ignore me and I don't quite know what to make of it. You act as if we've never even met before, or you stare straight through me as if I'm made of glass and I wonder what the hell I've done wrong. Then I start blaming myself, questioning my own actions, wondering if you're having second thoughts about our relationship. I appreciate you're busy and are usually surrounded by droves of fans, all desperately clamouring for your attention, but it hurts. Hopefully we can clear up any misunderstandings, to prevent it happening again...'

In Kim's opinion, she'd only asked what any girl would in the circumstances and wasn't being unreasonable, but it appeared she'd lit the blue touch paper. Ritchie immediately snatched his hands away and dropped them to his sides, the fury on his face leaving Kim in no doubt that she'd crossed an invisible line.

'For Christ's sake Kim, I have more important stuff on my mind and I don't need this ball of crap right now. Surely you must see that I can't neglect the other fans by spending all my time with you! You've already landed me right in the crap as it's been noticed by the powers-that-be that I've been 'otherwise engaged' when I should have been concentrating on rehearsals and soundchecks and creating those hits that don't just write themselves!'

Kim was gobsmacked, caught off guard as the burden of culpability was laid firmly at her door. Her mouth opened and shut involuntarily and she stared at him in disbelief.

'*I* have landed *you* in the crap? How on earth are you switching this around to make out it's all my fault? Sorry Ritchie, I didn't realise it was only me investing time and feelings in this relationship – I was labouring under the misapprehension that you felt the same way about me...'

'Oh Christ, don't be getting all emotionally heavy on me now, darling. You *know* the situation I'm in and that my job basically hinges on the all-important sexy and single image. What do you expect me to do?'

'I don't know Ritchie...maybe show me a little more consideration? To be quite frank, I'm shocked at your reaction. Can you blame me for wanting to know where I stand when you're constantly blowing hot and cold with me?'

'Oh, fuck this!' he snarled, shoving her off his knee so he could jump to his feet, swiping his drink from the table and sloshing gin onto the deep pile carpet. Everything about his demeanour spelled out A-N-G-R-Y.

'Shall I tell you something Kimberley? We've recently been informed that unless we miraculously hit number 1 with our next release then we're likely to be dumped by the record company. There's no other frigging labels queuing up to offer us a deal so *I'm* stressed out of my mind and *you're* having a pop at me because I've not smiled or said hello or been 100% glued to your side! Don't you see how it is?'

His voice was raised and people were turning to stare. Their road manager Gavin, a poor substitute for Barry who usually looked after the band when they were playing smaller, more intimate venues, swivelled his toady head around and managed to treat Kim to a death stare at the same time as his eyes looked her up and down as if she was a piece of meat. Kim felt so small, she wanted to cry. She felt awful for having a go at Ritchie for something so insignificant when the band's future was on the line and his head was all over the place.

Gingerly taking his left hand in her right, she stroked his fingers, desperate to make amends.

'I'm sorry, Ritchie – really, I am. I had no idea. God, you must think that I'm a real pain in the arse but I only wanted everything to be perfect between us – to right anything I'd done wrong. Honestly, I didn't mean to upset you. I'm sorry, Ritchie...will you forgive me? Please don't let anything spoil this amazing evening...'

For one frightening moment Kim thought he was about to shrug her off and leave her standing there like an idiot, until he sighed dramatically and then pulled her into his arms, lowering his lips to gently kiss the top of her head. 'It's okay darling. I'm like a coiled spring at the moment – all this tension and worry is making me tetchy. We'll leave it now and forget it ever happened. Now, give me a kiss and let me squeeze that peachy little arse of yours...'

The incident had passed, normal service was resumed and Kim breathed a huge sigh of relief. That was a mistake she wouldn't be making again.

She'd rather have *some* Ritchie than *none at all*.

They talked a little and occasionally their bodies were clamped together as they smooched again and the desire to tear each other's clothes off threatened to overwhelm them. Yet there was no offer forthcoming for Kim to accompany Ritchie upstairs and all too soon the night was ending. Eventually the rest of the band and one or two hangers-on disappeared until there were only a few stragglers left along with Kim, Ritchie, Sally-Anne and Bren – although Bren had passed out on a chaise longue in the reception area and couldn't be shifted - much to Sally-Anne's disgust who'd had visions of them making sweet love all night long and then waking up in his bed the next morning. Kim suspected Sal would have woken up to either a vomit covered pillow or a urine soaked mattress if she'd stayed.

With high expectations, the girls had long since cancelled their pre-booked taxi home – and now they were in a predicament. They'd anticipated staying over with Ritchie and Bren but suddenly Ritchie was outside flagging down a black cab which they knew, at this time of night, was likely to cost an arm and a leg, but neither of them wanted to say so. When Ritchie pecked Sally-Anne on the cheek and swooped in to give Kim a proper kiss, all she could think was that he was about to head back indoors to a luxurious hotel room, whilst they were disappearing into the night in a cab they couldn't afford, putting their trust in a driver who bore a disturbing resemblance to Charles Manson – and with all of their hopes dashed.

Yet again, Ritchie had avoided any commitment talk. Kim actually felt that she was further away than ever from any kind of goal, even if that was just exchanging telephone numbers or promising to send letters.

'Just what the fuck did you say to Ritchie in that hotel lounge?' Sally-Anne seethed once they were locked inside the cab and speeding away from Liverpool and the band. 'The deal was sealed and we could have had stayed the night but – oh *noooo* – you had to spoil it with your big, gaping cakehole, didn't you? Everyone heard him you know, raging at you for giving him unnecessary grief. And that slimy reptile Gavin said Ritchie was really riled and you'd be advised to shut your pretty little mouth. Thanks a bunch for cocking it right up for the both of us!'

Resisting the urge to bark that unless she'd been planning to have her wicked way with a comatose and non-consenting Bren then there hadn't been anything TO cock up as far as Sal was concerned, Kim shrank back, hoping against hope that the cab driver wasn't listening too intently. She didn't particularly want to feature in any unsavoury headlines in the Daily Shite the next morning.

'What are you on about, Sal?' she asked, hoping to placate her irate friend and wondering, yet again, what crime she was supposed to have committed. 'There was nothing to shout about - I only mentioned that there are occasions when he treats me like a complete stranger and basically wondered out loud why that was...'

'Well wonder to yourself next time, you daft cow! They don't need that crap, you know. They're busy as hell this week – studio time, personal appearances, a raft of interviews and visiting that children's hospital on Wednesday. Then they fly off to Sweden at the weekend. Do you think he needs you harping on at him over such trivial bollocks? Get a grip woman. There are thousands of girlies who would give their right arm to be in your privileged position and you can easily be replaced, like that!' She snapped her fingers in Kim's face for effect, just in case Kim couldn't comprehend how precariously balanced her relationship with Ritchie was. Like she needed reminding.

'For god's sake Sally-Anne, I have a right to voice my opinion and it wasn't anything controversial. I don't see why he couldn't just give me a straight answer!'

'Yeah, right...you carry on voicing your opinion and see what happens. See how long you retain his interest then...or whether he dumps you for someone who knows when to keep quiet.'

The worst thing was, Kim got it. Despite every fibre of her being screaming out that it shouldn't be that way – it shouldn't be *Yes Ritchie, No Ritchie, Whatever You Say Ritchie* – she knew Sal was right. She either put up and shut up or risk losing Ritchie's attention and affection – a gamble she quite simply wasn't prepared to take.

'Anyway, we made up in the end, and I don't think staying over was ever on the cards for us. He's terrified of jeopardising his position in the band by hooking up with anyone - least

103

of all a fan. Come to think of it, with the exception of Marty, we've never really seen any of the other guys with a woman, so maybe they're all trying to toe the line.'

Despite her protestations, Kim was actually beginning to wonder if *she* was the issue again. Maybe Ritchie didn't quite fancy her enough to take her to bed. The pounds had definitely crept on while she'd been working at Chris' Christmas Emporium as she'd developed a serious pastie habit, thanks to the bakery next door. She also had a huge spot about to erupt on her forehead.

Sally-Anne was still huffing and puffing and tapping her foot in annoyance, but Kim had just the tonic to cheer her up.

'Want to know a secret?' she teased, raising and retracting both eyebrows in rapid succession whilst tilting in to whisper conspiratorially, in case Mr Manson *could* hear their conversation and *did* plan on selling his story to the gutter press.

'Always!' piped up Sally-Anne, leaning in, all ears.

'Well, I have three! Firstly, Marty eloped and was married six weeks ago, on a beach on the island of Barbados! I know, I know...I can't believe it either!'

Sally-Anne was squealing and clapping her hands together like a hungry seal anxiously awaiting its dinner.

'Go on, go on!' she cried, as Kim paused deliberately to add suspense.

'Well...secondly...although there will be a relatively quiet start to the New Year, in July the boys are releasing a double A-side single which will consist of a collaboration with Saturday Munro – MASSIVE artist, as you know – and also *Falling* – our song! They're hoping for major chart success with this one Sal. And finally, they'll actually be embarking on a proper tour instead of piffling little gigs here and there! It's going to be a hell of a summer, with live shows throughout the country first, then on to the rest of Europe, before returning to the UK for a bunch of other gigs. Tickets go on sale next month, so we had better start popping the pennies in our piggybanks again!'

'Aw that's brilliant, Kim! See, now I know why I recruited you as my friend! Can't believe we will have to wait until the summer to see them again but this tour's going to be absolutely awesome - we'll buy tickets to every gig; be there to cheer them on every night of the tour. It's going to be fan-bloody-tastic!'

Kim wholeheartedly agreed but knew she would crumble if she had to wait HALF A YEAR to see Ritchie again. No way could she cope without him for six months.

There *had* to be something they could do.

Chapter 12

As luck would have it, one of Kim's precious days off coincided with a date the band were booked to perform a private gig for a clutch of minor celebrities and television extras at a country house hotel in Surrey. A friend of a friend of Nicky's Connor unexpectedly came up trumps with the information – this wonderful guy was apparently a physio for some aging soap star who'd casually commented that he was looking forward to seeing SMY live at his management's annual piss-up…and this had eventually filtered through to Connor, who couldn't believe Kim wasn't already in the know.

The cunning plan was to surprise the band – they were sure to be pleased to see their favourite fans and may even sneak them into the gig and, who knows, if the guys were staying at this fabulous five star hotel, which apparently had its own spa, orangery and *lake*, Kim and Sally-Anne may even be invited to join them in the lap of luxury. Fingers crossed.

On the day, the girls dressed up to the nines in their poshest outfits but still may as well have had GROUPIE tattooed across their foreheads, judging by the pitying glances and sympathetic smiles they received from the staff on duty.

Thankfully they were so early that nobody famous passed by while they were loitering on the steps and it was also a relief to note that no other fans were around to try and infiltrate this top secret gig. They *needed* to be the only ones. It was essential the lads weren't distracted by chatty autograph hunters and that there was no competition in the form of attractive, available women wanting a piece of their idols.

There was no back-up plan. The train fare and taxi ride to this place had cost a bomb and what remained in their purses certainly wouldn't stretch to a room in this hotel, not that there were any available, as the FULLY BOOKED sign on reception clearly indicated.

Whilst the girls hadn't expected a tour bus or fleet of limos, they were surprised when a clapped-out, ancient, sixteen-seater minibus arrived shortly after four o'clock. They knew sales had dipped but this was a real comedown.

Rubbing their eyes and with a chorus of yawns, the band hopped off one by one, accompanied by Marty's new wife, a sound engineer named Conrad and Greasy Gavin. If Kim wasn't overly keen on Barry, then she positively hated Gav. He reminded her of a long, slimy snake that had been dipped in chip fat. His sneery expression and oily, slicked back, dyed-black hair truly made her stomach turn.

Todd, Marty and Ady were first out into the cold, bundled up in chunky jumpers and winter coats, seemingly delighted to see Kim and Sally-Anne, making a fuss of them and posing for pictures. Bren was off the bus and then he was on again – who knew what on earth he was up to but Kim was sure she'd heard him call out sarcastically, 'Well this should be interesting Ritchie-boy!' She wasn't sure what he was appertaining to but then again it was hard to take someone seriously when they looked as if they'd recently slept in a ditch. Thankfully Bren scrubbed up well when required.

Just as Kim was beginning to think that they'd actually forgotten to pick up Ritchie en route, he finally appeared at the door of the minibus, zipped up his flying jacket and pulled up his collar, exiting the vehicle at a pace only a snail would be proud of. Unusual for him – he usually did most things at breakneck speed.

'Hi Ritchie,' she said shyly, not even attempting to second guess what reception she would receive from him.

Thankfully he smiled but it didn't quite reach his eyes. He looked agitated and nervous, as he raked his hand through his hair and cleared his throat. Now what?

'Wow, can't believe we're seeing you again so soon girls! How on earth did you find out about this gig? You never fail to astound me with your investigative skills! Shall we have a quick picture?'

When he placed his hands on their shoulders, as a member of staff kindly stepped in to take the photograph, Kim didn't feel any of his usual warmth radiating through and it all seemed too wooden and formal. Something was different, but she couldn't identify what it was. Had it thrown him off balance, their turning up unannounced? Or had Kim been given her marching orders but he was too much of a soft-arse to tell her to her face?

Before she could really say anything, the band members were all whisked indoors, leaving the girls outside, praying it wasn't about to sleet or snow.

'Shit. They could have bloody offered to sneak us in. There's only us two for gawd's sake – hardly likely to put them to any inconvenience. We can't stand here all night, freezing our bits off, hoping one of them might pop back out again. We'll miss the gig and they might head straight up to their rooms afterwards – and *we've* got nowhere to stay! Plan B, Kim.'

'We have a Plan B this time?' If they had, then she hadn't been made aware of it.

'Not exactly. Look, Plan B is that we try and butter up the staff here to gain access. Once we've got a foot in the door we're bound to bump into Ritchie in the bar or Bren wandering about somewhere, off his box, and then it's time to work our magic. You'll need to take that coat off and pull your dress down to give Ritchie a little more cleavage – you know how he likes a bit of flesh on show.'

'Piss off. What he sees is what he gets. I can't believe he was so remote when he arrived - like he was politely talking to a fan he'd never met before...'

'Oh, don't start all that nonsense again – it winds me right up. Remember, there was a time not so long ago when we would have given *anything* to be within a mile radius of one of the band. To even have our picture taken with them or receive an autograph – well, that was just a pipe dream! Since then we've achieved more than we could ever have thought possible...but ultimately we have to be thankful for what attention we do receive and bank those memories we're making along the way.'

'I still blush to the roots of my hair when Todd or Ady stops to talk to me or I'm cuddling up to Marty and Bren for photos...but with Ritchie it's different now. What's happened between us has irreversibly changed everything for me and I can't just switch it on and off like he's able to.'

Shaking her head in frustration, Kim squeezed her eyes tightly closed and was rewarded with a clear image of Ritchie in her head – except he wasn't smiling or giving her that knowing look. He was wearing a mask of indifference that totally messed with her mind. She didn't know whether she was coming or going with the man and yet she was supposed to crack on and accept it. Because if she didn't, she might lose him forever.

As the wind started to whip up an angry protest, the girls became increasingly snippy and frustrated with each other and Kim sincerely wished it was Nicky beside her rather than Sally-Anne. Nicky would tell it like it was, but was always on Kim's side. She wasn't sure where Sally-Anne was placed. Once or twice her mum had warned that she didn't trust the girl and had referred to her as a 'fair-weathered friend' with not a jot of loyalty in her. Kim had always leapt to Sal's defence but the girl's attitude was beginning to grate on her nerves and it occurred to Kim there and then that she and Sal were very different creatures with polar opposite morals and goals.

Never had Kim been so grateful as when Todd popped his dinky little head out of the door and said, 'You can't wait there, you two. It's supposed to hit minus one tonight and you'll literally freeze over. Come on in...there's a couple of hot chocolates waiting for you in the Mandarin Lounge. You can hide away in there until the guests arrive and I'll square it so that you can stand at the back of the gig while we perform. We'll catch up with you later in the bar as we're all staying over tonight.'

Kim wanted to throw her arms around him and plant a smacker on his baby face, and Sally-Anne actually did! Todd had remembered that they were there. He'd noticed the trees thrashing about and the heavy sky and hadn't wanted to leave them outside, suffering, as the temperature dipped even further. Hot drinks had been ordered and delivered to a table in a quiet corner of the hotel, where their presence wouldn't be questioned. Even with tougher security in place because a few mildly famous actors and television presenters had been invited, he'd persuaded the hotel manager to allow them inside for the evening, despite the fact that they weren't on the guest list. He'd apparently informed this panicky, high-pitched John Cleese lookalike that they were friends of the band and that any refreshments they ordered should be added on to his tab.

Kim would be forever grateful for Todd's kindness, thoughtfulness and maturity. Still so young in comparison to his bandmates, he was revealing himself to be the biggest man amongst them.

'Thank you,' she said, touching his arm, as he shoved their bags under the oval table where their hot chocolates awaited them. The rich, creamy hot liquid smelled delicious and Kim couldn't wait to spoon off the swirl of cocoa-dusted thick cream on top because it absolutely belonged in her belly. 'You've probably saved our lives!'

'It's nothing,' he assured her. 'Just a small token of appreciation and probably about time we gave something back in return.' He looked at her oddly then, shifting from one foot to the other. 'Ritchie...is Ritchie. And I'll let him know where you are.'

She thanked him again, as he rushed off to participate in the soundcheck. They could soon hear the verses and choruses of familiar songs permeating the walls of the hotel and Kim closed her eyes and sank back into the plush velour sofa, her hands warming up nicely around the mug, her heart mellowing at the soft and sultry tone of Ritchie's voice as he sang words of love and devotion...and regret.

'See, I told you! We've fallen on our feet here – good old Todd with his contacts and his flexible credit card.'

Sally-Anne's grating voice interrupted Kim's quiet moment and she was jerked back into the real world – a world where they didn't yet have a bed for the night.

'Yes, he's a diamond that guy - so generous and considerate. If only a touch of his magic would rub off on Ritchie. Let's hope he can conjure up a bedroom for us too or else we're in real trouble tonight.'

'Look, don't worry...we always come good in the end. If all else fails, we'll have to hide somewhere after the show until daylight and then make a run for it – although it won't come to that. No way will Todd or the others leave us to our own devices when they discover we're skint and stranded out in the middle of bloody nowhere...'

'But how will we remain undiscovered for the whole of the night when your snoring makes furniture vibrate?'

'Oh ha-ha,' Sally-Anne laughed, chucking one of the plumped-up cushions at Kim. 'Besides, I bet you a pound for a penny you end up in the sack with Ritchie tonight. How can he resist you in these romantic surroundings, with no doubt the best suite in the hotel and the biggest bed – he won't want that going to waste!'

'He's acting like I'm the last person he would ever want to seduce tonight, Sal, so I wouldn't bank on it. I think you and Bren are a safer bet, and he's probably high as a kite by now – allegedly.'

Sally-Anne sighed, nibbling her lip and mulling the situation over. 'I need to show him that some good loving from Yours Truly is equally as pleasurable as any Class A drugs; make him realise that sex with me would be the ultimate high...'

'Mmmmm...really? Well, best of luck with that.'

*

The audience was quieter than usual. From their distant viewpoint at the rear of the room Kim could see that the female contingent up front were pouting and making eyes at the boys, while all the menfolk, drinking steadily, looked bored as hell, with the exception of a rowdy bunch right beside them who talked throughout the entirety of the set. Kim was seriously tempted to smack them across their sweaty heads, to order them to shut their gobs and stop being so god damned rude.

At least the partygoers came alive at the end of the gig when the band performed the most popular and well-known songs from their repertoire and there was a rousing round of cheers and applause as the boys took a final bow.

As soon as they left the stage they were immediately guided out of the room and thrust into the lift, Kim and Sally-Anne unable to get close enough to follow. They had no option other than to wait at the bar and hope at least Ritchie and Bren would return for a nightcap.

If Kim's bladder had been stronger, the night could have ended very differently.

With no food to absorb it, the beer she'd knocked back had shot straight through her, so she promoted Sally-Anne to Chief Bag Minder and nipped out to the little girls' room off the main reception area. On her way back, only a few minutes later, she almost fell over Ritchie at reception, handing in his key card and checking out!

'Ritchie?' she said softly, tapping him on his left shoulder. Startled, he quickly spun around, almost wiping her out with the branded sports holdall slung over his right shoulder. He seemed surprised to see her again, and more than a little edgy.

'Kim!'

Resisting the temptation to sarcastically reply, 'Oh, you *do* recognise me then?' she adopted her best smiley face instead and asked, 'Are you leaving? I thought you were all booked in for the night?'

For once, he didn't look so sure of himself, as he signed the chit the receptionist had passed over to him and chewed on the inside of his lip.

'The others are staying, but I have to leave I'm afraid. There's stuff going on at home and I need to get back urgently.'

Kim actually felt her face fall in on itself as it crumpled up like a discarded tissue and her heart plummeted to her now defrosted feet. This was too hard. This was never going to happen. She had to accept it and move on.

Fighting back hot, traitorous tears, Kim replied, 'I'm sorry to hear that. I hope your family are all okay...'

'Come here.'

Clasping her hand, he guided her back towards the dining room and under the relative privacy of the sweeping staircase. 'I'm sorry,' he said, dropping his bag to the floor and reaching out to stroke her face, wiping away a stray tear with his thumb. 'There's been loads I've been trying to sort out and that's why I've been so distracted. It's not just my family issues – there's a load of shit going down with the band and my head's fucked. For what it's worth, I was hoping you'd be able to stay here with me, you know, tonight - while Barry and co. aren't around, laying down the law. Of course I was completely taken aback to see you outside – the last thing I expected was you and that bloody Sal turning up here tonight unannounced. No, no - it was, of course, a most welcome surprise to see YOU...and it meant that finally we could spend the night together and make good use of that four poster bed. I'd wake up tomorrow morning with you in my arms and everything would be perfect. But, as usual, there's a spanner in the works. Just our bloody luck.'

'Oh Ritchie, it feels like we're going nowhere and our relationship is doomed! It shouldn't be this complicated. There have been so many opportunities for us to make love; so many times when you could have taken me out or at least made more of an effort. If you don't want me then please be truthful and I'll leave you alone. I'll always be a loyal supporter of the band but I can't take any more of this...'

'Don't give up on me, *please*, Kimberley. I know I've been an idiot – messing you about because of my own insecurities and allowing my fear of being kicked out of the band to take precedence over your feelings. But we can work this out. I can't say too much at the moment but soon everything will be different. Trust me, Kim. Despite being able to belt out all of those love songs up on stage in front of the crowds, I'm not confident or comfortable when it comes to discussing my feelings *offstage*...but you mean so much to me. I couldn't bear to lose you.'

'I don't want to lose you either, Ritchie,' she sobbed into his chest, drawing away slightly to attempt to push her point across. 'But try to view it from my perspective – you've had literally years to do what you want with me and yet, it's never happened. It's like I'm not actually good enough for you. And I know that's true really. If you truly wanted me, we'd have been a proper couple by now...but as things stand, I'm still only a fan and that's all I'll ever be...'

'NO! That's just not true. Look, I suppose I could have slept with you, no strings attached, and my job wouldn't be on the line. I could have strung you along and used you for sex as and when I felt like it, but you don't deserve to be treated like some desperate little groupie. I know what I want now...and it's you, Kim. We have a humungous tour ahead of us next year to promote the Greatest Hits album – starting with a few gigs over here and then we're off to Europe and Australia...and then back to perform about another thirty gigs around the UK. It's a gruelling schedule, particularly with all the promotion and everything, but once that's over, there's nothing to keep us apart. Barry and all of the others can go to hell. So what do you say, darling - can you wait for me? It seems a shame to throw everything away at this stage when we've come so far...'

Kim wanted to say yes, but although her heart was in it for the long haul, her mind was telling her that she was likely to go crazy if things were to continue in the same vein; if she only saw Ritchie whenever the mood suited him...

'Have you got a pen and paper?' he asked, glancing over at the clock - clearly needing to make a fast exit.

Had she got a pen and paper? Of course she had! Along with her trusty camera, they were essential items in the Devoted Fan and Deranged Stalker/Groupie Kit. Except they were still in her bag which was with Sally-Anne, who was probably wondering where the hell she'd disappeared to (and who would most likely tear strips off her for allowing Ritchie to leave before she'd thrown herself on him).

'No? I don't suppose there would be anywhere to secrete them under that beautiful dress of yours,' said Ritchie, his hand gliding down the contours of her body, over her hip bone and round to her bum. 'Stay here a second,' he commanded, disappearing briefly, only to return with a leaflet and a biro. For one delicious moment Kim thought he was about to write down HIS telephone number, until he asked her to jot down her own. Oh well, second best result – at least it was marginal progress.

Leaning on Ritchie's solid, shapely back, with a trembling hand she scribbled her number on the leaflet and handed it to him. He folded it in half before bending down and tucking it safely into the side pocket of the bag which lay at his feet.

One last kiss – all too rushed and too brief – and then he was gone. A screech of wheels on the gravel outside confirmed his hasty departure, and Kim wondered who had arrived at such a late hour to chauffeur him back to the suburbs of Birmingham, when the minibus was still parked up in its allocated space next to the walled garden.

A commotion at the top of the grand staircase interrupted her thoughts and she swivelled round just in time to see wild-card Bren suddenly lose his footing and take a tumble…clattering down every step until he landed in a heap at the bottom. He immediately sprang up, unfazed, and put Sebastian, the duty manager, into a headlock, earning himself a filthy look from two passing old ladies – presumably they weren't part of the private booze-fest as they had a combined age of approximately 150.

Hot on Bren's heels were Todd and Ady, gathering up the contents of his pockets and offering up apologetic smiles to the old dears whilst trying to contain their laughter. There was no sign of Marty, but perhaps he and Ebony were making full use of the hotel facilities including *their* four poster bed and mini bar. Lucky old them.

Kim sighed. What she wouldn't have given to be frolicking around in a king-size bed with Ritchie. Please let him ring. It wasn't much to ask.

'You coming in, Kim?' Todd graciously held the bar door open for her and she thanked him, blushing as she realised she would be entering the room with three-fifths of *Show Me Yours* – another 'pinch me' moment. Surely Sally-Anne wouldn't be annoyed that she'd missed Ritchie when she saw what Kim brought her – particularly Bren!

Sal was over the moon – although Kim did play down the Ritchie incident, hoping her red-rimmed eyes wouldn't give her away in the semi-darkness. Within minutes Sal was engaged in a raucous drinking competition with Bren but the other party guests were as badly behaved and during the next ninety minutes Kim witnessed three men with their trousers on their heads, one hysterical woman threatening to snip off her husband's knob, a couple rolling around on the floor simulating sex, a YMCA dance-off and a bloody fistfight by the French doors. Hopefully no one was scheduled to appear on live television the next morning – it would take more than make-up to cover up the excesses of that evening.

Unfortunately, Bren's wandering eye meant that Sally-Anne was quickly abandoned in favour of a stunning young woman in a shimmering silver dress who sidled up to him and rammed her tongue down his throat. Apparently her husband had nipped outside for a smoke half an hour earlier and never returned.

Eventually Todd and Ady were surrounded by a sea of sultry females, all frantically paddling to grab their attention, and the girls were gradually elbowed out of the way and forced to admit defeat. They desperately needed help but there was no way on earth that either of them had the nerve to rudely interrupt and explain their predicament in front of these glamourpusses.

It was clear that Sally-Anne's plans to slide under the sheets with Bren (presumably while Kim kipped in the bathroom with her hands over her ears) were completely up the spout and in Kim's mind, there were only two options available – either sleep rough, resulting in certain death or, come clean to the boys and plead to be allowed to lay down their heads in one of *their* bathrooms.

'Christ. Sally-Anne, we're out of our depth here and, as lovely as Ady and Todd are, let's face it - we're on our own. Look, if Ritchie was around it would be a different story – I think - but we don't really know the other guys and to them we *are* still only fans. They might think we're going to rob them blind or snap them in their underwear while they're sleeping. We'd be encroaching into their private lives and that's a definite no-no. Oh gawd....what are we going to do?'

Still seriously peeved off with Bren (who was likely to be ejected from the room if he didn't refrain from trying to disrobe his little lady friend), like ancient knicker elastic, Sally-Anne snapped. 'Can't you telephone mummy and daddy to ask them to book somewhere over the phone for us to stay – you know, ask Papa to flash his credit card?'

'What? No, I bloody well can't! I'm barely speaking to them as it is. They'd kill me if I casually informed them that I'd ventured all the way out into the sticks tonight without making any firm plans - again. Anyway, I can't just ring home, pissed-up, at stupid o'clock and expect them to conjure up a bed and breakfast out of nowhere when everywhere is probably closed for the night. *I* don't even know where we are, let alone *them* having a clue where to start ringing around so don't be ridiculous! Anyway, if that's all you can suggest right now, then why don't *you* ring your mum and ask *her* to book us in somewhere?'

'And pay with what? Smarties? She has no credit cards and no money, you div.'

Last orders at the bar had clearly been and gone because the staff were suddenly clearing tables and stacking up glasses and gradually the room was thinning out. A prone, topless man was being carried out of the room and when Kim peered over to take a closer look, she realised it was Bren. For one awful moment she thought he was dead, until he suddenly tried to sit up and shouted, 'I need a piss!' as four breathless, sweaty men struggled to haul him out of the room. God, that guy was hardcore.

Unfortunately Todd and Ady had mysteriously vanished into thin air whilst they'd been watching Bren's antics. Presumably Greasy Gav had finally torn himself away from the freakishly tall red-head with the high-pitched laugh to shepherd his charges back to their respective rooms.

Shoulders sagging, bodies swaying due to excessive alcohol intake, they gathered their belongings and headed towards the main entrance. Sebastian was manning the front doors and Sally-Anne decided to try and appeal to his good nature.

'Sir...you know how you were kind enough to let us sit quietly in the Mandarin Lounge because we're such good friends with Todd...'

Discreetly stepping away from his guests, Sebastian replied in a hushed voice, 'I know you are fans, madam. Close friends of Mr Hargreaves would not have been loitering on the hotel steps for hours in frighteningly low temperatures. So let's not pretend otherwise. The band is blessed to have such a benevolent, attractive young chap as Mr Hargreaves amongst their numbers...' Sebastian's eyes began to glaze over and his face became all dreamy-looking as he appeared to disappear into some erotic fantasy in his head, before abruptly remembering where he was and snapping back into the present.

'Anyway...' continued Sally-Anne, undeterred, '...my friend and I have been disgracefully let down on overnight accommodation and we seem to have left our other money at home. So...seeing as that lounge was almost completely empty and we were impeccably behaved earlier...'

'No. The hotel is full, you are not paying guests – and you have no money to pay, in any event. It would be against health and safety and every other regulation and would present a security risk for our actual guests – many of whom are rich and famous I'll have you know. I'm afraid your request is completely out of the question and I must insist that you leave the premises with immediate effect.'

Kim's cheeks were ablaze, mortified at being ejected from such a beautiful establishment.

'I'm sorry,' she said, peering over Sally-Anne's shoulder. 'If we could ask the receptionist to arrange for a taxi to collect us then we'll be out of your hair soon...'

Nodding his agreement, Sebastian turned away to gracefully open the door for a legless middle-aged man being propped up by his good lady wife, whilst Kim and Sally-Anne shuffled miserably over to the front desk.

'Excuse me please. Could you possibly ring a taxi for us?' Kim asked politely, desperately wanting to be anywhere but there, where they had clearly outstayed their welcome.

'Where to?' abruptly asked the pencil thin girl behind the desk, her tired eyes looking Kim up and down as if she was a common prostitute.

'Er...I'm not sure actually. To the nearest train station, I suppose.'

'Wait!' Sebastian was beside them now, holding his hand up in a STOP gesture, clearly used to being obeyed by his minions. 'Could I have a word please, ladies,' he clicked his fingers and beckoned for them to follow him, and they trotted along behind obediently.

'Right you two, firstly, you do know that the ticket office and waiting room at the railway station are now locked up until eight o'clock tomorrow morning? And that there are no trains actually running until after nine?'

'Well, I suspected that might be the case,' Kim piped up nervously, 'but we literally have nowhere else to go...'

'And three women have been attacked there in the last year under cover of darkness...'

She didn't bloody know that.

'Well, we have no other viable options so we'll have to take our chances,' replied Sally-Anne, putting on her most downcast face; adopting a look that would have telephone lines jammed if it were used to front a charity appeal for abandoned puppies.

'Oh, cut that out,' admonished no-nonsense Sebastian. 'Look. I'm putting my job on the line for you pair but I can't have your deaths on my conscience. Now, we are going to head up to the residents' bar on the first floor, where you will sit quietly until it closes. When I return to relieve my barman of his duties you will both remove your shoes and take up a sofa each for the night. All alcoholic beverages will be locked up overnight, you will only have access to the ladies room and if you attempt to wander around the building then an alarm will be activated in reception and the police will attend. Do I make myself clear?'

'Yes,' they both nodded furiously in unison, not particularly relishing the prospect of being detained at Her Majesty's Pleasure.

Safely depositing them far away from the paying guests enjoying a nightcap in the residents' bar – where their brief hopes that Ady, Todd or Bren might be hiding out were quickly dashed – he flounced off to deal with a scuffle in reception, leaving them to heave a huge sigh of relief.

'We have got to stop doing this, Sal. My days of winging it are over.'

'You'd think Ritchie would be more concerned about your safety, him being so into you and all,' goaded Sally-Anne. 'You don't seem to be making much progress in that department, do you?'

Resisting the temptation to point out that *she* couldn't get Bren in the sack even though he was apparently doing anything in a skirt, Kim tuned out to Sal's witterings and fantasised about being tucked up at home in bed.

By the time they left the hotel, the sun had risen and daylight had replaced darkness, which at least meant they'd reduced their odds of being attacked and left for dead, although they were both crumpled and exhausted.

Sebastian's bark had turned out to be worse than his bite. He had asked the taxi driver to drop them off at his favourite greasy spoon café and handed them a crisp, new ten pound note with specific instructions to purchase two small breakfasts with the bottomless coffee option and to remain there for as long as possible, safe and warm.

Kim acted on a sudden urge to peck him on his rosy cheek to express her sincere gratitude for his unexpected kindness.

'One final piece of advice, ladies,' he added as he hastily backed away, holding his hand up to bid them goodbye.

'Yes?'

'Clean your teeth as soon as you are able to do so. Your breath is rank.'

Chapter 13

A watched pot never boils, and a gawked-at telephone never rings, Kim discovered, to her dismay.

Christmas was somewhat depressing. Her delivery from Santa consisted mostly of envelopes containing money (to put aside for gig tickets) and she had barely anything to unwrap on 25th December apart from chocolates, bubble bath and a litre bottle of vodka from Nicky, with the promise of a free haircut when the need arose.

She'd pinned all her hopes on Ritchie ringing to wish her Merry Christmas, if not before the big day, then at some point during the festive Top of the Pops or the Queen's Speech. Watching the band's appearance on TOTP (which apparently had been recorded mid-July during a mini-heatwave), she stuffed chocolate Brazil nuts into her mouth and tried to hold back the tide of misery that threatened to engulf her.

Her poor gran hadn't been well either, meaning she didn't even have her presence to lighten the atmosphere until Boxing Day, when the whole family paid her a visit, armed with gifts, turkey sandwiches and a Christmas pudding. Kim was shocked by her grandmother's frailty – she really did look under the weather and was unusually quiet. Consequently, they only stayed for a short time to allow the dog-tired, much-loved family matriarch to recuperate in peace.

Returning to Cheshire, Kim's family members dispersed to various friends' houses but Kim literally had nowhere else to go. Nicky was celebrating with Connor's family and all other mates and acquaintances had gradually fallen by the wayside.

Left to her own devices, she endured ten long minutes of a dire Carry On film before choosing to sit in silence instead. Boxing Day, and she was shovelling in salted peanuts, staring miserably at the multicoloured fairy lights flashing on and off, wondering where Ritchie was and what he was doing.

Would he be at home - his parents' house – tucking into finger food with his extended family? Or perhaps he was pissed up down the pub with his mates, screeching along to Slade? Maybe he was holed up with Ady or Marty, taking time out from the madness of Christmas to put down some lyrics – penning a future number one single that would catapult them back to the top of the charts.

Whatever he was doing, wherever he was...he wasn't with her and seemed to have forgotten, once more, that she mattered too.

Downing her tumbler of vodka and coke in one, she allowed the tears to run free. It seemed like the gift she would always remember from this particular Christmas was one of a Big Fat Nothing from a man who currently figured less in her life than even good old Saint Nick himself.

*

When the tour dates were announced, there was indeed a raft of shows to come – almost three weeks on the road around England and Scotland, forty dates throughout Europe, a month over in Australia during which there would be twelve live performances coupled with a significant amount of promotion, and then back to the UK for another twenty-five gigs. There were so many concerts, in far flung locations; the schedule was beyond gruelling and Kim imagined that it was an exhausting prospect for all involved. What the hell was their management's problem? And, most importantly, how in god's name could she attend even half of the UK gigs without breaking the bank?

Sally-Anne was now stacking shelves at her local Sainsburys whilst Kim was working in the office of a family run kitchen company, which mainly involved photocopying and making tea. It was boring as hell but the salary was decent and it had the added bonus of weekends off.

Kim and Sally-Anne bought tickets for fourteen gigs in total but were insanely jealous of certain other fans who somehow managed to book for even more. How in God's name did these people afford it? Maybe they robbed banks in their spare time or indulged in a spot of money laundering to supplement their income. Kim couldn't even stump up the cash for a new nail polish, let alone a trip to Newcastle.

By the time Valentine's Day arrived, both girls were single, skint and thoroughly depressed.

They'd forwarded lovey-dovey cards to Ritchie and Bren via the fan club but received nothing in return and neither girl had any secret admirers to boast of any closer to home. Kim was forced to endure a full half hour of Sally-Anne whining down the phone about her wretched life before she was able to hang up, whereupon the phone immediately rang again. Tempted to ignore it, as she really couldn't face any more earache, she eventually snatched up the receiver, excuses at the ready as to why she had to instantly terminate the call.

'Hello!' she barked, her patience wearing thin. 'You're through to the Summers' Family Mental Asylum! Please leave your message after the tone...*beeeeep*...'

'*Kimberley!*' interrupted a husky, familiar voice. A voice she adored as it belonged to the person who she loved more than life itself.

'RITCHIE!' she shrieked down the line. 'Ritchie, is that really you?'

'Kimberley Summers!' Ritchie laughed and she thought she'd never heard such a wonderful sound. 'I'm guessing you're pleased to hear from me then?'

'Oh Ritchie, you have no idea how wonderful it is to speak to you, especially today of all days...'

'Your card arrived, darling. It's beautiful...but then I wouldn't expect anything less from you. I don't really do cards – there's no time for me to go browsing for one anyway – but I wanted you to know I feel the same way. I miss you Kimberley and it's only the thought of seeing you again that keeps me going when I'm recording and rehearsing all day and long into the night...wishing I was at home in bed, with you wrapped up tightly in my arms...'

He never said why he hadn't rung earlier and it didn't occur to her to ask. By this stage she'd kind of accepted that this was how it was. He was a world famous popstar, she a lowly fan who'd progressed to 'friend' status. Someone who was also now his part-time love interest, fitting in haphazardly around his crazy life.

'I haven't had a day off since last year,' he continued, whilst Kim listened in and soaked up every precious letter and syllable that flowed out of his delectable mouth. 'They're killing us with this new itinerary and for the first time ever, it feels like a job rather than a passion. I'm merely an employee of a global corporation who want their pound of flesh and then some. Anyway, enough of my complaints! I've been so looking forward to speaking to you. Kimberley, queen of the little black dress and hottest female on the planet, will you do me the honour of being my valentine?'

'Of course I will, you goon!' she laughed, blushing a deep shade of burgundy at the fact she'd had the audacity to call him a goon. Barriers were definitely being broken down.

'Well, I was worried you might have given up on me and skipped off into the sunset with somebody more attractive and available, who could spoil you and seduce you every night of the week if they so wished...'

'You know I would never do that, Ritchie,' she soothed. 'For a start, there's no one on earth more attractive. And besides, I don't want anyone else and that's always been the case. I'll never love anyone more than I love you.'

'Glad to hear it, my beautiful, shining northern star,' he replied softly, his voice caressing her nerve endings, his breathing stoking up memories of how it felt to kiss him and feel his intimate touches. 'Do you remember when I practically caught you in my arms outside of that grotty pub in Croydon? It sounds so corny but our eyes met and I instantly knew I'd found someone special...someone who would shape my life...'

'I'm so glad you were there to break my fall. And when you serenade me with those wonderful words from the stage each night, I feel so blessed that you single me out and remind me of the very first time we met.'

'Kimberley, Kimberley....my girl. I wish you were here with me. I miss your smile and your cute little nose...and the wicked glint in your eyes and those long, sexy lashes...and the taste of those luscious lips...'

'Oh Ritchie, it's agony being apart like this with not a soul understanding how I feel. Sometimes it's like there's a chasm between us that's opening up more every day when surely we should be closing the gap by now. I only wish we could...'

'What? I'm on the phone! Can't it wait a minute? Oh lord, sorry darling, I have to go.' A commotion in the background. The sound of his name being called by another, deeper male voice. Doors banged and music cranked up.

'They want me to put some vocals down tonight and I'm being pressed to get a move on. It's been so good to talk to you and we'll speak again soon honey...'

'No! I can't believe we have to say goodbye already, Ritchie. Oh, okay...well if you really do have to go...'

'I *do* have to, I'm afraid. You take care of yourself Kimberley...bye darling,' he breathed, blowing a long distance kiss down the telephone line.

'Bye Ritchie.' She tried to reciprocate – to send him one back, so he could carry her kiss with him, wherever his travels took him.

But he was already gone.

Chapter 14

'Excuse me?'

Nicky stood before Kim, hands on hips, cheeks flushed, eyes bulging as she raised her voice and Kim shrunk back from the hostility and anger.

'Repeat yourself Kim, because I must surely have been mistaken. For one fleeting moment there, I thought you said you couldn't attend my hen party because you had tickets for a *Show Me Yours* gig on the very same night and that's where you would prefer to be. Tell me I misheard Kim. Tell me that you haven't chosen that fucking band over your best friend's hen night. C'mon then...I'm waiting...'

What could Kim say that could possibly paint her in a better light?

Of course she'd remembered when Nicky's wedding was due to take place. For Christ's sake, they'd all had enough dress fittings to etch that bloody date on her mind. Thankfully it wouldn't clash with any of the gigs she'd booked but stupid, STUPID Kim hadn't even considered the hen night. Nicky had banged on and on about her bestie organising a wild session in a city centre nightclub or weekend away with lewd party games and all manner of surprises, but she'd kept saying *two weeks before*, not an actual date, and it simply hadn't registered in Kim's mind.

Not only was there nothing planned, but Nicky was absolutely right – she wouldn't even be around for it.

'I'm sorry Nicky. I cocked up. I made sure, of course, that I was available for your wedding day but I didn't have a fixed date in my head for your hen night when I booked the gig tickets, so I'll be in London on the weekend in question. I don't suppose there's any chance...'

'What? Any chance I can move it to another date? Tell my Aunty Bernadette that she's got to cancel her ferry over from the Isle of Man? Move the WHOLE FUCKING WEDDING to accommodate your pathetic stalking schedule?'

'For god's sake Nicky, I'm not asking you to move the wedding. Don't be ridiculous! I only wondered if maybe you could bring forward the hen night by merely one weekend or perhaps delay it for a week? Oh, on second thoughts, delaying it would actually be the only option that would work for me, as it's the only weekend around that time that I'm free...'

'*FUCK OFF* KIMBERLEY! You are unreal, you are. You want me to shift it to the following weekend because YOU don't happen to have any concerts planned for then. Did it never cross your mind that I may already have plans? You know full well that mum's booked us in at Hilltops for a spa weekend!'

'Oh, god, I'm sorry. I clean forgot about that...'

'FORGOT? You have a very sketchy memory for most things these days, unless it's connected to your favourite topic. Tell me something Kim, if you had tickets for one of the band's gigs – say, the last night of the tour – and it clashed with my actual wedding day, which one would you choose?'

'Well...your wedding, of course,' Kim insisted, but she'd hesitated a second too long and Nicky missed nothing.

'No. No way. That's bullshit. Don't lie to *me*, of all people. The truth is that you would pick a snatched moment with Ritchie over the most important day of my life. I'm relegated to the shit-heap these days – along with everyone else, even your own family. So don't stand there and tell me otherwise, because you're a crap liar and I know you better than anyone.'

This was horrible. Any rows she'd had with Nicky in the past had been few and far between - the odd spat when they were drunk and incapable which was usually rectified over a greasy kebab on the same night. Just standard silly disagreements between friends that would be forgotten within hours.

This was different. Nicky was seething and, although there was a worm of guilt wriggling around inside of Kim, she was somewhat unrepentant. Nicky would do anything for Connor and they lived in each other's pockets – so why couldn't she understand that Kim would literally move heaven and earth to be with Ritchie?

The tension lay heavy in the air and Kim didn't know what to say to make the situation any less awkward, but in any case Nicky severed the conversation, as she gathered up her bag and her huge bunch of keys.

'Forget it, Kim. I'll organise the hen night myself, and it will be bigger and better than anything you could have managed because I'll be putting my heart and soul into it. And to be honest, it will be a relief if you're not there rather than hear you droning on about that fucking tosspot all night long. Oh and don't worry about wasting any more of your precious time being dragged along for dress fittings. You can stand down. I'm striking you off my list. I'll have one less bridesmaid and perhaps see you at the evening reception – if you can be bothered to turn up.'

An earthquake-like slam of the front door and Nicky was off, leaving Kim to stew in a potful of guilt, anger and loss. Somewhere deep inside she knew she had made a bad choice, but her time with Ritchie was so limited with so few opportunities for them to be together, that to surrender any of it seemed unthinkable. Even though she hadn't deliberately let Nicky down, in her best mate's eyes it was unforgiveable and Kim totally understood why.

And yet she'd still made that choice. She was a terrible, terrible friend.

*

With no further communication from Ritchie, Kim made a pact with herself that she would knuckle down and earn as much money as possible to fund her jaunts around the country. Her boss, Bruce, was highly surprised to find her volunteering to cover Nita's late shifts in the showroom on top of working every Saturday for the next few weeks. Nita was pregnant, sick as a dog and desperate for time off, so Kim became her new favourite person (and she earned herself a minor promotion in the process).

When Kim wasn't typing up quotes or attempting to sell kitchen cupboards and white goods, she was also pulling pints behind the bar in one of the local pubs. The Fox and Goose was full of domino obsessed, wrinkly old men and big-bellied darts players, but they were convivial, consistently polite and excellent tippers. God bless them!

Her dad was cautiously optimistic that she was turning over a new leaf. Her mum said to watch out for Ritchie snapping his fingers and see how quickly their daughter ran. Consequently, relations were still decidedly frosty at home.

She didn't speak to Nicky at all during those busy months but heard via her mum that all the wedding plans were coming together and that her best friend (if she could still call her that) was off to Dublin for a couple of days to celebrate with her hens. Despite everything, that hurt. Never in a billion years could Kim ever have imagined Nicky's hen party taking place without her there at the heart of it. Ritchie was definitely worth all of the stress and aggravation but still...

The top and bottom of it was that when she wasn't working, Kim was desperately lonely. Listening to the band's music, watching them perform on television...the thrill was always there but the man wasn't, and she had no one to talk to; no one to confide in. Sally-Anne was her friend but a little voice inside her head warned that anything she divulged in confidence wouldn't remain a secret for very long. Although Kim had defended her until she was blue in the face, she didn't actually completely trust Sally-Anne herself. Too often Kim had heard Sal make fun of others; there'd been far too many occasions when she'd pulled apart someone's choice of outfit or made sly comments about their weight behind their back. Then she'd been all sweet and friendly to their face, literally five minutes later.

'Do you think that old bird Hannah only possesses the one top?' she would ask, followed by, 'God knows why she has to drag that kid along with her everywhere. It's hardly likely to entice Todd is it, having a sprog in tow – unless that's why she does it. Everyone makes a fuss of the little princess and then mummy's the centre of attention...'

'Sally-Anne!' Kim was always shocked when Sal was mean about someone as kind, unassuming and harmless as Hannah. 'Don't be so bitchy. That's her daughter, and I don't think there's a husband or partner around to look after the poor mite. And anyway, the little one is so well behaved and so cute, singing along to all of the songs and making up her own dance routines...'

'Yeah, well...I'm sick of her occupying prime position in front of me, with her head popping up in half of my pictures. She's an annoying little...Oh hi Hannah! We were just saying we'd not seen you and Elizabeth around today.'

Kim couldn't understand how anyone could be so brazenly two-faced and it all made her feel extremely uncomfortable. Although she and Sally-Anne were mates and they'd shared a catalogue of experiences and plenty of belly laughs, Kim did begin to wonder if Sal was also secretly slagging *her* off when she wasn't around.

Surely not though.

However, Kim had noticed that Sally-Anne was suddenly thick as thieves with the Irish trio and, more worryingly, the Three Witches – and *they* never had a good word to say about anybody. Sal was constantly namedropping them and suggesting they all book gig tickets together (over Kim's dead body), seemingly desperate to infiltrate their friendship group and be seen as one of the Beautiful People. The last thing Kim wanted was to become a clone of anyone – particularly a member of a coven who got their kicks from tearing into fellow fans.

She wasn't about to let any bitchiness or bickering spoil the tour. Not only did this promise to be a phenomenal run of gigs but it was also time for her and Ritchie to shine as a couple.

Kim predicted it would be a summer to remember.

Chapter 15

When the band's Greatest Hits album was released, rammed with all their amazing songs and even a couple of bonus tracks that blew the girls' socks off, it did well in the album charts – in no small part due to the publicity bandwagon that rolled into every town and every city. Kim wondered why the campaign hadn't been orchestrated for the highly lucrative Christmas market but figured the management must have known what they were doing and concentrated her energies on admiring the new publicity shots. Taken at sunset on an idyllic Caribbean beach, the boys wore pristine dark dinner suits which contrasted against the powdery white sands and burnt orange sky and they all looked sun-kissed and sexy. Even Bren scrubbed up well and he'd been looking rather peaky of late.

But it was the dedication in the CD, cassette and gatefold album sleeve that stunned Kim, making her want to grab every family member, friend and colleague who had ever doubted her and yell at them: 'I BLOODY TOLD YOU SO!'

'This is for K…for her patience and support and love…always Your Ritchie xx'

She couldn't believe he'd done it. A public declaration of his feelings, for every single fan across the world to see. Anyone who bought the album and read the notes would think 'Wow! After all these years, someone has finally, forever captured Ritchie's heart. Who is this lucky lady?'

At last, he'd made a statement of commitment by undeniably acknowledging her existence. This wasn't some deluded fantasy she'd been entertaining inside her head. She wasn't a fan with a crush who was as gullible as she was pathetic. Kimberley Summers was to be envied and respected rather than pitied and made fun of.

All the waiting had eventually paid dividends.

This was real.

Chapter 16

The beginning of the tour was everything Kim wanted it to be: gigs 99% sold out, electrifying atmosphere each night and Ritchie was charming, tactile and attentive. It seemed to be a given that Kim would follow him backstage each afternoon when they arrived for sound-checking, where they would melt into each other's arms, making up for lost time by smothering one another with passionate, needy kisses and letting their hands wander to where they really shouldn't have been wandering, particularly in view of the close proximity of other band members and their entourage.

Kim was eager to please, to show him exactly how grateful she was for including his heartfelt words within the album dedications and at long last proving, in a roundabout way, how much she meant to him. Ritchie repeated how much he had missed her and she clung to him, never wanting to let him go. The other guys made themselves scarce when they were together and it was only her and Ritchie, locked in a world where no one could harm them or interfere or burst their perfect bubble.

Her parents still worried when she was away, anxiously awaiting her infrequent telephone calls. Kim was the first to admit that she was unreliable. It wasn't that she deliberately didn't call or that she enjoyed making them fret - it simply never crossed her mind, especially when she was in Ritchie's arms, his breathing and his heartbeat in tandem with her own.

Sunday had been a strange day from the outset. She'd awoken to an ominous feeling – a sensation that trouble was brewing; something unpleasant in the air. Hoping it wasn't about to be one of those stinking days when Ritchie would forget she existed, she tried to dispel that uneasy sense of foreboding and busied herself in the guesthouse, packing up stuff and chivvying on Sally-Anne, who had a tendency to flomp in bed until the very last moment.

As they were thanking the landlady of the establishment on departure, Kim's eyes were drawn to the collection of Sunday morning papers fanned out on a half-moon mahogany table in the hallway.

EXCLUSIVE! SECRETS OF BOYBAND *SHOW ME YOURS* REVEALED.

Caribbean wedding!

Drugs overdose and rehab!

Shit, shit, shit!

'Sally-Anne...*loooook!'*

Feeling sick to her stomach, Kim pointed to the horror headlines.

'OH MY GAWD!' screamed Sally-Anne at the top of her voice before snatching the nearest newspaper off the table.

Kim nervously chewed on her lip. Please don't let Ritchie be involved. He couldn't be. She was the only one for him, of that she was absolutely sure. But please say it wasn't him. They knew all about Marty's secret marriage and the drugs that seemed to rule Bren's life but as for the seedy romps, realistically, who knew what went on when they were touring overseas. The dirty dog could be any one of them, but if it was Ritchie, it would kill her.

'There's a newsagents on the corner dear. You can't take that,' snipped their suddenly hostile host. Clearly wanting shut of them now they had handed over the cash, she snatched back her newspaper, switching from spaniel to Rottweiler in a matter of seconds.

A mad dash to the local shop and they had a copy each but there was no time to stop and read until they were safely on the train to Northampton – they'd made it with only seconds to spare. Miraculously, they managed to bag table seats, where they spread out their Sunday rags and pored over them, scanning the print until they found the 'new' revelations.

Marty's marriage to Ebony was documented – no surprise there.

Bren's drug habit. Well, they knew he was off his head more than he was on it but, if the newspaper report was anything to go by, he'd been dabbling in all kinds since he was sixteen and had even done a stint in rehab, which was the real reason they'd cancelled the *Dirty* tour – not through exhaustion then.

Feeling more apprehensive by the second, Kim read on, greatly relieved to hear Bren was also guilty of the romps in hotel rooms with sex workers.

'Oh, well it's practically the law that you have to visit the red light district when you're in Amsterdam and there's always someone who ends up doing the business in a squalid hotel room when they've been smoking the funny fags!' Sally-Anne dismissed it as a load of old twaddle, clearly an expert on the subject – even though she'd never met a prostitute nor set foot in Holland in her life.

'It's not exactly a complimentary piece though, is it? I mean, where have they got all their information from? It's like someone's set out to do a proper job on them.' The accompanying individual shots of Bren were horrific too, clearly selected to make him look like a complete headcase, with his mouth hanging wide open and his unkempt hair stood on end.

'Well, they've been lucky so far to avoid a bashing in the trashy mags and papers. There was always bound to be stuff come out eventually.'

'Well I bloody hope that's all they've got to print because my dad will paste me if I end up in the Red Tops, snapped in a compromising position with Ritchie...'

'Oh yeah, because, like, they'd really be interested in *you!*' Sally-Anne snorted, treating Kim to a derisory look. 'It's hardly a major scoop is it? *Average girl enjoys snogs backstage off horny popstar at loose end!*'

'Thanks. That's really nice. Thanks a lot.'

They continued their journey in silence and Kim was relieved to see a few other familiar fans disembarking the train from another carriage when it pulled in to Northampton. It would be a pleasant change to talk to people who weren't so sharp-tongued and sneery. She was just about on speaking terms again with Sal by the time they finally arrived at their next guesthouse – which was grey on the outside, grey on the inside and possibly one of the most depressing places Kim had ever paid to stay in.

With no wish to remain in their tiny, airless room any longer than absolutely necessary, they fled out into the street again, keen to be anywhere but staring at the peeling wallpaper and cracked window pane. As they were approaching the theatre and passing a telephone box, for the first time ever, Kim felt an overwhelming urge to speak to one or both of her parents. '*It's like comfort food,*' she thought. Except instead of a bowlful of chocolate ice cream or slightly lumpy mashed potato she needed a good dollop of concern and familiarity.

Informing Sally-Anne that she would be with her 'in a minute', Kim slipped into the phone box and emptied her pockets of all the loose change to make the call.

The line wasn't great but she eventually heard her mum say, 'Hello.'

'Hi mum, it's me. Thought I'd give you a ring to let you know I'm okay. We arrived in Northampton about an hour ago and...'

'You were supposed to ring on Friday.' Her mum bluntly cut in, a strange, abrupt tone to her voice.

'Aw mum, you know what I'm like. I got distracted as usual – it's no big deal. I'm ringing now, aren't I? It's only been two days really...hardly makes a difference whether I call you on Friday or Sunday.'

'Your gran died on Friday evening.'

It was like her heart was being smashed, there and then, in that stinking red telephone box in an unfamiliar street in a strange town. The world as she knew it had ended and everything was spinning, as she gasped for breath and tried to make sense of what she'd been told.

'Did you hear me Kimberley? Your gran passed away.'

'But...but that can't be right. Gran was poorly but she was picking up, wasn't she? I thought the new antibiotics had started to work. How can this have happened? She's strong as an ox – she always said. I refuse to believe it. Not her. Not my gran.'

It was incomprehensible. The larger-than-life lady with the biggest heart who had always lived life to the full and who had smothered them all with her unconditional love - no matter how rubbish a granddaughter Kim had been of late. Yes, she'd aged, but she had so much more to give, many more years to be around on this mortal coil. It wasn't her time, she wasn't ready. Kim wasn't ready.

'She was admitted to hospital on Friday but didn't want to worry anyone, because that's who she was.' Her mum's voice cracked, the acute pain seeping through into her every word.

'Fortunately Aunty Joan panicked when she hadn't been able to reach your gran and drove over there on Friday morning, arriving just as she was being loaded into the ambulance. So at least she was able to accompany her to the hospital...mum wasn't alone in her final hours. We were on our way there when she took a turn for the worse – by the time we arrived it was too late...'

Mum's shuddering sobs physically hurt Kim. She couldn't bear to hear the raw agony and her own anguish seemed too much to bear.

'Pneumonia they said. They couldn't save her. She's gone.'

Tears rushed down Kim's cheeks as she tried, and failed, to imagine what it would feel like to lose a parent. Her mum was suffering so badly and she couldn't even console her. They were miles apart and she was way out of hugging distance...and yet again she felt the yearning for home. But the almost magnetic pull towards Ritchie was even stronger. She needed to be safe in his arms, to hear his words of comfort, to bury herself in his aura and pretend that this wasn't really happening to her family.

'I'll be back tomorrow...' she started to say, between gulps, but her mum wasn't interested.

'You said you would ring on Friday and you didn't. You could have come home and been with us, your family, where you belong...but you couldn't be bothered, yet again.'

'But it might still have been too late for me to see gran before she...'

'Your gran's been dead two days and you didn't even know it. We needed you, and you weren't here – as per usual. You're never here. Uncontactable and uncaring as always. I constantly asked you to make that trip over to gran's with us. You knew she wasn't well but she was WAY down your list of priorities. Always too busy, could never spare the time. And now you're too bloody late.'

'MUUUUM!' Kim sobbed, unable to deal with the level of her disgust on top of her own mountain of grief. 'I'm sorry - I really am. I loved gran and I'm heartbroken that I won't ever see her again...'

'It's always about *your* heart though, isn't it Kimberley? Once again you are acting like *your* feelings count more than any of ours. You don't have it in you to show an ounce of consideration for anyone else, do you? Me, me, me – looking after number one. Look, I have to go now. I'll see you tomorrow, if and when you get back.'

The line was dead. The phone had been slammed down and Kim could add nothing further. Although she was almost out of ten pence pieces, she could have got more, but it felt pointless. She would be home tomorrow.

The four mucky-windowed walls of the telephone box seemed to be closing in and she felt like she was suffocating. Gasping for air, she flung the door open and found herself a wall to lean against, where she wept into her hands and prayed that this was all some kind of sick joke.

'No, no, no....' she wailed, shoulders heaving, chest aching and legs threatening to give way beneath her shaking form.

'Kim?' Sally-Anne stood before her, head cocked to one side, looking puzzled. 'What's happened?'

Relaying the conversation, pausing frequently to wipe away tears and try to catch her breath, Kim felt a desperate urge to be sharing this devastating news with Ritchie instead. She wasn't even sure that Sally-Anne was all that sympathetic – yes, she hugged her and offered up the usual condolences and tissues, but her reaction felt lacking in compassion, particularly when her eyes were darting round, on the look-out for the tour bus. She was clearly itching to check the time on her watch and hotfoot it over to the theatre.

'You go,' Kim insisted, genuinely wanting her to leave. 'It's better that I have a few minutes alone to compose myself, to try to take it all in.'

Sally-Anne left, with a weak attempt at a 'Well, if you're sure,' and then almost hurtled into a lamppost in her haste to flee from the scene. She didn't do grief, it was apparent. If you wanted sunshine and giggles and a good time, then she was your girl. If your world was grey, verging on black and you were choked with misery - find another friend.

'You alright?' enquired a gruff voice, belonging to a large figure clumsily emerging from a nearby car - pulled up with all its hazards flashing. Kim tried to blink away the tears to identify the mystery person. Oh. It was Strange Geraldine, all flapping coat tails and pudding basin haircut (the granny perm had long gone) bounding towards her with something clasped in her hand.

'Just had some really awful news Gerry and I'm in bits – so no, not really. I'm not okay, but thank you for asking – it's much appreciated.'

Geraldine anxiously gnawed on her lip before awkwardly draping her arm around Kim's shoulders and she found herself squashed into this odd woman's massive breasts, which put even her own generous D-cups to shame.

'Don't like seeing you sad. You're always Mrs Chirpy. Not like me. I was born miserable.' It was difficult to disagree with that last statement as Planet Geraldine seemed to be a most peculiar place to reside. She rarely smiled or showed any signs of positivity or contentment, even when the band members were around and she was barging into them, taking thousands of pictures. It hadn't escaped Kim's notice that Ritchie often shied away from putting his arm around Geraldine when posing for photographs and that he seemed to be extremely wary of her idiosyncrasies and occasional musty smell.

Marty and Todd were overly kind to her though, instinctively recognising that she was merely different rather than dangerous. Almost certainly harmless – Kim hoped – and she'd become used to her scowly-at-rest face and curt, no-nonsense replies.

'Here, have this.' Thrusting a huge bar of Galaxy chocolate under Kim's nose, she started to back away, her soft side allowance for the current year clearly expended. Kim gratefully accepted the squashed slab – chocolate's chocolate at the end of the day - before Geraldine took off again in her old Escort. Kim thought about making a move then but her legs seemed incapable of working – almost as if she was wearing lead boots. She couldn't yet face the rest of the stage-door-gang, so she remained alone, propping up the wall, her heart aching for her wise and wonderful grandmother whose presence she'd taken for granted and whose cheery, wrinkly face would never greet her again.

As the heavy traffic ground to a temporary halt at the lights, she became aware of a male voice calling out her name. Glancing up, she was startled to see Todd, a front seat passenger in a white 4x4, concern etched on his handsome boyish face, enquiring if everything was alright.

'Yes,' she sobbed, because she didn't know what else to say.

To her surprise, the passenger door was flung open and out he jumped, instructing the unidentified driver to continue without him - the car park was only thirty seconds away.

'Kim? What's wrong?' For a young man he had exceedingly strong arms, which easily wrapped themselves around Kim, as she bawled into his shoulder. After a decent amount of weeping, he probed again as to what had occurred, and through her tears she attempted to explain.

'C'mon,' he said, removing her from the wall, whilst keeping one arm firmly around her shoulders. 'You can't stay here. You're in shock. Let's get you inside and grab a cup of tea.' In her fragile state, she would have complied with any instructions. She let him lead her down the street and round to the rear of the theatre, ushering her inside, away from prying eyes. As the stage door was closing behind them Kim registered the undisguised fury on

Sally-Anne's face and realised she was obviously pissed off because Kim had dared to step foot backstage without her. *Well, excuse me Sal for having a deceased grandmother.*

A hushed conversation between Todd and a member of staff resulted in a steaming hot mug of tea being swiftly delivered for Kim, who sat miserably on a tatty chair in a dressing room piled high with boxes of paper towels. He'd clearly drawn the short straw at this venue.

Todd momentarily disappeared, before thankfully returning and pulling up an equally tatty stool so he could sit with Kim, to quietly quiz her about her gran, listening while Kim explained how she had been the beating heart of their family and yet she'd neglected her, putting her own needs before those of her grandmother's. She was on her feet again then, shuddering and sobbing her heart out, with Todd's arms once more wrapped around her and his whispers of 'Ssshh' in her ear...and then suddenly the door burst open and she heard footsteps quickly cover the floor space. She was gently handed over and into the more familiar arms of her Ritchie, who held her and kissed her and assured her it was all going to be okay.

*

The grief came in huge tidal waves but Kim felt protected and safe in Ritchie's care and when they returned to the privacy of his dressing room, following Ady's immediate eviction due to the extenuating circumstances, she felt she was with the one remaining person who truly cared about her now – who didn't think she was a self-centred, selfish cow and who wanted her, regardless of her faults, of which there were plenty.

Covering her with kisses, Ritchie whispered words of affection and assurance. He said their relationship had made him a better man and Kim felt herself sinking into his chest, absorbing his body heat as they merged together. Somehow, this awful, life-changing news had brought them even closer and strengthened their bond. At her lowest ebb and sharing her innermost thoughts and feelings, barriers had been broken down. Even when engulfed by sorrow and regret, when Ritchie began to stroke and caress her body, she was surprised to feel herself respond with an almost urgent need to be touched intimately. Suddenly the kissing and over-clothes touching wasn't enough and her tongue seemed to take on a life of its own as she hungrily thrust it deeper and deeper into his mouth and she burned up inside as he pulled hard on her hair and used his knee to prise her legs apart and pressed himself against her.

'For fuck's sake Kim, I want to rip your fucking clothes off, here and now. All this abstaining is excruciating. Kimberley....Kimberley...' Ritchie gasped as Kim unzipped his jeans and delved in. He threw back his head and groaned.

'Wait, Kimberley. I had something to tell you tonight, although I'm not sure it's appropriate now, in view of what's happened.'

Reluctantly, she withdrew her hand and instead curled her fingers tightly around his belt loop. 'What is it, Ritchie?' She cocked her head to one side, wondering what was on his mind.

He thrust his hand into the pocket of his jeans and pulled out a folded piece of paper, pressing it into her free hand. Opening it out, she scanned the printed details and stared at him, puzzled.

'What is this? It confirms a reservation for a double room at The Mulberry. What's all this about?'

'Look at the date, Kimberley. It's tonight. For us. Me and you. Just a double bed and a Do Not Disturb sign - no interruptions from anyone. Fuck them all. Why should I let some knob in a suit dictate when I get to make love to my girl. Honestly, I've had enough of their shit...and we've waited long enough. I need to be with you Kim...and I know you feel the same...'

'Oh Ritchie...this...this is amazing...and so unexpected. I was beginning to think that we'd never, you know, consummate our relationship! That maybe you just enjoyed the fooling around backstage but weren't looking for anything remotely serious and that...well...you didn't quite fancy me enough.'

'Babe, you can *feel* how much I fancy you. I've only been reluctant to make a move because of all of the threats and restrictions and I didn't want you thinking that I *was* just fooling around. Christ, I've been such an idiot, obeying orders and denying us what we both really want. This special evening was planned so I could prove to you the depth of my feelings – a night of passion when we could lose ourselves in each other and forget everything else around us. But please don't feel pressurised darling. If you feel that now's not the time then it won't kill us to wait another week or month. I would never want to take advantage of you while you're emotional and vulnerable...'

'Ritchie. Ritchie Joe Clarke. Now is the perfect time for us and the notion that we should wait any longer is both unbearable and ridiculous. Take advantage of me all you like because I fully intend to take advantage of you! More than anything, I need to be in your arms and your bed tonight. Let some good come of such a horrendous, shitty day. I might cry relentlessly into your shirt before I rip it off your back...and afterwards I'm afraid I might bore you to bits with stories about my gran and her legendary slips of the tongue. But I've never needed you more than I do right now.'

She was torn apart, naturally, after receiving the devasting news that she was still struggling to digest. She was also worrying about her family and where on earth her place within them would be in the future, after this awful turn of events.

But she knew her gran would want her to live and love and celebrate life. And how better to do that than to spend the night with the love of her life - to fall asleep with him, wake up next to him and all things in between. Somewhere, up there, gran would wholeheartedly approve.

*

When Kim anxiously explained the situation to Sally-Anne – with every intention of helping her find somewhere less rammy to stay - she was taken aback to discover her 'friend' had already made alternative arrangements. The three Witches had invited her to kip on the floor of their room at their far superior guesthouse, rather than stay in the scabby 'dosshouse' they (Sal, actually) had booked. If Ritchie hadn't come up trumps then where would that have left Kim? Alone and still reeling from the shock of her loss, as the invitation didn't appear to extend to her.

Kim's head was all over the place. On the one hand she was nervously ecstatic at the mouth-watering prospect of spending the entire night with Ritchie – the wait was finally over. On the other hand, the sadness refused to go quietly and on a loop in her head were the cruellest of words: 'You're never going to see her again – you didn't even say goodbye.' There seemed no end to the torrent of hot tears but she hoped they would subside, if only for a short while, to allow her to fully enjoy the Ritchie Joe Clarke experience. Picturing the two of them naked and naughty, she blushed like an over-ripe berry. Not a good look on top of the red-rimmed eyes and drippy nose.

She recalled another of her gran's favourite sayings: 'Every cloud has a silver lining.' How true. It was the worst day of her life and yet also the best, all mashed up into one emotional rollercoaster ride, but she was determined to extract every ounce of pleasure from the evening ahead.

*

Something unthinkable also occurred that evening - for the first time ever, she missed the *Show Me Yours* gig, opting instead to mooch about in Ritchie's dressing room awaiting his return. She could hear the music thumping through the walls while the crowd chanted and screamed and it felt strange not to be there amongst their throng of admirers, singing her heart out. However, it was weirdly comforting to be alone amongst Ritchie's clothes and possessions rather than watching him captivate the audience out front. If she listened carefully she could still hear the intonation in his voice and the lyrics he delivered faultlessly as he lost himself in the music and it both calmed and consoled her in her state of grief. She felt far too delicate to be jostled about and deafened by the fans at the front of the stage.

The fans. She was still one of those but, apparently a friend too and now she was about to cross another line and do things which friends generally didn't do to or with each other. Would she become his girlfriend? Kim hoped she would be enough for him - that her inexperience wouldn't let her down and result in a complete anti-climax for someone who had reined in his desires for such a ridiculous length of time and who had surely been intimate with the most glamorous and perfect of women.

Please let me be enough.

Ultimately, it far exceeded anything that had popped up in her wildest, raunchiest dreams. Clearly sensing her nervousness, Ritchie took the lead from the outset, quickly and expertly removing her clothes and dismissing any insecurities she had about her body by praising and worshipping every inch of it, all the while kissing and tugging and squeezing and sucking. When she couldn't manage to release the last of his buttons with her trembling fingers, he simply ripped the shirt open and shrugged it off. When she struggled to unfasten the buckle on his belt, he gently removed her hands and completed the action himself, before guiding her fingers to the brass button, which she eagerly tore open. The removal of his sprayed-on jeans and designer boxer shorts was truly a joint effort.

When Kim eventually stood naked before him, shivering with anticipation rather than cold, his eyes widened and sparked and there was no look of disappointment there, merely wanton lust and appreciation. Finally, he too was naked and she was in awe of his magnificent body – shapely but lean, no bodybuilder but his muscles were subtly defined and his skin was smooth and glowed under the dimmed lighting in the room. Every inch of him was perfect, although frankly she was in awe of his equipment and quietly terrified about what he would be doing with it.

He led her across the room and pushed her gently down on to the bed, stroking and caressing as she writhed about underneath him, almost unable to bear the desperate demands of his kisses or the exquisite featherlike touches of his fingertips on her breasts. She could feel him pulsating against her pubic bone and then suddenly the intense pain as he entered her and she entered a whole other kingdom which was enchanted and magical and there were only other-worldly feelings of euphoria. But it still bloody hurt. A lot.

'Kimberley,' Ritchie said, pausing the proceedings and tilting his head to one side, surprise clearly registered on his face at the revelation that he had gone where no man had dared to venture before him. 'Are you still a virgin?'

'Yes,' was all she could shyly whisper in response, desperately wanting him to continue, the pain now a dull ache and the need for him to finish what he had started eclipsing all else.

'Oh Christ Kim, I'm sorry – I had no idea. Are you sure about this? Do you want me to stop?'

'NO!' she replied fiercely. 'Please don't stop. I...I should have said.' Pure embarrassment had prevented her from piping up that he would be her first – that she'd never wanted sexual relations with anyone other than him. Whenever an opportunity had presented itself in the past, her subconscious had told her that there was a better fit out there for her.

And here it was.

'No, no...it's okay. Jesus...I want you Kim, but only if you're absolutely sure.'

'*Please* Ritchie. Please don't stop. I want this more than anything.'

Sinking her fingernails into the soft skin of his back, she arched herself up to meet him again and he took her swiftly then. There was more discomfort but there was also pleasure, as the release finally came and he moaned her name like an animal in pain, his rapid breathing and the look of ecstasy on his face something she was sure she would remember for the rest of her days.

It wasn't the only time.

It was a night of passion and contentment...of fitting together and curling up tightly...of crying out his name and also murmuring it into his chest as she wept again at the intensity and depth of feelings that were swamping her on this most momentous of days.

It felt like everything had changed now and they were bound together and nobody could tear them apart. She was his and he was hers. This backseat passenger had been invited up front, they were shifting up a gear and boy, was she prepared for life in the fast lane.

*

The next morning Kim was sore and drained, both mentally and physically, but giddy that she had woken up in Ritchie's bed. A tiny part of her had expected him to say at some stage, 'Well, that was splendid, but off you pop now...mind how you go!' Instead, when he stirred, he instinctively reached out for her and croaked, in a still sleepy voice, 'You okay darling?' and as she nodded and tried to discreetly pull up the sheet to cover her chest, he gently removed it, told her again that she was beautiful and she felt something else stirring.

With breakfast foregone, all too soon they had to vacate the room – and Ritchie also had a tour bus to catch. The rest of the band and entourage were staying elsewhere and he'd arranged for the bus to collect him en route to their next gig. It was far less glamorous for Kim, who was forced to ring for a taxi from the hotel foyer and then cried like a baby and clung to Ritchie as they quietly said their goodbye-for-nows. She hoped anyone who witnessed their parting hadn't mistaken her for a good-time groupie who'd have gone with any one of the band who'd offered. She only ever wanted Ritchie.

Ritchie handed Kim a small gift bag as she climbed into the rear of the cab and her heart swelled as she immediately pictured an embossed box with an expensive piece of jewellery inside. One last kiss, the door was closed and the driver set off. Kim swivelled around so she could wave at Ritchie until the car eased off the gravel driveway and onto the main road. Her love disappeared out of sight and she felt her happiness evaporate in an instant, quickly delving into the bag to distract herself.

There *was* a small box – but Kim was disappointed to discover it contained a selection of chocolates rather than fancy jewellery. However, taped to the front of it was an envelope with her name on. Ripping in to it, Kim found two tickets inside – unfortunately, for gigs she knew she couldn't possibly attend due to her dire financial situation, lack of annual leave and, above all, the fact that her grandmother had just passed away and she needed to spend more time at home rather than less.

But it was sweet of Ritchie to do that.

And then there was the best gift of all.

Tucked underneath the tickets was a scrappy piece of lined paper with a wonky heart drawn on it, Kim's name in the centre, scribbled in that familiar, sloping handwriting and it was unbelievably touching...but underneath there was a mobile telephone number – *Ritchie's number* – OH MY GOD – and a message that simply read, 'Call me.'

The number was soon committed to memory, etched deep into the workings of Kim's brain and she itched to ring it but reluctantly accepted it was far too soon. She hadn't even realised Ritchie possessed a mobile – she'd never known anyone who did – but it was apparently so, and she still couldn't believe that she was one of the selected few he'd trusted with the number.

Back home, in a house that reeked of misery, with all curtains closed as a mark of respect and her mum drifting about in a zombie-like state, it was hard to believe that a matter of hours ago she'd been sheltered in Ritchie's arms, bringing him only joy, because within the walls of her family home she felt all fingers pointing. Kim's dad and Freddie's accusing stares clearly said, 'You didn't care enough to go and visit gran. You hardly ever rang her. Your selfishness compounded mum's sadness because you were absent and uncontactable when she needed you most.'

Desperate to ring Ritchie, to pour her heart out to someone who cared, she paced the floor of her bedroom until her mum roared up the stairs to pack it in before she wore holes in the brand new deep pile carpet.

Kim had tried to engage her in conversation, to explain how much she'd loved her gran and how sad she was for them all, but her mother was in no mood for listening. The atmosphere in the house was unbearable and at the root of it was the fact that Hilda Mary Owen had passed to the other side. Kim prayed she would find eternal happiness, wherever she came to rest – gossiping with her elder sister Maggie, eating her favourite plum jam butties and finally reunited with her loving husband Ron, the granddad Kim had barely known.

'I miss you gran,' she whispered, gazing at a Christmas family photograph taken a few years previously, when they were all goofy smiles and party poppers. Kim had been holding a piece of mistletoe above her gran's head whilst planting a smacker on her powdered cheek as Hilda chuckled, her eyes dancing and sparkling.

Nicky had called round one evening, to offer her sincere condolences and leave a sympathy card. She'd met Kim's gran on many occasions, during Christmas and birthday celebrations and when she'd tagged along on family day trips to the theatre or to the coast.

'I'm so sorry,' Nicky said, gently touching Kim's arm and she fought to stop her eyes filling up for about the billionth time that day. 'She was such a lovely lady and I know how much you'll all miss her. Please tell your mum and dad that I'm thinking of them – no, I won't come in thanks. The salon should have been closed today – day off - but we've ended up helping out with the re-fit and now I'm in desperate need of a bath.'

Kim had wanted her to stay but Nicky had disappeared quick as lightening, keen to get away from the House of Doom and the memories of long gone good times shared within its walls.

By the time Tuesday evening came around, the urge to speak to Ritchie was too much and she eventually caved and tried to ring him, three times actually – pre-soundcheck, post-soundcheck and immediately prior to the gig but on each occasion there was no answer and seemingly no facility to leave a message. Disappointment flooded through her veins and she tried desperately not to think of fans flocking around him, maybe even chancing a kiss. His slick moves on stage and the velvety tone of his voice could make a grown woman weep. She hoped there were no stunners in the front row who would catch Ritchie's eye.

Estimating the show would be over by ten-thirty, she tried one last time and – FINALLY – after a few rings she heard a breathless Ritchie pick up the call and pant, 'Hello?'

'Ritchie, it's me!' She was tearful. She needed him. It had been a tough few days and her heart and body were crying out for him.

'Kimberley! I think I missed a call from you earlier? I'm sorry darling, it's been manic today with one problem then another and we've only just come off stage. Bren went bloody AWOL after the soundcheck and Barry had to drag him out of some shitty pub in a rough part of town where even the police don't venture. Are you okay sweetheart?'

'No, Ritchie...I'm not.' A sobbing female on the telephone was probably not what Ritchie needed when he was still on a high from performing in front of a couple of thousand screaming fans but she couldn't help herself. 'It's been awful. I'm so sad about gran and everyone hates me because I've been wrapped up in you and the band rather than making a concerted effort to be part of this family...'

'Oh Kim, I'm sorry to hear that. It sounds hellish. But listen honey, I'm standing here freezing my ass off in only my boxer shorts and I need to get towelled down and into some fresh clothes. Can you call me again in an hour when I'm back at the hotel? We can talk in private then.'

Reluctant to let him go but accepting that his suggestion made perfect sense, Kim murmured her agreement. An hour later she was sitting in the hall, in her candy-striped pyjamas, counting down the minutes until she heard his voice again.

As Kim hovered anxiously by the phone, her mum paused on her way up to bed and Kim steeled herself for a tongue-lashing.

'Waiting around for him again are you? Wasting your life mooning over a man who, let's face it, seems to be calling all of the shots here.'

'Mum, please, I don't want to argue with you. Ritchie gave me his number – he actually gave me his number! No one else has it, he's never asked anyone else to ring him...just me. We've...well...we're becoming much closer and this is definitely a step in the right direction...'

'Oh please, Kimberley, who do you think you are fooling? People in normal relationships exchange numbers without a second thought...it's what *couples* do! Yet it's taken him this long to let you have it, for some strange reason. This isn't a relationship as far as he's concerned. He's clearly getting all the good loving without any real commitment or any of the day-to-day mundane stuff. Drill it into your head love - he wants you when he wants you, and only then. You're not a couple and never will be because he's using you - you're just too blind and besotted to see it.'

Kim wanted to bawl at her and defend Ritchie's honour and her role in his life, but her mum was already in such a fragile state and relations between them had deteriorated so badly, she didn't want to fight and go beyond a point where it couldn't be repaired. So Kim kept quiet and blinked back the tears and her mum's face softened.

'I know you don't believe me but I want to see you happy – single, married, climbing the career ladder, travelling the world or whatever makes you truly content – even if it's only nights out with your friends and dates with local lads. But I don't want *this* for you – this half-life, sat around waiting for him whilst the best of opportunities pass you by and you alienate everyone around you in your desperation to be loved by this charmer.'

'Mum...please go to bed. I said I'd ring Ritchie back at 11.30 and I'm already a couple of minutes late...'

She didn't mean to cut her mum off so abruptly but she couldn't risk missing any conversation with Ritchie.

The hard look was back. The pity was gone.

'Kimberley, I give up, you're a lost cause.' Alison's face sagged, her shoulders slumped and she started to trudge up the stairs. Kim would make it up to her one day, when her relationship with Ritchie was out in the open. One day her mum would appreciate how wonderful and kind Ritchie was, when he wasn't bogged down with work and contracts and managers who wouldn't have been out of place in the higher ranks of the SS.

*

Unfortunately, no matter how low Kim tried to keep her voice, she found it difficult to hold a private conversation sitting in the hallway, knowing her parents were eavesdropping up the stairs. What was a private time and place for Ritchie was most certainly not the case for her, which made it impossible to describe the awful atmosphere in the house and her mother's less than favourable opinion of him. However, Ritchie was able to read between the lines and made attempts to comfort her.

'It's okay, Kimberley. Life won't always be like this. Your gran knew how much she meant to you, I'm sure. I know you feel guilty and your family probably think I'm to blame for your absences but honestly, don't beat yourself up about this. You could never have predicted what would happen – none of this is your fault. God, I wish I could cuddle you and make you feel better...'

'I miss you Ritchie and I'm so sorry, but I can't use the tickets you gave me. I'm back in work tomorrow and what with everything going on at home...it's really not possible.' There was no way in hell Kim could afford the travelling expenses either but she wasn't about to admit that.

'Ah Kimberley, that's a bloody shame. I was so looking forward to seeing you and catching up where we left off. Are you sure there's no way you can wiggle your sexy little arse down to the south coast again? Surely your boss should be granting you a little leeway, what with your bereavement and all. If it's so bad at home then it would do you good to get the funk out of there...'

'Honestly Ritchie, I'd be down like a shot if I could but it's impossible. They're short-staffed at work and I'll need another day off for the funeral too. Besides, I'd feel awful coming without Sally-Anne because we've always booked everything together and obviously you can't be expected to provide tickets for her too. I couldn't turn up without her...'

'Why not? She's a monumental pain in the arse and she turns up without you!'

'What? No, we always agree on which gigs we're doing and plan everything together...'

'Well, she came to last night's gig without you.'

'No, she didn't...she couldn't have...'

'Kimberley, I'm telling you, she was there last night – you know how loud and lairy she is – you can hear her a mile off!'

Kim was flabbergasted. Why had Sally-Anne never mentioned anything? They'd spoken on the phone earlier and she'd never uttered a word about it. Come to think of it, there'd been a real racket going on in the background so Kim had presumed Sal was at work, but maybe she'd been elsewhere...like in a telephone box on a platform at a busy railway station.

According to Ritchie, Sal had been hanging out with the Witches, stalking the band's hotel after the gig. Sal had practically propositioned Bren in the foyer before he'd extracted himself from her grip and fled into the lift with his pants and his sanity (almost) intact. 'Surprisingly, he was relatively sober,' laughed Ritchie. 'And not *that* desperate!'

The subject was eventually changed and they moved on to discuss the magnificent night they'd spent together with Ritchie telling Kim exactly what he intended to do to her the very next weekend. She swallowed and trembled inside, relieved that their first encounter hadn't been their last.

Eventually, Ritchie yawned and said he needed to grab some beauty sleep, although Kim assured him that it was unnecessary because he was the most beautiful man on God's earth. He chortled and replied that she was one hell of a woman, that he ached for her and wanted to speak to her again before the weekend. 'I love you' was once more on the tip of Kim's tongue but she didn't want to say it until he'd said it first, and that wasn't happening yet.

Sleep seemed to elude her that night.

She tossed and turned thinking of Ritchie and their lovemaking, but every so often would be struck by a flash of fury as she remembered Sally-Anne and her devious lies and deception. Christ, she'd had to listen to the lying little cow's incessant moaning about not being able to make any of the mid-week gigs. They'd both agreed that a whole five days was simply far too long to wait to see the band again. When Kim had imagined SMY up on stage last night and wished with all her heart that she was there, Sal *had* actually been there.

What the hell was going on?

*

The funeral was arranged for the following Wednesday. Kim was ashamed to be relieved that the service and wake wouldn't interfere with her plans. A brief telephone conversation with Ritchie, whilst he was between interviews on his 'day off', confirmed that hotel rooms had been booked for the weekend and she would at least have two steamy nights of scorching hot sex to look forward to.

Sally-Anne kicked off, accusing Kim of dumping her friends in favour of a man. When Kim pointed out that she would have done exactly the same, given half the chance, her words were met with a derisory laugh and a claim that Kim thought she was better than the rest of them now.

'You've got to be kidding, right? I've never tried to lord it over anyone and you know that. If anything, I've always gone out of my way to be fair and considerate, so don't give me any of that old bull crap!' Kim was fuming. She could so easily have gone off and done her own thing but she'd tried to make sure Sal was included and this was the thanks she got!

'Anyway, I've a bone to pick with you, Sal. Why didn't you tell me you were going to the Guildford gig? I thought we booked everything together but you seem to have shifted the goalposts without bothering to inform me.'

Momentarily silenced, Sal was clearly taken aback. She was soon on the defensive though.

'I don't have to inform you of my every last move you know – Christ, you're so bloody needy sometimes. It was a last minute decision, when Rachell practically begged me to go and I thought, sod it - I'll ring in sick, borrow the money off our Dan, and go for it. You were stuck at home with your grieving family and I wasn't about to start rubbing your nose in it. *I'm* not that sort of person.'

Kim was beginning to wonder exactly *what* sort of person Sal was. She had a nasty feeling that if she delved a little deeper, she would discover that Sal had been sitting right next to Rachell, Nita and Justine at the gig - almost as if they'd booked their tickets exactly at the same time. Together. A while ago.

Something had altered between the two girls and it made for an uncomfortable atmosphere, even over the telephone. Kim suspected that Sally-Anne was positively green with envy at her blossoming relationship with Ritchie as almost every sentence she uttered was littered with scorn and sarcasm. An inner voice warned Kim that she should watch her back in the future as Sal was truly aggrieved that Ritchie had chosen Kim over her.

Still seething the following morning, looking for a suitable distraction Kim eagerly collected the daily newspaper from the mat, hoping there would be something inside to cheer her up.

RENTBOYS, BANKRUPTCY AND INFIGHTING

Secrets from the seedy world of SHOW ME YOURS!

How the once clean-cut chart-topping band fell from grace.

FUCKING HELL! Here we go again – splashed across the front page for all the world to see. Where had all this shite come from? This was not the distraction Kim was hoping for.

Heart in mouth, she steeled herself to read less than savoury details about her five favourite people. As long as it wasn't Ritchie, she could cope.

Rentboys: Ady. Good god, his mother would be devastated.

Bankruptcy: Bren. No surprise there. Those drugs don't come cheap and you can't go robbing houses to fund your habit when you're a world famous popstar.

Infighting: Ritchie and Todd. For god's sake, how had the rising tensions between the two of them completely slipped under her radar?

All fury long forgotten, Kim immediately rang Sally-Anne, and they picked apart the stories. This was not good publicity for the band; in no way could any of this be construed as anything positive. There's no such thing as bad publicity, Kim had heard it said – horseshit. This was damaging and destructive. She only wondered who was supplying the bloodsucking journalists with all this information. It was obviously someone who harboured a grudge and was really going to town on them, feeding every sordid secret they had

149

gleaned to the greedy gutter press, knowing how harmful it would be to the band's reputation.

Ritchie was furious when Kim rang him to discuss the weekend arrangements. Apparently the management were laying down the law and he said if the hotel rooms hadn't already been booked and he hadn't already made all kind of promises to Kim, it may have been necessary for them to cool it for the foreseeable future – at least until the very end of the tour.

As it was, Kim travelled to Newcastle by herself and flagged down a taxi outside of the station, to whisk her away to the hotel. Nerves got the better of her when she approached the reception desk; her voice was high and squeaky as she informed them there was a room booked in the name of Mr and Mrs Winters (although he may as well have said Summers – it wouldn't take a rocket scientist to make the connection). Kim almost wanted to hang around in the foyer for Ritchie to appear, purely to see the reaction of the snotty, stony-faced cow at check-in, who'd looked her up and down like she was a dirty whore and made feel particularly small. The look on the miserable trout's face when she realised exactly who 'Mr Winters' was, well that would have been a real treat.

Although somewhat less luxurious than their previous suite, it was still a well-designed, high-end room and Kim enjoyed unpacking and freshening up as she awaited Ritchie's eventual arrival. The novelty had worn off by four-thirty when she was panicking that she'd been stood up and worrying that she would be asked to foot the bill for the room. Her fears were unfounded though when, at four thirty-seven, there was a sharp rap on the door and as quickly as she opened it, Ritchie speedily kicked it shut again, scooping her up in his arms and swinging her around. She squealed and he placed her down, swiftly relieving her of her fitted top, pleated skirt and 70 dernier, black lycra tights, leaving her standing in the centre of the room in only her matching black bra and pants.

The blinds and drapes were open but, if anything, it only added to the excitement. Ritchie took a step back, deliberately licking his lips as he stared at her in the naughtiest of ways, and said, 'Let me look at you. Yes...you're as sexy and shapely as I remembered. Mmm...yeah...put your shoes back on...I like that.'

Even the tone of his voice turned her on and she could bear it no longer. After easing her feet back into the black patent high-heeled shoes, she took three steps forward and then undressed him, more confident than the last time, listening to his breathing becoming deeper and watching his lips part as his clothes fell to the floor.

It was fast, it was furious and it was fantasy stuff that she'd only ever played out in her head, never imagining for one minute that it could ever become a reality. When it was all over and they were tangled up in the bed sheets, sated and sheened in sweat, the magical spell was broken when Ritchie glanced at his watch and yelped 'Fuck a duck!'

'Christ, Barry will have my guts for garters! I was supposed to be at the sound check an hour ago!'

'Oh, surely for once they can forge ahead without you! The others are old hands at it now...'

'Kimberley, I'm the main fucking vocalist - the lead singer. Without me, the sound check *can't* go ahead! The other guys will be so pissed off, I'll never hear the last of it.' He was pulling on his clothes at the speed of light, while Kim was still blinking herself into action, wishing he would just crawl back into bed and ravish her again. This was where she lost him to his other world. This was when she became a fan or a friend again rather than a lover who'd familiarised herself with every inch of that irresistible body of his.

'I'll come with you,' she sighed, reluctantly sliding out of the comfort of the bed and reaching for her discarded top, skirt and underwear, although her tights seemed to have vanished into thin air.

'No! For god's sake, the shit really would hit the fan if I rocked up late with you in tow. I can hardly say that the traffic was shocking or I've had car trouble if we turn up together reeking of sex!'

Kim flinched. She was sure he didn't mean to snap, but he was certainly irritated by her suggestion that she should accompany him.

'Sorry,' she mumbled, crawling back into the bed and disappearing under the sheet. 'I didn't realise you'd driven here. I thought you'd hopped off the tour bus en route to the theatre...'

'Oh yeah, like that was gonna happen! *Er...why are we dropping you here Ritchie? Er...well I'm going for a quick shag before the main event...if that's okay?* Get real Kimberley! We're trying to keep this low key remember until the end of the tour – not flaunt it all right in front of their noses!'

Ouch. That bloody stung. 'A quick shag' – was that all she was? The pain inside her raged deep into the pit of her stomach and she desperately tried to keep her emotions in check but her tortured expression and glistening eyes gave her away. Ritchie's face softened and he leant over to gently stroke her cheek, still tucking his shirt into his jeans with his one free hand.

'Sorry, sweetheart. I'm stressed and I shouldn't take it out on you. Look, treat yourself to something from the mini-bar and I'll see you here after the show, when I intend to throw you back on this bed and show you exactly *how* sorry I am! See you later, sexy!'

He kissed her full on the mouth then, and he was almost – but not quite – forgiven. Grabbing his bag and his coat he flung open the door and then let it slam behind him, and Kim was left all alone again between the damp and rumpled sheets.

She felt strange. It all felt strange. The sex had been extraordinary but what followed had left an unsavoury taste in her mouth. Somehow it hadn't been the X-rated activities that had made her feel dirty but rather the fact that she'd been discarded like a used tissue once it was all over. She accepted he had a job to do and band members who relied on him - and hundreds of fans waiting to see him centre stage for a gig they had paid a considerable amount of money for. But still. This was all starting to wear a tad thin. The entire notion that people wouldn't understand if he had a girlfriend was making her feel like a grimy, shameful secret and she wondered if he ever intended to make her a permanent fixture in his life or if she was merely someone he thought he could hook up with from time to time.

Maybe she simply wasn't enough for him and she never would be.

Chapter 18

When Ritchie sang to her from the stage, the words took on a whole new meaning and Kim reckoned it must be blindingly obvious to the rest of the audience that he had a thing for her - that they'd been exploring each other's bodies and discovering new ways to excite each other that very same afternoon. Luckily, in the relative darkness of the room, no one noticed her blushes. Despite her earlier reservations, she was comforted by the knowledge that whilst there were legions of grown women – many far more attractive than her – screaming out Ritchie's name, she was the one he'd chosen to make love to. The only one he truly wanted.

She couldn't help but smile as she remembered the change in manner of the initially hostile receptionist when she'd exited the hotel with her body aching and head held high. The caked-in-foundation, orange-faced dollybird had been practically fawning over Kim, summoning a taxi and commenting on the pretty dress she'd changed into. In your face, rude girl!

Less pleasing was Sally-Anne's reaction.

Many of the fans had drifted away from the stage door area after Ritchie's arrival. Kim spotted his black Audi badly parked in one of the VIP spaces and wished she'd been able to travel as his passenger, but that hadn't even been on the table. Geraldine was still lurking about, chewing gum and looking like a stern, mad matron in her strange get-up of starched white shirt and crinkled blue pinafore dress, but Kim remembered her kindness and tottered over to say hello.

Gerry nodded in response, was initially silent and then suddenly blurted out: 'Sally-Anne and Rachell went backstage. Bren got them in. They've been in there hours so god knows what's been going on.'

With Bren, the mind boggled. Sex and drugs and rock 'n' roll. God help them.

They had a bit of an odd, stilted conversation about tour merchandise and Ady's trousers, Geraldine making no mention of both Ritchie and Kim arriving unusually late, albeit separately, and then, as she was about to make her excuses and wander off to hopefully catch up with some relatively sane fans, she heard giggling and clattering before the stage door burst open and out tumbled Sally-Anne and Rachell.

'I'll see you later, Sal.' Rachell deliberately ignored Kim and Geraldine, stalking off across the car park, tossing her mane of hair and wiggling her bum. The sound of gold-plated bangles jangling off her tiny wrists still rang out even when she was completely out of sight.

'Oh, you decided to show up then, did you?' Sally-Anne asked, with more than a hint of sarcasm and accompanied by the return of The Sneer. 'Thought you weren't going to bother.'

'Course I've shown up – I wouldn't miss another gig for anything! And it looks like you've been busy anyway, cosying up with Bren. I hope he didn't lead you too far astray.'

'What happens in a dressing room in Newcastle, stays in a dressing room in Newcastle,' she replied, pushing out her chest, clearly proud as punch and desperate to brag.

'Oooh...that sounds interesting!' Kim tried to humour her, determined not to rise to the bait.

'Do you and Ritchie actually think that no one knows the two of you are shagging? Are you really that stupid?' Sally-Anne was trying to goad her, although god knows what exactly she hoped to achieve by it.

'Sal! Don't be so horrible – what's got into you? It's not as if you've been hanging around like a spare one at a wedding – you've literally just been backstage with your favourite man! And you knew I'd be arriving late...' Glancing nervously over at Geraldine, aware that she was all ears and making no bones about it, Kim squirmed a little and hoped their strange acquaintance wasn't a full-on motormouth.

'Take no notice of her. She's just jealous,' Geraldine grunted, surprising Kim with her display of allegiance and earning herself the mother of all scowls from Sally-Anne. Trying not to smile, Kim cocked her head to one side and asked, 'Are we good Sal?'

Begrudgingly, she replied, 'Course we are, you berk,' and yanked Kim into an awkward hug. At least she was no longer breathing fire. Thank god for that.

Unable to hold her own water, Sally-Anne was quick to spill the beans as to the backstage antics. Kim was shocked to hear that Bren had taken great delight in kissing and touching up first one girl and then the other and all involved seemed happy with that situation. Apparently both Sal and Rachell had been more than willing participants. At least when he'd suggested that they make out with each other they'd both told him to Fuck Off. He hadn't taken it personally and had merely laughed and sent someone down to nab them more beers. Ever the party animal.

He'd also offered to buy them drinks at the hotel bar after the gig, so at least that was Kim off the hook. Thankfully, Ritchie had deliberately booked the two of them into an alternative hotel each night. Whilst part of Kim longed to go public and be allowed to mingle freely amongst the whole band and their entourage, it seemed privacy was crucial for Ritchie to let down his guard and escape from the full-on pressure cooker that was his position as frontman of the band - if only for a few short hours.

She returned to the hotel on foot but the journey was mainly uphill and by the time she launched herself into the revolving door of the hotel, she was sweaty and breathless. Purposely avoiding all eye contact with her new friend on reception - bloody hell, didn't that woman ever go home? - she darted over to the lift, jabbing at the button, longing to be back in the sanctity of room 212.

First on her agenda was to take another shower. Standing under the powerful red-hot spray, leisurely cleansing her skin with the complimentary mango and papaya scented shower gel, she hoped Ritchie would return soon, strip off and hop in for a thorough soaping session.

As the minutes ticked by, she accepted that wasn't likely to happen and to avoid wrinkling up like a manky old prune, she stepped out and wrapped herself up in one of the huge fluffy towels from the heated rail. The bed had been miraculously remade in their absence and Kim dived onto it with gusto.

'Come on Ritchie,' she urged him to appear, as if he could hear her or somehow sense her need for him, but was soon drowsy and struggling to fend off sleep.

She was awoken by a persistent loud knocking on the door. Squinting to read the time on her watch, she was astonished to see that it was almost one o'clock in the morning and realised she must have nodded off. Peeling her body off the damp towel, she grabbed the luxurious robe that had been provided and padded over to the door in her hotel slippers (freebies which were absolutely begging to be packed into her bag before checkout the next morning).

'Sorry darling,' Ritchie slurred, as he entered the room, swaying slightly and smelling faintly of alcohol and cigarettes. Too tired to even slip into the sexy little nightie she'd purchased in M & S with the last of her Christmas gift vouchers, she opted instead to throw the wet towel onto the nearby chair, discard the robe and slide down between the surprisingly dry sheets.

'Hey you,' she mumbled sleepily. 'Where have you been?'

'Drinking heavily,' was the smartarse reply that she didn't dare question. 'Bren had been stockpiling the beers backstage pre-show and a few of us stayed behind and got stuck in. That friend of yours is a bad one,' he said, waggling his finger, before collapsing onto the bed next to her.

Kim's heart almost stopped. Whilst she had been here, alone, waiting impatiently for Ritchie, he had been drinking with Sally-Anne and the others – including Ravishing Rachell whose looks almost stopped traffic. Sally-Anne had definitely had the last laugh – she knew full well Kim had been expecting Ritchie…and yet she'd happily let him linger, without so much as a call to the hotel to ask them to pass on a message. Kim hoped Sal would agree that they'd evened up the scores now – whatever crime she was alleged to have committed in the first place. And what the hell did he mean when he referred to her as 'a bad one'?

Suddenly she was wide awake with all her senses bleating. 'Was Sally-Anne misbehaving with Bren and Rachell again?' she enquired tentatively, hoping that had indeed been the case and Sal hadn't come on to Ritchie – surely she wouldn't do that though. She was still her friend, of sorts – wasn't she?

'Naw, he disappeared into the toilet with Rachell – classy. No, your mate, she got pissed out of her skull, blubbed like a baby because Bren wasn't taking her on, tried to snog Ady – and, trust me, she is NOT his type – and whipped out her tits for the roadies. Oh, and then she did her party piece – she vomited on Barry's best shoes. He wasn't best pleased, I can tell you.'

Bloody hell Sally-Anne, they'd never be allowed backstage again.

'Sorry Ritchie, she's not normally so badly behaved…'

'Oh don't worry about it. Meatloaf helped clean her up and then they disappeared for a while into someone's office – and there were strange sounds emanating from that room, I can tell you. And Barry's size 10s will clean. Trust me, I've seen much worse backstage.'

'I was waiting for you Ritchie, wondering where you were...' The words were out before she could stop herself, and she was really trying not to climb on his back over this.

'Oh enough grief please Kim...I'm shagged out and I need to sleep.'

She was strongly tempted to remind him that he'd be a lot less tired if he hadn't stayed out boozing until all hours, but she could see he was in no mood.

'Well I did wear you out earlier today, if you cast your mind back...' She trailed her fingernail down his chest, where the shirt was deliberately agape and the flesh it revealed was begging to be kissed and scratched.

'Mmm...yes you did...you naughty, naughty girl.' Ripping the sheet from her, he climbed on top, effectively pinning her down with his weight. She caught the twinkle in his eyes and the desire that shone out.

Not too tired then.

*

Another town, another hotel that would ordinarily have well exceeded her budget, but seeing as it was being funded by her sexy, popstar lover, she didn't need to concern herself with the astronomical bill.

She'd imagined them gazing into each other's eyes throughout breakfast as they fed each other berries and luscious spoonfuls of creamy Greek yoghurt. But Ritchie had insisted on calling up room service and a continental breakfast accompanied by a range of other delicious goodies had arrived within minutes, although very little had actually been eaten and her face flamed when she recalled what Ritchie had done with the honey. Two showers later and she was still a little sticky in parts.

Anticipating that they may perhaps travel on to Sunderland together, she'd allowed herself to believe that they were almost a proper couple in a real relationship, but then Ritchie had promptly burst her bubble, confirming his intention to drop her off near the railway station where she could meet up with her friend. Her heart had plummeted, not only with the realisation that they would be going their separate ways – albeit briefly – but that Sal would immediately take great satisfaction in commenting on the rather strange state of affairs.

At least they had left the hotel together, although her favourite receptionist had finally gone home and was no longer on the front desk to witness it.

Ejected from her coveted seat in his gleaming, top-of-the-range Audi, a bloody good distance from the station and a full hour before the train was due to leave, Ritchie planted a kiss firmly on her lips, before apologising for having to abandon her. He promised again that it wouldn't always be this way and then zoomed off into the Sunday morning traffic.

There were moments when she wondered if it had all been a figment of her imagination, that time spent with Ritchie, those snatched hours when she had him all to herself – but then she would look down at her cleavage and see the faint hint of a love bite marking the skin, or she would feel an aching in her wrists where he'd masterfully gripped them tightly as he'd taken her, calling out her name as the release came and nothing else mattered.

Back to the real world. A smirking Sally-Anne had located her nodding off in the foul-smelling waiting room, and was her usual subtle self.

'Oh, my god...look what the cat's sicked up...had a busy night did we?'

'Ha bloody ha. I'm absolutely knackered and will be taking myself back to bed this afternoon for the serious business of sleeping...'

'You missed a banging party backstage last night, Kim...drunken debauchery and all manner of stuff that would make your hair stand on end.'

Kim let her roll with it, wondering if her story would match that of Ritchie's.

'Course I was leathered and upchucked all over Bazza's best loafers. He had a real tantrum about that. And Bren kept trying to get his randy hands into my pants but I bravely fought him off...'

Oh really.

'...and your Ritchie was thoroughly enjoying himself...'

Do not rise to it Kim. She wants a reaction. She's goading again. But give her something to chew on.

'Oh yes, Ritchie had a particularly wild night. I can certainly vouch for that Sal...'

She left it hanging in the air - sometimes the less said the better – yawned, stretched and temporarily closed her eyes again. Ah, yes. That stopped her eyeballs burning.

'So what do you reckon to this morning's newspaper headlines then?'

Eyes wide open.

Oh no, not again. The look on Sally-Anne's face – *I know something you don't know* – she had gauged from Kim's reaction that she hadn't a clue and was clearly relishing her discomfort and anxiety

'I...I haven't seen the papers yet. I couldn't be arsed queueing up in the newsagents while I'm carrying this heavy bag. What? What did they say?'

Internally pleading – anyone but Ritchie (although preferably none of them because they were all very special to her, faults and all) – she mentally prepared for the worst.

'Oh they've proper outed Ady. You know how they played down the rent boys story and the kiss-and-tell from that bloke in Ibiza, claiming it was all tosh invented by some jilted ex-girlfriend? Well, there's photographic evidence this time. All these pictures snapped on different occasions, generally with the same guy. Kissing and holding hands and everything. I'm bloody sure it's that white-haired fella we all thought was dating his sister.'

'Poor Ady. He's so quiet and private, he'll be devastated. I wish they'd leave him alone. I mean, for god's sake, we're in the nineties now – times are moving on. Why can't people live and let live? He's a good guy and it shouldn't matter if he's shagging a man, a woman or anything in between. As long as it's legal and he's hurting no one, who has the right to judge?'

'Hear, hear! You'll make bloody prime minister one of these days Miss Summers. Anyway, there's more 'revelations' about Bren again. Christ, if that man's done as many drugs as they say then he's a walking miracle. Oh and there's also a big scoop about Todd!'

'Todd? What the hell could they unearth about Todd? He's the most inoffensive, charming man I've ever met!'

'He is that. But, guess what? You'll never guess. His name's not really Todd!'

'Get away with you! But if he's not Todd then who he is?'

'He is...wait for it...*Craig!* He has the same name as our postman!'

No way! I like the name Todd – don't get me wrong – but there's nothing wrong with 'Craig'. Why on earth would he change it?'

'Well it's actually quite dull. Apparently, he looked so young when they first formed the band – and he still bloody does – that they used to call him Toddler! And eventually Toddler became Todd and it stayed that way and nobody, until now, has ever realised that it wasn't actually the name registered on his birth certificate!'

'I'm surprised no one's discovered that earlier. He must have slipped under the radar. Anyway, whether he's a Todd or a Craig, I don't really care. It's a non-story and he's still a decent, lovely guy and they can piss right off, giving him unnecessary grief.'

'Where do you think all this is coming from, Kim? All this tripe that the gutter press seem to be publishing on a regular basis?'

'Search me. I'm sure someone has it in for them and is seriously trying to blacken their name. All these years of being the golden boys of pop who couldn't put a foot wrong and who sold their image as wholesome, clean-cut lads next door...and look what it's come to. If someone is trying to destroy the band then they're doing a bloody good job of it.'

'Not half. Their reputation is in tatters now and Rachell said ticket sales have taken a nosedive on this tour.'

'No wonder. They're doing about five thousand gigs. There were bound to be empty seats at some venues.'

'But at one time they could have sold out every venue five times over without even trying. At the moment they have heaps of publicity but, if anything, it's turning people off the band. Apparently the guys are worried and there's rumours circulating that their glory days are over and this could be their very last time out on the road.'

'NO! Surely not! That's rubbish - there's years left in this band yet.'

'I know that, and you know that, but the money men aren't impressed. Aw, look at the bloody screen – our train is delayed by forty-five minutes. What a pisser. I'm going to the shop for a can of pop. I'll be back soon.' Sally-Anne picked up her bag, hoicked up her jeans and tossed back her hair as she started to walk away.

Kim was almost relieved.

Then Sal stopped in her tracks. Turned around. Wicked intent evident on her face.

'Oh, there was another revelation in the paper actually. I almost forgot – silly me.' The glint in her eye was sly and deadly as she built up to delivering her killer blow.

'Apparently Ritchie-baby had a string of one-night stands when they were on the European leg of their last tour. Maybe not such a one-woman man after all then, eh?'

She laughed as she continued on her way, marching purposely towards the steps, while Kim's heart was given a good kicking and the ground beneath her seemed to shift. She dropped down onto a nearby seat, the pounding in her ears and head so loud that it surely must have been audible to every other occupant of the platform.

This really couldn't be happening.

*

Storm Ritchie burst into the hotel room earlier than expected, to find Kim and a billion crumpled tissues scrunched up on the king-size bed.

'Darling, I'm so sorry,' he began, but was ambushed by a variety of pillows and a torrent of abuse before he could complete his sentence.

'You bastard! You absolute fucking bastard! How could you? I trusted you and never in a million years thought you would betray me. While I was pining for you at home and counting the minutes until I saw you again, you were off shagging the nearest groupie! Clearly I meant nothing to you. Don't touch me, you stinking piece of shit!'

'*KIMBERLEY*!' Ritchie roared, pelting the pillows back at the bed and missing her head by inches. 'When I said I was sorry it wasn't an admission of guilt! I was apologising for you having to read shite like that, not because I'd done anything wrong! It's all lies, Kim – contrived crap to titillate the newspaper readers. Don't expect me to be holding my hands up for any supposed indiscretions any time soon because I've done nothing wrong!'

'What? Don't give me that! Why the hell would anyone bother making all of that up? I know there's truth in the other stories – Bren clearly has a drug problem, everyone guessed that Ady preferred boys to girls, Marty did of course get hitched and the whole name thing with Todd is obviously true because they printed a copy of his birth certificate and other supporting evidence. And you're standing there telling me that *your* story happens to be the only one that's complete fabrication! What do you take me for? A total imbecile? I loved you Ritchie, and you turned out to be a lying, unfaithful arsehole! You know what - I'm leaving. I'm not staying here with you in this fucking ostentatious, overpriced room for one minute longer...'

Swiftly catching hold of her forearms, Ritchie exhibited admirable defence tactics as she tried to punch him in the head and knee him in the bollocks, whilst sobbing loudly and regularly hurling insults. Eventually, all the fight seeped out of her and she folded into his chest, his arms circling her back, his determined voice low in her ear, uttering words to try and placate her.

'I swear Kim, I didn't do it. I would never do that to you and it hurts to think that you could ever doubt me. Christ knows what's going on at the moment. The papers are printing garbage about us almost every day and I don't know where it's all going to end. Yes, Todd's real name is Craig. Yes, Ady is in a loving relationship with a six foot four Scandinavian DJ who goes by the name of Nathaniel. Yes, Marty has a beautiful wife who prefers to stay out of the limelight. And, yes, Bren has a real problem with substance abuse and every other vice you can think of – although most of the column inches on him are full of inaccuracies and contain only a degree of the truth. But they had nothing to dish on me, and they wanted to find something. In the absence of anything remotely newsworthy, they invented crap they thought the public would want to read and, in the process, portrayed me as this terrible person who couldn't keep it in his pants. But worst of all, they hurt you and my family. And I'm now faced with the painful truth that you truly thought I was capable of such appalling behaviour.'

When she untangled herself from his arms, and stepped back to look him square in the eyes, she believed him. His face was earnest, his eyes glistening with unshed tears, his body language clearly that of someone who'd had a verbal beating for no reason other than he was famous. He looked exhausted with the stress of simply being Ritchie Joe Clarke.

'Promise?' she asked, her fingers tracing along his jawline, where the first growth of stubble scratched against her skin. 'Swear on my life and your mother's life that you didn't sleep with these women and that you've always been faithful to me.'

He took her hand and pressed it against his chest, where she could feel his heart beating through his striped cotton shirt.

'I promise, Kim. I swear. My life would be nothing without you and I would never do anything to jeopardise what we have. Please say you believe me. Don't break my heart.'

'Oh Ritchie, when I read what had been printed, I was devastated, humiliated and could have torn you apart with my bare hands. But I look at you now and I see you're being truthful and I'm sorry I didn't hear you out first before I threw my toys out of the pram. I love you Ritchie Joe Clarke. I believe you.'

Their lovemaking was tender as they took their time and savoured every precious moment, each desperate to deliver fulfilment – both yearning to be everything to each other.

On this occasion, despite sound checks and scary managers and every other problem that seemed to interfere with their private time, Ritchie was especially reluctant to leave their bed. He held on tightly to Kim, peppering her with kisses and words of affection. When he eventually threw back the covers and dragged himself away, he seemed genuinely sad to be apart from her, if only for a short while.

'If I could stay here with you forever I would, you know, but it's not that easy. Fame, success and money in the bank is all wonderful, but it comes at a price and everything else gets complicated. Just know, I would never hurt you in a million years and every second we're together is a second when I feel complete. I'm sorry, Kim.'

He bent over to brush her lips with his and she responded eagerly, before he gently eased her away.

'As much as I'd love to crawl back into that bed and have my wicked way with you, I'd better make tracks before we have Barry up here, shouting the odds and blaming you for my absence. I'll see you at the show darling and I'll meet you back here later for Round Two!'

'It's a date.' She heaved an almighty sigh of relief, happy they were now back on an even keel. 'Now get gone before I kidnap you and imprison you here forever.'

Flashing his dazzling smile before opening the door and backing out of the room, he left for the sound check and she instantly felt bereft. But there was another feeling bouncing around too, one that made her deeply uncomfortable.

She had genuinely believed Ritchie when he had looked her in the eye and assured her that the newspaper story was pure fiction. However, once she was alone again with only her thoughts and overactive brain for company, there was a tiny, niggling part of her that was not entirely convinced.

A seed of doubt had been sown.

Chapter 19

To make matters worse, Ritchie was seriously peeved that the rest of the band and backstage crew were also staying in their hotel, owing to some mix up with the original reservations made by the management company. Apparently Ritchie had carefully selected the boutique establishment, Grayson Gardens, as a romantic hideaway for the evening, and he was NOT happy that the 'riff-raff' had gate-crashed his private party.

'For God's sake Ritchie, stop pacing up and down will you! So the others are here now, so what? They all know we're kind of together and that I'd be staying here with you. Hang on - you *did* tell them that, didn't you?'

One look at his face, and she knew he hadn't.

'Oh, I see. So what exactly DID you tell them?'

'Not that it's anyone else's business, I said that I needed time alone to clear my head without the constant interruptions of a spaced out Bren, or bloody Barry knocking on the door, ordering me around and treating me as if I'm a child!'

'So they don't know you're here with me. Why the hell can't you tell them? Yet again I'm hidden away like you're ashamed of me...'

'Oh, not again Kim! Change your fucking tune will you. The last thing I need is a load of old shit from you, which is usually all about nothing. There's no pleasing you. I splash out on yet another top notch hotel room for us and you've still got a face like a wet weekend in Wigan. To be quite frank, I'm sick of listening to your persistent whining – you're not happy unless you're having a bloody good moan about something. And you know what - I don't have to sit here and listen to this crap...'

Panic set it as she saw him grab the reinforced handle of his sports holdall and she moved swiftly to wrench it out of his hands, hurling it over into the far corner of the room.

'What are you doing Ritchie? You know I've hardly ever complained, no matter what's gone on, but I'm entitled to have an opinion on *something*, especially when it makes *me* feel so bad. Please don't go. We can sort this out. I love you Ritchie.'

'I need a little fucking space, Kim. Piling all this stress on me, pushing me to my limits – you don't know when to give it a rest. Look, I need to get out of here. I'm slipping outside for a smoke and a chance to breathe. This is all too much and too heavy and it's doing my sodding head in.'

Hurt and bewildered, Kim sobbed into one of the pillows, berating herself for tackling Ritchie on his reluctance to publicly come clean about their relationship, whilst conceding that she had every right to question his odd behaviour. At least he *hadn't* taken his bag in the end. He couldn't have gone far.

The pungent smell of alcohol that followed him into the room when he returned a couple of hours later suggested he'd been knocking back the beers and tequila in the bar. It stung that he'd gone there without her - that he couldn't even show the other band members and touring staff that they were a couple and that she was important to him.

Apart from asking if she was okay (she nodded, but did he really think she was?), he didn't seem in the least bit concerned about her welfare, turning his back on her in bed. He was asleep within minutes, still fully dressed and snoring softly.

The loneliness overwhelmed her, even though she was beside the man she loved. This couldn't be right, but what could she do that wouldn't have him running for the hills? How could she ever explain how she felt when he didn't want to listen?

The space between them seemed vast, so she nuzzled into his back, unable to bear the lack of physical contact. She didn't want to cry again but tears slipped out relentlessly and she willed him to wake up and tell her how sorry he was. She wanted him to be repentant – to beg for forgiveness.

And yet he slept on, oblivious to her distress.

*

After a restless night, she finally peeled open her eyelids when she could feel Ritchie stirring underneath the bed clothes. For one dreadful moment she thought they still weren't on speaking terms, until he groaned and turned to face her, his sleepy eyes slightly bloodshot, his clothes crumpled on his body.

'Hi,' she said timidly. 'Morning sleepyhead.'

'Morning, beautiful. Christ, my head hurts. Can't believe I zonked out in these bloody spray-on jeans. I need to get them off.'

'Let me help you,' she offered, rising up and sitting astride him, loosening his leather belt, releasing the gold stud button and yanking down the zip.

'*Baby*,' he moaned, raising himself slightly to assist in the removal of the offending jeans and his designer jockey shorts, leaving him naked apart from his rumpled white t-shirt.

Dismissing the events of the previous evening, as she needed a short respite from the war raging inside her head, she initiated sex and it was as sensuous and passionate as ever, although Ritchie was thoroughly knackered afterwards, his hangover well and truly kicking in.

'That was amazing, as always, my Kimberley...' he gasped, holding his hand to his head and pinching his temple between his fingers. 'But you may just be the death of me one day, perfecting the art of seduction while I'm feeling somewhat delicate...'

'You didn't take a great deal of persuading,' she smiled, relieved that a temporary truce appeared to have been called. Should she mention anything or was it best left until another time?

'Look, Kimberley, I'm sorry about last night but you really pushed my buttons and when I feel under pressure, I explode. Let's leave it now and enjoy a cuddle before that phone starts to ring, and I have Barry in my ear, giving me a bollocking.'

She snuggled in, not sure if 'leaving it' was the answer, but knowing nothing could be gained by bulldozing on with her concerns at that moment in time.

They skipped breakfast again, feasting instead on each other, and all too soon the phone was buzzing (they ignored it) and then, sure enough, Barry was hammering on the door.

'Sorry love,' he said in his gruff voice, peering into the room after Ritchie had reluctantly padded over to open up, dressed in only his pants and socks. 'I hate to be the one to break up the party but this lad has a job to do and you're sapping all of his energy, Ritchie – get your frigging arse down to reception in twenty minutes or else we're leaving without you. Got that?'

'Oh, he's a bloody joy, isn't he?' Kim was unable to contain her sarcasm, as Ritchie kicked the door shut behind Barry and started banging around the room, collecting his clothes and muttering on about his life not being his own and being worked like a dog.

'He'll give me holy hell for this when we're on the bus. Do you have any paracetamol?'

She didn't, and chose not to comment on Barry's views on their relationship, such as it was. Their time together was almost over and they would be apart until Southport in a few days' time. Even then, Kim's dad was ferrying her to and from that gig as a favour, so there would be no overnight hotel stay then. And anything less now seemed such a comedown. Despite the small unfortunate hiccup, the time she'd spent with Ritchie had been precious and every tiny, miniscule part of her would miss the whole sum of this fabulous man.

*

He was off with her on Thursday. She could tell.

To rub salt into her wounds, her mum – taking the spare ticket originally intended for Nicky – was present to witness his strange change in mood.

Kim was surprised that her mum had accepted the invitation and olive branch. She'd also been apprehensive at the prospect of the journey there with her parents but the conversation flowed reasonably well and they arrived in Southport without anyone having been throttled. True to form, her dad parked in the cheapest car park he could find at the far end of the resort, but at least it gave Kim and her mum the opportunity to take a leisurely stroll along the promenade in the gloriously warm sunshine. Alison chattered on about the upcoming weekend away booked for her wedding anniversary and mother and daughter were united in laughter as Kim reminisced about a family holiday to Tenerife, when her eight year old self had disappeared and sent them into a blind panic – there were laughs all round when she was discovered munching her way through a second breakfast at the all-you-can-eat buffet, where no adult had batted an eyelid at the presence of an unaccompanied child in the dining room.

They recalled how much Kim's gran had loved Southport. She'd enjoyed thrashing them all at crazy golf and relaxing on one of the many benches in the lush and pretty gardens, watching the world go by whilst devouring her favourite mint-choc-chip Cornetto ice cream.

Her mum never even complained when they had to wait for hours for the band to arrive, even when she was forced to listen to Sally-Anne spewing out a litany of swear words for no apparent reason. Kim cringed and longed for the girl to bugger off. This increasingly unpleasant friend of hers seemed to take great delight in watching her mum squirm whenever she cursed. Kim would never have behaved so badly in front of Sally-Anne's mum. It was all about respect.

Sal wasn't exactly overly friendly towards Kim either, preferring to devote all her attention to The Three Witches - all huddling around, cackling, whispering and shooting sly glances. It wasn't for Kim...all this unnecessary cattiness and sarcasm. And she suspected that a little of the bitching was about her mum - and that simply wasn't on.

When *Show Me Yours* finally did roll into town, Kim struggled to catch Ritchie's eye, Sally-Anne and her new cronies determinedly rushing to crowd him, in a blatant attempt to blot her completely out of the picture. When Kim eventually slipped through a gap in the pack, tugging her mum behind so she could finally introduce her to Ritchie, he seemed nervous, possibly expecting a clobbering from this protective parent who mistrusted him. He clearly wanted to be anywhere other than faced with the mother of his girlfriend...or love interest...or recurring conquest...or whatever the hell she was.

He smiled and shook the hand of her mum, who was pleasant and polite, but Kim noticed she was checking him out with her beady eyes. Starstruck she was not. It was formal, awkward and excruciating and Kim was mightily relieved when her mum excused herself and wandered over to the nearest bench to take the weight off her feet. Kim longed for the return of the other Ritchie - the kind and loving man who occasionally put in an appearance and didn't drag her through the gates of hell.

Before she could think of anything witty or sarcastic or even *interesting* to say, he was mobbed by Sally-Anne and the other girls again and she was forced to observe from a distance as he insisted he really did have to dash, promising to sign and chat later. And then he was gone.

She'd missed the arrival of the other band members with the exception of Marty who'd waved and mouthed 'You okay?' to which she'd replied, 'yes, thank you,' whilst dying inside. Once the famous five were safely inside, Sal and the other fans were fast to disappear and Kim found herself alone again, with no clue what to do next.

Realising it was time to face the music with her mother and accept that Ritchie was an unpredictable heartbreaker with a selfish streak running right through him, she began to reluctantly walk away, only to hear the unmistakeable noise of Barry, bellowing out her name.

'KIMBERLEY! YES, *YOU*! Ritchie wants a word!'

Oh thank you, thank you, thank you! She was quick to return to the theatre and so pleased that she could have kissed him – although it may have made her retch. With obvious relief plastered over her face, she almost – but not quite - raised a smile from this most formidable of men.

'Thanks Barry,' she beamed, itching to go find Ritchie.

'Don't keep him long,' he growled, but he no longer terrified her. However, she was taken aback when he caught hold of her arm and added, 'Just be careful love. There's plenty of other fish in the sea. Try and avoid the sharks.' It was definitely a warning, but not one she wanted to dwell on. Undeterred, and focused purely on finding Ritchie and sinking into his arms, she ignored the words of caution and merely followed Barry down the corridors until they reached Ritchie's dressing room, where he deposited her at the door with a spectacular parting shot:

'And tell him that I've had enough of his shit.'

Knocking politely, because it felt like the right thing to do, she entered the room when Ritchie shouted 'Come in', only to discover him slumped forward in a wonky plastic chair with his head in his hands.

'Ritchie!' She instantly flew to his side. 'What on earth's the matter?'

'Everything and nothing,' was his reply, but he still didn't raise his head, and she stroked his hair and gently kissed his forehead, hoping to somehow soothe away all of his problems.

'Tell me,' she instructed, taking hold of his wrists and removing his hands from his face. 'You can tell me anything.'

'Aw Kimberley, what can I say? This tour hasn't been enjoyable at all. In fact, I'd go so far as to say it's been a long hard slog, and we're only a fraction of the way through. I'll never get used to seeing empty seats and unsold tickets either. Why are people so fickle, eh? They praise you and put you on a pedestal and then they kick it from underneath you and suddenly you're freefalling down to the bottom again. Right back where you started. *You're* the only silver lining in my sky full of clouds and I wanted to surprise you by booking a hotel room for tonight. Yes, I know home beckons because you're due in work tomorrow, but I thought maybe if I treated you to a taxi in the morning then we could spend some much-needed quality time together tonight – especially as it'll be our last opportunity for a while. The hotel is meant to be beautiful – apparently it's been voted best in the North West by 'industry experts'. And we have a superior suite with a sea view which I thought would be perfect. But then I saw your mum – my god, you look alike – and I realised that it couldn't happen and you'd be travelling back tonight after all. And it finished me off! I couldn't even speak, I was so disappointed...'

'Oh Ritchie, what are you like? There was I thinking you'd tired of me and all the time you'd been planning this! You *are* silly sometimes. We need to talk more rather than you shutting me out and leaving me to think the worst.'

'I probably handled it badly, but it doesn't change anything does it? You'll still be returning home with your mum and it's all been for nothing...'

'As if! Like I'm going to turn down a night of passion *in a superior suite* with you in favour of an awkward car journey with my parents. Look, they'll understand. I'll sort it and we'll stay over together and it will be wonderful. As long as you can bundle me into that taxi at the crack of dawn tomorrow to ensure I'm not late for work – or else I'll be given my P45 – again! The only problem is I don't have an overnight bag with me – no clean knickers or anything...'

'Well I wouldn't worry too much about those. We'll remove them now and you can stash them in that handbag of yours and then they'll still be clean in the morning...and I'll be horny as hell on stage knowing that you've gone commando under that miniscule little leather skirt.'

'Ritchie! You're a filthy animal! I can't do that!'

'You can, and you will. Now come here and let me do the honours...'

Kim actually found it quite sexy – and one thing of course did lead to another, but that wasn't something she'd be sharing with her mother.

'Ritchie, I have to go. My mum's waiting somewhere out there for me and she'll be having kittens.'

'Marvellous...go and find her and tell her all about the hot sex you've just had with the best ride of your life!'

'Yes, I'm sure that would go down a treat Mr Clarke, but if it's all the same with you, I'll keep it to myself - unless you fancy a pasting off my father later.'

'Christ, no! Now clear off, naughty girl, before you land me in even more trouble!'

*

Alison Summers was waiting patiently, tilting her head back to soak up the sun's rays when Kim appeared by her side. If her mum guessed what she'd been up to, then she didn't pass comment and for a moment they sat side by side in silence before words were said that made Kim appreciate how much she *was* actually loved by this woman who had brought her into the world – even if Kim could be difficult to love much of the time.

'I only want you to be happy,' her mum said quietly, whilst placing her slender hand on top of her daughter's. 'You've blossomed into a beautiful woman and – like me - you surrender all of your heart when you fall for someone. But please make sure that the man you're planning your future around is the right one. When I met your dad, I immediately knew he was the one and I've never, ever doubted him or his love for a single minute. Yes, there's times when he drives me up the ruddy wall, but he never fails to make me laugh, picks me up when I'm down in the dumps and has always got my back. Don't tell him I said this, but he's wonderful inside and out. If you can say the same about Ritchie then maybe he is your one, but if he hurts you, or lets you down or doesn't give you every last morsel of his love, then please don't settle for less. Because when he hurts you, he hurts me, and I can't bear it. You deserve the whole wide world – not just a tiny, remote part of it.'

Choked with emotion that rendered her temporarily unable to speak, Kim instead focused her attention on a crying seagull, swooping down over the water. For once she wasn't immediately on the defensive because she knew in her heart that what her mum was saying was true and that she only had her best interests at heart. Did Ritchie think she was the one? Or was she one of many?

'Try not to worry, please,' Kim eventually found her voice and attempted to reassure her mum, although she couldn't even reassure herself. 'I know you're only trying to look out for me and that you want me to find the perfect man and settle down and live my happily ever after. I want that happy ending too but it's not that straightforward so I can't promise it will happen any time soon. But what I do know is that Ritchie is an exceptionally special man and – believe me – there aren't many of those around. They broke the mould when they made dad, don't you know!'

Her mum smiled, but it didn't reach her eyes and Kim could see she worried that Ritchie would break her daughter's heart. The air was heavy with the weight of the issue that hung between them. Time for a rapid change of subject.

'Before I forget, I'll be staying over with a few of the fans after tonight's show – I should have mentioned it earlier but it completely slipped my mind. Someone dropped out so there's a space for me at their hotel, which is a gorgeous place by all accounts, so it would be a crime to turn it down! I'll borrow a few bits and bobs off the other girls and I can even share a taxi ride back to south Manchester early in the morning with someone who lives not too far away.'

'Right. I see.'

The grimace, the short sentences, then the abrupt silence - her mum clearly knew she was lying through her teeth. She should have come clean and admitted her sleepover would be with Ritchie – she was a bloody adult after all. But it would have felt like she was flinging her mum's words of advice back in her face and besides, how could anyone possibly understand how crucial this night was to their relationship, when he was about to fly off to foreign shores and she wouldn't see him for weeks on end?

'Shall we go and grab a coffee with your father?' Her mum seemed keen to move on, reluctant to call her daughter out on her barefaced lies and risk a return to all-out war.

No more was said on the subject and they strolled off in the direction of the funfair, where they found Kim's dad munching his way through a bag of doughnuts whilst watching the world go by. Then they ordered hot drinks in an overpriced café where Kim tried not to squirm on her seat, uncomfortable as she was, knickerless and in need of a hot shower.

*

Her mum's eyes barely left Ritchie throughout the band's performance, despite the enthusiastic show the others put on, particularly Bren, who looked like he hadn't slept in weeks and who was bouncing off the walls. In fact, the only comment her mother made about any other band member was: 'Hells bells, that drummer looks wired!'

Instinctively, Kim knew her mum was sizing Ritchie up, reluctantly accepting that he'd been at the front of the queue when good looks were doled out. Kim also knew that her mum longed to ram his microphone down his throat, for daring to have his wicked way with her only daughter, who enthusiastically opened her legs every time he snapped his fingers.

Ritchie had adopted his charismatic showbiz persona, beaming and strutting and writhing about, covering the whole stage with his rhythmic moves and positively filthy grinding, shirt open to the waist, baby-oiled chest glistening under the spotlight, seductive green jewel-eyes sparkling and illuminating the theatre. Kim didn't expect him to let her down, but still, she was quietly relieved when he slid over and unfalteringly sang the lyrics of *Falling* to only her, taking her to that place occupied by just the two of them. Without even glancing at her mum, she knew that her eyes would be wide as she listened and examined the lyrics, interpreting what they could mean and how they might influence her girl's future.

All things considered, Kim was fairly certain that her mum had enjoyed the gig, but when it was over, once the curtain had fallen and the house lights had come up, she looked at her mother and could see a world of worry in her eyes.

If Alison Summers could have chosen any life for her precious daughter, it would not have been this one.

'Come on,' her mum urged, as Kim wrestled her arms back into her jacket. 'You'd better say goodnight to your father and assure him yourself that you won't be doing anything silly with a certain gyrating popstar. At least nothing that's likely to appear in tomorrow morning's newspapers.'

She was joking, but Kim inwardly cringed. A raft of mucky stories concerning the personal lives of all band members had appeared in the national press and hardly a day went by when there wasn't a sickening piece tearing them to shreds or revealing sordid details about their sex lives. Bren and Ady seemed to have copped for the worst of it, with embarrassing tales of vigorous rumpy pumpy gone wrong (Bren) and a threesome in a seedy Birmingham hotel (go Ady! Who would have thought he had it in him?). Even Marty and Todd hadn't escaped unscathed, with stories covering everything from Todd's first girlfriend who'd been left broken-hearted when he'd dumped her in favour of a life of fame and fortune (not true – Kim had met her at a gig and she was really sweet, newly engaged and bore no ill-feeling towards her ex as they'd only separated because she'd wanted to concentrate on her studies) to Marty's 'massive' weight gain in his teens – which had been a case of him simply putting on a few pounds when he'd given up football following an excruciating knee injury (Kim thought he actually looked better with more meat on his bones as he was still only about eight stone wet through).

The allegations had re-surfaced concerning Ritchie, but this time in much finer detail, and Kim's mum had been furious when her daughter had dismissed them with a wave of the hand and a weary: 'It's a crock of shit, mum – not one single word of that is true.' She may have rejected them with a carefree gesture but inside she was churning, still unable to discuss any of it with Ritchie, for fear of fuelling another argument and making herself look like a tool for believing any old tosh that appeared in the press.

Kim's dad was unimpressed when he discovered Kim wouldn't be returning home with them. She knew he wasn't taken in by her fibs for one minute and would gladly crush Ritchie's windpipe, given half the chance. A frosty set of goodbyes was exchanged before Kim left her parents behind and made her way down to the Shoreline Hotel, providing her name as requested at the grand reception and accepting a key to a huge room at the front of the hotel, which did indeed overlook the sea and was definitely top end and very much off her affordability spectrum.

In the past she'd always made an effort to update Sally-Anne on her whereabouts but the girl had been acting so strangely towards her, Kim honestly didn't think that she would have afforded her the same courtesy, had the high heeled boot been on the other foot. Consequently, she'd slipped away without saying a word and couldn't give a fig whether Sal thought Kim was spending the night with Ritchie or if she'd presumed Kim had buggered off home in a huff with her parents after Ritchie's earlier reluctance to communicate.

Their friendship definitely wasn't what it had once been and she was yet another person Kim seemed to be drifting apart from.

When Ritchie finally made it back to the room, he was funny, attentive and loving, and Kim wondered how she'd ever doubted him. They made love with more meaning and intensity than she'd ever felt before, Ritchie maintaining eye-contact throughout, as if staring deep into her soul. He seemed reluctant to pull apart once it was over, so they snuggled up tight to watch a corny chick flick whilst quaffing champagne that had been delivered by room service, before he fell asleep in her arms and, feeling like a proper psycho, she watched him and listened to him breathe, for the umpteenth time admiring his unparalleled beauty and almost majestic presence, wanting to memorise every last part of him, from the slight blemish on his left cheek to the tiny scar on his right forearm.

As she was finally nodding off, he was coming to, and it wasn't long before he was seeking her out again, flipping her over and making her almost sob with the ecstasy, as he thrust time and time again, satisfying not only himself but all of Kim's needs. She offered little resistance – not that she would ever turn down any propositions from Ritchie.

It was the most passionate and perfect of nights and Kim never wanted it to end. Eventually she gave up trying to sleep and silently slipped out of bed, padding across the plush carpet to open the huge drapes covering the floor-to-ceiling window, gazing out at the breath-taking beauty of the coastline as dawn broke and the sun slowly emerged from its hiding place.

She knew this wasn't real life – knocking back champagne that probably cost more than her weekly wage, rolling about in a king-size bed between three hundred thread count Egyptian cotton sheets and watching the sun rise as the waves lapped against the shore. But for a few hours at least, she tried to pretend it was. However, she knew in her heart that even if all the ancillaries were stripped away and she was left in an empty room with only Ritchie by her side, she would still be deliriously happy. He could promise her the earth, but all she would ever want was him – just him, and no more.

Chapter 20

Of course, she hadn't made it into work that day. To her shame, she hadn't even placed a call to her boss to rattle off excuses. Completely distracted by Ritchie's insistence that she should return to bed and let him love her all over again before they parted for the remainder of the summer, she hadn't even considered doing the decent thing as far as her employer was concerned. When her body was spent and her heart was full, she eventually succumbed to sleep – only to awaken with a start to see Ritchie throwing his clothes on after his dreaded wake-up call.

'Sorry babe, time's up I'm afraid. As amazing as last night was, and as alluring as you look right now with your hair all tousled and your bare bum peeping out at me from under those bed sheets, I've got to run as we've a flight to catch later. Bloody hell, I'm cutting it fine – not even time for a shower, although I do like the idea of taking the scent of you and your sex with me all the way over to mainland Europe...'

'Dirty dog!' she joked, lobbing the empty condom packet at him, devastated he was leaving but wanting him to picture her teasing and playful rather than sad and whiny when he departed. Quickly burying her head in the plump pillows – remembering all too late the reason why she didn't drink champagne (not that she could afford it under normal circumstances) - she tried to stifle down the sobs in her throat and ignore the throbbing pulse in her forehead.

Unfortunately he had very little to pack up and was ready to leave in a flash. Despite her determination to stay strong, the tears defied her and plopped down on to the bedding, but Ritchie was soon at her side to wipe them away, soothe back her hair and promise faithfully that he would ring her, with assurances of course, that he wouldn't forget her while he was gone.

Somehow, his leaving this time felt different. She was used to hasty goodbyes and long absences – and basically not knowing where the hell she stood – but recently there'd been a tighter connection, more time together, a developing relationship. Whilst that whole little package was a vast and welcome improvement, it only served to remind her how far apart they still were in so many aspects; how he would soon be at the other side of the world and she would be left clinging onto virtually nothing.

After one final kiss, it was a 'See you soon darling,' and then he was opening the door.

But he didn't immediately dive through it and dash away, as was the norm. He paused, turned...and she covered her face with her hands to prevent him seeing the full horror of her puffed up eyes and blotchy complexion.

'Kimberley,' he said, using a gentler voice than she'd ever heard before. 'Kimberley, look at me – please. Just once...please...one more time.'

As she slowly lifted her head and eyes to meet his gaze, and squeezed out the weakest of smiles, he added quietly, 'Yes, one look. That's perfect...that's it. I'll take that with me.'

And then he was gone.

*

The next three months were the longest of her life. After the heavenly night in Southport, everything else felt like hell.

She'd remained in the warmth of that bed as long as she could before there was a real possibility she would be physically removed by a member of staff. Tempted to steal the sheets and never, ever wash them again – and she probably would have done if she'd had a big enough handbag – she put on the set of clothes that they'd removed together – knickers included this time around – splashed icy cold water on her seriously dehydrated skin and patted it dry with a soft and fluffy white hand towel, before taking one final look around the room and closing the door behind her.

Always a relief to confirm that Ritchie had indeed settled the bill on checkout, she accepted the 'Well done you!' grin from the far too perky receptionist, who clearly would have bedded Ritchie herself given half the chance, and steeled herself against the nip of the sea air as she reluctantly exited the main doors and stepped out into the real world.

Why the hell hadn't she accepted the money Ritchie had tried to press upon her for the taxi home? *Because you didn't want to feel like he was reimbursing you for your services,* a quiet voice piped up inside of her head.

Why the hell hadn't she brought enough money of her own to fund a taxi back to Cheshire? *Because you're potless until payday and, you'd originally anticipated that your father was to be your chauffeur.*

Luckily she'd managed to scrape enough cash together from the dark recesses of her handbag for the train fare and she'd eventually returned home with her tail between her legs, fretting about how she could make this right with her boss. She needn't have bothered. As she staggered up to her parents' house, legs wobbling from the overnight activities followed by the lengthy walk from the railway station, in the unsavoury clothes she'd set off in almost twenty-four hours earlier, she clocked her boss' shiny black BMW parked up at the head of the cul de sac. Bruce was smouldering inside, waiting, arms folded across his chest, tattoos displayed in all their glory.

She'd pretended not to notice him as she scuttled up the path, but he sprang out of his vehicle and thundered down the road towards her, and as she turned her key in the lock of their old, seventies style, wooden panelled front door, she heard him seethe, 'This is the last straw. You can either resign or I'll sack you Kim. I'll arrange to have your belongings forwarded on.'

Her disgusted, disappointed parents had treated her with contempt, refusing to speak to her, not even to issue threats that she either got a job or got out. And with Freddie now shacked up with his girlfriend, she lived a mainly silent existence in the home where there had once been so much love and laughter.

She held on to the thought that one day soon she would walk out of that house to live with Ritchie, never to return – not permanently anyway - and they would all regret the way they had behaved towards her and the love of her life. She prayed that Ritchie missed her even just a fraction of the amount that she missed him, and it seemed her prayers were answered with weekly telephone calls, when they whispered sweet nothings to each other and, at the other end of the spectrum, described in explicit detail exactly what they wanted to do to each other once they were reunited.

But the conversations were short and not enough to stem the daily flow of tears and the permanent, agonising ache in her heart.

Nicky's wedding day dawned on a bright, sunny Saturday and it hurt Kim more than she could ever have imagined that her beautiful friend was marrying the love of *her* life in an ancient stone church on the other side of town and Kim wouldn't be there. She longed to be having her hair done with the other bridesmaids alongside Nicky and her mum, sipping champers whilst locks were teased into wispy 'up do's' and make-up was carefully applied to glowing faces. She envied the other girls, no doubt resplendent in their stylish full length dresses, clutching tiny floral arrangements and humming along to 'Here Comes the Bride' and she shed a tear at one o'clock, when she knew Nicky and her father would be nervously

178

chatting in the back seat of the wedding car, as the driver circled the block several times to ensure they were late by exactly ten minutes.

The evening reception should have been a blast – in better circumstances she would have been off her face on double vodkas, staggering around nattering to all Nicky's family and friends, before they finally hit the dancefloor, hitching up skirts and embarrassing themselves to a spot of Village People or Black Lace.

Instead she felt awkward, uncomfortable and alone.

Her mum and dad seemed to want to chat to everyone (except her) and she was left in the corner for the main part - a real Billy-No-Mates. When she'd finally caught up with Nicky and her new husband, she'd wanted to throw her arms around her best friend, to offer up congratulations and tell Nicky how proud she was. But the words stuck in her throat and it was all she could do to reach out to squeeze her hand and tearfully say, 'You look stunning Nicky...so beautiful.' And she really did. Her ivory dress, with all its intricate beading and scalloped edges, was magnificently cut, to synch in her waist and reveal just enough of her chest to look voluptuous without being in danger of anything popping out. Her ash blonde hair was expertly styled and piled up on top and she wore a diamante tiara, with gold teardrop earrings hanging from her tiny lobes.

Perfect. She looked perfect. And she radiated joy and happiness, basking under the adoring gaze of her sexy new husband, who had discreetly excused himself for a moment.

'Thanks, Kim,' she replied. And although Kim was sure she saw her friend's eyes glisten for a second, it *was* only a second...and then she was gone, to seek out Connor and enjoy the rest of their celebrations amongst their loved ones.

With the exception of one or two mutual friends who stopped by to say hi, she remained alone for the rest of the night and frequently welled up as she observed bride and groom smooching along to their first dance, and later the group of bridesmaids, obviously inebriated, having a proper knees-up as they screeched with laughter and tripped up over each other's dresses. Even the sight of her mum and dad, slow dancing along to George Michael, made her want to openly weep and the end of the evening couldn't come soon enough.

Hurtling along in the taxi on the journey home, she remained tight-lipped, gazing out of the window, trying to imagine herself and Ritchie, exchanging vows and rings at the altar, greeting guests at their wedding party, and later enjoying their first dance as a married couple.

She tried so hard to create this fantasy, this perfect image in her mind…but it just wouldn't come.

*

More newspaper headlines – more bullshit.

If Kim had to read one more article about 'Troubled Todd' or 'Brawling Bren' or – worst of all – 'Randy Ritchie's Raunchy Nights of Shame', she honestly thought she would go mad. At least she could take comfort in the fact that Ritchie had in fact been tucked up in bed with her on the occasion of him supposedly servicing a 'lady of the night' in Northampton – a fact which Kim came to regret sharing with her rather straitlaced father, who bunched his fists, swore under his breath and then stormed out of the room.

Truths or lies, they were all damaging and there seemed no end to it. Every day, there was another story and it reached the point where she dreaded picking up her dad's newspaper from behind the door each morning in case there were more lurid accusations and reasons as to exactly why she should stay as far away as possible from 'that troublesome band'.

She missed working at Bruce's Bespoke Kitchens. God damn it, that job was the cushiest she'd ever had, she'd been good at it and it had paid well – but in reality no fulltime job provided her with enough annual leave to cover all the dates she needed to be free to attend the gigs and see Ritchie whenever he was available. It was impossible. However, skiving off and not even ringing in to explain her absence was inexcusable, meaning the termination of her employment had been inevitable. She felt so bad that she'd let everyone down though and hated them thinking that she was a terrible, lazy person who didn't give a shit about others. Fighting back the urge to turn up on their doorstep, break down and beg for reinstatement, she scoured the small adds and the shop windows until she eventually found temporary work in a packing factory which turned out to be the WORST job she'd ever had and she returned home each night, paler, stinkier and with an ever increasing display of spots covering her chin and forehead.

Her mum and dad never asked about her new job – maybe they thought it wouldn't be long before she would be resigning anyway, as soon as the 'Ritchie Joe Clarke show' was back in town. She was sad that that they showed no interest whatsoever in what she was doing on a day-to-day basis, but took comfort in the fact that her dad insisted on dropping her off at the factory gates when she was on earlies and never failed to collect her from the same spot when she finished lates. And her mum still cooked her tea and left it in the oven every evening, no matter what time she was due in.

The only relief – and the absolute highlight of each week – was those calls from Ritchie, when he would describe places and landmarks that Kim could only dream of visiting, and she would rant on about her bastard job and woefully tell him that the only thing keeping her going was the prospect of them being together again. He hadn't taken his mobile phone with him due to connectivity issues and it being ridiculously expensive to use to make international calls. Kim understood but wished she had some way of being able to contact him – although she would literally have been hung, drawn and quartered if she'd been caught using their house phone to ring a mobile number abroad!

When the band moved on to Australia, Ritchie's calls stopped altogether. Kim tried to put it down to cost, geography and time differences but it still hammered away at her heart, that lack of contact. She tortured herself, imagining him spending his nights off hanging out in the trendiest of clubs, surrounded by a bevy of beauties, while she slaved away in the noisiest place on earth and broke every single fingernail. Ticking off the days on her calendar, she made the mistake of counting the number of hours remaining before the band were due to return to the UK and ended up crying into her *Show Me Yours* cushion, which she had sprayed liberally with the intense, woody aftershave that Ritchie always wore, but which bore no resemblance on fabric to the powerful, intoxicating scent that she had inhaled from his skin.

Chapter 21

Four more nights. Three more days. Two more shifts. And then she could leave her godforsaken job in the workhouse/factory forever, treat herself to a trim at the hairdressers, slip into the brand spanking new scarlet cold-shoulder mini-dress and expensive suede boots (purchased from her mum's catalogue – paying back £2 a week for approximately five hundred years) and endure the tedious train journey over to Yorkshire to be reunited with her Ritchie.

Sally-Anne had apparently been 'out' every time Kim had phoned to speak to her so consequently they hadn't made the usual arrangements to travel together. In a strange way, Kim felt relieved that she wasn't dependant on Sal for anything. They were each in possession of their own theatre tickets and Kim would likely be sharing hotel rooms and beds with Ritchie. She'd still made provisional bookings at a couple of cheap bed and breakfasts though, in case he decided to head home immediately after the gigs. Silly state of affairs really, but better safe than sorry.

She couldn't wait to see him and wondered if he would be more tanned, even though it was winter in Australia. She knew he hit the sun beds on a regular basis because, let's face it, who wants to see a pasty looking popstar, but she pictured him darker and leaner since their last goodbye. She just hoped that she didn't look like some freakish, scary vampire next to him, thanks to the confines of the pet food factory.

'Wow Kim, have you put weight on?' Those were the first words out of Sally-Anne's mocking mouth when Kim stumbled across her together with Witches number 1, 2 and 3 at the train station in Yorkshire. Sal giggled, nudged Witch number 1 and stared Kim out. She felt a hot flush creep over her chest and face whilst her hands started to sweat. This was horribly unpleasant.

She didn't answer, lamely commenting on the weather instead. Sally-Anne told Kim to walk with them up the hill, but they sped on ahead, making a point of leaving her lagging behind with her heavy bag. Childish behaviour, but Kim didn't particularly want to show up at the venue alone so she tried to keep up the pace and ignore the awkward atmosphere between herself and the other girls.

When they arrived at the theatre, she was shocked to see Ritchie's car parked up close to the stage door – he was here already! Why hadn't he rung to let her know? Ignoring the sniggering of Sally-Anne's new friends, she sidled up to the wiry old man on the stage door, requesting that he please pass a message on to Ritchie Clarke that Kim Summers was here and waiting for him. Initially she wondered if the old boy had even heard because he failed to make eye contact, let alone utter anything in response. When he'd eventually stumped out and flung his cigarette butt, he disappeared into the bowels of the theatre.

After ten long minutes, he returned to inform her that Ritchie wouldn't be long and then the door was slammed in her face. Speechless and humiliated, she tried to laugh it off in front of the others, as if Old Smoke was slightly senile and hadn't understood, but it was blatantly obvious that they could see right through her painted-on smile and nonchalant demeanour, and she felt slightly sick that they had been there to witness her being left out in the cold.

When she'd almost given up hope, and Sally-Anne and her new crew had finally sidled off to buy chips, the stage door creaked open a few inches and Old Smoke beckoned her inside, where he insisting on frogmarching her to Ritchie's dressing room, presumably so she didn't pilfer anything en route. A sharp rap on the door and then her miserable companion scowled and turned on his heel to scuttle away just as Ritchie's voice from within shouted out 'COME IN!'

She couldn't help but notice that this dressing room had an air of disused classroom about it and presumably there were no riders in this particular venue to sweeten up the VIPs. My God though, Ritchie looked mighty fine. His beautiful long locks had been lopped, the new short, spikey style perfectly showcasing his model face and those sexy green eyes which seemed to glitter more than ever. He always took her breath away but suddenly she felt totally in awe and found herself to be sub-standard, self-conscious and lacking.

'Kimberley,' he rushed forward to fold his arms around her, almost crushing her with his strength and she longed to stay in that moment, to preserve the feeling that almost swallowed her up, clamped together with her great love after such a painful absence.

He was smiling when they did eventually tear themselves apart but his eyes were downcast and instinctively she knew there was trouble afoot.

'What is it Ritchie?' she asked, almost too terrified to hang around for his response. Supposing he'd met someone else? What if the time apart had made him realise she wasn't good enough for him or he'd weighed up his feelings for her and found that they weren't substantial enough to carry their relationship forward? She couldn't bear it; what would she do?

'Tell me Ritchie...what's wrong?'

'You're so intuitive, Kimberley. I didn't want to burden you with my problems but there's a lot of empty seats out there tonight and the management's having a shit-fit as the tour's making a loss. It cost a fortune to stage the Australian shows, but we made it back in ticket sales and merchandise. And we still have the advertising deals out there. But the European leg, and many of the UK gigs, have been a real disappointment. I guess the public lost interest in us – or bored of the endless media coverage and the scummy newspaper headlines.'

'Oh Ritchie, you'll bounce back – you know you will. Bands and trends come and go but if you write and record half-decent music there'll always be a market for you somewhere – it's finding out where you sit in this industry.'

'Ever the optimist, Kimberley! It's not the only problem though. Bren's sick – he's a mess. It looks like his hedonistic lifestyle has finally caught up with him and his body's letting him down and, worst of all, the record company won't fund any more stints in rehab. He can't afford to pay because he's been declared bankrupt – if you haven't already seen that in the papers then you soon will - and he literally hasn't a pot to piss in. The bottom line is that we're all miserable and disillusioned with the whole business. Our glory days are apparently over, we're sick of the sight of each other and the new music I'm writing is quite frankly, a pile of stinking horseshit. My inspiration seems to have fucked off with the ticket sales and Bren's cash. Sad isn't it?'

'Maybe Bren needs a break from the band and the dark side of the music industry – so he's not mixing in the same old circles, tempted by the same old vices. What's he going to do then, now he's skint? He won't lose his flat will he?'

'It's gone babe – along with the car and the Rolexes and all the other luxuries and fancy gear. He's back at his mum's again but she's tearing her hair out with him. Christ...what a mess...and I don't know where it leaves any of us. If we're dropped by the record company, we'll struggle to strike a new deal if Bren can't clean his act up. I've even suggested bringing in a new drummer to replace him while he sorts himself out – but the others say they won't continue without Bren.'

Christ, the situation must be bad if there'd been talk of removing Bren. He was an integral part of the band and to strip his colossal personality from the mix would rip the heart out of this group. Although he probably wouldn't have been as loud and lively without the use of illegal substances...

Kim desperately wished she could turn the clock back for him. If only he'd made wiser choices.

Ritchie's face looked pained and her heart went out to him. 'It's going to be alright Ritchie, you'll see. Something always comes up. At least you've invested most of your money so you'll be financially secure and the other guys seem to be doing okay. Bren was always a bit of a loose cannon but he's going to get through this and you'll be back up at the top where you belong soon. You've said it yourself, it only takes the right song at the right time and you're back in favour again, coining it in and riding high in the charts.

'God, I hope so.'

'At least you're back now. *We're* back together...and that's all that matters to me.'

'Kimberley,' he smiled. 'My Kim.' He cupped her face in his hands, appearing to study it carefully before continuing. 'You're one in a million...and it's been wonderful to see you again. We've had some awesome times together...'

Oh my god. She sensed there was a 'but' and her heart plummeted.

He paused, biting on his bottom lip, before removing his hand, automatically trying to rake it through his hair, forgetting there were now stiff spikes where once waves had been the order of the day. 'But I need to concentrate on my work – the band, my writing, even the possibility of a solo career. It's not good for me or my productivity to be spending so much time with you, because when I'm near you work is the last thing on my mind...'

He left the sentence suspended, right there, as if she was to complete it with the necessary words and make life easier for him.

Kim took a step back.

Shocked. Floored.

'Excuse me? What the hell are you talking about Ritchie? I've waited all these weeks...these months...these years for you. Are you saying you want to cool it now – is that it? Where is all of this coming from? Have you met someone else?'

'Of course I haven't! There's no one as lovely as you. But it's time I focused all my energies on my work rather than a woman – even you.'

'Is this what constitutes letting me down gently? Is that it? Don't you want me anymore?'

'Don't be ridiculous, Kimberley. You know that's not the case. But it wouldn't be fair on you either to force you to take a back seat. My feelings for you haven't changed...it's just...'

'WHAT? It's just *what?*'

'It's...it's...oh Christ, I don't know. You, and me...well it's too much of a distraction. I can't seem to summon up the inspiration, get the artistic juices flowing. I need to be fully engaged; totally in the zone.'

'Surely our relationship should inspire you! If your feelings were anything like mine you'd be writing songs of love that come straight from the heart – lyrics crammed with raw emotion...the joy of falling in love, the ecstasy of making love, the constant ache when you're apart, the injustice of having to keep it all under wraps...'

'But the record company doesn't want love songs! I've penned loads of those and they're all on the backburner until I can come up with something that will have teenagers up on their feet. They want catchy little tunes that holidaymakers will be chanting on the beaches. Dance beats that will be blasted from car stereos as posers whizz along with the sun roof down and the wind in their hair. Songs with a retro feel that will fill the floor of every nightclub in every town. Music that will make the youth engage again. That's what they want! Something quality but catchy and unforgettable.'

'Not like me then. It would seem I'm absolutely, one hundred percent forgettable.'

'No, no you're not – don't say that! If there was any other way...' He cradled her in his arms and she clung to him, her chest heaving, wondering how they could have reached the end already when she'd thought their real relationship was only just beginning.

'Oh Kimberley, don't cry. I'm so sorry darling. I don't want to hurt you...'

'Then don't break my heart for god's sake! Especially if you genuinely do still want me. It doesn't make sense to break it off, if you still feel the same. None of this makes sense.'

'I thought I'd be doing the right thing, keeping my job – and keeping the others in a job – knuckling down and securing our future, setting you free to live your life without the shackles of my world holding you back. You're young, you're beautiful and you deserve so much better than this. You need a guy who can devote all his time and attention to you. This is no life for you...'

'No! If it means losing you then I'll happily pay the price. All these feelings...all that waiting...all this time – it can't have been for nothing...'

He gave no response but a mixture of sadness and confusion clouded his face. She could see he was torn but she couldn't let go – she *wouldn't* let go.

'Don't end it Ritchie. Please. Me, and you, we're good together and we can ride this storm and any other that blows our way. You – you'll be everything you want to be and me – well I'll sit quietly in the background waiting, until the time is right. The limited hours we'll spend together will be all the more special for it and I promise I won't ever nag you or make you regret this decision.'

A smile. Thank goodness. That smile that broke a thousand hearts and almost smashed hers to smithereens.

'I don't deserve you. Kimberley. Helen. Summers. You are alluring, astonishing, and arguably the best sex I've ever had! Ow!'

She swiped his chest with the back of her hand, with no intention of hurting him, but her grandmother's ring left a small red welt in the 'V' formed where the two sides of his shirt had been deliberately left open. Instinctively, her lips were drawn to the mark and she leant forward and let her tongue flick over it, tasting his blood, whilst her hands reached around him to caress his muscular back. He swallowed hard, swore and his breathing quickened. She knew she had him back – even if it was only a temporary reprieve.

What followed was fast and frantic and neither of them gave a toss whether anyone barged in and saw them, semi-naked and bent over the chair. No one did catch them in the act, but the risks they were taking made it all the more thrilling. Ritchie had never slapped her behind quite so hard and she'd never dug her nails in to his flesh quite so deeply.

Unfortunately, because the sex was so urgent it was over far too soon but at least Ritchie seemed calmer, as they curled up in the chair together, heartbeats and pulses gradually returning to normal.

'I'm sorry, Kim,' he repeated, tucking a stray hair behind her ear and lowering his lips to kiss one of her drooping eyelids. 'My mind's been in turmoil but I was silly to think that I'd ever be able to let you go'

'You should have talked to me, Ritch - you and your spontaneous decisions will be the death of me. There I was, like a kid at Christmas, bursting with excitement at the prospect of being with you after such a prolonged separation...and there you were, about to dump me from a great height!'

'Don't worry, I would rapidly have come to my senses and been down on my knees begging for you to take me back!'

Still recovering from Ritchie's shock plan to press pause on their relationship, without so much as a discussion or a hint of what was to come, Kim tried to smile and swallow the hurt he had inflicted, desperate for them to be back where they were – as precarious a place as that was. He needed reassurances now though. It was important that he understood what they had was pure solid gold and that she'd never want anything more. He had to know that she'd wait forever, if that's what it took.

'You, Ritchie Joe Clarke, are hot-headed, highly strung and hard to understand at the best of times. You know I'll always forgive you Ritchie. I would always take you back. You, and me. We're one.'

*

It transpired that he hadn't booked anywhere for them to stay and Kim's disappointment was compounded. It shouldn't have been a surprise, with all the crap that was bouncing around in his head, but it hurt to think that they might have to spend this long-awaited night sleeping in separate beds, in different hotels.

However, Kim's provisional bed and breakfast booking had expired while they'd been otherwise engaged in his dressing room - a quick call to the landlady from Ritchie's mobile confirmed that this was no longer an option for her. The frown lines that etched his usually smooth forehead and the tapping of his foot suggested he was a little concerned and none too happy. He remained silent, rubbing his left hand over the sexy stubble on his chin while she wondered what was so difficult about inviting her to stay in his room. She didn't care if he was sharing it with Ady, or Bren or a six foot gorilla with a foot fetish...*anything* was better than being left to her own devices after dark in a strange town with limited funds. What was wrong with this man?

'It's not ideal, with the other band members there, but I guess you can come stay with me at our hotel. Ady and his partner are booked into the bridal suite for their anniversary so at least I have a room to myself. We'll have to smuggle you in though. At this stage of the game, I don't want anyone thinking that I'm not totally committed to this band and I definitely don't want the press getting wind of it and seeing your good name dragged through the dirt in the Sunday rags...'

The band's return from the other side of the world had unleashed fresh, unsavoury revelations and when Kim had read them she'd just wanted to scream, STOP! Whoever's doing this, just STOP!

Bren's fight with a nightclub bouncer in Birmingham. Ady's dad disowning him because of his sexuality. Todd's one night stand with a beautician from Copenhagen. Marty's caution for shop-lifting when he was thirteen – now THAT surprised Kim! Ritchie seemed to have escaped relatively unscathed this time around but it worried her. He was no saint, of that she was fairly certain. It felt like there was a time bomb, ticking away, counting them down to some sordid, slanderous juicy headline that was going to rock his world. And probably hers too.

The thought of a cruel exposé on herself and Ritchie actually brought her out in a cold sweat. However, even though her parents would be terribly hurt and embarrassed, a small part of her was ceasing to care. A tiny voice inside her head pointed out that if the worst should happen, at least the world would know that she belonged to Ritchie and he belonged to her and it would finally all be out in the open. They could venture out in public as a couple, go on dates, jet off on holiday, maybe even live together. And perhaps there would be a grand wedding (or even a smaller intimate one) further down the line and two or three cherub-like children. Yes, she definitely wanted children, who were sure to be insanely gorgeous if they were blessed with Ritchie's first-class genes.

So let the reporters do their worst – it could turn out to be the best thing that ever happened to them.

*

Despite the underwhelming ticket sales, the concert crowd made some serious noise and the sheer volume and exuberant participation more than made up for the fact the theatre was only two-thirds full. It was therefore a happy, adrenaline-filled Ritchie that bounced off the stage and into his car, aided and assisted by a worryingly reserved Barry. Kim actually thought it was an imposter. He was one of the loudest people she knew, and she knew Sally-Anne.

As agreed, she arrived at the hotel half an hour later, relieved that there were no fans hanging around on the steps waiting for autographs – no mad stalker hoping that Bren might invite them in, take them upstairs and give them a good seeing to. To be honest, she didn't think Bren would be fit enough to see to himself, let alone anyone else. When he'd passed her earlier, his eyes were bloodshot and he was staggering around, like a bluebottle that had been blasted with half a can of fly spray. He made her heart ache. She wanted to beg him to please get help and get clean – once and for all - but then again, if she'd lost her home and practically everything she owned, she'd probably be drowning her sorrows and searching for the next high too.

Ritchie seemed twitchy and nervous until they were safely in their room – she liked that, being able to say it was 'their room' – where he visibly relaxed, his shoulders dropping by about three inches and the tension seeping out of his body. It seemed their earlier conversation and the raucous crowd at the gig had done him the world of good as he was relaxed and absolutely the best version of himself. He poured her a large glass of red wine so dark it was practically black, chinking his glass against hers as he made a toast: 'Cheers Kimberley. Here's to us!' US! She liked that even better. It was an enormous relief to hear that there was definitely still an 'us'.

'Sorry about before – you know – me having a wobble and all that. I don't ever want to lose you but sometimes it feels like I'm cracking up with the whole work situation and the mounting pressure.' He took her left hand in his left hand and squeezed it gently, as his gaze lingered on her face and she marvelled yet again at the good looks that had been bestowed upon him. Those unique green eyes that sparkled and shone in her dreams. Those perfect, pouting lips that were the softest she'd ever known. The jet black hair that always looking immaculate, whatever the style.

'I understand Ritchie, but please don't do it again. You hurt me, and it blindsided me. Promise there'll be no more wobblers?'

'Promise,' he grinned, placing his glass down on to the coffee table, and Kim mirrored his actions.

What followed was the sweetest night of love imaginable. The pace was slow, the mood was intense and the passion was amplified by the separation they'd endured and their eventual jubilant reunion. This time she cried tears of pleasure as this man, who she loved so deeply it tormented her when they were apart, insisted on giving all night rather than receiving; devouring and worshipping her body, batting away her hand as she tried to cover her plumper belly, insisting she was beautiful and goddess-like and the most perfect example of woman he had ever known.

When morning came, she was bleary-eyed, hungover and physically stretched from the activities of the night – but pain and pleasure went hand in hand where Ritchie was involved. They cuddled and he talked at length about his favourite places in the world and how he hoped to show them to Kim one day. They then took it in turn to sensuously massage each other's neck and shoulders before crashing back onto the pillows and drifting off to sleep whilst still holding hands. When they next awoke, to the persistent ringing of the telephone - the hotel reception delivering Ritchie's much-hated wake-up call - the headaches were more muted and the pain in her thighs had subsided to a dull ache.

'Shit! I have to get out of here soon. My train leaves in an hour Ritchie.'

'Aw babe, don't go yet. I need you here with me. You've no idea how I've struggled to cope without you while I've been away. I've missed your beauty, your body and this cute little blemish on your breast that makes me want to kiss it...again...and again...and again...' His lips blazed a trail starting at the base of her neck...down over her clavicle...and on to the area just above her right nipple, where she'd always had a tiny mark that she'd hated...until now.

'Seriously Mr Clarke, I have to get up and go. I know it's only five minutes from here to the station, but if I miss this train I'm screwed as the next one's not for another four hours. Bloody Sunday service!'

'Oh yes...you're definitely screwed. Three times last night wasn't it? Now come here and let's do something about that Sunday service...'

He reached for her and she responded in kind. Despite the clock ticking and her body aching, she could never pass up the opportunity of a lovemaking session with Ritchie. This one didn't disappoint, but more than any action, it was his words that were significant. He described how he'd pined for her when they'd been separated and said he'd never felt this way about anyone in his whole life and it scared him half to death. He'd never been so candid about his feelings before and at one point she thought he was actually going to say the 'L' word. Running his fingers through messy waves of Kim's hair, he pecked the tip of her nose and whispered, 'Kimberley. Kimberley Helen Summers. You're incredible and irresistible and sometimes I think I don't deserve you. Kimberley…I...I...'

'What Ritchie?' she urged him to say the words she'd been desperately longing to hear.

'I...I've fallen for you so badly darling. I've fought it all the way but I just don't want you ever to doubt me and the strength of my feelings.'

Well, not quite love, but they were getting there.

She finally persuaded Ritchie that she had to vacate the bed, but he followed her around the room, lifting up her hair and tenderly kissing her neck as she fastened the buttons on her top, sliding his hand up her skirt as she attempted to dab perfume on her wrists, resting his chin on her shoulder and reaching his hands around to cup her breasts as she dragged a comb through her bedraggled hair. Feeling more in control of the situation than ever before, she turned around and pushed him firmly on to the bed, but as she stood over him, giggling, he wrapped his legs around hers, trapping her against him, circling her waist with his arms and bringing his head down to rest in the comfort of her belly.

She wanted to hold him there forever, to stroke his hair, to drop kisses onto the soft skin at the nape of his neck, to let him breathe into her. Somehow this was more intimate than the sex.

'Ritchie, I love you, but I really do have to leave.'

She kissed the top of his head and reluctantly tore his hands away from her body. When he looked up his eyes seemed filled with pools of sadness and something else she simply couldn't read. Her beautiful, emotional, complex star. Her reason for being.

'I'll see you down to reception,' he said, catching her by surprise, as he usually remained in the room while she stole out of the building like a cat burglar. She watched him throw on his sweatshirt, jeans and chunky black socks - so effortlessly casual and yet so spectacularly attractive, even when unwashed and exhausted. They held hands on the way down – taking an unnecessary risk if he didn't want them to be seen together – and he accompanied her through the main doors and outside, where he kissed her on the lips one last time, in full view of the reception staff and a handful of passers-by, and she stood proud as a peacock as they said their goodbyes.

'See you later Ritchie...oh Christ!' She hadn't realised how close they were to the flight of stairs in front of the hotel and as her heel slipped over the edge, she staggered backwards, in true slapstick fashion.

Although it felt like she was moving in slow motion, quick as a flash, Ritchie's strong hand grabbed hold of her wrist, hauling her back to the safe house that was his body, and even though her heart was still pounding at this near miss, she was awash with relief that she hadn't made herself look a real tit in front of their captive audience and hadn't broken a leg or two on the way down. He pulled her close and she nuzzled into him, never wanting to be anywhere other than in his arms.

'When you fall, I'll catch you,' he whispered, reminding her of the very first night they'd ever met, when he'd saved her from tumbling to the ground and later, of the personalised message he'd added to her photo. Her saviour. Her hero.

Her Ritchie.

Chapter 22

Almost skipping round the corner to the station, Kim glowed from within as she recalled explicit details of the previous night, savouring the newfound power she'd seemed to wield as they'd left the room and exchanged their goodbyes on the steps. Not even the menacing scowls she received from the wicked witches as she clattered onto the platform just in time to hear a grumpy voice announce a thirty-five minute delay for their train could dampen her spirits – although she did lament the fact that she could have languished for an extra half hour in bed, snuggled up with Ritchie rather than hanging about on a rather bleak, blustery platform with people who didn't seem to like her very much.

Kicking her heels, she chatted to a rather subdued Sal and tried to make polite conversation with Anika, Rachell and Justine. Storing up enemies and bearing grudges was exhausting. She didn't have to like them. Life would be so much simpler if they could all try and be civil to one another, although she sensed that her name would be mud as soon as her back was turned. Shrugging internally – it was something she couldn't change and she therefore reasoned that she would have to lump it and try to let it glide over her, like water off a duck's back, she offered them all a polo mint and then listened to Sally-Anne moaning about her period pains. To be fair, she did look rough – although that was possibly a result of the previous night's alcohol consumption – and the others didn't give a toss. Kim dug deep into her holdall and plucked out a couple of furry painkillers and a lukewarm bottle of lemonade. Her offerings were gratefully received and they moved over to a couple of recently vacated seats on the platform, where they chatted about this and that, and Kim briefly saw a glimpse of the old Sally-Anne, although the bitchiness and sarcasm returned with a vengeance as soon as she began to perk up.

Eventually Justine was dispatched to go and find a hatch or a shop from where she could pick up a bottle of pop that wasn't completely flat and a gossipy Sunday newspaper. Within a matter of minutes she was back, racing towards them - Kim presumed she'd forgotten to take money.

'Headlines...Bren...fucking hell...' she panted, brandishing the paper in front of their noses, and they all quickly huddled round, desperately scrambling to read the big story.

Not one of them could have anticipated what was thrown out there in black and white, emblazoned across not only the front of the trashy rag but also the subject of a double page spread inside.

Bren had a secret child. A two year old son. And not only had this wild, bankrupt, drug-addled, bloody brilliant drummer actually fathered a child, but mum of said son was none other than CALLIE. One of them! Beautiful Callie with her cascading blonde hair, hour glass figure and impossibly long legs. Callie who, despite the looks that could give Cindy Crawford a run for her money, was essentially just a quiet girl from a respectable family who was no different to the rest of them. *Callie* for God's sake. The devoted fan who had turned her back on the band and suddenly disappeared off the radar.

No wonder they hadn't seen sight nor sound of her since the end-of-tour party back in the summer of 1990.

Fair play to her though for keeping Bren's secret, for not bleeding him dry at a time when he still had money in the bank. She'd also apparently been approached by the newspaper for her version of events but the only comment she'd given was that she'd never asked anyone for anything and simply wanted to be left alone to bring up her son. For his part, when tackled by the paps, Bren had apparently gushed that Callie was a wonderful mother who had refused to take a penny from him and that his one regret in life was that he was too darn selfish and irresponsible to be able to step up and deal with fatherhood.

Some unscrupulous photographer had lay in wait for her as she'd left home, attempting to hide away in an oversized hooded top. She looked stressed and weary on the photo but not particularly surprised that she'd been unearthed. Maybe she'd been pre-warned they were about to swoop, or maybe she'd been expecting that day of reckoning since the moment those two blue lines had appear on the pregnancy test wand and her world had turned on its head.

They were all shocked, more so because it was someone they'd known. When she'd disappeared from the scene they'd all presumed she'd gone on to forge a dynamic career for herself or bagged a handsome millionaire businessman to fund a lifestyle of luxury. None of them could ever have guessed that she'd had a little Bren growing inside her womb - that she would always have a part of Bren that no one else could ever take away.

Kim wondered if Callie loved or *had* loved Bren – if her feelings were similar to those that she had for Ritchie – but Callie had made the difficult decision to do what was best for her child. How sad if this girl had truly fallen for the loose cannon. If Kim had to choose between Ritchie and a baby would she be able to let Ritchie go? If she ever found herself in such a situation she would hope that Ritchie would stand by her and they could raise their child together. But in all honesty she couldn't be sure about that - her relationship with Ritchie was all over the place.

And contraception had always been high on his list of priorities. She'd gone on the pill as soon as sex was on the agenda but even then he'd still insisted on using condoms too until she'd practically waved her pill packet in front of his nose to prove he could take her at her word. She'd been terrified of getting caught out anyway – the fallout from any pregnancy would have been momentous. Ritchie would have freaked, her father would probably have belted him and she would surely have died of embarrassment if it had been splashed all over the newspapers. The thought of dirty nappies, maternity bras and squeezing out another human hadn't appealed to her either back in those early days.

It was an unusually subdued Bren who was last off the minibus when the band – minus Ritchie - arrived later that afternoon. He never particularly looked well anymore but he was even paler than usual and his eyes were shiny and circled with red rings, his body language giving everything away. Without ceremony they were all ushered into the back entrance of the theatre, while the fans gossiped about Bren's secret sprog and all the other details of the band's private lives that were being spat out on a regular basis.

When Ritchie still hadn't arrived two hours later Kim started to panic that he may have been involved in an accident and wondered how on earth they could manage on stage as an instrumental four-piece. She'd tried to contact him from the payphone in the reception area several times but apparently, the mobile phone she was calling was switched off, and she'd heard sniggers from the usual suspects every time she'd failed to reach him.

She walked away, downcast and desperate to know where he was.

Relief surged through her body when she finally saw his Audi zipping round the corner, almost wiping out a parking attendant in his mission to reach his destination before Barry spontaneously combusted with anger at this very, very late arrival.

She wasn't expecting him to make a fuss of her, as he quickly exited the car, slamming the driver's door with such force it practically made the wing mirror rattle, but she did anticipate a smile, a few words, a whispered apology or possibly his hand reaching for hers to ensure she followed him backstage. A gesture to assure her he was okay – that they were okay. But he kept his head down, powered on through the assembled fans and said nothing to nobody – not even her.

Surely he'd already known about Bren's son – so presumably this wasn't the reason for his strange behaviour. He may have blanked her in the past but he'd always said hello to the other loyal fans who'd waited for him and had a smile and a wink at the ready. This was definitely new and really not a good sign.

Had there been trouble between the band members? Or issues with the record company and/or management? Were there 'problems' at home, as he'd mentioned previously? Or was it because of the low uptake for tickets again for tonight's gig (the box office lady had claimed that sales had been dismal and said they were lucky the show was still going ahead).

He didn't turn around once as he was steered inside and the last she saw of him was the back of his head as he rushed up the stairs and out of view, before the door banged shut and the fans began to disperse. She longed to knock on and beg to see Ritchie but there was something in the air and she sensed she wouldn't be welcome. It would have been humiliating if she'd been brushed off with a 'Sorry love. He's too busy to speak to you.'

Panic set in as she realised she hadn't sorted out her overnight accommodation, yet again. When the hell would she learn that she couldn't depend on Ritchie? She loved him, but the man was unreadable and unreliable much of the time. It would serve him right if he came looking for her later and she'd already checked into a guesthouse, meaning the luxurious double room that he'd no doubt booked in some pricey hotel would go to waste. Yes, that's what she would do. It would teach him a lesson and she wouldn't be worrying all night.

Of course she didn't stop worrying. Whatever the reason behind Ritchie's behaviour, there was no viable excuse for it and she was devastated at how easily he was able to switch off his feelings for her and be totally unconcerned about her welfare. Even when she'd booked into the 'Templeton' and had a clean and pleasant single room with ensuite at her disposal, she couldn't shift the feeling of gloom, that weighed down on her chest like a heavy box packed to the brim with pieces of broken heart and broken promises.

When the band took to the stage later, it was blindingly obvious that their hearts weren't in it and the lacklustre crowd, many of whom could barely even be bothered to clap, let alone scream or cheer, weren't exactly a morale booster.

Ritchie's eyes were completely devoid of their usual sparkle. Even at a distance Kim could see they were dull and vacant and the expression on his face – on each one of their faces – said *I really don't want to be here. Please say this will all be over soon.*

Despite the fact that she was front row, centre stage, he managed to avoid all eye contact with her too, ensuring his eyes remained fixed on the back wall of the theatre for much of the show, as if he didn't dare look around the room and acknowledge her presence. It was confusing and crushing all at once and she sensed the return of that familiar blame she always eventually insisted on shouldering for anything Ritchie did wrong. Had she said something out of turn the last time they'd spoken, that had made him think she wouldn't be there for him when he needed her most? Had she given the impression that she wouldn't be supportive and understanding and always have his back? Had he looked at her, the last time she'd woken up by his side and thought, *Jesus, I can do better than this?* All that power she'd held in her hand when they'd parted on the steps had turned to dust and slipped through her fingers.

But most crushing of all was when the familiar strains of *Falling* resonated throughout the theatre and she waited for him to fix her with his stare as he always did - to sing those tender words which meant he cared and that everything was going to be okay.

Please Ritchie, look at me. Please Ritchie, don't let me down.

Except when he reached the old familiar lyrics, he didn't glance around - he didn't even look at the back wall. He didn't do anything other than close his eyes whilst he sang, and the only noise in the room was his voice, the instruments and the sound of Kim's heart smashing and hitting the floor.

*

An idiot – that's what she was. If past experience had taught her nothing else, it should have made her realise when to pursue something and when to leave it well alone.

She'd waited, along with all of the others – there seemed to be more people hanging around at the stage door than there'd been inside the theatre – and hoped and prayed that she'd got it wrong. Whatever problem there was it was HUGE but surely it had nothing to do with her. Perhaps Ritchie had merely zoned out throughout the show, singing their favourite song on autopilot, not even registering the words tumbling out of his mouth. So she'd stayed...and watched as the band flashed by and on to the minibus, whilst Ritchie was protected and shielded and shoved into his car by an unusually flustered Barry.

Determined to make him look her in the eye, she walked on quickly, to position herself on the corner of the one way street he would have to venture down, to ensure he couldn't miss her as he checked right before pulling out.

He didn't look at her – he looked *through* her, and she froze, abandoned and humiliated, as he accelerated down the side street and turned on to the main road at the T-junction.

Gone, he was gone.

Kim eventually started to retrace her steps back to the theatre, only to come face to face with Sally-Anne, who was headed in the opposite direction. She and Rachell were linking arms, looking for all the world as if they'd been best buddies forever.

'I can't believe they've just buggered off like that – it's well out of order!' Sal scowled at Kim, as if the band's hasty departure was somehow her fault and Kim, already fragile, could only nod and hope she wouldn't have to make meaningless conversation with these two girls who clearly resented her. Thankfully, they stomped on past, sly stage whispers and mocking laughter following in their wake. They couldn't have done a better job of kicking Kim when she was already down and she really did feel wretched to the core.

How she longed to see a friendly face. Hannah had been around earlier – without her lovely daughter for the first time ever – but she'd disappeared immediately after the show and Geraldine hadn't made it because she was apparently at a family wedding (that girl had family? Who knew?). Everyone else Kim was vaguely acquainted with either wasn't there or seemed to have vanished as quickly as the band did. In the face of such misery, there was only one option left open to her.

Time to go and buy a massive bottle of cheap alcohol to sneak into the guesthouse and then drink until she passed out.

Chapter 23

With a thumping head and a heart that was clocking up twice as many beats as it should, Kim was sweating out neat vodka when she staggered out of her overnight accommodation the following morning. Unable to face any kind of solid food, especially not sausages and fried bread, she'd also departed on an empty stomach.

Luckily, the next show was only around an hour away so she decided to take the bus to avoid bumping into Sally-Anne or any of her so-called mates at the train station. On arrival, she found a mediocre hotel on the outskirts of the town and booked a single room. She no longer expected anything of Ritchie Clarke. Not after the previous evening. Gone was even the tiniest slither of hope that they would be reconciled and end the day drinking champagne in a hot tub within a magnificent hotel suite.

Whilst the hotelier agreed to let Kim leave her luggage, she wasn't officially allowed to check in until after lunchtime so decided to pound the streets in an attempt to blow away the cobwebs, or at the very least completely purge herself of all the excess alcohol fumes.

It didn't work; twenty minutes in and she was on the verge of collapse. After treating herself to a takeaway coffee from a backstreet snack bar, she took up residence on a damp bench, where she shivered the morning away, accepting a tissue from a kind-faced old lady who'd perched down beside her. Kim hadn't even realised she'd been crying. Old Lady didn't probe but introduced herself as Dora and proudly told Kim all about her grandchildren. The conversation was a welcome distraction. Apparently Sarah, the eldest granddaughter, had jacked in her studies, taken off backpacking around Europe and settled down to have babies with a Spanish artist. They'd recently opened a gallery on the outskirts of Barcelona and she was deliriously happy. *Good old Sarah*, Kim mused. Shedding her old skin and putting herself out there – grabbing life with both hands and refusing to let disappointing exam results hold her back. In more ways than one Kim envied her...and Nicky...and all the other girls she'd knocked about with at school. Free to live their lives. They weren't weighed down and restrained by the chains of loving Ritchie, hampered by their inability to let go of this stunning but stupendously selfish man – no matter how badly he behaved.

She was a lovely woman – Dora – who reminded Kim so much of her own grandmother. My god, how she yearned to feel the arms of her gran around her and breathe in her old familiar smell – a combination of white musk and home-baked custard pies. What she wouldn't give to hear her say, 'Now Kimmy, don't let this boy walk all over you...'

After Dora ambled off to catch her bus, Kim was overwhelmed with loneliness and was almost tempted to ring her mum just to hear her voice. Another thirty, forty, fifty minutes passed by and she finally dragged herself up and headed back to the hotel, which was actually a diamond of a place sandwiched between two shitholes. She initially lay down on the perfectly made bed because all she wanted to do was hide away from the rest of the world, but she wanted Ritchie and the rest of them to see she was made of stronger stuff, so she decided to get up, freshen up and show up.

Changed into her favourite 501s, stripy fitted t-shirt and slightly scuffed leather ankle boots, face made up and smile painted on, she took a deep breath and wandered on down to the theatre, where she discovered that she had missed the arrival of the band – Ritchie included – and the only remaining fans were Sally-Anne and the Witches, hunched up on the steps, pouring over the pages of a crumpled newspaper.

Dear God, not again.

When they looked up and noticed Kim there was no pleasant greeting, only a burst of laughter, satisfied smirks and a slow shake of Sally-Anne's head. Kim could see she was in for a real treat.

'Well, well,' sneered Justine, with sly intonation in her voice. 'Your ears must be burning…we were just talking about you.'

'Oh yeah...how so?' She tried to brazen it out. The girl was clearly itching to provoke and about to lob some poisonous comment in her direction.

'Didn't know whether you'd dare show your face today in the circumstances...'

What the hell was she harping on about?

'Why wouldn't I show my face? And what circumstances? If you're meaning those unsubstantiated rumours concerning Ritchie on the European tours then I'm really not interested, particularly in some crap about him supposedly bedding a different woman every night...'

She could see they were all loving it, obviously party to some bollocks from the morning papers that she hadn't yet read and probably didn't want to if it was all about Ritchie. The situation between the two of them was already dire.

Sally-Anne was quick then, up on her feet and bounding down the steps so she was almost face to face with Kim, all traces of friendliness and pleasantry dispersed with, as she looked ready to go into battle.

'How could you, Kimberley? You must have known! Didn't you feel the slightest bit guilty when you were dropping your silky knickers for Ritchie Joe Clarke? Have you no conscience?'

What the actual fuck was going down? Mystified and downright bloody annoyed – because Sal *knew* Kim hadn't the foggiest idea what she was talking about – Kim made an attempt to swipe the newspaper from out of her hand but wasn't quick enough.

'For Christ's sake Sal, if you've got something to say then just spit it out. I'm sick and tired of all this bullshit.'

'Oh you're sick and *tired* of it, are you? Girls – listen – Mrs 'I'm better than you because I'm shagging the lead singer' is sick and *tired...*'

'Just pack it in Sally-Anne. Do NOT try and imply that I've ever made out I'm better than anyone else, least of all you, because you know full well that simply isn't true. There have been times when I've gone out of my way to sneak you backstage when you had no business being there - when my name was the only one on the invitation...'

She regretted her choice of words as soon as they were out of her mouth. Her snappy response was the red rag to the raging bull that was Sally-Anne.

'Oh, did you now...fucking hell...well maybe I should be worshipping at the feet of the high and mighty Kim Summers then, seeing as I have this huge debt to repay for all the millions of favours she reckons she's done me. My amazing friend Kim felt sorry for me – poor little old Sally-Anne - and tried to invite me into her club. Well you know what, *Kimberley*, I don't want to be in your fucking club because I have morals and decency and I would never, ever screw around with a MARRIED MAN!'

'What? Me neither! There's no way I would ever involve myself with anyone who was married...'

And then the penny dropped.

She couldn't be talking about Ritchie. No way could she be referring to Ritchie.

Her open-mouthed silence seemed to unnerve them all and even Sally-Anne, their newly elected pack leader, took a step back, presumably in case Kim went ballistic.

'Please let me see the newspaper.' She held out her shaking hand and Justine stood up and wordlessly passed it to her. Like vultures, they circled then, sniffing around until they could smell blood. Waiting to attack.

For a moment Kim screwed her eyes shut, unwilling to open them and be faced with the black and white print that she knew would destroy her. When she finally plucked up the courage to read the headlines, she realised she wasn't prepared.

'SHOW ME YOURS!

ROCKSTAR RITCHIE'S SECRET WIFE.'

Hearthrob's girl revealed for the very first time.'

Oh my god. No. Just no.

It couldn't be true. Not Ritchie. Not this.

She slunk down on to the steps again, barely able to read the text, her eyes burning and awash with tears.

There wasn't much else on that front page.

Turn to Page 4. Yes, yes that's what she would do. She would turn to page 4 and she would read all the crap and it would become perfectly obvious that the article was merely another part of this witch hunt – this attempt by persons unknown to rip the group apart and ruin the lives of all five members. They had barely anything to throw at Ritchie so they'd paid some tart to claim she was married to him when they'd no actual proof and it would all be revealed as garbage and the newspapers would have to pay unprecedented damages to Ritchie and the guys...

Except there *was* proof.

Page 4, in all its glory, was a collage of photographs of Ritchie and his WIFE through the years. A very young but still recognisable Ritchie with his arm around a blonde pig-tailed girl – both in their school uniforms, for fuck's sake. They'd apparently been teenage sweethearts. Another, clearly taken at a house party somewhere judging by the floral settees, cheap cider bottles and hi-fi unit, and there they were - both togged out in double denim and flashing their toothy grins for the camera. Then came a horrible strip of grainy photo booth snaps where they were both pulling stupid faces on all but the bottom one where they appeared to be sticking their tongues down each other's throats. Next up was a sickly sweet image taken on a beach, capturing them both in their skimpy swim gear, licking ice cream from the same massive cone,

And finally, the worst two pictures of all.

Firstly, a copy of their Marriage Certificate, confirming all of the gruesome details.

And secondly, a close-up from their wedding day, where this woman's hand was placed on top of Ritchie's, displaying her huge rock of a diamond alongside a simple gold wedding band. Even in black and white, it was a beautiful picture. Ritchie carried off his morning suit and cravat combination to perfection and SHE – Kim couldn't bear to read or say her name but it was apparently *Michelle* – looked so pretty, with masses of blonde hair tumbling down onto her shoulders, the sweetheart neckline of her dress revealing just a hint of her perfectly formed, perfectly sized breasts – a dress Kim could never have worn without resembling a bloody serving wench.

She wanted to be sick.

Her stomach was a washing machine on a fast spin cycle and she could already feel its meagre contents threatening to rise up and spew out onto the steps.

She really must have looked a fright because suddenly Sally-Anne's arm was around her and she could hear the insincerity of her feigned words of sympathy. 'Oh you poor cow, you really didn't know? What a bastard eh? Let's just hope there's no kids involved...'

Oh Christ, she couldn't bear it. There was no mention of any children in the article but supposing they did have them – Ritchie and this *Michelle* – and these little ones were being kept out of the spotlight. Even if they were childless, how could Ritchie have a wife that he'd never, ever mentioned? How was it even possible that he could have concealed this most damning of secrets throughout all the years she had loved him?

Reading and re-reading the article, her heart fractured a little bit more with each snippet of information. They'd apparently been together since they were fourteen and, rather than living with his parents as he'd claimed, the love nest was a massive house tucked away from view down a secluded country lane where SHE preferred to stay, out of the limelight, riding her horses and walking her dogs on their FOURTEEN ACRES, rather than accompany Ritchie on tour. Well that was very fucking convenient for him. They had, however, enjoyed a fortnight together in a luxury hotel on the band's recent Australian trip. Celebrating their wedding anniversary.

So *that's* why there'd been radio silence when he'd been out there – SHE had been with him! Kim couldn't even hope that they were estranged or living separate lives. They were very much still together. A couple. A married couple. A committed married couple.

She wanted to scream.

The last thing she needed was Sally-Anne and those mean-faced witches – correction, BITCHES - offering her their brittle shoulders to cry on. Pretending that they cared and were outraged on her behalf, when she knew without a shadow of a doubt that they were lapping it up, deriving pleasure from every ounce of her misery.

'I need to speak to Ritchie,' she muttered, pushing Justine away, feeling an urge to smack her in her pouty mouth when the girl asked, 'Is that wise Kim?'

Refusing to engage her in any further conversation, Kim swallowed the mouthful of something nasty that had risen up from the depths of her stomach, dropped the crappy newspaper onto the ground, and marched away, headed towards the stage door at the rear of the theatre. She knew they'd followed her though. God forbid they might miss any tiny part of the pre-show drama that was about to unfold, which promised to be even more entertaining than the gig itself.

There was no sign of anyone around and, of course, the door was firmly closed. Anguish, fear and blind fury were transforming her into a shaking, hysterical mess and waiting around on the off-chance someone might nip out for a cigarette or a stroll was absolutely not an option.

So she hammered on the door until the adjacent window rattled in its frame.

Nothing.

More hammering. Still nothing. More bloody hammering. Distant noises inside the building but no one appeared to answer her distress call. Drastic action was called for.

'*RIITCHIEEE*! she screamed, pounding until the heel of her hand felt like it was about to explode. 'RITCHIE CLARKE!'

She would kick the fucking door off its hinges if that's what it took to get someone to wake up and find out what all the commotion was about. She launched her foot, wincing with pain as it connected with the door but it wasn't enough to stop her. She was going to kill him.

It didn't take long then. A member of staff, surely familiar with dedicated and desperate fans banging and screaming to be let in, sensed something dangerous in the tortured noise and violence of her actions which alerted them to the possibility she was probably slightly unhinged and likely to do herself damage if not swiftly dealt with.

A bulky, stern-looking woman in an ill-fitting suit yanked open the door and Kim thoroughly anticipated a whack in the chops. She didn't care. She'd gone beyond that.

'I need to speak to Ritchie Joe Clarke NOW!' she screeched, attempting to force her way in – but hitting a brick wall in the form of this woman's abs of steel.

'He's busy, love. They're about to do their soundcheck. You can't come in here anyway - it's for artists and management only. Maybe hang around later for an autograph or a picture...'

'*Are you kidding me?* The last thing I want is another mugshot of that lying prick! But if you don't let me in or he doesn't drag his skinny arse down here right now, I promise I will scream and shout out here all bastard night until everyone knows exactly WHAT he is. He wouldn't want THAT ending up in the papers now, would he?'

'Listen sweetheart, I don't know who you think you are and why you reckon you're entitled to backstage access when clearly it's a restricted area, but if you don't step back then I'll have to use force, and if you persist in causing a scene then I'll have no option but to call the police...'

'*RITCHIEEE...RITCHIEEE...*' Kim continued to shriek, figuring she had nothing to lose at this stage. 'Ritchie Joe Clarke, come and speak to me now, you spineless, gutless, lying fucker! It's *Kimberley* by the way, in case you need me to narrow it down. Forgot to tell me you had a wife didn't you, you two-timing twat! Show your fucking face, you piece of shit!'

Scary bouncer-woman acted on her previous threat and gave Kim an almighty shove. She stumbled but managed to remain on her feet, unwisely deciding that throwing herself at this menacing obstacle and attempting to move her solid bulk whilst screaming blue murder would be the way to gain a backstage pass.

She presumed quite a crowd had gathered behind her, from all of the tittering and gasps and cries of 'Oh my god, she's lost her mind!' but they were the least of her worries. This tank-like woman decided the best strategy was to catch hold of both of Kim's wrists tighter than any set of handcuffs could ever restrain her, and just as she looked set to hurl Kim across the car park, she heard a pair of angry feet thundering down the stairs, accompanied by Barry's voice: 'Bloody hell Linda, let her go! She has a point and I for one would pay good money to see her tear strips of that lad upstairs. You'd better send her in before the bloodhounds sniff out this front page scoop and we're all out of a job. Jesus, where's my sodding blood pressure pills?'

Released from Linda's vice-like grip, Kim was off the starter's blocks then, tearing past Barry to pelt up the stairs. Very kindly, one of the staff had labelled the dressing room doors so she knew exactly where to find *him*. Thankfully the door was unlocked as Kim exploded through it and came almost face to face with an ashen faced, dishevelled and bleary-eyed Ritchie who looked far from his usual sparkly, perfect self.

'YOU DIRTY BASTARD!' she roared, wellying the nearest item she could grab hold of at him – luckily for his sake it was a flimsy notepad and not a glass ashtray or full tin of hairspray. He still retreated to the other side of the room, eyes wide, hands attempting to rake through the lacquered prickly points of his hair. Nervous, rattled, frightened...what a frigging chicken. If there'd been an unlocked window to climb out of, he'd have been gone like a shot. Coward.

'How could you?' she sobbed, blinded by steaming hot tears. 'How could you let me think that you were mine, when all the time you had a wife in the wings, waiting for you to come home? Did I mean nothing to you? All this time – all these years – you've been stringing me along...'

'Oh come on darling, we had fun – it was good while it lasted. It was never meant to be anything serious...and I never really lied to you...'

'NEVER REALLY LIED TO ME?' She was incredulous. What planet did this man originate from?

'Because I didn't suspect that you had a little wifey tucked away and didn't ask, you weren't obliged to tell me about *Michelle*, were you not? That constitutes telling the truth in your books, does it?'

'Look Kim, we had a good run, but it's come to an end now, no harm done.'

'No harm done? You've repeatedly cheated on your wife, abused her trust and made her look a fool! And what about the damage you've done to *me*? I loved you Ritchie, I truly loved you and you're the only man I've ever said that to…'

'You loved the idea of copping off with a famous pop star Kimberley – they all do, in the end. It's dream-come-true territory. It's…'

'*THEY* ALL DO! Who the bloody hell are *they*? Is this your way of telling me that there are many more women like me dotted around the globe, nursing their broken hearts tonight after finding out their man already belonged to someone else?'

'I'm not *their* man…or *your* man…I'm fucking sick of being labelled this and that – as if I'm not an actual person in my own right!'

'No Ritchie…you're not *my* man – I was duped. Because all along you belonged to *Michelle* – you were *her* man.'

'Listen Kim, I don't belong to anybody. No one person is anyone else's to own, like they're a piece of property…'

'FUCK OFF, you deluded little arsehole! You have a certificate that binds you to someone else – it's what being married is all about! This isn't about you and your needs, you egotistical, lying prick. It's about the other people you've hurt, the damage you've caused, the lies you've told that have literally ripped me apart. Because you see, no matter what anyone else said about you – no matter how many times I was warned off or was told I deserved better – I believed you Ritchie…I believed in us…'

'There was no US Kimberley – let me state that loud and clear.'

How could he be so cold and cruel? This stranger, stood before her – albeit at a safe distance – breaking her spirit, shattering her world. The very man she'd trusted and depended on, despite all the damning articles and murky rumours. The man she'd anticipated spending the rest of her life with…and he thought it perfectly acceptable to treat her like scum.

The big, hiccupping sobs that escaped from Kim's mouth took even her by surprise and she felt the pain slice through her body like a machete through butter.

It was the first time since she'd burst in that she actually saw a glimpse of humanity within Ritchie when he fell silent and had the decency to look guilty. His features softened and she registered the pity in his eyes, but she didn't want pity. She wanted to be able to turn back that clock to a time when she was clueless and believed every lying word that tripped off the tongue of this unscrupulous unsavoury man.

Tentatively he moved forward, into her space, crouching down to look up at her from under thick black lashes, the familiar twinkle almost back in those exotic green eyes.

'Look Kim. It's not ideal, but when all of this has calmed down and the world's press isn't watching, maybe we can hook up again...you know, have a little more fun together?'

Kim tried to prevent a strangled sob escaping from her throat, as her cheeks burned and her hands curled into tight little fists at her side. She struggled to maintain her composure in the face of such audacious arrogance. Such insular selfishness.

'You fucking what?'

The realisation that he'd badly misjudged the situation, with the vile words he'd uttered to fill the awkward gap, quickly dawned upon his face...about three seconds before Kim hurled herself at him and started throwing punches, determined he would feel the full force of her anger and a little of the unnecessary pain he had no qualms about inflicting.

He quickly caught hold of both of her wrists with shouts of 'STOP IT, YOU MAD BITCH!' and 'FOR CHRIST'S SAKE, GET A BLOODY GRIP!' She aimed her knees at his groin instead, still trying to cause him actual bodily harm, even whilst under restraint, all the while screaming like a banshee.

It felt like a long time, but it was probably less than a minute before she was gently but firmly removed from Ritchie's grip and pulled into another man's arms. Marty patted her back as he rocked her, his voice soothing, his manner calming.

'Ssshh now Kimberley...it's going to be okay. Ssshh now, it's alright.'

Eventually the sobbing subsided and she raised her head to meet Ritchie's glacial stare. He was looking at her like she was the problem here - as if she was the one who'd done wrong.

'I loved you,' she repeated, quieter now but no less passionate. 'Every bit of me loved all of you. And I waited for you. All those wasted years. You promised me we'd be together once this tour was over; you told me there'd be nothing standing in our way. All lies. All fucking lies.'

He had the grace to look marginally ashamed again but said nothing, not even pathetic, meaningless words of apology.

'Just answer me this, Ritchie. Why did it take so long to bed me if all you wanted was a bit of extracurricular fun? We were both consenting adults…so why wait?'

A pause. A clear of the throat. His eyes darted across to Todd, who'd quietly entered the room and was stood with his arms folded across his chest, eyeballing Ritchie, a look of pure unmasked hatred on his youthful, once-innocent face.

'I tried to resist you Kimberley, but I couldn't – and that's the top and bottom of it. I honestly tried to do the right thing and leave you untouched but you were persistent, I'll give you that. No matter how often I blanked you or attempted to walk away from the situation, you never gave up…until you finally wore me down and I gave you what you wanted.'

Even above the ringing in her ears, she heard Marty's sharp intake of breath and Todd's snarl of '*You fucking wanker*' before he flew at Ritchie, although Marty was quick to intervene, hastily pulling the two men apart before real violence erupted in the room. Ritchie lost his balance and, unfortunately for him, staggered into Kim's pathway, just as she began to retch. Marty hastily handed her the waste paper bin but he was a second too late and projectile vomit sprayed all over Ritchie's designer jeans and top brand trainers.

'For fuck's sake, you stupid bint! What is wrong with you?'
'BAARRRY…BAAAARRRRYYYY…' he shouted for their esteemed manager as if this older, experienced, formidable guy who had more than earned his stripes, was only a minion expected to do his bidding and be at his beck and call. He clearly had no respect whatsoever for the man who'd kept them all in line and worked his nuts off for them while they'd reaped all the rewards.

A damp flannel was produced from somewhere and Todd carefully wiped Kim's brow and around her mouth, all the while insisting that she shouldn't worry, they would sort the mess out. Barry's voice then: 'What in god's name is going on here? Fuck's sake – let me find someone who can clean this up.'

'Get her out of here Baz.' Ritchie's words were venomous and cutting and he was glaring at her now, as if she was dirt, as he attempted to scrub his jeans and de-sick his shoes with a packet of wipes he'd found on the window ledge. He seemed far more concerned about his precious designer gear being ruined than breaking Kim's heart.

No love in his voice or in his manner - not even *like*. Just disgust and then dismissal.

When Barry was sure there were no visible signs of any vomit on Kim's face or clothes, he took hold of her arm and steered her towards the door. She was too weak to resist but made the mistake of taking one last look back at Ritchie and wished she hadn't.

Those beautiful eyes were narrowed and he resembled a sly, sleek feline, spitting and showing her his claws - letting her know *exactly* who held all the power.

A calculating, cold creature who was now maintaining his distance and warning her to stay the hell away from him.

It was over.

They were done.

PART THREE

FOE

(1995)

Chapter 24

Once they were away from the dressing rooms and out of earshot of Ritchie, Kim saw a very different side to Barry. The brisk, rude, obnoxious Barry was temporarily replaced by a kinder man, who surprised her with his words.

'I'm sorry love, I really am. You know, those five boys back there are like sons to me. I've no children of my own – never wanted any and sure as hell wouldn't have had the time – but those lads...well, I've history with them, wiping their arses and trying to keep them out of the shit since the early days. I think the world of them. They're good lads on the whole and I've always been proud of them all, even Bren, who has the most generous heart inside that broken body, but right now, I'm ashamed of Ritchie. Addictions, stalkers, prostitutes, behind the scenes battles and egos – they've all given me headaches and high blood pressure over the years, but it's what I'm paid for and I can deal with everything, no sweat. And I'll fight anyone who wants to take a cheap pop at one of my boys. But how Ritchie's treated you – it's immoral and abysmal and I *told* him he had to do the right thing. He knows all too well what the other four think of him too and that they've all, at one time or another, threatened to walk, because of him. Please don't think he wasn't warned. He was ordered to nip it in the bud on multiple occasions but, in true Ritchie fashion, he took it to another level instead, and to hell with the consequences.'

Barry's compassion, on top of everything else, was hard to take. She needed to make her escape and fill her lungs with cool, fresh air.

'You go now, love. Get yourself a drink and pull yourself together. It pains me to say it, but you deserve better than Ritchie Joe Clarke, the black sheep of our dysfunctional *Show Me Yours* family. Stay away from him now and don't ever give him the opportunity to hurt you again. I'll see you out Kim - mind how you go.'

She tried to thank him but couldn't speak; the words were lost somewhere in the tormented sobs clogging up her throat.

There was an audience to greet her outside. It appeared that the noisy disturbance had attracted every fan in the vicinity and every passer-by in the street, but she kept her head bowed, fleeing out of the car park and into the nearest pub. No amount of cold water splashed on her face or layers of make-up haphazardly applied in the toilets could disguise her swollen eyes or even out her blotchy skin tone, but the large glass of Cognac – not usually her alcoholic beverage of choice, but her mum always swore by it in times of crisis – helped to steady her nerves, as she tried to hide herself away in a dark corner of the bar area.

'Kim?' She looked up to see Hannah and Geraldine draped over the table, concern etched on Hannah's kindly face, a dark scowl making Geraldine's features look even more menacing than usual. Hannah's little girl, Elizabeth, was going from table to table, collecting beer mats and singing to herself. Oh, to be that innocent again and so easily pleased!

'We're so sorry Kim. You must be devastated. We honestly don't need to know all of the gory details but wanted to see if we could help in any way. Is there anything we can do?' Hannah gently covered Kim's hand with hers in a motherly way. Christ, how she needed her own mum right now.

'We can shout abuse at Ritchie during the show if you like or trip him up in the car park afterwards?' Geraldine bobbed her head up and down vigorously as she spoke. Kim had no doubt she actually meant it and was touched that this weird but well-meaning woman was prepared to face-plant Ritchie in retribution for the pain he had caused.

'Thanks for the offer Gerry. It's tempting but I wouldn't want anyone ejected from the theatre or arrested on my account.' She tried to smile, to express her gratitude, but immediately felt the need to cry again.

'I had no idea! How could I have been so stupid?'

'Nobody knew, sweetheart,' Hannah assured her, swiftly producing a pocket-sized packet of tissues to wipe away the tears. 'You weren't stupid – you're anything but. As much as we love Ritchie, he had no right to treat you like that. You deserved the truth, to enable you to make an informed choice rather than be a victim of his deception.'

'I'd have stayed well away if I'd known he was married, I swear. Okay, I may have flirted like my life depended on it…perhaps even sneaked a few cheeky cuddles and a peck on the lips. And obviously I'd have been flattered by the attention, but there's no way in hell it would have led to anything else. His poor wife – I feel like such a bitch. A foolish, gullible, easy bitch.'

From Geraldine's blank expression, it quickly became apparent that she had no experience to draw on with the opposite sex (or same sex) and she wouldn't have known what flirting was if it had jumped up and slapped her across the face. Hannah was sweet but her world was centred around her young daughter and she had been single for as long as Kim had known her. How could they ever understand what Kim was going through?

They tried to persuade Kim to eat with them but the notion of any kind of food entering her mouth turned the inside of her stomach to porridge again. She did, however, promise to meet them outside of the theatre pre-show, so she wouldn't have to take that walk of shame, down the aisle to her seat on the front row, all by herself.

Eventually they left to take the little one to the park and the other punters in the pub gave Kim a wide berth, presumably because they thought she was a total lunatic, sobbing into her glass, swearing like a Sex Pistol and rocking in her seat. She longed to be anywhere but in this depressing, jaded seaside resort on a Sunday evening but even so, she still couldn't bear to head home and allow her tickets to go to waste. She may no longer be welcome backstage but still felt the urge to be out front when the band took to the stage. She loved the music and she loved every single member of the band. The prospect of walking away from this life, and even Ritchie – *especially* Ritchie – was simply too painful to contemplate.

Geraldine and Hannah were seated at the opposite end of the front row and Kim found herself squashed between Sally-Anne and the loudest man on the planet who managed to spill his drink on her twice, nudge her in the ribs three times and sneeze over her coat only once, but once was enough. Apart from an initial cursory nod, Sally-Anne didn't bother to acknowledge her presence, let alone enquire after her welfare. She purposely turned her back on Kim and proceeded to lean over to whisper conspiratorially to her new friends, in an obvious move to exclude Kim from their exclusive club. Fine. She didn't want to be a member anyway.

The moment the house lights dimmed, Barry took to the microphone to introduce his 'sons' and the first chord was struck, Kim felt the sweat begin to trickle down from her armpits and a feeling of pure panic set in. A tightening of the chest, constriction of the throat and a heart that raced and thudded, threatening to burst out of her body right in front of Ritchie, as if to show him: 'Look. Look at what you've done.'

Ritchie shamelessly managed to avoid all eye contact with her throughout the entirety of the show, whilst winking and smiling at everyone around her. Kim could have stripped off naked or screamed she had a gun and wasn't afraid to use it and he still wouldn't have glanced her way or displayed any form of genuine emotion on that smiling, crowd-pleasing, fake-ass face of his. His eyes gave him away though. Of course there was no trace of any guilt or regret in those iridescent pools of green, but they looked heavier than usual and there was definitely dark shadowing underneath them, partially disguised by layers of thick stage make-up. He looked tired and stressed and that in turn took its toll on his performance. He never usually put a foot wrong or sang a note out of tune but more than once he danced to the right when he should have danced to the left and one melancholy album track was sang in completely the wrong key.

Kim thought that she would throw up again if he eyeballed anyone else when it came to singing *Falling*. But she needn't have worried - it had been cut from the set. Despite being a firm fan favourite, it had been wiped from the show, as Ritchie was attempting to wipe Kim clean out of his life.

It was undoubtedly a blessing in disguise, although it practically killed her. He would, almost certainly, have ignored her again throughout, and probably always would now. The alternative was even worse. He may have serenaded another girl during *their song*; picked out another fan who was either completely irrelevant to him and presented no threat to his marriage, or someone he was lining up to be his next secret lover.

In the scheme of things, to an outsider, the missing song would seem like something and nothing.

But to her it was everything.

She'd had so very little of him to lose that it felt like the cruellest, most unimaginable loss of all.

Kim cried again, silently, and no one noticed.

She sat firm in her seat for the remainder of the show. She didn't belong down at the stage, enjoying the party with the other fans – she no longer knew where her place was.

What she should have done after the show was leave immediately and put as much distance between herself and Ritchie as was geographically possible. What she actually did was summon up all the energy she could and headed round to the rear of the theatre to join the small crowd that had gathered there.

But she stood alone, on the periphery, looking on.

Geraldine beckoned her over but Kim pretended not to notice. As much as she appreciated the kind gesture, she didn't want sympathy from a virtual stranger. Sally-Anne was hanging about with her newly formed clique but Kim decided to approach her, in the hope she would demonstrate a degree of solidarity, but she merely scowled, stepped away and continued to gossip with her new friends, who cast vicious looks in Kim's direction, making her want to shrivel up and hide away. Clearly Kim was a leper now as far as they were concerned - trouble with a capital 'T'. Sally-Anne was not prepared to show her any compassion or loyalty and their longstanding 'friendship' had clearly been a sham. They were all effectively chucking her under a bus. No way could they hang around with someone who Ritchie would be avoiding like the plague. No matter what he'd done, he was still their crush, their hero, their fantasy figure, who could do no wrong – and she guessed that they would all be vying to take her place once the dust had settled.

It wasn't long before the band exited the theatre, but it felt like forever.

Marty was keen to get away, politely but firmly declining all requests for photographs and autographs, but surprisingly, he did make a beeline for Kim.

'You okay?' he whispered, his concerned eyes scanning her face, no doubt taking in the dishevelled hair and tear-stained cheeks. His strong, caring hand rested on her shoulder, as she replied with a barely perceptible nod – unable to speak for fear of disintegrating before him.

'Do you still intend coming to tomorrow's gig?'

A nod again – *please don't make me speak Marty.*

'Do you have somewhere to stay tonight? Yes? Good. And then what? Have you booked accommodation for tomorrow?'

No – god no. She'd not even considered it. The rail travel was organised but she'd been dealing with her sleeping arrangements on a very much day-to-day basis, always clinging to the hope that Ritchie might surprise her with a room for the two of them somewhere special.

She shook her head, searching for words. 'I don't have plans. My mind won't work – it's all fog. I don't know what I'm going to do...'

'Then might I suggest that you go home, Kim. Go – be with your family. Create some space between him and you. Try and rest tonight, if you can, but tomorrow take yourself as far away as possible from all of this madness...'

He reached into the pocket of his jeans, removed a folded up envelope and pressed it into her hand, curling her fingers over the white paper and its contents.

'Take this Kim. It's not much but none of us really carry any cash these days – and Bren doesn't actually have any – but we all chipped in with what was lurking in our pockets. Use it to buy a decent meal or a coach ticket home. Don't let him win sweetheart. There will be other greater love in your life and a time when you will forget all of this pain.' Marty leant over and she felt his lips graze her cheek in a gentlemanly fashion, kindness running through his veins. If she hadn't been so despondent she might have revelled in the moment when she received his barely-there kiss (something never before bestowed on any other fan).

'Take care,' he whispered and then he was gone, a handful of fans hot on his heels. Inside the envelope she discovered a twenty pound note, a ten pound note and two crumpled up fivers, along with a selection of pound coins and fifty pence pieces.

His kindness and generosity almost choked her and she quickly stashed away the money in the side pocket of her shoulder bag, wiped her blurry eyes with the sleeve of her jacket and raised her palm in a goodbye gesture as the boys boarded the minibus. Ritchie was positioned between Barry and Ady, hiding away – like the chicken-shit he was – and he never glanced up, not even once. Todd was barely on board before the door clunked shut, the horn sounded and they were off.

As the vehicle passed her by, she willed Ritchie to turn his head to the window, to exhibit a morsel of remorse, but he didn't have it in him – that much was clear. His face was set hard, his chiselled jaw rigid and his eyes stony as he stared straight ahead.

Cheers Ritchie. Thanks for breaking my heart and ruining my life.

*

She'd returned to the hotel, to endure a hot, tetchy night tossing and turning, tears gushing, grief screaming out of her body. By the time the sun came up, she was quiet and still. She had nothing left to give but the sorrow was swelling and spreading around inside of her like a cancer, eating away at her until all her strength and spirit was diminished.

On auto pilot, Kim listlessly gathered up her belongings and checked out. Somehow she managed the walk to the railway station and to board a train because suddenly she was on her way to Birmingham, making her way to the next gig. She simply didn't know what else to do. Thankfully, there was no sign of Sally-Anne throughout her journey – she'd had her fill of this two-faced cow's sarcasm and vitriol.

A daily newspaper had been abandoned on the seat by its previous occupant and Kim's heart sank when she saw its big scoop was actually a continuation of the story about Ritchie and his 'stunning wife'. Feeling like the pain might just slay her, Kim still turned to the inside pages and read on, about this 'adoring' couple's deeply private lifestyle away from the world of *Show Me Yours*. How they'd bought and tastefully renovated the seven bedroomed house with its own swimming pool and stables (she was a keen rider – as was he, but not in the traditional sense). He'd continue to stay with his parents on a regular basis to fool the press, while Michelle was stashed away in their multi-million pound luxury pad with its mile long approach, sweeping driveway and naturally afforded privacy, secreted away behind dense woodland - and apparently you would never find it unless you knew it was there.

As the train whizzed through the green and pleasant countryside, Kim wondered if she was anywhere close to where Ritchie and Michelle had put down roots. It was laughable really – those times when he'd mentioned 'problems' back home and she'd presumed he'd meant at the modest detached house his parents owned in a quiet suburb of Birmingham. Oh god yes, there'd no doubt been problems at home – probably when Michelle uncovered evidence of the latest floozy he'd picked up when he was touring Europe or when she suspected he was screwing around on home turf. Bastard.

On arrival at her destination, Kim was directed to a cluster of guesthouses and tourist accommodation, eventually stumbling across a stylish boutique hotel which was surprisingly competitively priced. She checked in, deposited her bag and immediately made her way outside again without showering or even applying a fresh face of make-up. What was the point in titivating herself up or looking her best? Who would actually care?

Shops, bars, restaurants – she passed them all on her way to the theatre but hadn't the heart or the money to eat, drink or make purchases. She kept on plodding even though she knew in both her head and her heart that the last place she should be was in that toxic environment, amidst all the bitching and backstabbing, surrounded by complete strangers and the worst kind of enemies - those 'friends' who she had naively trusted but who had ultimately betrayed her.

But still, she walked on…and on…until she turned a corner and caught her first glimpse of the theatre over the road. Kim stopped, abruptly. An invisible wall had been constructed.

Her mouth was dry but her hands were clammy. There was a loud ringing in her ears which seemed to dim her other senses, her blurry eyes struggling to focus.

You'll be okay. You're a survivor. If she kept repeating that mantra then surely it would be true.

She could do this.

And then her heart began to gallop in her chest and any breath she was about to expel was violently sucked back into her body. The panic within her rose up and it took all her efforts not to scream blue murder, right there, right then.

She couldn't do this.

Abandoning all her best intentions, she took to her heels and ran, as fast as she could.

Back round the corner, back down the street...running, running, running...until her breath came in short, sharp rasps and she could run no more for fear of pegging out on the pavement.

When the heavens decided to open, she took sanctuary in a phone box, the usual rank smell of piss pervading her nostrils and threatening to permeate her damp clothing. A sudden desperate need to talk to home, she fumbled around in her bag, dug out a selection of sticky silver coins and slotted them in to the box, urgently hammering out the old familiar number, waiting to hear the tone which would signal she was connected.

Come on, come on! Please don't be gassing with Mrs Henratty next door or drinking tea out on the patio, taking a breather between the washing up and the ironing.

'Hello?' Oh thank god, someone had picked up, but it was Freddie. What was he doing there? He was living in sin with Rochelle now – at her parents' place in the granny flat that

220

had been recently vacated by granny, who'd shuffled off to Northwich to shack up with an old boy she'd met at bingo.

'Freddie! Is mum there? – I need to speak to her urgently...please tell her to come to the phone...'

'She's not here. You can't speak to her.'

He sounded snappy and irritated, but then he always seemed to be on a short fuse – although maybe that was only with her.

'Oh god, put dad on then please...but hurry up Freddie...'

'He's not here either. For Christ's sake, Kim...it's their silver wedding anniversary trip – remember? Not that *you'd* be interested...'

Of course. They were away for a long weekend, booked months ago – three days at a five star hotel in Morecambe, the seaside resort where they'd honeymooned on the cheap all those years ago. Returning to the scene of the crime. Mum had talked of nothing else for the last few weeks and yet it had completely slipped Kim's mind.

'Look,' Freddie barked, impatient as hell. 'I've only nipped in to check the house and pick up those jeans mum was altering for me. Was there something you wanted? I take it you *do* want something – because you never ring when you're off being a groupie...'

'I...I...I just needed mum...I mean I really wanted to...'

''Fucks sake Kim, spit it out! I've not got all bloody day.'

'I wanted my mum or my dad...' Kim whispered, tears plopping onto the collar of her black chiffon blouse, as she wrapped the telephone cord round and around her finger, so tight it was in danger of cutting off the circulation.

'Yeh well, tough shit. It's a bit too late to start playing the devoted daughter. Hopefully, they'll be taking a stroll down the prom now or tucking into a nice mixed grill. Speaking of grub, I'm starving and we're supposing to be calling at the chippy on the way back so...'

Pip. Pip. Pip. The high-pitched tone in her ear warned of imminent disconnection if she didn't pop more coins into the telephone slot, but she had none immediately to hand.

No more money. But then again, no more words.

Before Freddie had the chance to say anything else, the line was dead and he was gone.

Right. Well that was that then. No comforting words from a parent to assure her everything was going to be okay and that she wouldn't be a laughing stock. No stern but loving advice from her mum, reminding her that the relationship with Ritchie had been a noxious and tenuous one that she should've binned years ago. No huffing and puffing from dad and an angry threat that he would punch Ritchie's lights out after giving him a piece of his mind.

Okaaaay.

With a heavy heart, Kim exited the phone box – to the relief of a scrawny looking woman who was hopping up and down, from one leg to the other, either desperate to make a call in there or about to use it as a toilet as had many more before her. Kim retraced her steps, albeit at a much slower pace.

Her hotel was a long way off and she was still unable to muster up the courage to venture anywhere near the theatre so she dragged her feet into the nearest pub, where she nursed half a lager for several hours, earning daggers from the middle-aged barman who clearly wanted her out of there, staining the atmosphere – of which there was little.

She eventually moved to another pub, where she didn't even buy a drink, but was left well alone in a dark corner, the young bar staff clearly unconcerned, so long as she didn't decide to cause them any problems.

Lord knows how many hours passed but only when she felt sure the band had definitely arrived and the fans dispersed from around the stage door, did she dare step outside again and slowly return to the theatre. She was shocked to see from a cursory glance at her watch that it was shortly after seven o'clock which meant any familiar bodies would be securely inside and it was safe for her to approach.

The light had eventually faded, the temperature had dropped considerably but she was in no hurry to shift indoors. What was a little bit of cold when you were dead inside anyway?

Support act finished, interval over, the main event was just beginning when she finally entered the auditorium, the familiar drum beats pounding in her chest. As per usual, the hardcore fans down near the stage were screaming and cheering, but instead of creeping down the aisle to take her place on the front row of the stalls, she slipped in to one of the empty rows at the rear to take in the show, although most of it passed in a blur.

It was safe to say, her participation days were well and truly over and whilst she adored the four good men playing alongside him and would always appreciate the hands of friendship that they had proffered, Ritchie was a stranger to her now – a lying, cheating, dirty stranger. It was unfortunate that she still loved him.

When the usual fans rushed the stage towards the end of the show, Kim was forced to witness Ritchie thrusting and gyrating in front of an over-excited, screeching Keeley, who almost dissolved when he brushed her hair with the tips of his fingers. Those fingers that had done unspeakable things to Kim. Those fingers that had stroked, prodded and pinched her…

That touch she would never know again.

The bile began to rise in Kim's throat. She knew she really did have to escape this time.

She actually *couldn't* do this anymore.

The cold air slapped her around the face as she exited the theatre and Kim felt like she was seconds away from slumping to the wet ground in a big, shaky, hysterical heap. She wanted the tears to stop pumping, she really did, but they were relentless, and it was all she could do to lower herself down on to the damp step and not howl like a wolf.

'*KIM! KIMBERLEEEEE..*'

What was she going to do? She longed to go home but was trapped within the confines of this bloody city – where Ritchie had been born and bred and grown up to believe that he could treat women like whores. Her belongings were back in her hotel and her rail travel was booked but only for a train due to depart the following day, and that would only take her as far as Gloucester the next day in any event. Not home. What a mess. She so badly wanted out of all of this and yet it was hopeless.

'*KIMBERLEY SUMMERS…KIMBERLEEEE…*'

She was sure she could hear her name being carried along on the breeze but was so screwed up and confused, it could possibly have been a figment of her imagination.

Her arms folded across her chest, she rested her throbbing forehead on them and tried to shut out the world, as she continued to weep and disintegrate in the cool evening air.

A pair of hands firmly removed her own from her head and then clasped them tightly. Blinking away the latest torrent of tears she noticed a pair of dainty feet clad in sparkly black pumps on the step below and as she slowly lifted her head, she was astonished to see Rochelle crouched down before her, kind eyes reassuring that she was here now - someone had arrived to take care of her.

'Where have...how come...why are you here...?' Kim was bewildered – grateful, but bewildered.

Rochelle smiled in response and gently pulled Kim up on to her feet. Her soft hands closed around Kim's tear-streaked face and the warmth of her touch radiated through.

'Come on Kim. We're taking you home darling. Let's get you in the car.'

Too weak to protest and so relieved to be rescued from this monumental mess of her own making, she allowed herself to be led and guided by Rochelle, as she steered her round chattering groups of people congregated on the pavement, ensuring she wasn't knocked down whilst crossing the busy main road.

'Here we are,' soothed Rochelle, opening the rear door to Freddie's clapped-out Escort, bundling Kim in and making sure she wasn't about to leap out of the other door and straight into the oncoming traffic.

Freddie turned around as Kim sank into something squidgy and familiar on the back seat - her duvet and pillow. Wow...Rochelle was a real life saint.

The tears bucketed down again as the enormity of walking away from this life, and the idol who'd captured her heart, well and truly sank in.

'Sorry Freddie,' Kim sobbed, apologising for so much more than simply dragging him down the motorway when he had to be up at six a.m. for work. She was apologising for the shoddy way she'd treated him and the rest of her family - and for not listening to a single one of them when they'd all tried to warn her off Ritchie, encouraging her to find love and happiness elsewhere. It was also an apology for what was to come - because although she may have been fleeing from this theatre on this night and waving goodbye to her fandom life together with all her hopes and dreams of living happily ever after with Ritchie, she was still consumed with her love for him and likely to be in a pretty battered state for the foreseeable future.

'You dickhead,' Freddie muttered, but there was a hint of kindness in his eyes, which made Kim realise quite how fucked up she really was. If Freddie was showing her sympathy and compassion then she really was in trouble.

'I'm so sorry,' she repeated, 'but thank you for coming and rescuing me when my world collapsed and I had no one else to turn to.'

'Don't thank me, thank Rochelle. When I said you'd called but I'd got rid of you quick-smart she wiped the bloody floor with me – said there'd been an exclusive story in one of the papers about that twat of a singer you'd been seeing who apparently had a wife stashed away that no sod ever knew about! Gave me a right bollocking she did and said we couldn't just leave you in shit-state in a strange city. Insisted you needed to come home...'

'Well, those *were* my words but as soon as I mentioned that bastard had a wife, it was Freddie who did the whole 'No fucker hurts my sister' performance, snatching his car keys and his coat while I fetched your duvet and pillow. In fact, you should curl up and rest now Kim. You look exhausted.' Rochelle affectionately squeezed Freddie's thigh as she spoke and Kim was grateful in that instance that a lad as gawky and daft as her brother had found someone as level-headed and wonderful as this girl.

'Anyway, luckily you'd jotted down part of your itinerary,' Rochelle continued. 'But we only had destinations and theatres to go off. We were just keeping our fingers crossed that we'd make it before the end of the gig and that you would still be here. To be honest, it's been a pig of a journey, but it could have been a heck of a lot worse had you been at the other end of the country.'

'Thank you for coming. When the truth was outed and I looked into Ritchie's lying eyes and knew I'd been had, I wanted to run. I love him so much, Rochelle but he didn't love me at all. I was nothing to him...just another girl who'd fallen under his spell...'

'Sssh darling...there'll be plenty of time to talk later. The important thing is you're safe and you're going home. Try and sleep a little now.'

They were almost out of town when they remembered that Kim's unpacked bag was still in her hotel room. Freddie swore and performed a u-turn, following Kim's vague directions to the modern building on the leafy little back street, where Rochelle went in to see the landlady. Thankfully, the slightly suspicious individual eventually agreed to hand over Kim's belongings on payment for the room and they were all mightily relieved when they were able to drive away and Freddie could slot back into the line of traffic heading out of town. Unfortunately, this journey involved passing by the theatre again and Kim couldn't stop herself - she had to look. Compelled to take one last glance at the building where Ritchie was probably at that moment, even in his more subdued, anxious state, lapping up the attention from the girlies at the stage door, his shirt unbuttoned to the waist, his radar switched on - ever-ready to catch the eye of a pretty girl.

It hurt that she probably wouldn't ever see the band again. The four other guys were hugely talented musicians but also decent, caring people and she'd miss them forever. Even Bren. Above all else, it was the knowledge that this was the closest she'd ever be again to the man she loved so furiously, so unwaveringly, that it gripped her heart and tortured her soul.

She couldn't live without him. She didn't *want* to live without him.

Chapter 25

Grief. It was killing her. She was mourning for something that was dead and buried – her running joke of a relationship with Ritchie. For Kim it had been alive and real and something to build on whereas for Ritchie it had been nothing concrete – merely something he had been willing to cut the legs off the minute the heat was on him.

Her parents had returned to find Freddie and Rochelle having temporarily taken up residence, watching Kim like a hawk, discreetly ensuring there were never any sharp objects left around and rationing headache pills.

Her mum and dad hadn't seen the papers while they'd been away, completely oblivious to the storm that had wrecked Kim's world. They were naturally furious and her mum cradled her daughter, matching her tear for tear. Everyone desperately tried to persuade her to eat but for the first time in her life Kim had no appetite. She heard her mum whisper to Rochelle that it was as if Kim had given up on living and Kim conceded that was probably a fair statement. After all, what was left when Ritchie and the band were removed from her life? She had no job, no money, no home of her own, no friends and worst of all, no partner to share the rest of her life with. What was the point in anything anymore?

'Why did he do it?' she'd cried, sobbing in her mum's arms, allowing her tears to soak through the soft fabric of the well-worn blouse.

'Because he could,' her mum had replied, her voice breaking as she witnessed her daughter's agony. 'He had everything already but he still wanted more. Even though he had a happy marriage and the perfect life away from the glare of the media, all of that talent and sack-loads of money, he knew he could have more and he took it, regardless of the damage he would cause.'

'I was so naïve, mum. Such an idiot. He played me well, I'll give him that. I believed his bullshit and despite all the evidence to the contrary, I truly thought we had a future together and that one day we would go public and blissfully settle down as a couple. He was careful though, so careful, because he never said he loved me – not once. Sometimes he acted in a loving way, used words that implied he loved me and made love to me as if I was the most beautiful girl in the world, but he never actually said he loved me.'

Kim's mum openly winced at the notion of a sexual relationship between her daughter and this man she despised. She'd guessed they were sleeping together but it was still difficult for her to hear.

'You're not an idiot Kim – far from it. You're honest and faithful – everything he's not – and you took him at face value. Ritchie Clarke was playing a game but you were genuinely opening up your heart to him, falling victim to all of his flattery and promises. What girl wouldn't when faced with one of the most attractive, supposedly eligible men in the country, showering them with attention and making all their best moves? If it hadn't been you it would have been someone else.'

'I told him I loved him though mum. For goodness sake, who doesn't say it back in the most tender and private of moments? Why didn't he feel guilty about what he was doing?'

'He has no conscience darling - no moral code. You're an attractive girl and he wanted you – that's the bottom line. The streak of decency that runs through other men is missing from this guy. An honest, honourable man would think, 'W*oah...best take a step back. What started as harmless flirting is now getting out of hand - and I'm a happily married man.*' But that particular trait usually found in rounded human beings appears to be absent from Ritchie. He may be beautiful and glossy and charming on the outside but underneath he is mean and sly and very, very ugly.'

'Do you think I meant anything at all to him mum?'

It was a tricky question. Alison had only met him once and her opinion of him had mostly been formed from newspaper articles and the way he had treated her daughter – badly.

'Kim, the honest answer is, I really don't know. You're a gorgeous, bubbly, lovely young woman – at least you *were* bubbly until he drained all of the fizz out of you. It's easy to see how he would have been flattered by your attention and attracted to you but...'

'Because it went on a long time mum and he could have stopped it, if he'd thought I was becoming too clingy or there was a chance he'd be busted. I didn't get it at the time but there *were* occasions when he completely ignored me, probably when he was scared his cover was about to be blown. But still, the affair continued and sometimes I saw a far more sensitive side to him, when he was caring and gentle. What I don't understand is why he carried on seeing me when it would have been easier to cut me loose. And why add the lovey-dovey message for me on the album sleeve, which surely she must have seen? He was taking unnecessary risks.'

'Kim, men like him thrive on risk – it's what drives them. The risk of being caught floods them with adrenaline and they love it. I'm not saying he didn't have any feelings for you, but I think the only person he loves is himself. I can't help but feel sorry for his wife...'

'Don't, mum,' Kim sobbed. 'I'm so ashamed that I did the dirty with someone else's husband. She probably thought he was devoted to her but now she knows he's been unfaithful to her for years. I feel like such a terrible person!'

'Don't be ridiculous darling. How could you have known? Your father and I thoroughly disliked this smarmy show-off and we were sure he was playing around but we never for one moment imagined that he was a married man. Hopefully this wife of his doesn't know anything about you...or any other poor, unfortunate souls he may have strung along...'

'Those women in the papers,' Kim howled, burying her face in the duvet. 'All those reports about the groupies while they were away on tour in Europe. I questioned him and he went nuts – turned it on its head to imply that it was me who had trust issues! I bet he invited the prettiest girl in the audience up to his room every night. Oh god, it's unbearable, the thought of him doing those things to other women...as if the wife isn't bad enough...'

'Well, there is still the possibility that they *were* all just invented by the press or someone who really disliked him, to try and rubbish his character...'

'Knowing what I know now mum, I think it was probably true and he was trying to throw me off the scent with the accusations of mistrust.'

'Bloody cheek of him when he's been putting it about round the bloody world...sorry darling...but it makes my blood boil – knowing what he's put you through.' She paused, to stroke Kim's fuzzy hair, which was in dire need of a wash.

'Kimberley, I have to ask. Were you sensible when, you know, you were with him? You did..ahem...use something?'

Too exhausted to even blush, her desolate daughter nodded miserably. 'He was quite careful about that mum. I was on the pill anyway – sorry, I should have told you – but sometimes he still whipped out a condom, even in the heat of the moment. Bloody hell, he must have kept Durex in business.'

Her mum wasn't too exhausted to blush.

'I'm glad about that Kim – you have enough to contend with, without worrying about babies or STDs and...'

'...and he would definitely have given me a dose if we hadn't practised safe sex, if it's true he's been shagging half of Europe.'

'Ahem...quite. Kimberley...I'm glad we're being straight with each other, me and you, about all of this...but please don't have this kind of discussion with your father or you'll give him a bloody heart attack. He's already on the edge, raging about what he's going to do to this philanderer when he gets his hands on him – I had to take his car keys from him yesterday to stop him from hurtling off to Birmingham with his cricket bat...'

'Just as well. The band were in County Durham last night. It would have been a wasted journey.' She wiped her eyes with the scrunched up corner of her duvet cover and swallowed back another huge lump of grief.

'I love him mum – I still love him. No matter what he's done and what a bastard he is, I just can't switch it off. Don't worry, it's over. I could never turn a blind eye to a wife and he was quite clear that we were finished once I'd vomited on his shoes – but only after he'd suggested we could take up where we left off once all of the fuss had died down...'

'Jesus, the man has no shame.'

'You're right about that. No shame, no heart. But my shattered heart is unfortunately still saturated with feelings for him. And although I hate him for what he's done...I still can't stop loving him.'

A sudden wail of hysteria erupted from inside of her and bellowed out across the room.

'I can't live without him mum! I can't bear the prospect of never seeing him again. I'll never again hear him say my name or kiss me...or feel like the luckiest girl in the world in his arms. I just can't do it. Life isn't worth living without him in it...'

'Don't you say that Kimberley!' her mum replied in her sternest voice, catching hold of Kim's mucky face. 'Don't you ever say that. You think that now, of course you do. But you won't feel like that forever. There will come a time when you'll know you're in a better place and you'll realise what a waste of space he was, with his smooth talking and his fancy pants. He's nothing special really once you remove his flashy popstar mask - just another chancer with a line for everything. A con man who never deserved your love. One day you'll find true love and you'll realise that all of this was merely a practise run for the real thing.'

'How do I live without him though mum? How do I haul myself out of bed each morning knowing all that lies ahead is another day without him in it? How do I sleep at night knowing we'll never be together again? And how do I fill those long hours of nothingness in between, and accept that he never loved me and had always loved another woman? How do I even begin to go on without him?'

Her head hurt. Everything had changed in the space of a couple of a days and her life, as she knew it, was effectively over.

'You'll find a way Kim, and we'll all be here to help. I love you so much my darling girl. I won't let you accept that Ritchie Clarke was the best – because the best is yet to come.'

'Thank you mum – for looking after me and never saying 'I told you so'. We haven't exactly seen eye to eye of late and you could so easily have washed your hands of me after the way I've behaved...'

'You don't have to thank me for goodness sake, you're my baby girl. When you're fifty years old you'll still be my baby girl! We only ever wanted what was best for you. I know you thought we were permanently on your back and that we always had the knives out for Ritchie – but he treated you dreadfully. We genuinely wish he'd proved us wrong, Kim – that he'd spoiled you and demonstrated what spectacular boyfriend material he was. But he couldn't even ring you on your birthday, let alone send a card. There were no Christmas presents or flower deliveries and, worst of all, no demands on your time. We accepted that he had a somewhat unusual job and lifestyle and that he was exceptionally busy and away more than most. But surely that would have warranted two hour phone calls in the middle of the night, or unannounced visits when he unexpectedly had time off or couldn't bear to be apart from you for another minute. We wondered where he was at Christmas – of course he wanted to visit his family but he could have occasionally taken you with him! And he knew very little about you and your background, making no effort to integrate himself with *your* family and friends. It was so upsetting, knowing you were prepared to accept such diabolical treatment - this kind of low level attention. He had the best of both worlds...'

'...and his other world was his life at home with his doting wife. Meanwhile, I sat by the phone willing him to ring and feeling my heart drop to my boots every time he didn't pick up when I called him. I'm so thick, so gullible.'

'No. You're too clever and too honest for him.'

Kim's parents had never once blamed her or said 'I told you so' but she still felt thoroughly ashamed and unworthy of their understanding and forgiveness.

She also agonised over every minute she'd spent with Ritchie during every minute she was attempting to survive without him. Replaying each episode over and over in her head, her cheeks flamed as she recalled how manipulated she'd been - how she'd defended him to everybody else but chosen to silence herself when any issues arose, for fear of his wrath. She remembered all the moments she'd thought were precious – moments which were now tarnished with her newfound knowledge - and cried until her throat was raw and her eyes felt like pin cushions.

Her parents tried to protect her but inevitably there were occasions when they weren't around – like the day she found a pile of her dad's daily papers and her mum's weekly magazines dumped in the bin outside. She dragged them out and tortured herself, reading various articles about Ritchie and Michelle - interviews with them gushing about how their love for each other had weathered all storms, including Ritchie's many infidelities throughout their European tours. When questioned if there'd been any lovers when the band had gigged in the UK, he'd said of course not – the sweaty sex sessions abroad had been opportunistic and meaningless. He would never have risked his marriage by playing away so close to home. When asked if any of his extramarital couplings had honestly ever morphed into a full blown affair, his wife had smugly replied that when he had the finest steak waiting for him at home, why would he ever want to settle for a cheap, greasy burger elsewhere.

Christ. As if she couldn't feel any worse.

The words were painful but the pictures were the hardest to stomach. In one publication, this so-called loving couple had been glammed up for a photo session at home, styled to within an inch of their life. Toasting each other with champagne in their ultra-modern kitchen. Curled up together on an enormous leather settee in front of a log burning fire. Hands and feet entwined as they lay facing each other on a king-sized bed supposedly giggling at some private joke.

The images broke Kim's heart all over again. He knew she would see this. He clearly didn't care.

One newspaper article did almost cheer her up. It featured a picture of Ritchie with a lovely, shiny, whopper of a black eye, complete with a fairly deep cut through his oh-so-perfectly plucked eyebrow. The story was that he'd tumbled down stairs after partying a little too hard with the band but that didn't wash as they were barely on speaking terms even before Michelle had popped out of the closet. Kim refused to believe that they'd suddenly bonded again and hoped that Michelle had actually thumped him good and proper. He was so vain, he'd be gutted about any mark that might possibly tarnish his glossy image.

As the days and nights dragged on Kim felt like she was heading down a dark, dark tunnel with no light at the end of it and no way back. Her future looked bleak and even if she'd actually had a job, how could she have showed up for work in this state? Her outward appearance was bad enough, but inside she was a broken mess, and it wasn't something that could be easily patched up.

It was therefore a relief one evening when her bedroom door slowly creaked opened and Nicky's head bobbed round, her eyes full of sadness and concern. Kim badly needed her friend, who was armed with a huge box of chocolates and a litre of dirt-cheap vodka.

Any animosity between the two girls seemed to vanish in an instant as Nicky raged 'Oh Kim, how could he? The fucking shitty, twatting, lying bastard,' and Kim at last felt that there was someone on her wavelength. Nicky matched her glass for glass and the two girls winced as the lethal liquid burnt a trail through their insides, promising the hangovers from hell,

'I'm so glad to see you,' Kim hiccupped, sloshing vodka all over the carpet. 'I thought I'd lost your friendship forever and you'd never forgive me...'

'Don't be so frigging stupid, Kimmy-Wimmy. I was mad at you – hell, I was incensed with you – but I've loved you like a sister since you stole my best marble at primary school and that will never change. You fucked off to Crazy Town for a while and I couldn't get through to you...but I knew we'd sort it out some day. I only wish it was under better circumstances.'

233

'I can't believe I dipped out on your hen night and being your bridesmaid because of my own selfishness, shutting out everyone besides Ritchie...oh god Ritchie...I miss him so much Nick. He was all I ever wanted, and now I've lost him. Except he wasn't mine to lose...what am I going to do Nicky? I can't survive without him...I just can't...'

'You can and you fucking will, my beautiful, messed up friend. When you're ready – even if that takes a year or ten – you'll bump uglies with someone else. Probably a random guy you meet when you're out on the razz. But eventually you'll find Mr Perfect – The One – and you'll know what true love really is. Let me tell you...my Connor gets right on my nerves sometimes with his natural history programmes and his unnatural need to go out jogging at every available opportunity – I mean, who the fuck actually does that for pleasure? But he's wonderful actually, a real star if I'm honest. And you will find your star one day, little lady. And I'm not talking about a star up on stage – a stupid, tossing, prick of a pop star who pops his little willy out that often I'm only surprised it's not caught a chill yet – I'm talking about a genuine, kind, thoughtful, gorgeous man who WILL move heaven and earth for you but WON'T give you a selection of STDs.'

'Oh Nicky-Nick...you have such a way with words. But I'm disease-free, thank god...and Ritchie's willy was huge and I don't want anyone else's...ever...'

'How do you know?' Nicky demanded, stuffing a praline heart into her mouth. 'You've had no other willies to compare it to, so how do you bloody know? I'm telling you, one day you will be back on the market for willies and you'll wonder why you ever put up with that over-used, worn out husk as long as you did. Fact.'

It was good to see her – so good – and it was the one positive thing to come out of the whole sorry mess. Unsure as to how Nicky could forgive her and why she would even want to, Kim was incredibly grateful that it appeared their friendship could be rekindled, although she didn't doubt it would be a long, slow process to return to where they were, if they ever could.

It transpired that Nicky had called their house every day since she'd heard about Ritchie's double life. One of the girls in the salon had casually gossiped, 'What about that Ritchie Clarke eh? Had a little Trouble-and-Strife hidden away all of this time!' and Nicky had dropped everything she was doing mid-perm and rushed to the telephone to speak to Kim's mum - who'd barely left her daughter's side in her hour of need.

Kim could only wonder at how Nicky managed to crawl out of bed and into work the morning after they demolished the litre of sub-standard vodka. Luckily, she was unlikely to be reprimanded as she now part-owned the successful salon. At least Kim could die slowly under the covers and didn't have anyone on her case. Her parents reckoned it was exactly what was needed, a get-together with Nicky and a chance to be some version of the old Kim again.

Another surprise was a short note through the post from Geraldine. It was brief, gruff, but sweet. She said she hoped Kim was okay and added that everyone missed her - *that* Kim highly doubted, but she appreciated the sentiment. There was no address included for a response, but she gathered Gerry wasn't much of a writer anyway.

Sally-Anne was conspicuous by her silence. Not a phone call, nor letter - nothing. Their friendship appeared to have been purely band related and once Kim's days of pursuing *Show Me Yours!* were over, so apparently was any kind of relationship with Sal. Kim had once thought that they were mates but it had been completely one-sided. She had been useful to Sal on the way up, when everything was rosy and exciting - when her 'thing' with Ritchie was opening doors and allowing them access to a world she was desperate to be part of. Once the plug had been so brutally pulled, Kim was no longer of use to her. Sal had moved on to others who were better connected and she wouldn't risk her place in the order of fans by hanging around with a nobody, especially someone who Ritchie was likely to be avoiding at all cost.

A small part of her had felt sad – they had so much history together. So many shared adventures, up and down the country. They had been exciting times and no one else understood because they weren't there, seeing what they saw, feeling what they felt.

But a much bigger part of her was relieved. Once she'd started to doubt Sally-Anne and realised that she was probably gobbing off about her behind her back, it had soured their friendship and Kim had begun to accept that if they hadn't had *Show Me Yours* in common, they would have never been friends in real life. She certainly wouldn't miss trying to gage Sal's mood, or being sacked off in favour of the Witches or the Irish girlies...or having to endure her acid tongue and endless supply of sarcasm.

There were no good days, but some days were worse than others. Kim would often wake up after a fitful night's sleep and literally squawk all day, crying out for what she'd lost - what she'd never really had. She listened to the band's music non-stop, tearing herself apart with

Ritchie's voice and the lyrics she remembered him singing to her. There were other days when she raged from morning until night, calling Ritchie and his stupid horse-face wife fit to burn, when the rest of the band would come under fire as well, for guarding his secret – even though it wasn't their secret to tell. Kim would shout and scream at the injustice of falling for a singer who moonlighted as a professional liar.

And then there were times when she would simply stare into space, vacant and empty. Times when she truly believed there wasn't the remotest possibility of ever getting over Ritchie.

But it was the people who loved her who kept her going. Her mum using up the rest of her annual leave purely so she could stay at home to nurse her 'sick' daughter. Her dad laying carpets at odd hours so he would be around when his wife wasn't. Nicky singing silly songs down the telephone and visiting every other day, with a constant supply of horror tales from the salon. Even Freddie calling in as he was 'passing by', popping his head around her bedroom door to ask how she was doing. 'Shit' was more often than not her reply, and he would usually enquire if she'd like him to hire a hit man to terminate Mr Clarke.

Kim was miserable as hell but knew she had to make an effort to allow other people to continue with their own lives, so she began to shower and dress each morning and helped her mum out around the house, finding it was easier to keep busy than dwell on what had broken her.

She couldn't envisage that there'd ever be a day when she would be happy again, when the burden of grief would lift and some measure of joy would enter her life. But she was trying.

When Nicky booked her in at the salon, she eventually caved, even though there seemed little point in looking nice when there was no one to appreciate it. Nicky blasted her for that and delivered a lengthy lecture on how she should be doing it for herself, NOT for anyone else. Kim stopped complaining and let herself be pampered.

When her dad insisted they all venture out on a family walk, she refrained from protesting too loud and agreed her muscles needed strengthening and her skin occasionally deserved to see daylight.

And when Rochelle offered to buy her a nice pub lunch, she smiled and said that would be lovely, even forcing herself to eat more than a sparrow's portion. Undiluted misery was definitely the best diet she'd ever been on. She'd hardly been able to face the prospect of food, with the exception of the odd slice of toast or chopped up banana, so she'd lost heaps of weight. Unfortunately, it had sailed past the point of looking good on her, and she knew she now looked haggard and gaunt. So she thanked Rochelle and made a real effort to eat the lasagne, which was thankfully authentic and tasty.

It was all progress. If someone had told her two weeks ago that she would be venturing out in public again, she wouldn't have believed them. She knew the next step would be to find a job, but who would want her working for their company? Lethargic, miserable and tearful – hardly an asset to any future employer.

The most painful hours were at night time, when the house was in silence and everyone was asleep in bed and she was all alone in hers, picturing Ritchie spooning his wife, both of them contented from all the sex and the mutual free-flowing declarations of love. She tortured herself with images of the two of them together, not only doing the x-rated stuff, but the more mundane events like shopping together and sharing a bottle of wine over supper before flomping on the sofa to watch a film or discuss their respective days.

And sometimes she would simply remember – what it felt like to be caressed by Ritchie, to feel his passion and ardour. To be the one he wanted. And she would miss him more than ever and wonder if she would ever feel anything for anyone like that again.

Chapter 26

According to information derived from newspaper gossip columns, the tour had limped on to a quiet, miserable end and the very last show, which was usually full of pranks and high jinks and always very, very loud, was somewhat lacklustre, each band member apparently looking like they were desperate for it all to be over.

It therefore came as no great surprise when the 'former chart-toppers' quietly announced, via their management, that they had mutually agreed to go their separate ways.

No press conference. No **BREAKING NEWS**. No dramatic *SHOW ME YOURS TO SPLIT* headlines emblazoned across the papers. No TV special, documenting their journey.

Despite the fact that Kim had walked away and would probably have never seen them perform live again, it all seemed so impossibly sad – that a band with such passion and promise in the early days, with such an immense amount of talent and brilliance between them, could fade away in such an undignified, pathetic fashion. The below par chart positions and astonishingly poor ticket sales had all pointed in one direction that said THE END but it had never seemed possible...and she wondered how the other devoted fans would cope without them. What else did the likes of Geraldine and Sally-Anne really have in their lives? Somehow she couldn't see the friendship between Sal and the other girls lasting the course once their common ground had been removed.

How was it even possible to return to normality when they and many others like them – and Kim – had lived and breathed those five guys for as long as they could remember?

And what would happen to Bren without the only thing keeping him financially and physically alive? The band was his anchor. Without them to cling to, his purpose, his status and his small income was gone. Kim feared for him, she really did.

However, there wasn't much time to mourn the loss of the band before the next bombshell was dropped and Kim found herself watching Ritchie and his wife, side by side being interviewed on a daytime chat show, supposedly to discuss him embarking on a solo career, exclusively revealing that they had been trying for a baby for the last ten months.

TEN FUCKING MONTHS!

One hysterical phone call to Nicky at her workplace and her friend and confidant was around like a flash as soon as she'd finished her last cut and colour for the day, armed with two bottles of wine and a family sized bag of crisps.

'That fucking fucker!' she raged, kicking off her shoes as she stormed into the bedroom. 'How was he ever likely to get his Mrs up the duff by poking you? God help any child with him as the father – a few crappy nappies and he'll be dipping his wick elsewhere again, you can bet!'

'I wish I was having his baby.' There it was, out in the open - the new thought that kept popping in and out of her head. 'Then I'd have a part of him for always...something SHE could never have. He'd be tied to me forever instead of being able to forget me – the desperate little groupie he used and abused whenever the urge took him...'

'Oh yeah, and knowing him, he'd firstly deny he was the father, then insist on a DNA test...and then he'd still refuse to see the child or accept him as his spawn...and you'd end up fighting him through the courts to try and recover maintenance while he quietly emptied bank accounts and declared himself penniless. And then you'd be left barely surviving hand to mouth with a screaming baby dangling off your hip while he'd be off living the life of riley...'

'Oh Nicky, I know. Deep down in my heart I know that's exactly how it would be…but it doesn't stop me...'

'...and just when you're at your most weak and vulnerable – when you've no job, no money and no proper home to call your own, all responsibility for this baby ultimately resting with you, as the only real parent this child would ever have - when you've hardly slept for about two weeks solid because baby is teething or puking all night, you'd open the door one morning to a load of paps on your doorstep and find all the mucky details of your sex life plastered across the papers. And cute little Ritchie would come up smelling of roses like he always does while you're branded some dirty little money-grabbing slapper and your dad's arrested for murdering Ritchie with his own bare hands...'

'Okay...I get it, I get it...please…no more!' Nicky always kept it real and brought her to her senses – zero bullshit whilst still managing to remain compassionate, loyal and funny as hell. God, Kim had missed her.

It was so incredibly painful though to see Ritchie and this woman as a real life couple, smiling at each other and touching each other with agonising familiarity. To think they had been together all the time he had been getting it on with Kim. The bare facts made her want to weep until she passed out.

The wife was quite attractive, Kim later conceded. With her high cheekbones and pouty lips, she was certainly striking. But her horsey face and ridiculously long mane of hair meant she didn't look too dissimilar to the poor creatures she cantered around on, Kim thought bitchily, glad there were elements to criticise. And she had seriously dark roots and spindly arms too.

She also looked the hard, steely, no-nonsense sort. Kim was glad that *she* was much softer round the edges. Mind you, Michelle had probably learned to be tough to handle Ritchie and his escapades. He had been completely unfazed by any curve balls the seasoned presenter had chucked at him, skilfully dodging all questions about his infidelities and shrugging off the issue of the cut above his eye which had suddenly appeared in the dying days of the band, sticking to his story that he'd fell whilst inebriated. If that was down to a fall, Kim would show her bare ass in Selfridges' window. She knew that it was virtually impossible to sustain a cut like that from falling, even with a spectacularly bad landing – more like his stupid lady wife walloped him and her ring sliced his face real nice.

That face though...Kim knew every inch of it...every contour, every bone, every change in skin tone, every hair, every last millimetre of it. But the fake television smile – she hadn't recognised that one – and definitely not the simpering, supposedly adoring one he had reserved for his wife. She only knew the smile he'd always had for her. The way he parted his lips to reveal a glimpse of those whiter than white teeth. The way his bottom lip jutted out slightly, while his head tilted to one side and his eyes sparkled. That was the smile that belonged to her.

But it was over. Over, over, over. She kept on telling herself. And despite the fact that his face was imprinted on her memory and always would be...she guessed that soon Ritchie wouldn't even be able to pick her out in a line-up.

Nothing, nothing, nothing. That's what she'd meant to him.

*

So the band was defunct, her heart was broken and she was swamped by feelings of worthlessness and despair. Above all, she felt unloved - despite the displays of affection and loving words she unquestionably received from family and friends.

The worried whispers, the telephone calls and conversations when they thought she was asleep - she felt guilty that her grief was infecting her family, replacing their status quo with constant worries about how little she was eating, how rarely she smiled...how reluctant she was to return to any kind of normality.

Even though she and Nicky were close again, there was still the elephant in the room – the atrocious way Kim had treated her and badly let her down – and they skirted around the issue until one evening when Nicky arrived, a woman on a mission, her face set in a determined grimace as she lifted the lid on Kim's shocking behaviour and the ever-constant shame she carried with her.

'Look, I'm going to say this, because it needs to be out in the open. We will have the conversation, we will discuss it once, and then it's finished - no grudges to be held, no lingering resentment,' she informed Kim, pouring them both a huge glass of a very yellow wine – it was to be hoped it *was* actually wine. Kim *had* been a shit friend after all.

'Right, this isn't easy, but here goes. You hurt me Kim. More than I could ever explain. We were sisters – not by blood but in every other way – and yet you trampled all over my feelings and were notably absent when I needed you most. From the days we used to play Kiss Chase with all the boys at St Mary's...to the Saturday trips into town when we were finally allowed to catch the bus by ourselves. From sharing a bowl of Alphabet Spaghetti in front of the telly to practising our terrible dance routines in your bedroom. We did everything together and I thought it would always be that way. You used to make me roar with laughter and I remember making you giggle so much you wet your knickers on the roundabout at Dunmore Park.'

She sighed, squeezing on to the end of the bed, where Kim sat cross legged, awaiting but dreading what was to come. There was no denying she'd been a selfish, heartless bitch, but it was still difficult to hear how she'd damaged other people, all in the name of love.

'But all that changed when HE entered your life. To begin with, when he was only a favourite pop star you were admiring from afar, well I could get on board with that and the hero-worshipping was something else we would share for a while. And even when you'd

241

started the crazy stuff, like scarpering off to London when you were still a teenager, frightening your poor mum and dad half to death…well there was still a small part of the old Kim to hang onto. But not for long. Because once you met that unscrupulous bastard and he had you in his sights, there was no room for anyone else. No awareness of anyone's feelings. He ruled your world – if he clicked his fingers, you'd go running, even if it meant letting down your family, your colleagues and me. You'd changed; you weren't the same girl any more. And the worst of it all was that most of your time was spent moping around, angrily trying to defend a man who clearly had less than honourable intentions - a shit-house who treated you like dirt and who messed with your head.'

Kim wanted to speak - to apologise - but didn't dare interrupt. It was only fair to allow Nicky to clear all of these pent-up resentments off her chest - anything that had been festering within her needed to be outed and exterminated before they could move on and be the best friends that they had once been.

'Kimberley, he was a total head fuck. One minute he wanted you, the next minute he didn't. One minute he was all over you, the next minute he looked through you as if you were invisible. He demanded that you stop putting him under pressure, but then he was jealous because you were merely speaking to one of his band mates or any other male on the planet. This is hard for me to say this to you – because you know it yourself and it's like rubbing salt in your wounds – but he didn't want you, not really. Not in the right sense. The trouble was, he didn't want anyone else to have you either, so you could never move on with your life. The slightest inclination that you were becoming pissed off with the shameful situation and he had you either guiltily begging him for forgiveness or he was fawning all over you – unable to let you go, even though he had a *wife*. I know you didn't know that at the time, but my god, there was no getting through. You wouldn't accept any criticism of him at all and you were so ratty with everyone else because of your own misery. But even though I barely saw you and you made no effort to check in on me…it never crossed my mind that you wouldn't be there for my hen do - that you wouldn't be following me down the aisle in your super-slinky bridesmaid's dress, holding my bouquet as I prepared to exchange vows with Connor. We used to prance up and down in your mum's glitzy dresses, remember, and pretend we were brides? Pillowcase on head and everything. And ultimately I had to do it all without you…'

'I'm so sorry Nick...I'm thoroughly ashamed, particularly at messing up your hen do. I would have been there for you as your bridesmaid, but if we're being totally honest – and I know that's the point of this chat – then I probably would have been physically present but my heart and mind would have been elsewhere - with Ritchie. I'd have resented the time spent away from him. I don't expect you, or anyone else, to understand but I HAD to be there when I could, on the tours, because I was never able to see him away from that life. I feel sick telling you that Nicky – I really do – admitting to what a scummy person I'd become and how badly I let you down. If I could turn back the clock I'd give anything to relive that time again and share those special hours...but honestly, when I saw you at the evening reception, I couldn't have been prouder - you looked so beautiful and I was so happy for you both...'

'It was the best of days and nights Kim, nothing will ever change that and I know what a lucky sod I am to have found Connor – particularly when I think about the tosser you fell in love with – but I genuinely missed you. And even when we spoke at the reception, me and you, I still missed you – because the Kimberley there wasn't you. She wasn't the funny, upbeat, madcap, faithful friend I'd known practically all my life. In her place was an imposter with a hard face and an awkward manner, who didn't really want to be there. And although nothing could have spoiled that day, when I thought about it afterwards it hurt Kim - it really hurt.'

'Again, I'm so sorry - you're right; I definitely wasn't myself. Ritchie hadn't only stolen my heart but also the best parts of me that made me who I was. Unfortunately what was left were the shitty bits and scrag ends that weren't worth anything to anybody. Nicky, I was hopelessly in love with this guy and he was all I could think about...and there were moments and occasions which felt like the best times of my life...but looking back, I realise there were many more days which felt like the worst times. My life was constructed around him – when he wasn't around I was so empty and lonely and I couldn't explain to anyone how that felt. How could I expect anybody to understand when I didn't understand myself?'

'He was breaking your heart right from the beginning you know. Sure, he dressed it up, the heartache, with passionate lyrics and meaningful looks and stolen moments...but he was already damaging you right from the outset. I blamed you at the time, for everything, and it seemed doubly worse because, although *I'm* far from a saint, I'm fairly certain I would never have made you feel as irrelevant and excluded as I did. But with hindsight I can see

243

you weren't the only one to blame. He was the one putting you through it all – more of my anger should have been directed towards him rather than allowing you to cop for the lot. And for my part, I was wrapped up in all of those wedding plans and I didn't notice how tortured and lonely you were – that you were going through something and maybe needed some help...'

'To be quite frank, I wouldn't have wanted to hear that – any offer of help would have been thrown right back in your face because I couldn't bear to hear the truth. In my mind, I loved Ritchie and he loved me, and that's all there was to it, and none of you knew what you were talking about! Christ, I was so blinkered, determined to close my mind to the possibility that our relationship might be all one-sided...'

'You wouldn't hear a word against that knob...and I used to ask myself, how can she think this is all normal? Why can't she see that this is a seriously unhealthy relationship? How can she not doubt the integrity of this man for one instance, when the warning signs are everywhere, when the newspapers are full of his shagathons across Europe...'

Kim cried again then. Noisy, messy sobs that came from deep within.

Nicky was right, it *was* all difficult to hear, and no matter how many times Kim apologised, she couldn't revisit the past and make it all better.

Eventually – 'Thank you for letting me rant at you Kim. To be fair, you've sat there and taken it, and never answered me back once – which is most unlike you! Please know though that it was never to hurt you back as some form of twisted revenge – it just needed to be said.'

'I get that Nick...and I'd rather you say it than keep it all inside. Oh god, the shame and the guilt is horrendous - I don't even know why you're still talking to me. I have to admit, I thought I'd lost you forever...'

'No, not forever, just for a while. I had to take a step back, let you get on with things. I reckoned either he would come to his senses and start to treat you right...or you would wise up and sack him off – not imagining how it would all eventually pan out. The bottom line is you're my best mate, Kimberley Helen Summers, and you always have been. I've never had another friend like you, either before or after The Ritchie Years, and no one could ever replace you. Please don't wallow in guilt forever though or I may have to beat you to death with your collection of *Show Me Yours* albums.'

'You are lovely you are Mrs Flanagan, and even though I really don't deserve the Best Friend status you have bestowed upon me, I am gladly taking it back because honest to god, I couldn't bear to lose you again. No matter what happens in the future, I promise you faithfully, I won't ever let you down again...'

'You'd better not, Ms Summers, because I have another status to bestow on you, if you'll accept the challenge?'

'Oh god, what is it? Tit of the week? Mug of the century? Do tell.'

'Erm, not quite but I confess I may have called you worse over the last year or so. No, it's hopefully something much more complimentary and befitting of you these days. So here's the thing...how will Godmother to the most beautiful child on earth do you?'

'WHAAAT!'

'Yep, you heard it lady,' she grinned, scooping up a bottle of the plonk and spinning it around to reveal the non-alcoholic description on the label. 'Mrs Connor Flanagan, wife to 'Flanners', worst cook but best hairdresser in the north west, is about to become a Yummy Mummy and YOU are going to be the cool, calm and collected godmother that our little spud will need when he or she can't get their own way with ma and pa...so you'd better get your act together and bring those nappy changing skills up to scratch!'

Much screaming, screeching, squealing and jumping around ensued, so much so that Kim's mum came sprinting up the stairs, wondering if one of them was murdering the other...only to join them in their celebrations, elated to hear Nicky's wonderful news.

And it *was* wonderful – at last, something to brighten up Kim's day which would offer a glimmer of hope for the future. New life and new responsibilities.

She and Nicky had done 'The Conversation' and they could put the whole matter to bed. The time they'd been estranged, when Kim had believed their friendship to be dead and buried, had only made them appreciate exactly how lost they were without each other, and what Kim had presumed was a permanent divorce, had in fact only been a temporary separation until she was back on track again. Nicky had suspected this to be the case all along and had simply boxed up her sadness, put it to one side and waited for the day when they could let bygones be bygones and return to where they were.

Surprisingly, Kim didn't feel resentful that Nicky was having a baby with the man she adored whilst her own dreams had gone up in smoke. This child would be born into a comfortable, loving family, with doting parents who were true soulmates. If Kim had carried Ritchie's baby, she would have ended up like Callie, only with slightly less dignity – she surely would have hounded Ritchie until the day he died for the unforgiveable act of abandoning his own child.

Kim was exceptionally proud, not only of Nicky and everything she had achieved but, on a more personal level, of the fact that Nicky and Connor were putting their trust in her to stand up and take care of their child if, god forbid, the worst should happen. Hopefully it never would, but it still meant that they believed she was a decent, trustworthy, stable human being who would never let them down and it was the catalyst to make her sit up, have a word with herself and realise she couldn't allow herself to be this weak forever. There was much for her to put right, bridges to build and a job to find – she was currently an emotional and financial freeloader and that had to stop.

*

For the first time since her world was blown apart, she wanted to dress up nicely and burst out into the big wide world. First stop was her former job at the kitchen showroom, where she discovered her ex-boss struggling to navigate the computer system – a fraught Nita had abandoned post to rush home to care for her sick child.

'Hi,' she said sheepishly, noting the raised eyebrow she received in response and the look of wariness on his face, clearly wondering if she was about to either sue him or effect some kind of revenge.

'It's okay, I'm not here to cause trouble Bruce – quite the opposite – and I should have come before now. Firstly, I want to apologise as I was completely out of order, not turning up for work like that, especially when you'd already given me numerous second chances and been so understanding about time off and flexibility. It's no excuse and I don't expect you to forgive me but...you see...I wasn't quite myself then and I allowed my feelings for a certain person – who ultimately wasn't worth it – to rule my heart and my life. He was a very persuasive man and I was completely taken in by his lies. I'm sure you've heard what a bastard he turned out to be.'

Shuffling a bunch of documents, Bruce nodded awkwardly. Of course he'd heard – all the world now knew what a fool she was.

'Nita showed me the newspaper love. Even though I was angry, I wouldn't have wished any of that on you and I don't know how that swine got away with it for so long. I hope you've shown him the door now Kim?'

'Well...*he* kind of showed *me* the door once the cat was out of the bag and I flipped. Still thought he could keep me waiting in the wings though, in case he had an empty bed one night and needed some company. That's the sort of man he was – he is. Hurts a tad though.'

'You're a good kid. You don't need some flashy popstar promising you a good time and delivering nothing. Get yourself down to that Zone nightclub on a weekend – I'm sure you'll find someone better in there.'

'Ha-ha, I don't think so, but thanks for the advice. Anyway...firstly I wanted to apologise for my state of mind clouding my judgement and consequently letting you down. And secondly, I wanted to thank you for giving me the job – the opportunity – when I really needed one. For what it's worth, I really liked working here. It was one of the best jobs I ever had – and believe me, I've had a few – and I only wished I hadn't been such an idiot and put you in a position where you had no alternative but to fire me.'

'Ah Kim. I wish I hadn't had to. When you were actually working, the customers loved you – we all did – and you were actually good at what you did. No hard feelings eh love?'

'No, no of course not. And if I ever own a house and need a new kitchen, you'll be my first port of call.'

They shared an awkward hug and then parted on extremely amicable terms (once she'd corrected an error he'd made on a customer quotation, which was sending the whole system into disarray). It meant a lot to her that he bore no grudges. She only wished there was still a position for her there...but even if there had been an opening, she could hardly expect him to reinstate her after the last palaver, good man or not.

The next step was to spend the money she'd been given by the band in her hour of need rather than preserve it as a souvenir. She guessed Marty and co. would approve when she purchased chocolates, wine and bubble baths for her parents, brother, Rochelle and Nicky, of course. They were only small gifts but it was the gesture that mattered and each recipient was clearly touched (even Freddie – mind you, he'd always been touched, as in not quite right in the head). It had been so long since she'd thought of anyone but herself and Ritchie and *Show Me Yours* that she'd forgotten what pleasure there was to be derived from putting a smile on someone else's face.

She truly was incredibly proud of herself for actually spending the money rather than keeping it forever and framing it but, more importantly, she used the last few pounds to buy a perfect bunch of pale pink roses to take to her grandmother's final resting place. It was a wet, windy day when her father drove her to the graveyard, but Kim was oblivious to the typically English weather. Whilst her dad remained in the car, she crouched down and poured her heart out, repeatedly apologising for neglecting her gran in favour of the man who would ultimately break her heart. As the rain tipped down, so did her tears. She felt emotionally drained after the visit, but it was something she'd been desperately wanting to do since the awful, awful day the truth had been outed.

'Miss you gran,' she whispered, as her dad eased the car slowly down the gravel track and out into the traffic. 'Love you, always.'

*

'Look I'm sorry I suggested it, but I don't think being surrounded by Ritchie's face and all this band paraphernalia is helping you much on your road to recovery.'

Whilst Kim accepted her mum was probably right – it was difficult to move on and attempt to forget Ritchie when his face adorned every wall of her bedroom, which was also piled high with records, tapes, mugs, scrapbooks and all kinds of SMY merchandise – she wasn't completely ready to leave that part of her life behind just yet. Her role as partner or lover or merely part-time mistress - or whatever she'd been to him – well, obviously that was history...as was the friendship she'd believed they'd once had. However, she wasn't prepared to close the book on her fandom status, whatever anyone believed was best for her.

She knew it was the sensible thing to do, and there were times when she stared at Ritchie's face on her wall and he seemed to be mocking her, saying, 'Stupid girl...as if I'd actually be interested in a nobody like you...' On those occasions she became so possessed by anger that it burned from within her, branding her soul and sending ripples of fury throughout her body. She despised him then - more hatred for one man than she would ever have thought possible.

But she was holding on to all she had left of him. And she didn't want to let go of Todd, Ady, Bren and Marty either. They were amazing men who she'd loved too – although not in the same way she'd loved Ritchie of course – and she couldn't simply turn her back on them.

There were other times when she couldn't believe she'd been to bed with this poster boy, opened up her heart to him and told him she loved him. Was it a dream? Because sometimes it felt like one, being so far removed from her ordinary life back at home. The whole notion of being singled out by an idol and entering into a relationship with him – well, it was the stuff dreams and fantasies were made of. This wasn't the reality for an average, run-of-the-mill young girl who didn't mix in those circles. So how had her dreams come true? And how had those dreams evolved into a nightmare? It all seriously boggled her mind.

She used the hours when she felt more positive to compile and deliver CVs and job applications. She *had* to find paid employment and not spend the rest of her days sponging off her mum and dad. She *needed* a job to pay her way, to start to live again and regain some self-confidence and stability.

Just as she was becoming rather despondent at the lack of response to her wad of applications, she received a call from a local cafe and – boom! She was in! The owner was impressed with her covering letter and varied work experience (vast number of jobs)...and this lady being an acquaintance of Nicky's mum hadn't hurt at all.

From day one, Kim and Carol hit it off like a house on fire and she enjoyed her new job immensely. If there'd been time to daydream she would have been sucked back down that dark tunnel again, so she worked like a dog, determined to keep her mind and body active. She also wanted to actually keep this job and prove to any doubters that she wasn't a complete loser after all.

Within days of commencing employment at Nice Slice, Kim discovered that Carol was well aware of her backstory and consequently wanted to nurse her back to health, with words of wisdom and as many pies as Kim could stomach. They didn't talk much about Ritchie until day seven when Kim broke down and wailed that she still missed him, even though he was a real dick-driven, duplicitous, dirty fucking bastard. Carol completely empathised with Kim – her own husband had buggered off with a woman twenty years his junior while his too-trusting wife had been manning a stall at their daughter's school bazaar. Poor Carol. Poor Kim.

Kim's parents hoped that she had turned a corner. They couldn't bear to watch her going through such agony and were desperate for their old daughter back but Kim truly believed they'd unfortunately seen the last of that girl. The old Kim was gone, to be replaced by a storm-damaged, battered, broken down version of her former self. She'd been changed forever.

Thankfully the crying had subsided – it was far too exhausting and would have made holding down a steady job virtually impossible. Unfortunately, when the tears ground to a halt and the emotions were kept in check, what remained was an agonising, aching emptiness. It was the worst kind of pain – like a toothache that starts in the epicentre of a huge molar but gradually bleeds out into the gums...and then the jaw...and then up into the ear canal until the person is literally consumed by the pain and can take no more – it started at the gaping, open wound that was shot through her heart but spread throughout her bones and tissue and glands and into her head and brain...until she felt like she'd had as much as she could take and silently begged for an end to her suffering.

But how could she explain that to anyone? Even the people who loved and cared for her the most could never begin to understand the loss because they'd never experienced the intensity of her feelings for Ritchie.

So she battled on. Her loved ones, the prospect of becoming a godmother for the first time and her new job were what kept her going through it all.

The days became weeks became months and before she knew it they were approaching the end of another summer and even though her love for Ritchie and her pain had not diminished in the slightest, she realised that she must have taken a few momentous steps on the road to recovery when she decided to pack away everything relating to Ritchie and the band and handed it to her dad to be stored up in the loft.

She had made the grave error of sifting through an overstuffed bag of photos and mementos. Every single picture of her with Ritchie, every personally signed item from him, every shower gel she'd pinched from luxury hotel suites they'd fooled around in – they all tortured her and unfortunately signalled the return of The Tears – and she knew she had to stop self-inflicting if she wanted to come out the other side.

So the very next day, that bag and everything else band-related, was consigned to the Haul of Memories that was gradually filling up the loft space. If she'd stopped to think about it too much, she'd have changed her mind and been delving back in, retrieving favourite photos, re-reading personal messages from Ritchie, remembering what she'd lost – what she'd never really had.

When Nicky learned of her progress, she'd insisted on taking Kim out clothes shopping to celebrate, although Kim had been initially reluctant to agree. Almost every slinky dress, tiny skirt and low-cut top she'd purchased for as long as she could remember had been bought with Ritchie in mind and any new purchases seemed rather pointless when she had very little money still and no intention of going anywhere to wear any new glad rags.

But Nicky was insistent. She had other ideas.

'Look, I intend to spoil you and you'd better not object. Nothing will give me greater pleasure than to prise you out of that bobbly dressing gown and into a pretty dress. Besides – how will you be able to join us for Lyndsey's birthday bash if you don't have anything new to wear?'

'Oh Nicky, I can't go – not on a proper night out. I'm barely strong enough to make it to work and yesterday I had to literally force myself to take a stroll round the park with dad because he'd been on my case. With very few exceptions my world has been contained within these four walls for the last few months and it feels like it's all expanding far too quickly...'

'Oh, what a load of old poop! What you need is a good old knees-up with me and the ladies from the salon – a chance to get dolled up and tanked up and forget all your troubles, if only for a few hours. And don't talk to me about expanding too fast...'

She cradled the obvious baby bump contained within the fabric of her elasticated waist trousers and expelled a huge sigh. '...because if I continue to expand at this rate I'll end up carrying a twenty stone baby by the time I'm full term. Anyway, we're going off piste...the bottom line is that you desperately need a filthy night out and I'm exactly the person to organise it – although naturally I must remain stone cold sober, probably bore you all to death moaning about my chronic indigestion and then sneak off home in a taxi before the clock even strikes ten.'

'Ahem, you're not really selling it to me Mrs Flanagan. What'll I do then if you bugger off home?'

'The girls will totally look after you, as will my little sis, who's coming along for the ride...so you'll be in safe hands, don't worry. Darcy's a proper little Mother Hen these days so she won't let you out of her sight. They're all under strict instructions to make sure you're full to capacity with alcohol and grooving away on that dance floor all night long. Trust me, this is the best kind of medicine for a broken heart – and you'll be so rough the next day you won't even be able to think about Ritchie...'

'No, I'll just have the Hangover From Hell to add to my list of problems come Sunday morning and I'll be even more weepy than I normally bloody am...'

'You're not getting out of it buddy, so brace yourself.'

Nicky had that steely, slightly bonkers look of determination in her eyes and Kim knew it was pointless to resist – besides, if a night out took her mind off Ritchie, if only for a few hours, she accepted it would do her good. Nursing her broken heart was leaving her listless and lethargic and she needed to dip her toe into the real world once more.

'I'll feel like such an idiot though Nick. All those girls knew I was head over heels for Ritchie and I told everyone who would listen that he was The One – because I really thought he was. They probably all reckoned I was seriously deluded and look – now they've been proved right. A fool, that's what they'll think I am. I can't bear the prospect of everyone sniggering and laughing at me and wondering how I could ever think it remotely possible that a man like Ritchie could be interested in someone as mediocre and plain as me.'

'Hey, firstly, you are far from mediocre, and most women would kill for your looks. And secondly, these girls are good 'uns you know – hand-picked by yours truly. There's never been any sniggering or laughing behind your back, in fact they actually look on you as a minor celebrity, in a 'I can't believe I know someone that's shagged Ritchie Clarke!' kind of way. I can't promise you won't be inundated with questions about the size of his dishonourable member, but I *can* promise those girls won't ever judge you and will always have your back.'

Kim did actually believe her. The girls Nicky employed were lovely, loyal and more likely to be supportive than sarcastic, unlike past so-called friends whose unsavoury behaviour and unnecessary put-downs she'd endured for far too long.

Yet again, she wondered why she'd ever wasted so much time and energy on her fake friendship with Sally-Anne, who didn't have a loyal bone in her body. Sal was also a mean, two-faced, obsequious liar and the only person she cared about was herself. The one good thing that had come out of Kim's awful situation was that this piece of work was completely out of her life and she would never have to listen to her bullshit again.

Nicky and the girls who surrounded her were in a different league altogether.

Chapter 27

'Stick another tenner in the kitty ladies and I'll order the next round in!' Marnie was keen to get tanked up before they'd even left The Fox. By the time they reached the nightclub it would be carnage.

She'd seen Nicky's eyes glaze over as she'd belched and yawned and tried to stay awake. Poor cow. Girls' nights out clearly weren't much fun when you were pregnant, alcohol was strictly out of bounds and you were struggling to even participate in the dancing, never mind clamber onto a chair, as per Lyndsey, who was thrashing her arms about and singing along at the top of her pipes to a vintage Culture Club number.

Kim was definitely on the rocky road to Totally Shitfaced, calling off at Slurring Central and Puking Parkway, but it felt good to numb the pain for a while.

Of course, she'd had a moment (lasting approximately forty-five minutes) earlier in the evening, when the girls had dived on her, demanding to know how the hell she'd managed to worm her way into the trousers of a world famous popstar when they couldn't bag the strong and silent lad from the garden centre. Was he good in bed? Did he talk dirty? Did he treat her to one of his classic stage winks just as he reached the point of orgasm? And had she chucked darts at his posters since his deception was uncovered and spread the word that he only had a teeny tiny willy?

Very quickly the tears had turned to laughter and after a quick visit to the ladies room for Nicky to repair the damage to Kim's make-up, she'd staged a comeback, determined to enjoy herself, despite the ever-present hollow feeling inside.

The girls had moved on to discuss who amongst them had the hairiest legs and the topic of Ritchie and Kim's sex-life had been shelved, thank goodness.

By the time they reached *Loopy J's* nightclub, she was a little unsteady on her feet, one or two of the girls were loud and lairy (Marnie and Lyndsey) and they were all ready to rave and misbehave, particularly Sunita, who'd acquired a Pat Sharp/Tina Turner wig from Christ only knows where. They were also minus Nicky whom Kim had taken pity on, escorted to the taxi rank and gently pushed into an awaiting cab, promising to fill her in on everything she missed the following day – if Kim could remember anything.

Once they'd paid their pounds to the miserable chain-smoking woman on the door, they selected their spot for the evening – equidistant between the bar and the toilets and next to the main dancefloor – and it was her turn to get the round in. She presumed Nicky had chucked a wedge of money in the kitty before she'd left because they definitely had more in the pink and white spotty purse than they'd started off with at 7.30 pm but, anyway, it was all good.

'Two Jack Daniels and Diet Cokes, one orange Bacardi Breezer, one bottle of Bud and a pint of your finest lager please,' Kim yelled to the nearest barman, who seemed to be trying to dodge customers rather than serve them.

'You do realise that there is no such thing as fine lager in this establishment, don't you?' chuckled a familiar voice in her ear. Spinning around, she came face to face with someone she hadn't seen in an age.

'Oh my god! ADAAMMM! Hello yooooo!' she cried, throwing her arms around him and hugging him as is a pissed person's want – too tight and way longer than necessary.

'Ha-ha, you're already drunk, woman! Long time no see, eh?'

'I can't believe it's you! What the devil are you doing here?'

'Yes, I can assure you, it's definitely me. And, on occasions, I do let the other lads drag me out around town and force gallons of beer down my neck! What are YOU doing here? You don't still live round here, do you? I presumed you'd upped and moved away...'

'This is the first time I've been out on the lash round here in years! Nicky organised a ladies night out for Lyndsey's birthday – although Nick has now waved the white flag and returned home to her lovely, luscious husband, but we'll let her off because she is with child. Darcy's here too – you remember Nicky's sister – look! There she is – attempting the splits in front of that slobbering stag party – and some other girls from Nicky's salon. They're all so nice and they've been ordered to take care of me because I can't take my ale, as you can probably see...'

To prove her point, Kim stood back to let him watch her sway in her stupidly tall heels, realising she was grinning like a goofy fool, swishing her hair from side to side in time with the eighties music.

'Oops!' she giggled, bumping into a couple of guys attempting to make their way to the bar. 'Sorreeee! See, Adam – this is why I need looking after....I've only had a few and I'm totally pished! Spent ages getting ready and beautifying myself and now I probably look a hot, sweaty mess...'

'No, you look beautiful Kim,' Adam quietly assured her, taking hold of her free hand and guiding her back to the bar to avoid any further collisions. 'But then again, you always did.'

She remembered then – the secret feelings he'd harboured for her and the slight matter of her breaking his heart. The tears when he'd quit his job at the shop and walked away from her, without ever looking back. This buff, funny, kind man who she'd trampled all over in her quest to possess Ritchie Joe Clarke. And he really was buff. Adam had always been an attractive guy who women were drawn to, although he never knew his worth or how hot he truly was. But he'd matured into something spectacular. His fair hair was longer and tousled and with natural blond streaks and he'd clearly been away on holiday to somewhere hot and sunny as he had a spectacular tan to accompany his new-look locks. A turquoise polo top, sporting a tiny designer motif, hung loosely over a pair of faded jeans that clung to him in all of the right places. Ooh, he had stubble now too...and Kim found herself wanting to reach out and stroke it. Bloody hell, she needed to lay off the alcohol – jumping on an old friend and colleague, as handsome as he may be, was not the answer to her problems. Her heart was still in pieces and snogging the face off someone other than Ritchie would only be a quick-fix rather than a permanent solution. Still...Adam was very easy on the eye and had always made her laugh like Basil Brush on drugs whenever she'd worked alongside him or they'd messed around in the pub.

'You're too kind, Adam,' she replied. 'You always were one of the most thoughtful guys I ever met...'

'Ha! My girlfriend would probably disagree. She's always telling me I need to up my game!'

Oh. He had a girlfriend. Of course – why wouldn't he? He was fit and fabulous and it was inconceivable that he hadn't yet bagged himself a babe.

'Noooo...no way. Adam Foley...let me tell you...' Slurring her words, badly, she moved a step closer to him, grabbed hold of both of his hands and squeezed them tightly. '...because it's really, really important that you know. You, Mr Foley, just need to keep on being your wonderful self – your game is already *waaaay* up.'

And without even thinking, she leant over to peck him on the cheek, giggling at his surprised reaction, before she managed a 'Bye-bye, Ad the Lad' and staggered back to retrieve the beverages from the bar, hugely relieved to see Lyndsey coming to her assistance, as there was no way in hell she could have carried everything back to those thirsty party animals, not without smashing at least half of what they'd ordered.

'Oh shit, I've not paid!' she remembered, thinking hells bells, that barman really WAS dozy, failing to take the money from her before she did a runner. Honest to a fault, she shouted over to Dozy Dan, who was still trying to avoid making eye contact with any potential customers, only to be informed that 'him over there' had paid for the round of drinks. He pointed directly at Adam, who lifted his glass, smiled and mouthed 'Cheers!'

Raising her own bottle in response, whilst managing to tip half of its contents down onto her shoes, she beamed and let herself be dragged off to the dancefloor, laughing as the girls shouted, 'Who the fuck was *that?*', proud to have been seen with such a ten-out-of-ten, fine figure of a man and knowing that everyone must be wondering how the bloody hell little old Kim attracted not only sexy singers but the sexiest man in Cheshire to boot.

*

It wasn't pretty the following morning – in fact it was downright ugly and Kim hadn't felt so hungover in an incredibly long time. Wired from all the sugary alcopops, it had taken her at least two hours to nod off...only to wake up in a pool of cold sweat, make-up smeared all over her clean pillowcase, still in her best dress, which truly was NOT designed for sleeping in. At some point during the night it had ridden up around her waist, leaving what could only be described as a belt of angry welts around her middle, and actually peeling the bloody thing off was a challenge in itself. She suspected she may have caused a minor disturbance when she'd arrived home as her bedroom light was still switched on, coins were scattered all over the carpet and the contents of her bag had been tipped out on the stairs. And to her utter amazement, she appeared to have returned with only one shoe. Quite a feat in itself.

When she crawled out of bed to grab a glass of water and fresh pyjamas, a violent protest erupted in her head and the effort of actually moving was all too much in her delicate state.

She gingerly slid back under her duvet, flashbacks of the previous evening mocking her and reminding her of every silly drunken stunt they'd pulled.

Warm-up session at *The Fox* followed by the main event at *Loopy J's*. Nicky heading home in a taxi (lord, she would be on the phone soon, demanding all of the juicy gossip). Darcy attempting the splits and showing her ass to six leery lads from Newcastle. Lyndsey having a full-on barney with a bouncer after a hard-faced bitch nicked her drink and he refused to do anything about it, swiftly followed by Lyndsey's noisy ejection from *Loopy's*, although she was eventually allowed to return. Marnie getting it on with a guy she'd known from school but then deciding she preferred his mate. Sunita attracting shed-loads of men but rebuffing every single one as no one could hold a torch to her ever-loving husband, waiting patiently at home with the kids.

And then there was Kim.

Had she *really* draped herself over Adam, planted a kiss on his cheek and told him his game was *waaaay* up? Christ, she hoped he didn't think that was a euphemism. She cringed as she remembered doing a nifty little dance for his entertainment and groaned at the memory of him attempting to hold her upright at the bar.

As the effect of the alcohol completely wore off, she became ever more morose and the gap at the side of her where Ritchie should have been tore her up. It was all well and good getting slaughtered down town, making merry with friends and temporarily taking her mind off HIM ...but the next day it was payback time. Not only was she seriously regretting those last vodka shots and the greasy donner kebab meat, but the ferociousness of her hangover intensified her misery, making her want to go to sleep and never wake up.

When one of the band's songs played out through the radio in her bedroom, the pain was almost intolerable as she listened to Ritchie's velvety voice preaching that everyone should follow their heart and find true love. Thanks mate, she thought she *had* found it. But he buggered it right up.

It was a long day, even after she'd filled Nicky in on all the gory details and the headache had dulled slightly. Even when she'd forced down a sizeable portion of her mum's infamous homemade steak pie, accompanied by mash, peas and several gallons of gravy. Even when she'd managed a nana nap on the rug in front of the gas fire in the living room while dad watched the Antiques Roadshow and mum attempted to scale the Great Ironing Mountain of England.

By the time the ten o'clock news began, Kim was relapsing and the head-pounding and sweats were back with a vengeance. Why did anyone drink alcohol when it ruined them like this? Two drinks – that would be her limit if she ever touched the booze again, and not a drop more.

She would certainly not be accompanying the girls on any more nights out – at least not for the foreseeable future.

Death by stinking hangover was not a dignified way to go.

*

The following Saturday, there she was, in *The Fox* with the girls, despite all her protestations and determination – they wore her down in the end. But she had learned a lesson from Piss Up Number 1, avoided all shots and tried to pace herself throughout the evening.

She'd been so sure she couldn't put herself through it again at the beginning of the week, but by Thursday had started to question what she actually had to look forward to at the weekend, if not a night of giggles and shenanigans, in the company of Nicky's friends. Nicky of course was excused from her role as Chief Drunkard in view of her pregnant state, but she informed Kim that she was intending to live her social life through *her* now, until her child was at least twenty-one. Kim gave it six months postpartum before her partner in crime would be slipping into her glad rags, abandoning Connor to the night feeds and exploding nappies.

Creatures of habit, the girls commenced drinking at *The Fox* again and finished up at *Loopy J's*. Darcy's best friend, Kayleigh gate-crashed their party and she appeared to know everyone everywhere so there was never a dull moment. The girls treated Kim as if they'd known her forever; she'd become an honorary member of their friendship group and she appreciated how they'd welcomed her into their fold with open arms.

It had been another difficult week, to say the least. Taking small, hesitant steps...she'd been going forward into a new life...and if she'd stopped to measure her progress at all and

259

compared where she was then to where she'd begun, she'd have been immensely proud of herself.

Then Kim suffered a huge, hurtful setback.

Wednesday. Front page of the newspaper. Lead article. Whacking great big headline.

POPSTAR RITCHIE'S SECRET AFFAIR

Plummeting heart, rising bile, thumping chest.

She forced herself to look further than the headline and almost passed out when the accompanying picture jumped out of the page and screamed 'YOU, YOU, YOU!'

No. No. And no again.

It was blurry, it was black and white, but it was definitely Kim and Ritchie in all their glory pasted across the front page.

He was holding her hand as they exited a hotel lift on what was obviously the morning after the night before. The camera didn't lie – they clearly hadn't been there for a business meeting. This was no innocent moment captured as their paths crossed in the hotel lobby. The touching, the eye contact, the body language and dishevelled clothing all pointed towards an illicit liaison - a night of passion between two very willing participants.

Her hand clamped to her mouth as she remembered the morning in question, which was the very last time she'd stayed with Ritchie and he'd accompanied her outside…prevented her tumbling down the steps…pretended he cared.

As her knees gave way, Kim fell back on to the stairs and burned with shame. She'd always dreaded this moment and had prayed it would never happen. Some women might relish seeing their private life splashed all over the papers – they might even build a living on it.

But she wasn't one of them.

She searched the text for her name but was surprised and relieved to find that she was only described as a 'mystery female'. Thank god she was a woman of mystery rather than a woman of the night, because that surely would have finished her father off.

Whoever had taken the photograph had done so at some distance – maybe a member of the hotel staff who'd sold it for a quick buck or, god forbid, a scumbag from the paparazzi.

There were numerous mentions of 'sumptuous surroundings' and 'luxurious five star suites' but nothing of what actually went on within the walls of their room or pictures of the housemaid holding up their bed sheets and pointing to tell-tale stains or anything sordid like that.

The real stab wound to the heart came towards the end of the piece when the reporter had asked Ritchie to comment on the article and the accusation of the full-blown extra-marital affair. Rather than maintaining a dignified silence, he had delivered the quote of all quotes:

'Whilst many of the details contained within this article are factually incorrect, I accept that I have made mistakes which have caused considerable pain and distress to my beautiful wife. I sincerely regret the meaningless one night stands and the shame this article has brought upon my family. Michelle is my best friend, my rock, the love of my life and my absolute world. I would ask that the press please respect our privacy at this difficult time.'

There was so much contained within that one paragraph that crucified Kim.

Apparently she was a mistake. He had merely added Kim to his lengthy list of one night stands rather than confess to any meaningful relationship. He regretted the time they'd spent together - the moments, the hours, the nights were all consigned to the dustbin in one vicious swoop. She was never the love of his life – obviously – and she hadn't even come close. It was all about *Michelle*. She was his whole world, whilst Kim wasn't even a tiny speck within it.

He was a liar, a big fat liar. All the rest of the shite may have been true, but they had shared much more than one night. It had gone on for years between them.

Firstly, the Will They Won't They initial stage when he'd seemed reluctant to enter into a sexual relationship. She still didn't understand his reasonings or his reluctance when he was prepared to drop his pants for other, nameless women throughout Europe, and probably the rest of the planet to boot.

Then the second half of their 'relationship' when they'd dived into all of the sex with gusto, and he'd promised her the earth whilst at the same time giving her nothing really, apart from the odd orgasm and moments, few and far between, when he'd revealed a tender side and she'd really believed that he'd been letting down his guard and she'd finally made a breakthrough.

She was heartily sick of crying over this man, who clearly wasn't worth the angst, but the tears refused to abate and streamed down to soak her t-shirt and remind her that she would never be free of her feelings for Ritchie, never able to truly move on. She would always be looking over her shoulder and waiting for her name to be dragged through the gutter press.

Christ, she'd reached a new level of hatred for this bastard. Yes, of course, she loved him still. But the fury that engulfed her was like no other – like acid bubbling up and burning through her veins. Her muscles tensed and threatened to pop through her skin, she was grinding her teeth, every hair on her body seemed to be standing on end and she could hear herself breathing way too fast. Every bit of her was panting, pulsating, pain-ridden...and if Ritchie had been standing in front of her there was a very good chance she would have attacked him and he may not have been able to defend himself against her rage.

The opening of the front door took Kim by surprise and she looked up to see her mum there – her mum who was supposed to be at work, but who'd returned unexpectedly, brandishing a copy of the godforsaken newspaper – the dirty rag that employed unscrupulous people to ruin other people's lives – and by the look on her face she was none too happy.

Like a stinging slap to the cheek, mum's sudden appearance was enough to bring Kim round a little and she remembered that she wasn't the only person they were hurting with their bullshit and big revelations.

'I'm sorry mum. I didn't know anything about this and was obviously unaware at the time that someone was secreted behind a pillar taking pictures of us. I'm so sorry and feel so ashamed. They've made me out to be a loose little slapper who just wanted to show him a good time but I loved him mum and....'

'Stop!' Raising her voice and her hand, Kim's mum interrupted the stream of apologies and with a surprisingly calm voice she continued.

'I know you loved him – we all knew. And of course you were unaware that someone was sneakily taking snaps to make money out of you. That goes without saying. Listen, it doesn't name you in the article, but even if it did, it wouldn't matter to us. We're proud of you honey...the way you're trying to make amends and forge on with your life, even though you've been to hell and back. We've always been proud of you, even when relations were difficult between us and we struggled to stand by and watch Ritchie walk all over you...'

'But if they start naming names then everyone will be talking about me...and it will be your good name dragged through the mud by association...'

'Look Kim, if anyone dares to take a pop at you or is anything other than kind to any of us then I'll make sure they're bloody sorry. If they're not careful they'll feel the full force of your dad's fist, because you are the victim here, whose only crime was to fall hook, line and sinker for what is known as a cad...a playboy...a player...or whatever they call them these days. *He* was a married man with an eye for the ladies who had *you* hanging around, waiting in earnest for him when he always knew it was destined to end in tears.'

'Some of the stuff that's been printed though...it makes me feel like none of it was real and Ritchie words were so cruel. He dismisses me like I'm an insignificant little groupie. *Meaningless,* for Christ's sake.'

'Right, young lady, you can stop this nonsense. If you'd been this desperate little groupie, Ritchie Clarke would not have been ringing this house to speak to you. If he'd wanted to escape your clutches then he wouldn't have given you his number. If you were the one doing all the running then why was he booking five star hotel rooms for the pair of you? You know, and I know, and everybody else who matters knows, exactly what the truth is. As soon as I saw this load of old tosh in the newspaper I took an extended lunch and dashed home, because I knew how distraught you would be - but this is enough now. If you sit here any longer, dissecting it all and tearing yourself apart with questions and recriminations, then you're doing yourself no favours. Now throw on some clothes and drag a comb through your hair because we're going to hit the shops for an hour and grab a doughnut on the high street. And YOU are going to ring Darcy and accept her kind offer to join the girls again on Saturday night. Got it?'

Which is how Kim found herself in *The Fox* with half a lager in her hand.

Once she'd recovered from the initial shock of the photograph in the newspaper, she picked herself up with a vengeance, allowing her mum to treat her to a cute little playsuit and glittery high heels for her night out. Kimberley Summers set about the everyday business of living.

263

She even managed a hint of a smile on the Saturday night when her dad gasped theatrically, and told her she looked like a supermodel as she was on her way out of the door. And mum's opinion was clearly visible in her eyes – *Ritchie doesn't know what he's missing.*

Very merry, but not legless, by the time they reached *Loopy J's*, she danced and sang her way through the DJ's selection of golden oldies, only making her excuses and disappearing to the toilets when a *Show Me Yours* floor filler blasted through the speakers. This was obviously something she would have to get used to. She couldn't erase their back catalogue and many of their earlier hits had been huge and were always going to pop up on the playlist in venues of this kind.

'You okay hun'?' Darcy had tottered behind in her strappy heels and was peering into Kim's face, checking for tears or signs she was about to go and have a meltdown in the nearest available cubicle.

'I'm alright...just about. It's been a hard week.' Well, that was a bloody understatement.

The evening had begun with the other girls venting their anger at the audacity of Ritchie to prefer 'Shergar' (Michelle) to her good self. They'd all seen the picture and the columns of crap and were determined to make it clear exactly whose team they were on. Lyndsey had even been making up rude lyrics to sing along to the band's hits, to alter every line when Ritchie sang about love. Every *Your love makes me stronger...* became *You disappoint me with your tiny donger* and each *Missing you more than I can say...* was overridden by a *Piddling on your smarmy face...* God love them.

And now Darcy was doing her level best, even under the influence of half a bottle of Malibu, to keep Kim's spirits up as the evening rattled on.

'Come here sweetie,' she ordered, throwing her arms around Kim and leaving her with no option other than to bury her head in Darcy's fake-tanned and shimmered shoulder, almost suffocating with a mouthful of her backcombed hair. After allowing Kim a decent amount of time to wallow in self-pity, she then dragged her up the stairs and back into the bar area, to the cheers of the other girls and a gang of good-looking men they'd apparently infiltrated.

And smack bang in the middle of them was none other than Adam.

Bell Lane Minimart Adam. Former friend and colleague Adam. Adam who'd seen her seriously worse for wear only one short week ago.

Adam.

He made Kim laugh within the first few seconds, saluting her as she was on the approach and then poking his tongue out. It warmed her heart to see him again.

'Hello you,' he said, holding out a bottle of beer. 'I took the liberty of ordering you this after I'd spotted you earlier. I hope you don't mind.'

'As if! Any time you feel like buying me alcohol, never resist that urge!'

They clinked their bottles together and she smiled, delighted to be back in her old friend's company, excited that she would probably be in for a good session of flirting and horsing around, flattered that Adam had cared to include her in his round. Extracting drinks from the tight-arse toads in their neck of the woods was virtually impossible.

They made small talk and fooled around...and suddenly her friends and his were staging a drunken dance-off and the two of them had been backed into a corner on their own. It was dark, but she took a long, hard look at him – that handsome face, those caring, smiling eyes...and that seemingly perfect body, encased in the snuggest of jeans and a fitted slate grey button-down shirt...and she thought, what a lovely, lovely man. It wasn't necessary for him to have his hair cut and coloured by the top stylist in the city. He didn't need to have his shirt ripped open to the waist to expose a tanned, waxed chest. The trainers he wore were expensive but purchased from the sports shop in town rather than a poncy, place-to-be-seen store on one of the most expensive thoroughfares in Birmingham.

Adam needed no gimmicks or money thrown at him. He was perfect as he was, comfortable in his own skin – not trying to be someone else.

'I'm surprised your lucky lady lets you out on the town with this rabble every weekend.' She was fishing for details but hoped that wasn't too obvious.

'Well...that's no longer an issue as we've gone our separate ways since I last saw you. It just wasn't working out.' Adam's reply was brief and to the point and Kim noticed he didn't seem particularly heartbroken about the split.

To her surprise, she felt something jump for joy inside of her and it was all she could do to stop herself from leaping up, punching the air and shouting, 'YES! Get in there! He's a free agent again!' Instead she tried – she hoped – to look reasonably sympathetic, offering up words of condolence.

'Ah, I'm sorry to hear that Adam. That's a real shame.'

And then he did something strange. He tucked a stray hair behind her ear but didn't take his hand away...and his gaze met hers and he said nothing for a moment. He just stared. It wasn't uncomfortable - nothing freaky – but it was like he had something to say, yet the words simply wouldn't come.

And then Marnie fell over and couldn't get up for laughing and the moment was gone. Like someone had put another fifty pence piece in the Conversation Meter and they were off again, gassing like the great friends they'd once been.

'No worries,' he assured her. 'The relationship had run its course and we both knew it was time to call it a day. She's a great girl but I think we're both kind of relieved it's over. So what about you then? What brings you down to the cheesiest nightclub in the west on a Saturday night when you could be having it large in some private members bar in London with a certain popstar who stole you from under my very beaky nose?'

Was he taking the piss? Surely he couldn't have missed her very public humiliation at the hands of the man she'd thought she'd be growing old with?

'Do you not know?' she almost whispered, barely audible above the boom of the music. 'Do you not read the papers?'

'Actually no,' he frowned, looking at her intently. 'Well I try to avoid the red tops as they're usually rammed full of a load of old tripe. Why, what's been occurring? Has something happened to my arch nemesis?'

'If only,' she sighed, determined the tears would not make an unwelcome appearance and that she would stay strong. 'Turned out you were all right to think there was something suspect about him. He's a married man Adam - he had a wife all along...'

'A *WIFE*?'

The DJ had cranked up the volume which meant it was difficult to hold a conversation without shouting and sharing the intimate details with hundreds of other clubbers. Kim took Adam's hand and led him up the next set of stairs and through the double doors, to the quieter, chill-out area, where there were only a couple of heavy rockers necking in the corner, and a bored young girl behind the bar chewing on her neon pink nails.

They huddled together on a threadbare, hard-as-nails settee and she told him the whole sorry story. It was the only way forward, to own her mistakes, acknowledge her stupidity and admit that she'd been flattered and fooled by a prize knobhead but never loved by him – as evidenced by his announcement to the world in newsprint that she'd only ever been an easy lay and nothing more.

'Twat,' Adam remarked, scowling as she laid bare all of the facts and shared with him the many doubts she'd had about Ritchie during their time together but how she'd sat on them, still unable to let him go. How she'd thought she'd be the one to make him want to settle down...when he was, in fact, already settled down – albeit with someone else.

'Such a trusting, gullible, blinkered, Ritchie-loving idiot, that's me,' she attempted a wobbly smile, trying to make light of the pain she had felt...and still felt. With one swift movement Adam had closed the slither of space between them on the ripped settee and squashed her against his chest, his arms around her holding her as if they would never let her go...and she felt safe there – anchored and calm.

Eventually they pulled apart and smiled at each other.

'Ritchie Joe Clarke is the unluckiest man on earth you know.'

'Erm...how so?'

'He is the unluckiest man on earth because he had you and allowed you to walk away...and one day he will wake up and realise exactly what he's lost. To have *you* love him and then to lose that love...it may take time but that's seriously going to hurt, I'm telling you.'

'Oh Adam, you're so sweet and kind. Thank you for listening and for being your usual awesome self. For being so caring and understanding and non-judgemental...'

'And handsome, don't forget handsome...'

'Ha-ha, yes, handsome, that's definitely in there...incredibly handsome.'

Eventually they conceded that they must return to their friends before a search party was launched, and they were greeted by shouts of 'Oy-oy!' and 'Your fly's undone, Bad Ad!' from the bunch of lads. The girls apparently hadn't been worried at all. From what they'd seen of Adam and heard about him, they'd judged her to be in safe hands...but if those hands had been anywhere other than round her waist then it was an actual criminal offence not to disclose all details in the kebab shop later. Apparently.

Kim felt lighter – freer – for having confided in Adam and somehow it had helped glue the bond even tighter between them – the bond that had been severed when she'd unintentionally hurt him in the past. They danced together and giggled like a couple of school kids in the corner and she was disappointed when she heard Lyndsey shout, 'Jesus, look at the time! I've got to be up again in three hours to do a car boot sale with my dad!'

She didn't actually want to leave.

Causing chaos in the kebab shop, the two groups of friends eventually abandoned the remains of their pizzas and donner meat and wandered on down to the taxi rank, girls linking arms with boys...Adam linking arms with Kim. She wasn't ridiculously drunk this time and it felt fun - and fun was certainly what had been missing from her life. After confirming that her home telephone number was indeed still the same one he'd memorised when he was besotted with her, Kim and Adam hugged goodbye at the cab rank, Adam promising he would be in touch very soon.

'He's a cutie, that Adam,' slurred Marnie, hiccupping alongside her, the taxi driver watching her carefully in his rear view mirror, presumably in case she was about to throw up on his leather upholstery. 'If you don't want to be his girlfriend then can I have him?'

'Oh, he doesn't want me as a girlfriend - that's old hat now. We'll just be friends who enjoy each other's company and...'

'Friends my ass! You'll be ripping his kecks off by Christmas, you will. And very nice kecks they are too. Seriously though, if you two don't get it together then there is something seriously wrong in this universe. You make a gorgeous couple and he's most definitely into you...'

'Don't be silly.' Kim shook her head but couldn't hide her smile, at the notion that Adam might still be that way inclined towards her and at the idea of the two of them becoming a couple. Highly unlikely, after what she'd put him through.

Adam was a cracking guy and a real catch, whereas she, as a Ritchie Joe Clarke reject, was very much damaged goods.

Chapter 28

Peaks and troughs. Achievements and disappointments. Good days and bad. Rays of sunshine and piss-pours of rain.

Like a dog owner whose cheeky little mutt hadn't yet been housetrained, Kim never knew from one day to the next what would be awaiting her the following morning. Would she be swearing and raging at the vile content of some newspaper article or magazine column? Perhaps she'd be crying buckets after listening to the lyrics of some random crappy song, lamenting her lost love and howling his name into her pillow? Or maybe she'd be stopped in her tracks by the sight of an item of clothing that bore more than a passing resemblance to something Ritchie had once worn?

Worst still, she might pass someone in the street and suddenly her nostrils be filled with the scent of the aftershave that Ritchie favoured ('Twat – For Men')? Or she might simply be shot through the heart by a bullet in the form of a revving car engine - a noise that would take her back to a time and place when that sound had either signalled Ritchie's long-awaited arrival or his dreaded departure.

Or would she feel numb inside, all day long? No relief, no escape, no way out.

The good days were those spent with Adam, when they arranged to go shopping or to see a movie together. Sometimes Adam's flatmate would use his work's van to drive a bunch of them out to a country pub for a Sunday carvery, where they would pile their plates high and rehash the events of the previous evening, when they'd painted the town red with their friends and laughed until dawn.

She was still hurting and very fragile and Adam, to his credit, never once tried to push the boundaries of their friendship or come on to her.

The trouble was, in time, she found herself wanting him to, and that stunned her more than anything.

It was hardly surprising that a single young woman would yearn to be kissed by someone as wonderful as Adam. He was, after all, a virile and staggeringly sexy young man with a heart of gold...and that body of his was just crying out to be jumped upon.

What came as a shock to Kim was the sudden thunderbolt of a possibility that she could ever want anyone other than Ritchie. Her mind struggled with the suggestion that she might actually enjoy being in another man's arms and bed. The depth of her love for Ritchie, the way the relationship had been so cruelly obliterated and the huge empty crater left in its wake, had her absolutely convinced that there could never be anyone else in her life. She would never want another man in that way, and surely never love them to the same degree. He was the love of her life after all.

But she did. She wanted Adam. She'd finally admitted it to herself but it was a secret she hugged close to her chest, declining to share it with anyone else, not even Nicky. The worst part about it all was the realisation that she actually felt guilty for being attracted to Adam! Betraying Ritchie – that's how it felt. And how ridiculous was that? How could she possibly betray a dirty rotten toe-rag who was already married when she met him? This was a man who'd lied and abused her trust and accused HER of being the one with the problem. A shit-bag who'd been getting it on with a whole selection of women across the globe and who'd not only wanted to have his cake and eat it, but who had also been greedy enough to take a bite out of everybody else's buns too!

She'd wondered if Adam felt the same way about her or whether they were basically back in the Friendship Zone. Surely they wouldn't be practically joined at the hip if it was purely platonic? Her sensible head warned that he'd only recently come out of a relatively serious relationship so he was probably just killing time in between girlfriends and enjoying the laughs without any commitment.

Except there were days when she wasn't always much fun to be around. Luckily Adam was the best listener and allowed her to soak his shirt with her tears and he always, always managed to say exactly the right thing and inevitably cheer her up.

And gradually she found she cried and regretted less...and laughed and planned for the future more.

There were moments like when he was regaling some funny story about a rugby buddy who'd lost half of his teeth and she sat, gazing at him, appearing to listen intently - all the while wondering what it would feel like to have those luscious lips of his cover hers or to feel his strong, bulky arms around her comparatively slender body and she had to bite her lip to stop herself saying, 'For the love of god Adam, just kiss me!' She was willing him to sense the change in mood, but if he did, he chose not to pass comment or take her up on her silent offer and she found herself becoming increasingly frustrated.

They still flirted, particularly when they had gallons of alcohol sloshing around inside of them, and there were moments when they were close and she imagined that they were a couple. They'd slow-danced at the end of Marnie's birthday party supposedly so that neither of them would be landed with a lecherous relative or slightly odd acquaintance when the lights went down. But somehow the distance between them was closed, until her head was on his shoulder and his lips were in her hair. And she felt safe and loved and those moments were precious – you could keep your slobbery, saliva-filled kisses and your wandering hands. This was real.

And yet, the following day they were back to fooling around amongst friends, making no mention of the previous evening.

Maybe she should have blurted it out – confessed how she felt and then dealt with the consequences.

But her mind was muddled and stopping her from taking that step.

And ultimately, if Adam did feel the same way, she couldn't risk hurting him again. He deserved way better than a woman on the rebound who still loved another man – a woman who may finish any relationship before it's even legitimately kicked off because her heart still belonged elsewhere.

The situation was removed from her hands when their blended circle of friends unanimously voted on an overnight trip to Blackpool, travelling by train and staying in a budget hotel. The day pretty much involved monkeying around and drinking heavily, merrily traipsing from pub to pub showing off all of their best dance moves alongside groups of tipsy pensioners. It was the funniest, happiest of days which gave Kim a taste of what she'd been missing out on when all her time and money had been spent on the band and she'd foregone a huge part of doing what teenagers do - hanging around with their mates, leaving stresses and responsibilities to the adults.

By pub number eight Kim and Adam were equally mortal and they broke away from the crowd to head off to the nearest fried chicken shop, where they fed each other chips that had clearly been cooked in oil that hadn't been changed in an age. When they staggered back to the hotel, he chivalrously escorted her back to the girls' room but instead of returning to where the boys were to sleep, he followed her inside and they collapsed on the double bed together, cuddling without any prior thought or discussion.

'Night-night, beautiful,' whispered Adam.

'Sweet dreams, handsome,' replied Kim.

When the others returned in the small hours they *apparently* (because Kim subsequently had no memory of the incident taking place) hammered like crazy on the door until Adam shouted 'Bugger Off' while she merely grunted like a pig before settling back into a deep sleep again. Satisfied that they were both safe and well, the rest of the party bunked down together in the boys' room – although Kim suspected they coupled up and she did NOT want to know what had occurred in those beds throughout that night.

When Kim and Adam awoke around dawn, realisation dawned that they were in fact sharing the same bed, although still wearing most of their clothes, thus saving major embarrassment. Kim slipped out of bed first to do the necessary in the bathroom, vigorously scrubbing her teeth to rid herself of her beery breath and spraying herself with exotic smelling perfumes and deodorant, in an attempt to mask the stink of deep fried chicken. As she exited the bathroom, wearing the matching cherry-patterned strappy camisole and pyjama shorts she should have donned much earlier, Adam entered it, clearly wishing to freshen up quick-smart, although he looked and smelled mighty fine to Kim.

Fidgeting with the television remote, flicking between a dire Sunday morning political chat show and a bunch of ancient cartoons, she felt surprisingly tense and shy, unsure as to what she should say or do when Adam re-emerged. Perhaps she should sit casually in the chair by the window or maybe perch on the end of the bed, all calm and nonchalant. In the end she switched off the television, hopped under the covers again and slipped one of her camisole straps down over her shoulder in an effort to look reasonably sexy. She hoped Adam could take a hint.

When he reappeared, clad only in his t-shirt and boxers, it was all she could do to stop herself dribbling – he really was an incredibly handsome guy. Her heart went out to him when she saw that he too was hovering around looking nervous and awkward so she patted the bed and ordered him to get back in, before he froze. Thankfully it broke the ice and he grinned and did as he was told.

Suddenly they were face to face, nose to nose and naturally their lips were next to connect and she was powerless to resist – not that she wanted to. It was one of the most gentle kisses she'd ever known and as his thumb tenderly stroked her cheek and his other hand reached out for her fingers under the covers, something just seemed to fall into place. It felt right. And after only a moment of gazing at each other in wonder, their lips met again and again, each kiss more hungry and intimate than the last. Sometimes, when they paused for breath, he pulled away from her a fraction, smiled and then seemed to study her face intently – maybe searching it for any sign of doubt or regret. Kim felt sure there was none.

And whilst she felt definite stirrings underneath the bedclothes, she was happy that it went no further. Adam was affording her the time that she needed. She was battle-scarred and bruised and needed to learn how to trust again before she entered into another sexual relationship...and although she knew she could trust Adam with her life, it was imperative they let things progress slowly. There was no need to rush, after all.

They returned from their cheeky trip away a fully-fledged couple. Kim's mum and dad were overjoyed, their faces lighting up like Blackpool Illuminations when they saw the pair of them together, Adam's arm casually hanging around Kim's shoulders, hers hooked around his waist. They were so relieved that their daughter was back from the brink. She'd realised there were decent men out there and that Adam was very much one of them.

Whilst she still ached inside for the savage loss she had endured, she couldn't have been happier than she was with Adam, never for one moment doubting his commitment, his fidelity or the strength of his feelings.

Sex was still temporarily off the menu. They'd discussed it and there was no denying they both desperately wanted it but Kim was determined they wouldn't be booking any pay-by-the-night fancy hotel rooms. She'd been there, done that, bought the t-shirt/fancy underwear. There was no privacy to be had at her parents' place, and not much more at Adam's flat but Kim didn't want to be hurtling into a sexual relationship at breakneck speed in any event, because it had been mainly JUST sex with Ritchie and very little else.

Besides, even though she had every expectation that the sex would be spectacular, for the time being it was enough to concentrate on the kissing and touching, finding many, MANY other ways to pleasure each other. The gentleness and kindness of Adam was in stark contrast to the cruelty and self-centredness of Ritchie. When Adam touched her it was never rushed, never greedy, never on purely just his terms.

A few weeks into their relationship, while they were tangled up with each other on the settee in his flat, savouring long, slow kisses and enjoying an hour's blissful peace and privacy, Adam cleared his throat and then opened up his heart to her.

'I love you Kim. There's no point in me waiting weeks or months before I tell you. Because I know now. It's how I've always felt. There's something about you that makes me feel like I've arrived – you know – like I was on a journey not knowing where I was headed, but I've reached my destination now. This is where I was meant to be – with you. No one else. Only you.'

The honesty of him - the way he looked at her and his pupils dilated as he revealed everything and held nothing back – coupled with the downright raw sexiness of him left her deliriously happy but speechless. She'd never expected to feel this strongly about another man, particularly not so soon, when she was still fragile and frightened of falling in love again. But Adam *got her*. He knew she was mixed up and scared and he was insistent that she said nothing in return.

'Please Kim,' he said. 'Don't tell me you love me until you are absolutely certain...and I know you're not there yet. These things take time and I suspect you're still kind of hung up on that lying bastard. If and when you do say it, those words will be everything to me and I'll be bloody ecstatic! But only do so when you're positive you really mean it and he's completely, one hundred per cent out of your system. Not before then - not yet.'

So she didn't feel under pressure, even though he'd uttered that precious statement first – even though she knew deep down that she loved him. It was important that she loved him equally though and not only as an extremely fanciable friend who she was crazy about and who was there for her when she needed him. She had to know for sure that she no longer loved Ritchie Joe Clarke in any capacity before she declared her love for Adam.

Adam's patience and understanding enabled her to pace herself. He gave her the space that she needed whilst providing the companionship and love that she'd never known before.

She really didn't miss turning in to bed and being overwhelmed by fear and loneliness. It was a relief to fall asleep dry-eyed and not wake up on a pillow soaked with tears she'd shed in the dead of night.

Of course there were lapses – moments when she'd feel a pang for her former life. Times when she'd recall something Ritchie said or did and suddenly the memories were so vivid that it was almost like she was there with him again. She'd hear a mention of Birmingham or see a male model on a poster with dark hair and green eyes, or an Audi would whizz by her in town and she'd instantly see flashes of Ritchie, feel intense spears of pain.

But her life was changing for the better now and she truly believed she was finally moving on. For the main part she was happy. Loving Adam and having Adam love her in return was more than she could ever have wished for. She knew she was a lucky, lucky woman.

*

And then the Ritchie Joe Clarke show rocked up only a few miles away from where she lived.

She'd severed all ties with the *Show Me Yours* community, which meant the only information she'd had concerning the band was that which she'd struggled to avoid in the press or on television. The fan club had been dissolved around the same time as the band, to be replaced by an information service that reported on each of them individually, but she'd purposely kept her name off the mailing list. The last thing she wanted was to be receiving any updates regarding solo material or promotional events – it was all irrelevant to her now.

So when she happened to glance in a record shop window and found herself eyeballing the man himself, dressed from top to toe in biker leathers, sneering at the camera whilst professing to play an electric guitar, she nearly keeled over in shock.

Occupying much of the huge pane of glass was a mammoth poster of Ritchie, underneath which was a short printed list of scheduled personal appearances - one due to take place next month at an outdoor concert only ten short minutes away down the road.

'Holy shit!' she squealed, shopping bags dropping to the wet pavement as she stepped closer to the glass to check her mind wasn't playing tricks on her. Nope, poster still there. Ritchie still having the audacity to turn up on her patch for his 'work' - when he would NEVER have gone there for pleasure, even if she'd begged and pleaded. Apparently, it was to be his first live solo appearance to promote his single and album...and that in itself felt strange – that she'd been unaware he had new music due to be released. She hadn't even realised he'd ever seriously considered going solo, although it should have been no great surprise after the demise of the band.

Kim had arranged to meet Adam for lunchtime drinks and realised she probably looked slightly deranged as she flew into the busy pub, desperate to impart her news.

'That lying, cheating no-good arsehole! Have you seen it? Have you? The poster in Hitzone's window? He's apparently playing Wolsey Park as he's got a frigging solo single coming out...and he's top of the bill. The cheeky fucking bastard!'

Tossing the shopping bags onto one of the empty chairs, she almost burst a blood vessel trying to digest the information and deal with her emotions.

'How fucking dare he! He knows full well that I'm from this area – Christ knows, I told him often enough. And yet he has no qualms about turning up here, stirring up feelings, hurting me yet again. Has the man no shame?'

'Well, clearly not,' Adam responded quietly, carefully placing his pint glass down onto the table. Kim noticed he'd barely touched his lager, even though he'd probably been waiting ages because she was late - as usual.

'I can't believe it Adam. After everything he's done, does he really think he can turn up out of the blue and everything will be hunky-dory? It really does beggar belief!'

'But apparently it's only one of many gigs that's been lined up to promote his album.'

She'd been digging in her handbag, searching for her purse, even though she knew Adam would probably insist on paying for her drink. But suddenly her head shot up and she was on high alert. Before she had managed to put her brain in gear, she was firing bullets at the wrong person.

'You knew? You fucking knew about this and you didn't tell me?'

'Of course I didn't bloody tell you! What purpose would it have served? Your *Show Me Yours* days are over and you're supposedly moving on, trying to forget the man. So no, I didn't tell you because I didn't think you'd want to know. And obviously I didn't want to upset you...'

'Oh yeah, like that's the reason eh?'

'And what the bloody hell is THAT supposed to mean?'

'It means that it suited your purpose – that you didn't mention it because you didn't want Ritchie back in my life again!'

276

'Back in your life again? Kim, he's MARRIED. You found out and quite rightly erased him from your life...but he was never going to give HER up for YOU...no matter how wonderful you are...'

'Oh thanks for that – it's made me feel much better. You know what, you had no right to keep this from me. I'm an adult and can make my own choices - I don't need you protecting me all of the time.'

Silence. Adam's face was a furious shade of red and the pint remained on the table, abandoned.

'You're absolutely right Kim – you're free to make your own choices and I won't stand in your way. I suppose this was inevitable. Christ, he only pops up in your life on a poster in a shop window and you're already a changed woman.'

She was still angry but guilt was already setting in. She shouldn't have ripped into Adam – he was the good guy.

'Look Adam, I know you meant well but I shouldn't have had to find out like this. I'm seething that he doesn't give a toss about it opening up old wounds for me, but I'll try to keep calm and see what he has to say for himself...'

'*You mean you're actually planning on going to this gig?*' Adam was incredulous that Kim could even consider drifting within a fifty mile radius of Ritchie after what he'd done to her, let alone engage him in conversation.

'I have to Adam...no, please...listen to me. I have to because I want answers. I *need* answers. When it all imploded, it was brutal and it was over in a flash – which meant I was trying to tackle him on it whilst I was still trying to take it all in myself. I was angry and he was on the defensive and it was only later that I wished I'd said *this* and I wished I'd asked *that*. You know what I mean?'

'No Kim, I don't know what you mean. When both parties are decent human beings then yes, I suppose when a relationship breaks down, each needs to know exactly what went wrong. Nobody should be left in the dark and everyone is entitled to answers for the sake of closure. But this is Ritchie Shithead Clarke you're talking about. The man who kept you as his secret girlfriend year on year whilst his wife waited patiently at home *and* he bedded god knows how many other unsuspecting young women who also probably thought they were in with a shout…'

'Stop it Adam! I know what he did, I'm not stupid. But I have to see him one more time. I need to look him in the eye and ask if he ever really felt anything for me – if there hadn't been a wife, then would there have been a chance for us? I know it sounds crazy but I just have to know. And whatever he tells me – whichever way it goes – then I'll have my closure.'

Adam's face crumpled as all the fight seeped out of him. He looked defeated and sad and at that moment in time Kim hated herself for inflicting more anguish on him. But she couldn't help herself.

'Kim, I can't keep putting myself through this. It's too hard. Too painful. I have to walk away before it destroys me.'

'Walk away from what? Don't do this Adam. We've had an amazing time together and I've felt…well everything I thought I'd never feel again. You know I'm over Ritchie and of course I've moved on. But this is just something I've got to do.'

He shook his head, resigned to the unavoidable outcome.

'Kim, you may have moved on to some degree but you're lying to yourself if you think you're over him. You haven't even begun to get over him. I see that look in your eyes and I know it's still him…and maybe it always will be. Even though you've come on in leaps and bounds and you've learned to live your life without him in the forefront, he's still always there in the background. And I can't accept this. I can't wait around forever on the off-chance that you'll finally stop wanting him. He still has such a hold over you – whether you like to admit it or not – and as soon as he's back on the scene, I'm discarded. It's relegation time for Adam again - despite everything we've shared. Can you really be sure, if he left his wife tomorrow, that you wouldn't forgive him and take him back? Please be honest with me.'

Oh god, she didn't know, and that was the worst of it. In her head she knew of course that Ritchie was an accomplished liar who'd do it all over again in a heartbeat. Someone who'd hurt her relentlessly without even batting an eyelid.

But her traitorous heart still clung on to the memory of the two of them together and no, she couldn't be sure that she wouldn't crumble in his arms again, given half the chance.

Her silence spoke volumes to Adam, who stood up abruptly and cleared his throat, his watery eyes documenting the struggle with his emotions.

'I just can't do this anymore Kim. I'm calling it quits.'

As he proceeded to shuffle out from between the table and chairs Kim lunged forward to grab his arm. She couldn't lose her lovely friend like this, not over this. Life without Adam in it didn't seem like much of a life – he made her laugh, he took care of her, he listened, he loved, he cared.

'Please Adam, don't do this,' she pleaded, pulling at his tan suede jacket – the jacket they'd chosen together when he'd decided to update the contents of his wardrobe in view of the 'extremely stylish woman on his arm'.

'I just need those answers. For god's sake, you know I hate Ritchie for what he did, for how he treated me...'

'Remember that fine line between love and hate? Well that's where you're at. You shouldn't love him, you shouldn't hate him – he has to be nothing to you before you can get on with your life and love again.' He gently uncurled her fingers, hesitated and then bent down to kiss them. She felt like she'd swallowed a whole egg – the lump in her throat was huge but the void in her life would be immeasurable.

'You need to get over Ritchie and I need to get over you. I'm not sure either's going to happen but we have to try...because we both deserve to be happy, just probably not together.'

'Oh Adam don't say that, it sounds so final! I can't bear the thought of losing you. I'll miss you so much...'

'I know you will – and the feeling is very much mutual. I think you do love me, in your own way, but it's not enough – not in the same way I love you. It's a shame, because we – me and you – could have been awesome. But it's obviously not meant to be and we both have to wake up and smell the Nescafé.'

Tears were plopping down her cheeks, because deep down she knew he was right and, to be fair to him, she had to let him go. But she was up and in his face before he knew what had hit him. He wiped away her tears with his thumbs and she wept words of apologies, before burying her head in his chest, hoping he'd let her stay there forever.

Eventually he took hold of her shoulders and eased her gently away.

'I'm sorry too,' he whispered, before turning and walking out of the pub and out of her life.

Kim cried all the way home, dreading the moment when she would have to inform her family that she and Adam had split, for good.

There was no shouting, no recriminations – even when they found out about Ritchie's gig and Kim's desire to have it out with him. Her dad just nodded grimly and her mum tutted and said, 'Well it's not ideal, but if it's what it takes to get this man out of your system then maybe it's the thing to do...'

Loneliness descended upon her as night fell and she curled up like a foetus on her duvet, wide-eyed and wondering what the hell was wrong with her.

She'd allowed the most wonderful man to slip away from her, again, and although she'd hurt him unintentionally, she'd still hurt him, and that stung. She was a cretin to let him go, and when she considered the possibility – no, *probability* – that he would eventually meet someone else, marry them and most likely raise a family with them, it made her feel physically sick.

And yet, if she could press rewind and play that day again she'd probably still have walked the same road, because she had to see Ritchie again and attempt to fill in those blanks - and this would probably be the best chance she ever got.

The trouble was, she could still remember what it felt like to be in Ritchie's arms. If she closed her eyes she could still feel his lips brush hers and his fingertips trace the outline of her face. The memories were so vivid still that she could almost hear him breathing there beside her...his chest rising up and down...his heart beating as one with her own.

But he wasn't there. She was alone. And maybe that was her destiny.

Chapter 29

What on earth had she hoped to achieve by swanning off to see Ritchie? Had she really believed that he would man up and face the music? For goodness sake, when had he ever been known to lie down and take his punishment?

Of course he wouldn't speak to her! *Of course* he would do everything in his power to avoid making eye contact or conversation with her! At best it was painful, at worst it was humiliating.

She'd arrived ridiculously early, determined he wouldn't escape her interrogation. She would pin him down and speak to him civilly, finally establishing whether he'd only considered her to be a bit of fluff on the side or whether she had in fact ever touched his heart.

Besides a small number of *Show Me* Yours fans – identifiable by their old tour t-shirts and excitable demeanour, Kim was sickened to see Sally-Anne and the Witches already on site, awaiting Ritchie's arrival. It was excruciatingly awkward but these girls were veritably rubbing their hands together at her discomfort, sniggering and whispering and having the cheek to look down their noses at her. More than once she thought she heard them use the word 'slag' as they glanced over in her direction. Sal never actually uttered a word to her face – not even to say hello. Kim couldn't believe this girl had stayed at her house once upon a time, been welcomed by her family and trusted to keep Kim's most guarded secrets because she'd considered her to be a genuine friend.

Worse still, there weren't enough fans waiting outside the main gates to lose herself in any crowd until Ritchie arrived. Just her and them and a few locals with their autograph books and biros.

When Ritchie finally did turn up in a brand new, customised Audi, the security guard opened the gates to let him drive through...and Kim didn't know who was most surprised when they were all allowed to tailgate in – the little crowd or the big star.

Almost as if they'd been instructed what to do in the unlikely event Kim ever popped back up again, Sally-Anne and her cronies promptly sprang into action and surrounded Ritchie, fiercely protecting him, as he was led away by the bubbly young girl whose badge identified her as Event Coordinator. Ritchie pretended he hadn't seen Kim and quickly disappeared into a mobile dressing room, briefly reappearing a couple of minutes later, but only to beckon Sally-Anne and her associates into his lair! Leaving Kim on the outside - uninvited and clearly unwanted.

Quite a turn-up for the books.

Who did he think he was? And who did they think they were? Nasty little cows.

'Excuse me...'

She hadn't notice the elderly couple sidling up to her, the lady waving a pen and a leaflet in her right hand. 'Do you think he'll be back out to sign for us or is he likely to stay inside with his friends? Sorry, you are a fan aren't you?'

A fan? Not really. Not anymore. In the early years, yes, before she'd morphed into a Friend-of-Sorts, before apparently shagging her way to Fuck Buddy status, ejected from that seat by the emergence of a faithful old wife. Kim presumed she was now more Foe than Friend, not even worthy of a smile or a kind word, let alone an explanation or apology.

She was an absolute *Fucking Nobody* now.

Consigned to the shit-heap for committing the Category One crime of loving a man who she hadn't known was married to someone else.

'I...I was a massive *Show Me Yours* fan back in their heyday...'

Well that was the truth. She'd loved that band, as an entity, before Ritchie had wormed his way into her underwear and hacked away at her heart until it bled. The band was so much more than one person – he was the frontman but they were the main men. Wherever life took her, she would always treasure the memories she'd made with the other guys and wish only the best for them in the future.

Wandering away from the OAP strangers, she treated herself to an ice cold slushie and killed time mooching around the stalls, watching the other artists in action. And then she half-heartedly sat through Ritchie's set. There was no denying his voice and stage presence commanded attention, and the new songs were good (but honestly didn't have the energy of the old *Show Me Yours'* hits)...but she couldn't feel the same about his performance. He'd ruined that for her now. The audience were also pretty reserved and disinterested until he wound up with a couple of the band's old classics, and suddenly they were all up dancing and singing along.

She'd parted from the crowd by then, although if she squinted she could just about make out Sally-Anne and the other Devil's Daughters bouncing up and down at the front. When she started to head round the back, to make her way towards Ritchie's changing cabin, Kim had a real stroke of luck, stumbling across an old school 'friend' manning the security gate at the rear of the stage. Lyndon had always been a bit of a knob, but she was never so grateful as when he asked 'You here with Ritchie Clarke then?' Kim nodded and he proudly ushered her through, clearly believing that she was still doing the business with Tosspot and therefore treating her like a minor celebrity, by association.

It was all worth it, to see the look of horror on Ritchie's face when he came jogging off stage and ran smack bang into little old Kim, almost knocking her off her feet.

'Hi Ritchie...not planning on catching me this time?'

She'd rarely seen him stuck for words. He always had so much to say for himself. Still panting from his exertions on stage, he was hot and shiny and she knew he'd be desperate to go and strip off, clean up and grab an iced drink.

So she barred his path.

'Don't worry, this will only take a second,' she assured him, enjoying his discomfort. He took a hasty step backwards, presumably in case she planned to slam her fist into his pretty little face. She was sorely tempted, but had far more dignity than he gave her credit for.

'Get a grip Ritchie, I'm not about to do anything stupid. Not now. Getting involved with you and allowing myself to be strung along for years...well, I do believe that used up all of my stupidity allowance. But there's something I have to ask...and I feel you owe me an honest answer. It's the least you can do after the disgraceful way you used me, lied to me and tore my heart apart.'

He had the grace to look marginally ashamed and when she eyeballed him she saw something else there too - a look of affection possibly? A glimpse of that tender side he liked to keep so well hidden? Whatever it was, it wasn't enough. Kim wanted answers.

'I loved you Ritchie – god help me but I did. It's ridiculous really, but I need to know whether you felt anything too or, conversely, if I meant nothing whatsoever to you. Don't be afraid to say if that's the case by the way – it may not be the kindest thing you've ever said but at least it will be the truth, for once in your life. Whatever your response, at least I will know once and for all before I completely erase the memory of *us* from my mind.'

He raked his hand through his damp hair and part of his fringe fell forward, tumbling into his eyes. In the past she'd have reached out and brushed it to one side with her fingertips and one thing would have led to another. She resisted the temptation to touch him now and kept her hands firmly on her hips, showing him who was boss, even though she was quivering inside.

'Well? Say something then!' She was losing patience with him already. How difficult could it be to give her a straight answer? Jesus, the man should have been a politician rather than a singer.

There were a few raised voices behind here and she became vaguely aware of two members of security staff and Gimpy Gav fast approaching but was determined to persevere anyway.

"Ritchie, I need to know why you did it. Did I simply imagine those rare moments when you gave the impression that you cared? Or was it all just one big fat lie right from the off?'

'Kimberley...look...you know you meant a lot to me but my life was complicated before you came along and although I never set out to hurt anyone, I found myself in an incredibly difficult position and...GAV! There you are! I know, I know...we need to get going...'

He'd seen a lifeline and grabbed it like a drowning man, the fucking coward. Saved by Mr Toad, universally despised road manager and complete and utter tosser.

As she stared at Ritchie then – at a man she'd never really known – she lost any last remaining ounce of respect she might ever have retained for him. He couldn't even do that one small thing for her – deliver one truthful sentence. It was so little to ask in return for such a lot that she had given to him.

Until he'd spotted Gav racing to his rescue, he'd been about to reel off some first class bullshit. She'd never have known if any morsel of it was the real deal or if it was all yet more pathetic, inexcusable lies. What a pointless exercise this had been.

The funny thing was, as she swiftly turned and left – determined she would have the satisfaction of walking away from him, rather than the other way round – and she made for the exit as fast as her wobbly legs would take her, she thought she heard him call out her name.

'Kimberley.'

But she carried on walking; there was no turning back.

Previously she would have swung around and been ready to run to him as soon as he clicked his fingers...but no more.

He'd made a fool of her for the very last time.

It was weird that it didn't hurt as much as she'd expected it to. In fact, it felt like a colossal weight had been lifted from her shoulders. She was free. There was no fanfare, no celebrations, no jubilations...just a sweet release from the pain that had always accompanied her intense feelings for Ritchie.

*

Later that day, when she tried to explain everything firstly to her mum and then secondly to Nicky, she could see they were struggling to understand. Both of them viewed it all in black and white and couldn't really comprehend how she could be so desperate to see Ritchie one minute and then be so sure she was done with him the next.

But she knew.

It had been a long and arduous journey but she had finally reached the end of the road.

When she'd seen him there, by himself, faltering and panicky...and looking for all the world like a rabbit caught in the headlights, she'd realised he was never the man she'd believed him to be and therefore never the man who could have made her truly happy. The hatred she'd felt for his wife had been replaced by pity, because this weak and pathetic woman was continuing to endure Ritchie's lies and infidelities, presumably because she loved him and was afraid to let him go.

Whereas for Kim, it was at last well and truly over.

She felt sad that she'd wasted so much of her life on a man who was incapable of loving in the same way. She felt ashamed that she'd treated many people abysmally in her pursuit of someone whose heart was made of stone.

But more than anything, she was full of regret because she'd lost the one good man she'd ever had when she'd picked Ritchie over Adam that day. She'd ruined the best thing that had ever happened to her – she knew that now, although her judgement had been clouded at the time. The most beautiful man, inside and out, who had genuinely loved all of her, all of the time – not just the bits of her he could use for his own pleasure, to satisfy his own desires. The most caring, considerate, kind human being who was incapable of telling even a little white lie – whereas lying was second nature to Ritchie, who was incapable of telling the truth.

On the grapevine she'd heard that Adam was seeing a dental nurse from the posh side of town. Kim had strolled past the practice a few times one day to try and catch a glimpse of this new girlfriend but regretted her actions when the woman came bounding out of the front door at lunchtime. She was, of course, blessed with a tiny, dainty figure and had translucent blonde hair which she wore scraped up in a swingy little ponytail. And her naturally pretty, heart-shaped face was lit up by whiter than white, perfectly straight teeth. Why couldn't she have been a munter? It would have made Kim feel so much better.

She missed Adam, god how she missed him. Achingly so. She longed to hear his voice, his laugh, his footsteps…but she knew she had to do the right thing and leave him be.

She'd had her chance with him – so many chances – and buggered everything right up. He, more than anyone she'd ever known, deserved true and everlasting happiness and she couldn't interfere with that. She'd never find out how their story could have ended, their lovemaking would only ever happen in her imagination...and there would be no opportunity to tell him those three words he'd waited so long to hear.

'I love you,' she whispered to her memory of him. 'I love you Adam Foley.'

PART FOUR

FINAL

(2018)

Chapter 30

'Any idea where my phone is, mum? I promised I'd message Jock and Vaughan about the rugby.'

'How would I know where it is Matty? I've barely seen you the last three days and when you've been home you've been holed up in your room. May I suggest that you try removing a layer of debris off your carpet and you might just strike lucky – that's if you're not lost forever underneath the mounds of dirty washing or infected by the mould on the collection of plates you seem determined to stash away until you've collected a full dinner service. I tell you what, if you're not out of there in an hour shall I send in a search party?'

'Ha-ha, very funny old mother of mine...now where on earth did I...oh that's it! I can hear it ringing!'

'I know, I'm the one ringing it, you tool.'

'Mmmwwwahh. You beauty! Cheers mum...what would I do without you?'

'Starve and have no friends?' Handing over his sandwiches, Kim longed to smooth down the stuck-up tuft of hair on his beautiful fair head but instead tutted in mock disgust at his inability to arrange his life into some kind of order. She loved her lads – her life's work – and didn't really mind running around after them. Which was just as well, because Matty, her eldest, was high maintenance even for a seventeen year old. Although at seventeen she came complete with a whole other stack of problems...

'*Will!* Get a move on if you want your father to drop you off! If you're not ready he'll leave without you...' As if. He'd never yet missed a ride with his dad and he was in his penultimate year at school. Will may have been two years younger than Matty but he was bright as a button and a dab hand at twisting his parents round his little finger.

Thundering down the stairs came their not-so-little ball of energy, chestnut hair expertly gelled into place to impress the *ladyeeez*. Kim noticed he'd dropped the name of the girl he sat beside in Maths into most conversations in a casual 'Tara said this...' and 'Tara said that' kind of way and it was a dead cert that he had his sights set on this lovely young girl who worked in the local takeaway at weekends. If nothing else, he might bag a few extra chips out of it.

'Do you want me to pick anything up from the shop on the way home tonight love?'

Ah. Kim's other half, looking dapper in his tailored pin-striped suit, straightening his favourite navy silk tie that Kim had bought him last Christmas and dropping a featherlike kiss on to the crown of her bed-head.

How she loved him. There were of course occasions when she thought he was purposefully trying to drive her round the twist, but on the whole he was a modern day saint – especially putting up with the three of them. He might watch and play more football and rugby than she would like and snore like a rusty chainsaw when he'd downed several pints at the Spinners on a Friday with his mates...but on balance, she had many more faults than him.

And even though his hair had greyed – so much so that it looked as if his head been dipped in silver paint – and he had a few wrinkles that had taken up residence on his incredibly handsome face, he was still as gorgeous as the day she'd first met him and she knew what a lucky dog she was.

'If you're going anyway, buy chocolate. Big bar. No nuts.'

They played out this little farce almost every day – she would tell him to buy chocolate but only if he was calling in the shop anyway, and he would visit the shop specifically to pick up chocolate, and chocolate alone. Because he was that kind of guy.

'See you later love. And maybe that chocolate might earn me a little snuggle tonight eh?' He leant in for a proper kiss – still full on the lips – and treated her to a cheeky wink whilst Will shoved two fingers down his throat in a vomit-inducing piss-taking gesture.

'Get a room,' he groaned, covering his eyes, presumably so he wouldn't be scarred for life.

'We *have* a room,' Kim chirped back at him. 'But it's full of most of your belongings after you decided to have a sort out and dumped all your gear on us.'

'I'll take it to the charity shop at weekend,' his dad sighed. 'Just add it to my list of jobs. Bye love, enjoy your day off.'

A mass exodus out of the front door and then they were all gone, to their respective jobs and places of education. Switching off the radio – Kim generally loved music playing in the background all day long but Wednesdays were blissful, when she liked to savour the peace and quiet for her first free hour of the day – she collected her coffee from the machine and pottered through to their living room to sink deep into the corner of the L-shaped leather settee, inhaling the solitude. She adored all of her compact family unit but my god, it was a treat to have time to herself!

This was her favourite part of the house. The way the sunlight slipped through the horizontal wooden blinds, painting the room with golden stripes....and the collection of dark framed family photographs that were in stark contrast to the off-white walls they were hung from. They'd replaced the fireplace only a few months earlier and the chimney breast was now covered in a modern but tasteful ivory and gold textured wallpaper which matched the super-plush champagne rug that Wiggle, their over-eating, slightly flatulent, golden Labrador liked to sink into after Kim had meticulously cleaned and towel-dried his paws at the living room door.

She adored this living space. It was a family room and her lovely family had enjoyed many precious hours in here over the years. Confidences had been shared, tears wiped away, laughter had rung out and board games had been played. Most evenings when she returned from work she would dive upstairs and melt into a scalding hot bath, before drying off and sliding into her favourite fluffy dressing gown and slippers. Then she would return to her designated corner of the settee to relax and invariably nod off whilst curled into her equally knackered husband. His job was demanding - Kim still wasn't sure exactly what it entailed but she knew it was something in computers and that he was in charge of IT for several huge manufacturing firms, working on a strictly freelance basis, which meant that he too was basically his own boss. She was so proud of him. After changing career path a couple of times he'd finally returned to college to re-train and look at him now! He'd grafted his way up the ladder and was remarkable at his job, apparently.

Mind you, she worked bloody hard too. Kim still struggled to believe she was actually sole proprietor of her own successful business! Her very own cafe and catering set-up. When Carol had suddenly thrown in the towel and Kim had still been there, clinging on but drifting aimlessly, her boss had made her an offer she simply couldn't refuse. After careful consideration over several glasses of Chardonnay in the pub with her mum, dad, Freddie and Rochelle, Kim had borrowed the money and purchased the business for a stupidly low price, complete with fixtures and fittings, and hey presto, one businesswoman! Okay, she knew it wasn't the Ivy, but once she'd passed her driving test they'd expanded into outside catering, and also the shop next door, which led to them making and delivering approximately five billion paninis per week, on top of providing cakes and cookies for numerous businesses within a ten mile radius. She'd surrounded herself with an amazing team who had all the baking and cooking know-how whilst Kim mainly dealt with the business side and fought for accounts at massive money-spinning venues across the region.

Who would have thought it though? Certainly not Kim, that's for sure. After a shaky start when many people had written her off as a no-hoper, she'd suddenly gathered speed and momentum and once she realised she actually had a talent for it, there'd been no stopping her since. She wasn't raking in millions but could boast a decent profit after only the second year of trading and Kim's salary combined with her hardworking husband's income meant they lived a comfortable lifestyle whilst saving to put the boys through college and university. They did, however, wish to enjoy the fruits of their labour while they still could and therefore intended to take their feet off their respective accelerators as soon as the bulk of the mortgage was paid off.

They were kidding themselves building up a university fund for Will. He'd never exactly been academic and when the school careers advisor enquired as to what his ideal job would be in the not too distant future, he'd instantly replied 'Holiday Rep'. Bless him.

Brew finished, life contemplated, Kim forced herself up and into the kitchen to load the dishwasher, switching the radio on as she flitted about.

'I see you stumble and I'm there waiting...'

And off it went again, instantly.

'Shit. Wow. Not heard that bloody song in years.'

It was true. As the lesser played number on a double A-sided single, unless the listeners were of a certain age and had been dedicated *Show Me Yours* fans way back when, they were unlikely to have remembered the song at all as it had practically faded away into obscurity. And it certainly wasn't ever played on the radio any more. It was always *Tantalising* that made it on to the airwaves as it had been a collaboration between the band and Saturday Munro – a young girl with big ambition in the eighties and nineties whose music had stood the test of time and whose image had evolved over the years to ensure she was always, always relevant.

Well...dear god...that took me by surprise and dredged up a few unwelcome memories...

Over the years the better known hits of the band had continued to receive radio play and were also still blasted out at functions and in nightclubs as the resident DJ treated themself to a cheese-fest. And over time Kim had become desensitised, able to hear them and accept them for what they were – cracking pop songs that filled dancefloors. She no longer had an aversion to the sound of Ritchie's voice; it had ceased to have that effect on her decades ago. There were no associations to sordid liaisons or broken promises...no tears, no hatred, no love. In fact, quite often she found herself smiling as she blanked out the image of the man who'd broken her heart and recalled the other four wonderful and talented band members – the boys who'd become men. Except Bren of course, the boy who'd never quite got the hang of growing up.

But this song...this track was in a different league. It was from a time and place that was buried deeply within her. An old wound that had been plastered over with true love that had come later. She hadn't heard this in years and yet, suddenly, she was back there, drenched in memories of days and nights that she didn't particularly want to re-visit, but they were always there, somewhere, hidden, waiting to drill through and remind her what a fool she'd been.

Those words. How she'd lapped them up when he'd sang them to her. How she'd seriously believed they were deeply personal between the two of them - that they were truly on the same wavelength.

The way he'd looked at her. His eyes, his body language, his intentions. Ideally she would forget that she ever loved someone like Ritchie Clarke but it was impossible as he was a significant part of her past that she couldn't simply erase because it hurt to go there. There was no altering the fact that it all happened, however long ago. And even though Ritchie had lied, deceived and played her, it had still all happened to Kimberley Helen Summers - no one else. Her feelings were her own and consequently so were her memories.

From time to time she wondered if she ever popped up in Ritchie's memories or if he'd ever had any regrets about the despicable way he'd treated her. Probably not. She didn't believe Ritchie had ever possessed a conscience. As far as she was aware, he'd never gone on to have any children (at least none that he knew about) – although she'd certainly never kept track of him since the day of his solo gig when she'd finally let him go.

He was too selfish a man to nurture and bring up other human beings who would need his undivided attention...but if he *had* made babies then maybe one day it may have occurred to him that at best he had treated Kim badly, at worst with contempt. It may have made him think how devastated he would be if his own child were to be the victim of such a deliberate deception by the person they loved.

Still, he couldn't hurt Kim anymore. She didn't love him, she didn't hate him...he was merely an egotistical, heartless man from her past who didn't deserve any further consideration from her...and he certainly wasn't getting any.

Besides, she'd loved Adam now much longer than she'd ever loved Ritchie and he made her smile and love life rather than weep and suffer the worst kind of pain imaginable.

Adam. Her husband. After all of these years she still loved to say it.

*

Following her painful split from Adam, there had been a couple of years when they'd both gone through the motions of cracking on with their lives, once Kim had been able to rid hers of all the toxicity.

Adam had three girlfriends during that time – not that Kim was keeping count – and each time she heard there was someone new in his life it was like another wound inflicted. She couldn't bear it, but she had to, because she had no right to stand in the way of his happiness.

She dated one guy, Aaron, for all of six weeks before confessing that she was still in love with her ex (Adam, of course) – which he took quite badly and told everyone she was a dull, frigid chubber. The next time Kim ran into him he wasn't looking too good himself. Either he had fought with a door and lost or someone had clearly shattered his nose, although no one would admit to it. Kim's dad, Freddie and Connor were all high on Kim's list of likely suspects, but almost a decade later she discovered that gentle pacifist Adam had been furious to hear what was doing the rounds and had actually waited for Aaron outside of his crummy flat and punched him full-on in the face. Good lad.

Reluctantly, she'd admitted to Nicky that she'd felt precisely nothing for Aaron right from the outset but had taken a chance on him because he was supposedly gorgeous, although he just didn't rattle her lust bucket. After that disastrous coupling she'd withdrawn from active dating and relationships and made do with the odd meaningless snog in a nightclub...but even that lost its appeal very quickly and she decided she'd rather go home with a kebab and a hangover than any man other than Adam.

Nicky and her mum could see through her fake smiles of course and knew how much she was missing Adam. Her best friend forced a confession out of her one day whilst they were stuffing in slabs of chocolate cake, admiring the brand new kitchen Connor and his brother had recently fitted.

'You love him, don't you? Adam I mean – not bastard Ritchie.'

'Yes, of course I do. But I'm too late Nick...I had my chance and I blew it. In fact I had several chances and I blew them all. By the time it finally dawned on me that he might be The One, we'd gone our separate ways – and I've been paying for it dearly every day since.'

'I knew it! Your eyes – they give everything away, you know. I can see how unhappy you are, deep down. And it's not a raging, raw, Ritchie kind of pain...it's more of an anguished acceptance which makes you look dead inside...'

'Bloody hell, it's that bad eh? Nothing I can do about it though. I can't exactly ask him to dump his latest lady in favour of me – not with my track record. Anyway, for all I know, they might be deadly serious about each other. He may be completely smitten and mapping out a future with her...'

'Or he's equally as miserable as you are and is trying to save face amongst the lads by strutting round town with a stunner on his arm...when all he really wants is you...'

'Oh cheers, that makes me sound like a real ugly mush! It's a bloody good job I know what you mean. Anyway, it's a lovely idea but wishful thinking I'm afraid. He made it perfectly clear that we were definitely over, for good, and that there was no going back for him. To be honest, I don't think he'd ever really believe me now if I told him I loved him. As far as he's concerned, there isn't a hope in hell of moving past the spectre of Ritchie Joe Clarke...'

'Oh Kim, you have to try – because you'll regret it for the rest of your life if you don't. You two were made for each other and yes, sure, it's taken you a while to cop on to yourself and allow any other man access to your heart...but Adam might just relent and forgive you. I'm telling you, he's still in love with you. He might have had other girlfriends but he's never truly got over you.'

Nicky wore Kim down in the end. She accepted that she couldn't continue with the half-life she was living. Even if there was only the faintest of chances that Adam might still be interested, then she had to go for it. She accepted that she had to be the one to go cap in hand to Adam though. It had to be her who contacted him and not the other way round. She'd hurt him too many times, wounded his pride and made him feel second best when all along *he'd* been her destiny.

Nicky rolled her eyes in disbelief when Kim informed her that she was writing a good old-fashioned letter to Adam to explain how she felt. It wouldn't be right to turn up at his flat or ring him out of the blue and she certainly couldn't follow him round town on his lads' night out like a deranged stalker or lay in wait for him when he exited the gym. She wanted to get it down on paper – to pour her heart out and have him read it, make a quiet decision on his own without bowing to pressure...and be able to screw her missive up and toss it in the bin if he really was completely done with her.

So she stuck a first class stamp on it, popped it in the post and waited. It should have arrived Tuesday. By Wednesday she felt sick with fear that radio silence meant she'd not only made a holy show of herself (again) but also that he'd finally fallen out of love with her.

It was only on the Friday night, when she was a complete snivelling mess, that she discovered Adam was actually away on holiday and not due back until the following weekend! It really did feel like the longest two weeks of her life, anxiously waiting for his return. Even the lengthy periods she'd idled away striking the days off until she saw Ritchie again were a piece of cake compared to this torture – and the suspense was killing her.

Eventually she received a response by text but, although Adam probably meant well, it was somewhat inadequate.

Thanks for your letter. I need some time to think. I'll be in touch, Ad x

He'd obviously read it straight away and then pinged off the text so she wouldn't think he was ignoring her. That was him all over, always considering the feelings of others. But it clearly wasn't a cut and dry situation for him. He hadn't been bowled over by her efforts at reconciliation, read the words that had poured from her heart and thought *'I still love her. This is it...she's the one...it was always her.'*

Patience was a virtue that she really didn't possess, but in this instance she had to suck it up and allow matters to take their course on Adam's terms, in Adam's own time. But it was shit.

At the end of another interminable week Marnie insisted on dragging her along as her plus-one to a friend's engagement party, although Kim was seriously reluctant to even leave the house, let alone celebrate some other lucky git's happiness at having found their soulmate. Blah.

But there was apparently no one else available to step into her shoes, so she found herself prised into one of Marnie's skimpy holiday dresses, with her hair in a beautiful 'up' do – the benefits of having hairdresser friends – arriving at the local bowling club, which had been titivated with balloons and banners for the special occasion.

They'd been there precisely ten minutes, in which time they'd said hello to the happy couple, Sam and Sam (true story – Sam, the big burly bloke who was a primary school teacher and teeny-tiny Samantha, his former teaching assistant), purchased two drinks each from the bar and grabbed a table on the periphery of the dancefloor, when Kim glanced across the room at a noisy party of lads sidling over to the bar. To her horror, she saw Adam in the thick of them, looking hot and heavenly in a loose black shirt over charcoal jeans, effortlessly cool.

'Shite!' she didn't want him to think she'd come to the party deliberately to 'accidentally' bump into him. She had to get out of there.

Too late. Obviously sensing a pair of beady eyes boring into the back of his head, he'd turned around and looked over in their direction, his brows raised as his eyes met Kim's.

She forced out a feeble smile and raised her glass in an attempt at a matey gesture before quickly grabbing hold of her friend's arm.

'Marnie, we have to leave...now! Adam's here and he'll think that's the only reason I am. He'll feel under pressure and bolt for the door and meanwhile I'll reek of desperation and...'

'Oh don't be so bloody ridiculous...of course Adam's here! He's the cousin of Man Sam...ooh, did I forget to mention that?'

'*Marnie!* Of course you did!' Kim hissed in response as she realised she'd been done up like a kipper. 'You knew all along, didn't you? That's why I'm here! That's why you insisted on strong-arming me along on a Saturday night when I should have been propped up in front of X Factor, munching my way through a family sized tub of toffee popcorn. Oh Marnie!'

'Sorry,' she grinned, although clearly not sorry at all. 'Oh look, he's coming over...it might just be your lucky night'

With dread in her heart and sweat on her palms, Kim glanced up to see Adam approaching their table.

'Hi Marnie. Hi Kim. I'm surprised to see you both here. I didn't realise you knew either Sam that well...'

'Hey Adam. To be honest, I don't actually know them at all. I'm only here because Marnie begged me to come along. I had no idea you were related to Man Sam...Marnie did though, didn't you my wily little friend?' Marnie squealed as Kim pinched the skin on her hand under the table and glared at her.

'Okay, guilty as charged,' she admitted, holding her hands up to surrender. 'But I did it with best intentions. You two are driving us all crazy! YOU love him...and YOU love her...and there's no longer any reason for you to be apart. And yet you're both bloody dithering and worrying about getting hurt again when there's really no need. Everyone can see that you're perfect for each other and belong together – and that you're both in it for the long haul. Now for god's sake, sort this out – tonight – the pair of you, before I bang your heads together or set Nicky on you! Please don't waste any more time...there's been so much of it lost already...'

And with that, Marnie stood up and threw her arms around Kim, whispering into her ear 'You've got this. He's a keeper and he loves you.' Of course, she was fighting to be heard over the pounding of the music and consequently ended up broadcasting it to half of the room, but Adam gentlemanly pretended he hadn't caught it . He also received a hearty hug and although Kim couldn't make out what Marnie said to him, he nodded and then broke into the brightest of smiles. Marnie almost skipped away then, clearly pleased with her matchmaking skills, leaving the former couple awkwardly in situ – Adam still standing and Kim still on the edge of her seat, wondering what on earth would happen next.

What did happen was Adam reached out his hand and took hers, leading her across the dancefloor, out of the room, and over the car park to a wooden bench that faced out onto the bowling green.

They sat side by side and he broke the initially awkward silence.

'The letter – it was unexpected but welcome...and wonderful.'

'I didn't know if it was the right thing to do but figured I had to do *something*. I felt bad though, knowing you had a girlfriend. I didn't want to upset the applecart.'

'Ex-girlfriend. It was short and sweet. Halle was – is – a lovely girl but she's not the girl for me – none of them were. It was pointless going out with anyone really because I could never commit to them long-term. In fact, I couldn't even commit to them emotionally at all. So we broke up shortly before I flew out to Crete with a couple of the lads. A holiday was what I needed – to escape from everything and everyone. A Greek getaway where I could knock back the beers and soak up the sun. And whilst in Malia I had a little time to think, on the few occasions when I was actually sober.'

'Was there...did you....I mean were there any girls while you were away?'

'If you mean did I sleep with anyone...I'm not going to lie...yes, there was one girl. We kissed a couple of times over the duration of the holiday and then on her last night we had sex.'

Ouch. That really, really fucking hurt. And Kim had no right to complain. He'd been a free agent, after all, with no one to answer to.

'Sorry Kim. I didn't do it to hurt you – never in a million years did I think you'd be in touch again and I'd decided that was for the best. What can I say...we were on holiday, it was fun but we were careful, it was great but not mind-blowing, and we kissed goodbye without either of us ever mentioning staying in touch. It was what it was.'

'I've always wanted you to be happy Adam, which is why I didn't attempt to make contact earlier – even though I've known for a long time that I loved you. Since we broke up, I've tortured myself, picturing you kissing other women, falling for them and loving them. It's been tough but I've always said to myself, as long as Adam's happy then that's all that matters. But hearing you speak about sleeping with someone else, and so recently too...listening to those words actually come out of your mouth...it hurts so much it makes me feel sick.'

'And yet I had to listen to blow by blow accounts – literally – of you and that spawn of Satan doing the business, over and over again...'

'Touché. I'm so sorry. I wish I could go back and change a lot of stuff in my past. Top of my list would be reversing the damage I did to you. I guess you've just served up a carefully cut slice of revenge.'

'No, Kim. I've never sought retribution, never. I was simply trying to get on with my life. Deliberately hurting you – well that was never my intention. I've always loved you far too much for that.'

They were silent again then, brooding over each other's sex lives and wishing there weren't so many regrets.

'So.' Kim closed her pale hand over Adam's tanned one that he had casually placed on her leg, the slightest touch of him sending shockwaves throughout her body.

'So.' he replied, budging up closer until they were thigh to thigh. 'The big question - where do we go from here?'

'That's precisely what I'm asking Adam, but it has to be your decision, because my letter literally spelt out my feelings. You're all I ever wanted, even though I was slow – painfully so - to realise it and succumbed to distractions along the way. You're the sweetest, kindest, most loving man I've ever met in all of my life and - don't let this go straight to your head - I do believe that you're also the most handsome, sexy, intelligent male on the planet. When I'm with you I'm a better person – the person I used to be before I became Ritchie's-Bit-Of-Stuff-Kimberley – obsessed and depressed. And that's because you bring out the very best in me and show me how fabulous life could be, if only I'd go with the flow. When I'm with you I feel like I can conquer the world and I can't stop bloody smiling because I'm so proud and so, so in love with you. Losing you the second time was the worst thing ever and to contemplate spending the rest of my life without you...well, that makes me unbelievably sad. I thought I'd found love with that wazzock but honestly, it was nothing compared to what I have with you – what we *could* have together. It was shallow and shameful and its foundation was a bed of lies, but with you it's so deep, so honest and the two of us...well, we are one heart, not two – if you know what I mean. We fit perfectly together and all I want for the rest of my life is you, me and our babies...together.'

She had to steel herself for the likelihood that he wouldn't give her that third chance. Who would blame him if he decided she was more trouble than she was worth?

'But if you don't believe me, or you feel you can't trust me...or if you have genuinely moved on and you don't love me anymore...'

She stopped to regain her composure. Her voice had shook as she realised exactly what was resting on this.

'...if you don't love me anymore then I'll accept your decision Adam, no hard feelings. I'll always love you but if I have to let you go then I will – I would never want to hurt you again.'

For one awful moment it seemed she was screwed. When he didn't instantly reply she thought he was turning her down.

Until his face was suddenly millimetres away from hers and they were almost nose to nose...and his free hand crept up to stroke the waves of her hair.

'So exactly how many babies were you thinking of then?' It was pitch black but he was so close she could see that his eyes were smiling as his hand slid down and under her hair, to caress her neck and make her want to cry out with longing.

'As many as you want. As long as I'm with you I'll cope with a houseful of little Adams.'

He kissed her then, gently and exquisitely and she sensed that everything was going to be alright. No - everything was going to be amazing. As the music blasted out from inside the clubhouse, she pulled him against her and whispered that she would very much like to start trying for those babies sooner rather than later, and that he had better start planning another holiday.

'Honeymoon,' he said. 'Let's plan a honeymoon.'

*

There were only two babies in the end.

They had a dream wedding and a fantasy honeymoon courtesy of both sets of parents and a huge withdrawal from Adam's building society account. Kim's meagre savings covered the deposit and bond on their first rented home...and they were up and running. Luckily for them the business was a success from the outset, as Kim discovered she was pregnant six months into the marriage. How they coped in those days was astonishing really. Kim was trying to work most days either riddled with morning sickness or later, with a young baby attached to her hip. And Adam was grafting long hours in retail and coming home to a flat that was a tip, a particularly vocal and overtired baby and a thoroughly exhausted wife. But their home was filled with love and they were content, and Adam never once complained about the absence of a clean work shirt or lack of food in the fridge.

Once Matty was a little older Kim's mum stepped in to look after him two days each week and Adam's mum held the fort every Friday. Kim and Adam had very quickly become frustrated with forking out for a flat that they didn't actually own which meant a move was on the cards, especially once they spotted a beautiful old house in need of renovation in a leafy street not far from where Kim's parents' lived. The place was a mess but structurally sound and had great potential and although they had to call in tradesmen for much of the essential work, they weren't afraid to get their hands dirty and were ably assisted by family and friends.

They were mostly living in their bedroom (the first room to be completed) when they discovered Kim was pregnant with Will. It came as no great surprise as they couldn't keep their hands off each other and hadn't wanted a huge gap between the kids so contraception was all but forgotten. Ignoring the look of horror on Alison Summers' face as she contemplated chasing after a headstrong toddler whilst rocking a screaming baby, they celebrated with fish and chips before making plans to accelerate the works on the rest of the house.

They had a tricky year then. The company Adam worked for was undergoing major restructuring which basically meant longer hours without so much as a hint of a pay rise, and Kim was rushed off her swollen, throbbing feet. The morning sickness seemed never ending and she found herself crying over the most trivial of issues whilst worrying herself into a frenzy about financial and practical matters. Dionne, the lady who baked most of the cakes for the business, announced she was taking early retirement when her husband unexpectedly took ill. Kim's dad was poorly for months with a serious chest infection. Freddie and Rochelle entered into a trial separation.

But after Kim gave birth to their beautiful bouncing baby boy number two, everything started to fall into place. Kim accepted that she couldn't work more-or-less full time until the boys were at least of nursery age and decided to make the most of her time with them. She'd recruited another fabulous baker and temporarily ceased to tout for new business until she was in a position to deal with it herself. The house was looking good and they'd even spruced up the garden so it looked inviting and pleasing to the eye rather than like a scene from Jumanji.

And then Adam trudged in from work one evening after a hellish day, confessed he hated his job with a passion and declared he wanted out. Kim understood. She knew life in the supermarket had been bringing him down and the prospect of slaving away there for the remainder of his years seriously depressed him.

He'd worked it all out though. Evening lessons at the local high school followed by home learning and revision into the small hours. Kim supported his decision – of course she did. He'd always been there for her and backed her in whatever she wanted to do...and now he needed her to do the same. It obviously put a strain on their finances and she soon found herself taking over many of Adam's home chores to free up some study time for him, but they managed. By sheer hard work and determination he quickly gained his qualifications and found himself employed by a company that actually cared about staff morale.

Once he had experience under his belt and the time was right – i.e. they'd carved up the childcare between the two sets of grandparents again and Kim had returned to her business and was busting a chop to bring in more contracts and cash – he ventured out on his own...and had never looked back. So now they both loved their jobs but they'd paid their dues and were looking forward to slowing down the pace in the very near future.

They had a good life – a life she'd almost forsaken in the pursuit of someone who'd wanted her love but had no intention of ever giving her any of his.

Chapter 31

After a quiet stroll down memory lane, Kim jumped up to let Wiggle out into the garden before heading for the stairs. She needed to shower and dress before driving into town to search for a suitable birthday present for Nicky.

Wonderful Nicky who had been Kim's best friend since primary school and who would probably remain so until her kids shoved her in a nursing home – and even then Nicky would no doubt be in the adjoining room, banging on the walls and ordering her to wheel herself in for a gossip about the old boys across the corridor.

Okay, they'd experienced a little hiccup – all Kim's fault (and Ritchie's) of course – but it had only strengthened their friendship and made them both acknowledge that what they had wasn't worth losing over any man, especially not the likes of 'RJC' (Nicky had refused to refer to him by his actual name for nigh on two decades, and had to stop calling him 'Twatface', as there was a real danger it could have ended up being her eldest child's first word).

Nicky had delivered a fair-haired, blue-eyed angelic baby girl three days after her due date, followed by a not so angelic bruiser of a boy two years later and finally another gorgeous girl three years further down the line. Estelle, Jason and Phoebe really were beautiful kids but then how could they go wrong with their inherited genes? Kim and Adam were god parents to those three whilst Nicky and Connor were god parents to Matty and Will. They always joked that the four of them were parents to all five children and existed in one big happy family...so much so that Freddie reckoned they should all set up a commune together where they would be happy-clappy and wear flowers in their hair whilst growing their own vegetables and drinking their own piss.

Perhaps not.

Kim wondered what on earth she could buy Nicky for her special day. Maybe a spa treatment – she was always beautifying other people but rarely had the time or energy to pamper herself.

A frantic hammering at the front door interrupted Kim's train of thought and she did the standard checking-who-it-is-through-the-front-window-first thing before contemplating opening her house up to a possible persistent salesman (or woman) with the gift of the gab.

Nicky! – Speak of the devil. Kim was surprised to see her at this hour on a Thursday morning when she should have been at the salon. She waved at Nicky through the glass and then opened up the porch to let her in.

'Hello you! What brings you here on a workday? I know you're the boss but I hope you're not skiving off again!'

Nicky slipped past Kim, immediately heading into the kitchen to put the kettle on. Kim closed the door firmly behind her friend and then followed her through the house, noticing that Nicky hadn't yet said a word...and when her friend turned around, the expression on her face was grim. Kim's blood ran cold as she realised that something was very, very wrong.

'Have you seen the news this morning babe?' Nicky's voice was quiet and deliberately soothing but it was only making Kim more nervous and she was immediately overcome by The Fear.

'No – why? What is it? Oh my god...has something happened? It's not the boys is it? Tell me it's not my boys! Or Adam? Please god don't let it be any of them!'

'No, no it's not Adam or Matty or Will. Or your mum or dad. And no, it's none of my brood or Connor or any of our families...'

'So what's going on Nicky? Please tell me. Something dreadful has clearly happened, judging by the expression on your face. Is it the business or...oh my god Connor's not having an affair, is he? Surely he wouldn't because he adores you and, anyway, that would hardly make the news and...'

'Kim...stop...please. Quit guessing because it's nothing you'll be expecting. Sit yourself down, there, at the table while I make you a brew...because what I'm about to tell you is going to come as a shock...and I'm so sorry I have to break it to you. The thing is...'

'Oh god, please hurry up and tell me what the thing is!'

'Kim, my lovely Kim. There's no easy way to tell you this but...well...you'd find out soon enough and I don't want you to hear it when you're on your own.'

Nicky cleared her throat and crouched down in front of her. Kim bit her lip nervously as her friend continued.

'The thing is Kim...Ritchie died this morning.'

Kim sat, open-mouthed, hearing the words Nicky said but failing to understand their meaning. She felt like she was on a carousel – the spinning, the dizziness, the sensation of suspension mid-air as her surroundings became blurred and confused.

'Did you hear me Kim? Did you hear what I said?'

'Are you joking Nick? I know you hate the man but this is taking it a tad too far! And I know for a while I wanted him wiped off the face of the earth but that was only wishful thinking. Someone like him will outlive the lot of us, I tell you...'

'Do you think I'd ever joke about something like this? I'm serious Kim – it's true. The breakfast show reporter said Ritchie had a massive heart attack in the early hours and was rushed to hospital but pronounced dead on arrival. He's gone love...it's true.'

She was serious. She wasn't messing around.

'But he can't be...he's Ritchie Joe Clarke. He's larger than life, he's full of life...he's...he's invincible...'

Kim's voice sounded so small – barely an audible whisper.

'He's only fifty-two. He's a perfectly healthy man who's never had any medical issues, as far as I know. There's never been any mention in the media of any nasty diseases or life-threatening disorders – not that I've been following his life since the day I called time on loving him, but I'm sure it would have been plastered all over every red top and gossip mag if he'd been suffering from a heart condition or anything that may have brought on an attack.'

'Probably all that extra marital shagging...anyone who spends as much time in the sack as he did, well it's got to take its toll eventually...'

'He's fifty-two,' Kim repeated numbly. 'Fifty-two. There must be some mistake. I bet he's sat at home, laughing because it's all part of some elaborate publicity stunt and he'll pop up on the six o'clock news all full of himself because he had everybody fooled.'

Nicky said no more but stood up to switch on the television – and there it was.

Breaking news: *Eighties heartthrob Ritchie Clarke dead at the age of 52. Star suffered fatal heart attack at his country home.*

Old photos of Ritchie were being displayed on screen. The newscaster was talking about tributes flooding in from other stars and his peers in the music industry. No comment as yet from other band members. Flowers were already being laid by tearful fans on the steps of the recording studio where he made his last solo album. A helicopter was circling over the house deep in the countryside where Ritchie had spent his last days. *His last days.* A telephone interview with *Barry* of all people – he sounded genuinely upset and said all five of those lads had been like sons to him and that he was deeply shocked at the news of Ritchie's sudden demise as he'd only spoken to him several weeks ago, when he'd seemed his usual animated self.

So it was true. It was real. Ritchie was dead.

Kim was floored. She couldn't speak. Vaguely aware of Nicky placing a hot drink in front of her and then a hushed telephone conversation between Nicky and her mum, who'd apparently just heard the news herself and was concerned about how Kim may react, she flicked from channel to channel watching the same news, worded differently, accompanied by clips of the band on Top of the Pops and footage of a tearful fan clutching a bouquet of red roses outside of Ritchie's mum's house – his dad had long since passed away. Eventually settling on Sky's rolling news, Kim curled up into the armchair as flashes of her past life illuminated the inside of her head and she remembered the first time she had met him outside of that Croydon pub, when she'd had no idea what she was starting.

Eventually Nicky had to return to work, albeit reluctantly. Kim assured her she was fine - it was a zillion years or so since she'd been involved with Ritchie after all – and Nicky hugged her so hard it was on the verge of hurting. By massive coincidence – allegedly - within five minutes of Nicky's departure, Kim's mum arrived and she was soon rustling about in the kitchen keeping herself busy while Kim remained in a zombie-like state glued to the flat screen tv.

After a while, her mum could stand the silence no more.

'I know you keep saying you're fine Kimberley but you don't look fine to me. You're not crying and you're not screaming and shouting...in fact you're not saying anything at all. But I know you...and you're clearly in shock.'

'Mum, I swear, there's nothing for you to worry about. Yes, of course it's a surprise – but I'm sure it will be for many people who've never even had any involvement with Ritchie at all. Anyone who's relatively famous and who dies so young, well, it's always going to cause a ripple of shock and it's far worse for his fans. But I'm not part of that group anymore – I'm just someone who spent time with him and who followed the band all over, when I was young and stupid.'

Kim purposely played down her part in Ritchie's history because, all things considered, it had been a minor one. She had something to compare it to now - a real bona fide, mutual respectful relationship that had lasted the course, not a fleeting dalliance with someone she'd hero-worshipped. Someone who had emotionally abused her. Treated her like dirt.

There had been no real love there, not on his part anyway. Real love was what was between her and Adam. It was not what had gone on between her and Ritchie.

'Look Kim, we both know how you felt and what he did to you. You may have, thankfully, fallen out of love with him and fallen in love with my handsome son-in-law, but losing anyone that you've ever loved at any point in your life, even when they've trampled all over your heart and left you with nothing but warped memories, well it hurts and no one would blame you for shedding a few tears...'

'Mum, I stopped crying over Ritchie a long time ago. Yes, I thought I loved him at the time and yes, I was devastated by his betrayal, but for the last twenty-odd years he's meant NOTHING to me. My marriage to Adam has been more than I could ever have dreamed of or hoped for. When we exchanged vows at the altar in St Cuthbert's and left that church as husband and wife, it was only the start of the most wonderful journey we've been on together. Do you think we could have enjoyed such a successful marriage if I'd still been nurturing feelings for Ritchie? Adam trusted me when I assured him that period of my life was over and I would never let him down.'

'Kim, you're as white as a sheet, your hands are shaking and you've taken to biting your lip again – I don't think I've seen you do that since those dark days when that man was riding roughshod all over you. But it's the look in your eyes that's killing me – the haunted stare of a woman who's had her heart broken all over again...'

'Oh god mum, I'll burst into tears if it makes you feel any better! It's sad, I admit, that Ritchie's passed away when he's barely even into his fifties and I can't begin to imagine how broken his old mum must be, losing her son so suddenly. I even feel sorry for his wife because, let's face it, she's been with him most of her life, through thick and thin – from huge success to fall from grace, from nation's sweetheart to pantomime villain, from the dream wedding to the nightmare of countless infidelities. And just as they've finally settled down to their quiet life in the country, Ritchie's snatched away from her without any prior warning. She's the one suffering now.'

Her mum's over-exaggerated sigh declared that she clearly didn't believe Kim but would let it rest for now. 'Well you won't mind if I switch that TV off then, will you? Right, now get yourself ready and we'll head off to town to try that new coffee shop by the side of Next – size up your competition!'

Kim wanted to vehemently protest when her mum turned off her news source; she wanted to stay home, by herself, and watch every single snippet of information released about Ritchie's final days and listen to every last tribute that was paid.

It was ridiculous, but she didn't know why she felt that way.

Chapter 33

On Adam's return from work, Kim immediately knew by his pained expression and awkward body language that the news of Ritchie's passing had reached his ears. If he'd thought 'Ha! The fucker's dead – there is a god after all!' he never said it, but then Adam never would, because no matter what he thought of Ritchie, at the end of the day her lost love had been someone's son, someone's husband. After the initial 'Hi' and exchange of kisses he merely asked 'Did you hear the news then?' to which Kim replied, 'I did and it was a bit of a shocker – his poor family.'

And then he stared at her, as if trying to assess how she was bearing up – whether any suppressed feelings were about to reveal themselves and take him back to the days when she'd hurt him, without meaning to - and Ritchie Joe Clarke had caused her to do that.

When Kim headed that particular ball of thought off at the pass, and moved on to make the usual daily small talk about traffic, office politics, the diabolical television scheduling and what was for tea – Chinese takeaway as she hadn't been able to think straight to plan anything in advance – Adam seemed to exhale a sigh of relief and accept that the conversation was over, before heading up to change into his pyjama trousers and faded Homer Simpson t-shirt.

Kim had been glad to shift the conversation on but everything still felt strange and she didn't know what to do. She couldn't confide in Adam without worrying him and the boys were only interested in how long it would be before she fed them and, to be fair, they barely knew who Ritchie was, or that *Show Me Yours* had been a massively successful band back in their heyday. It felt weird – that people had been born since those days and knew nothing of the impact those five guys had made on the charts and on the lives of so many - to think that there were people in the world who'd never even heard of them!

Matty had drifted in from college, howling with laughter after watching his best mate Shirty fall from his pushbike and bust his nose (boys do have an odd sense of humour). He'd merely said 'I hear the old geezer from that band pegged out today – you know, the flashy one that Uncle Fred said you had a thing for,' and Kim thought 'Yeah, that's an understatement if ever I heard one...'

And when he mentioned it to Will, who'd emerged from the kitchen with a second bowl of Frosties, Kim's youngest had responded with a bewildered 'Who?'

There had been texts from Nicky, Freddie and Rochelle (and more from her mum of course) but she could only manage a stock reply of: 'Of course, I'm absolutely fine!' when she was acutely aware that actually, she wasn't fine at all.

Kim and Adam avoided all news bulletins throughout the evening, acting as if nothing notable had happened that day. They turned into bed and she snuggled into his back, as she did every night, and prayed that sleep would soon come and this day would finally be over.

*

It didn't of course – she lay awake for hours, a ball of raw emotion lodged in her throat and a head rammed full of memories and mistakes. She kept picturing Ritchie lying serenely in his coffin, stripped of his designer shirts and obscenely expensive jeans, a shroud covering the beautiful body of his that she had known so intimately, his dazzling green eyes shut forever, his mouth closed for eternity – and that was the part that pained her the most.

Never again would the world hear his voice.

Ritchie Joe Clarke had sung his last song.

*

The next morning Kim looked dreadful and no amount of make-up could disguise the under-eye bags and blotchy skin. But she still headed to the café on autopilot to assist with prep, before rushing off to see an office manager about possible catering for monthly board meetings. It was only as she left the posh office block, with another job successfully in the bag, that she had the mother of all meltdowns when she absentmindedly switched on the radio and was blasted with the *Show Me Yours* tune she had always tried to avoid – the ballad she would forever associate with that testing period of her life…

Tears streaming down her cheeks, she was forced to pull into a supermarket carpark, where she released her seat belt, collapsed onto the steering wheel and cried her bleeding heart out, cursing Ritchie, for daring to hurt her like this when she'd thought he would never be capable of reaching her again.

When she wasn't exactly spent, but at least fit to drive in a reasonably safe manner, she rang to postpone her other appointments for the day, before shifting the car into gear and setting herself on course to return home.

The boys both had plans for the evening. Matty was off to his part-time job at the multiplex whilst Will had his usual rugby practice followed by a catch up with his mates. After she'd made some necessary enquiries online and over the telephone, she awaited Adam's return with trepidation – he wasn't going to like what she was about to say.

He'd had a shitter of a day too but Kim needed to discuss everything with him.

Over her finest vegetable curry they made small talk before Adam jumped in and pre-empted her strike.

'Go on then, spit it out. You've something on your mind and I've a feeling I know what it relates to. When I asked if you were alright earlier you assured me everything was peachy but your eyes are red and you've clearly been crying. It doesn't take a clever dick with a huge IQ to work out why.'

'I'm sorry Adam. I can't lie, it *is* because of Ritchie, even though I hate that I feel this way. His death has floored me and I can't seem to get my head around it. He is – was – of course someone from my past but knowing that he's gone, so suddenly, has hit me like a ton of bricks and although I thought I was fine, the truth is, I'm everywhere. Sad, angry, confused – all the emotions are there and I don't know what to do with them.'

'You're supposed to feel nothing, remember? No love, no hate – you're meant to be immune to him…'

'I am…but death…it does strange things to people. I obviously don't love him anymore and I've not cared enough to hate him in a long time…and yet this…'

'…and yet this means he wins again.'

'Wins? How the hell does he win? He's bloody dead Adam – I don't see how he wins in any of this.'

'He's making you feel stuff that you shouldn't Kim. Even in death he's drawing you in and creating a divide between us.'

'Don't be ridiculous Ad. We're too strong for anybody or anything to come between us. Our marriage is as solid now as it ever was...'

'So what's the plan then? Hide away at home and mourn him until you're all cried out? Spend all day every day listening to his music whilst mentally reliving every precious minute the pair of you were together?'

'I want to go to his funeral Adam.'

A moment of eerie silence before the point of eruption.

'HIS FUNERAL? Are you crazy? Why on earth would you want to be there unless you're desperate to see the other band members again or maybe you think you should be in attendance because all his other loved ones will be there and you'll fit right in...'

'I don't expect you to understand because of the history I had with him, but I feel that I have to go...'

'No. No, you don't *have* to go – you *want* to go and that's something entirely different.'

'But it's not because I'm still in love with the man or I'm heartbroken because I'll never see him again or anything like that.'

'Then what the hell is it?'

'Adam, I'm struggling to explain but I feel a compulsion to be there – to say goodbye and let go of the past, no matter how disgracefully Ritchie behaved...'

'You supposedly *had* let go...you said your last goodbye when he tried to dodge you at the solo gig and you finally came to your senses. And how are you going to know when and where the funeral will be held?'

'His family have released a statement to say they welcome fans to gather outside of the church, although the service inside will be a private one. They're keen for the media to show how popular and loved Ritchie still was and details of the service will be published soon. Fans are discussing it on the band's forum too and one girl who lives near his mum says the funeral will take place at the church the family still attends. This girl apparently spoke to Ritchie's uncle who has confirmed it. I've rang the train station for some travel times and I can shift a few things around at work so it won't affect anything of any great importance...'

'You've got it all worked out, haven't you? This isn't a discussion - this is you telling me you're off to Birmingham to attend your dead lover's funeral, no matter how I might feel about it.'

'For goodness sake, he's deceased! He can't hurt either one of us now and he's certainly no threat to our future happiness…'

'You honestly just don't see it, do you? Even now, he still has this hold over you. Your desire to be close to him for one last time totally eclipses your husband's feelings…which makes him the clear winner in my books. In the race for your heart he'll always pip me at the post, and I'll always be the runner up. I shouldn't have allowed myself to become complacent. Stupid Adam – took his eye off the prize and failed to see the dark horse charging up from behind – the phenomenally vain Ritchie Joe Clarke, always destined to snatch you from right under my nose.'

'Dark horses? Race for my heart? What the fuck are you gibbering on about Adam? In all the time we've been together, there's only ever been you for me. I've never wanted another man, be that Ritchie or anyone else. But I know for certain that I would always regret it, if I didn't travel to Birmingham to see him off on his final journey – to pay my respects.'

'He wasn't and isn't worthy of respect, least of all yours and I'm telling you, Kim, I really don't want you to go.'

'Don't do this Adam. Please accept that my presence at his funeral is no reflection on how I feel about you.'

'And do you think his wife is going to welcome you with open arms to the big star-studded event? When you've always done your utmost to stay out of the newspapers and lie low since the affair, how do you think you'll feel if you end up humiliated in the Daily Drivel, pictures of his Mrs trying to throttle you at the graveside?'

'She doesn't know who I am, does she? And, let's face it, I am one lone woman at that church who will probably be lost amongst the hundreds of others who fell for Ritchie's lies…'

Although said in jest in an attempt to lighten the atmosphere, it only caused Kim to pause a moment and recall how she'd naïvely believed she was the only one for Ritchie – what a mug she'd been.

'So what purpose will it serve? Hanging around in the cold like a groupie again...hoping for a brief glimpse of the other band members...'

'That's not why I'm going and you know it. If they do happen to be there then I'll probably say hello because they're all decent guys and they took care of me when I was in a mess. It would be good to see them again – even in such awful circumstances.'

'I notice you said 'I'm going' in that sentence and I'll say again, I don't want you to. You know I never put my foot down about anything but this is important to me Kim. You don't belong in that other world now and seeing everyone again will just dredge up a load of unpleasant memories...'

'I have to go Adam...*this* is important to me.'

'Then I guess you'll have to make a choice, won't you?'

Adam's clenched jaw and open hostility frightened Kim. She'd never seen him so incensed.

'And what's that supposed to mean?'

'It means you have a decision to make. You can either stay away from the funeral to spare your husband's feelings...or you can flit off down to Birmingham, against my wishes, and see the great man's coffin and mix with others who will always know you as Ritchie's bit-on-the-side rather than the wonderful woman I married. But if you choose the latter option then this won't end well. It will kill me if you go and I'll know for sure then that I was never 'the one' and it was always Ritchie. So don't expect to come back and pick up where we left off...'

'Oh come on Adam, this is getting silly now. And to threaten me and suggest that I loved Ritchie more than I love you...well it's absolute bullshit and you know it!' Kim's face flushed with anger. She was incredulous at Adam's outburst and the very notion that one hour at a funeral could endanger such a rock-solid marriage.

'If it feels like a threat then I'm sorry. But as I'm sure you vividly remember your level of suffering at Ritchie's hands, well I can't forget how long it took to mend my broken heart...and I don't think I can do this again.' He shook his head, as if he couldn't believe he was actually having this conversation with Kim, who'd been his rock for all his married life.

'Adam please...there's no need for it to be an either/or. It's just one day – actually less than that – but it's somewhere I *have* to be and it's not as if I'd ever have the opportunity to do it again if I didn't go and later regretted it...'

'There's no talking you out of it, is there? You're clearly not prepared to take my feelings into consideration...' Adam's broad shoulders had slumped and his eyes were downcast as he seemed to realise he was fighting a lost cause.

'Listen Adam – Ritchie's hold over me was lifted and obliterated many moons ago and you're the last person I would ever want to hurt because you and the boys are everything to me, so please don't imply otherwise. This conversation is completely getting out of hand. *My* wish to attend this funeral should not be the cause of all this aggravation...and if it's likely to cause a permanent rift between the two of us after twenty years of bliss...then there must be a serious flaw in our relationship.'

'Maybe you're right...perhaps we weren't as strong as we thought we were...'

That took the wind out of her sails – she hadn't expected him to agree with her.

'Oh for god's sake Adam, you're my husband and I love you and that's all there is to it. I'm sorry you don't like the idea of me attending the funeral but I've given you my reasons – as best I can – and I will only be gone a few hours and then we can literally put it all to rest. Now eat your bloody tea and stop being so pathetic.'

The rest of the meal was picked at in silence before Adam scraped back his chair, stood up and shifted into the kitchen to transfer the plates to the dishwasher. Claiming a stinker of a headache, he announced his intention to have an early night and disappeared upstairs. They'd always gone up to bed together so it felt like a real black mark against their marriage, with its previous clean slate. She knew it was because he was hurting but then again, so was she.

It left her with time on her own to think and unashamedly drink almost a full bottle of cabernet sauvignon. Never in a million years would she purposely hurt Adam and she knew she could put a stop to it by venturing upstairs and apologising. She could tell him that he was absolutely right – Ritchie's funeral was no place for her. Besides, she couldn't stand to see Adam so confused and distraught and be the orchestrator of all that misery.

But she couldn't do it. Inside she was raw and aching and for some inexplicable reason she was mourning the loss of a man who had almost destroyed her.

Whatever happened, she needed to say a proper goodbye, in her own way, by herself.

Chapter 34

After a thoroughly miserable week when she and Adam barely exchanged a few words and the atmosphere in the house became unbearable, Kim nervously boarded the train to Birmingham, filled with dread at the prospect of seeing Ritchie's coffin and absolutely anticipating she would be a blubbering mess by the end of the day.

At least the boys hadn't picked up on the tension between her and Adam and had merely laughed when she'd said where she was going.

'Mum, you're an embarrassment, you absolute groupie!' they'd joked and she'd winced. 'Can't believe our own mother is that desperate she has to go and mourn some z-lister she had a thing for in the eighties!' It was all a little too close to the knuckle for her liking and she could only smile and add, 'The band were once a huge part of my life and I'm guessing there will be lots of fans there who I'll recognise from the old days.'

They had indeed been a massive part of her life but in truth it felt like someone else's life when Kim looked back on it. The businesswoman she had become, content and surrounded by her loved ones, was a vastly different person to the young girl who'd travelled the length and breadth of the country, initially desperate for a glimpse of the band or a quick autograph, later holing up in hotel rooms with the heartthrob lead singer, who dealt out more pain than pleasure.

By the time she arrived at Birmingham she already felt wretched and couldn't believe she was actually only a fifteen minute taxi journey away from the church where Ritchie would arrive by hearse rather than tour bus. A lone tear trickled down her face as she remembered him speeding down the street in his shiny black Audi – god he loved that car.

The taxi driver was a jolly guy, eager to chat about his grandchildren and all their achievements. He warned Kim that it would be rammed where she was headed because there was a celebrity funeral taking place at the church on the corner – 'that Richard guy who sang with a band in the 1980s. Had a cracking voice and they released a few catchy tunes – shame they suddenly disappeared off the scene...'

'That's where I'm going,' she'd croaked as she'd tried desperately not to cry again.

'Oh, did you know him then?' Well at least she looked more acquaintance than fan.

'I used to – years ago. Ex-boyfriend,' she mumbled, but recognised it felt good to say that aloud. Because even though nobody else had ever acknowledged that status, that's what he'd been to her. He may never have referred to her as his girlfriend and had been quick to distance himself when it suited, but from Kim's perspective they'd been in a relationship, albeit a toxic one.

'Must be upsetting then, for you. And shocking – he was only young wasn't he?' Rhetorical question – she was spared having to answer.

Colin the Cabbie picked up on her misery and swiftly changed the subject, proudly telling her that his grandsons had recently been selected for the school footie team. The journey actually passed quicker than Kim would have liked – suddenly she was in no rush to see a wooden box containing the lifeless body of a man who had loved life so much.

'Bye love,' said Colin as she eased herself out of the back seat and handed over his fare. 'You take it easy now and don't be upsetting yourself.'

*

The clouds drifted apart and the sun shone through as Kim attempted to pull herself together and slowly headed for the narrow footpath that led to the church.

The sun always shone on Ritchie – he continually came up smelling of roses while others were left to suffer for his sins.

A small pack of photographers had assembled on the lawns and one or two glanced in her direction as she passed them by, presumably to ascertain whether or not she was a person of interest. She was quickly deemed to be a nobody and all heads then turned away to check if anyone worthy enough for them was following behind. Kim doubted it. She was so early she was only surprised she hadn't gate-crashed the previous service.

There was a modest crowd around the main doors to the church, which appeared to be closed and manned by two tiny old guys dressed all in black – a far cry from the bouncers and security that held back the masses on tour when the band were riding high at the top of the charts.

Kim hovered, unsure of her next move. Most of the invited guests were yet to arrive and she suddenly felt far too shy to be approaching the gathering near the doors. She guessed they were all fans as many seemed to be dressed in the band's old tour t-shirts but she had no idea if Sally-Anne or any of the faces she knew from her time around the band were amongst them. Had they all moved on and discovered there was life after *Show Me Yours*? Maybe all of these people - many already visibly distressed and sobbing into tissues - would turn out to be complete strangers and she wouldn't be welcome if she tried to infiltrate their group.

When she looked at the pictures emblazed on their shirts she instantly experienced a pang for a time when she was merely a young fan crazy about an amazing band who were on the cusp of becoming the biggest popstars on the planet...and she could almost feel the excitement of rushing out to buy the latest single or the exhilaration of sitting in a crowded theatre, waiting for the boys to explode on to the stage. The atmosphere. The lights. The screams. The band. The memories.

'Kimberley? Kim Summers?'

Jolted out of her reverie, Kim swung around, more than a little apprehensive as to who might know her by name so far from home.

Instant recognition - even though their paths hadn't crossed for longer than she cared to remember.

'Callie? Callie from Surrey? Oh my god, is it really you? You look amazing!'

She really did. Her blonde hair was cut considerably shorter into a razored bob that was both sleek and stylish. She had aged, of course, but she'd matured spectacularly well and her figure was as trim as it had ever been – no wonder she'd caught Bren's eye. Her slate grey dress clung to her, a black tailored jacket over the top to keep off the chill. Kim couldn't believe this was the very same woman who'd made a child with Bren - my god, their son must be in his twenties now!

'It's me! Long time no see, Kim. You look fab too...you've hardly changed at all.'

Kim knew that wasn't the case - but it was nice of her to say so anyway.

'Thanks...but you're far too kind. God Callie...this is a real blast from the past! How are you keeping?'

'Oh...so-so. You know how it is. How about you? How's life been treating you?'

'I'm okay. Older, wiser – I think. Christ Callie, it's been bloody decades since I last clapped eyes on you! It only feels like yesterday that we were teenagers, when the world was a simpler place and all that mattered in our lives was the band. Do you remember those days?'

'How could I forget them? It was all Top of the Pops, videos and pen pals back then…and we somehow managed without mobiles, the internet and social media! Give me a good old-fashioned record to play any day rather than a bloody digital download. And it was theatre rather than arena tours back in the day so nothing seemed quite as impersonal and the band were much more accessible. Although maybe it would have saved some of us a lifetime of heartache, if we *hadn't* been able to access them quite so easily…and my time following them around wouldn't have been so abruptly cut short due to the minor issue of my unplanned pregnancy.'

'I guess that did kind of put the mockers on you charging around the country and slipping away for a bit of nookie with your beloved Bren. Honestly, no one even suspected you two were close until that night in Croydon when you certainly gave everyone something to gossip about!'

'Didn't I just. We'd kept it quiet – well, as quiet as you can keep it when the guy you're seeing is Bren – and I liked it that way. Naturally I had delusions that I would be the woman who'd make him grow up and settle down. And I loved him – of course I did. The pregnancy was unexpected though. My dad went crazy when he found out that Bren was the father and said I could at least have picked a reasonably sane member of the band!'

'Bren was wild though, wasn't he? The epitome of the pleasure-seeking rockstar, enjoying the hedonistic lifestyle…'

'And I thought I could change him – silly me.'

'You'd fallen for him. You weren't to know what you were up against. Did he freak when he found out about the baby?'

'Oh god, yes – he disappeared on another binge, turned up on my parents' doorstep three days later, all apologetic and carrying the biggest teddy bear you've ever seen, pleading for forgiveness and promising he would turn over a new leaf, if only for our child. I believed him at first because I knew that he loved me…and I kept on giving him more chances, even after the fourth or fifth relapse. But after I delivered our beautiful boy I knew I couldn't expose this innocent bundle of joy to the excesses and inconsistencies of Bren...I had to let him go.'

'Oh Callie, you were so brave to break away from Bren and go it alone as a single mother...'

'It wasn't easy but it was Bren who actually instigated the split. He cradled his new-born son, placed him gently back in his Moses basket and then began to talk...and he was the most coherent and sensible I've ever known him to be. His admission that he couldn't be a proper father and he didn't want to be an improper one either – well, it was stuff I already knew but hadn't wanted to confront. We agreed it was for the best – to my father's great relief – and we both cried our hearts out. He left us that day for the last time and immediately resumed his erratic lifestyle, whilst I buckled down to take care of our son.'

Despite her magnificent outer shell, Kim could see that loving Bren had taken its toll on Callie. She was standing tall and desperately trying to maintain her composure but her eyes filled and she trembled as she spoke of her heartbreak.

'You're a strong woman, Callie. It takes courage to step away from a relationship when there's a child involved – even when that relationship is so damaging...'

'It was necessary. I loved Bren from the moment I first laid eyes on him – before the band hit the big time there were appearances on the nightclub circuit, which is where I first stumbled across them and I was captivated by this young man who was full of mischief but bloody fierce on those drums. I knew he was a bad lad but our eyes met and we flirted and frolicked...and I thought I'd won the jackpot when he asked me out. For goodness sake, propositions of that magnitude don't happen to quiet little country girls like me. I was so sure I'd be forgotten the minute he left the club and I'd never hear from him again but he rang! And I was smitten from our first meet-up, even though it was difficult to arrange anything because they were always so busy and always on the road. When we did get it together, sometimes it was as wild as you'd expect with Bren, but he also had a softer side, reserved only for me. He could be the most caring, gentle guy when we were alone and his true self was exposed. However, once fame beckoned it was a weird time. The powers-that-be imposed a complete embargo on girlfriends and suddenly I was demoted. I'd always been a fan but still, it felt pretty strange hanging about around stage doors when I'd only just vacated Bren's bed. It was challenging to say the least, keeping our relationship a secret and accepting that I couldn't always be a part of his world, if you know what I mean?'

Oh Kim knew what she meant alright. She recalled the feeling of limbo, when she was neither one thing nor the other, caught between two worlds, belonging to neither.

'Yes, I totally understand...'

'Ah yes, you and Ritchie...'

'You heard then?'

'Sorry Kim but EVERYBODY heard! Well, apart from the wife of course. I believe he made a beeline for you and you never stood a chance. Unsurprisingly most of the other girls were jealous as hell because you landed the star prize – the main man; the heartthrob who they all had pinned to their bedroom walls...'

'Hardly the star prize in the end though, as it turned out...'

'Who are you kidding? Even if they'd known he was married they would still have wanted him and taken him to bed, given half the chance. I could see you weren't like that Kim...even from our brief conversations at stage doors it was obvious you were a decent girl with morals. It wasn't all about the sex - you'd fallen in love with Ritchie and wanted the whole package, not just his body and his best moves.'

'I did – I loved him and I told him. But he never said it back, because he didn't love me. At least you were lucky enough to be confident of Bren's feelings for you.'

'Ultimately it wasn't enough – love – in our case. When love comes up against addiction it invariably loses. And even though he obviously adored our son it wasn't enough to make him stay clean...so he may as well never have loved either one of us at all.'

Callie smiled sadly, seemingly reflecting on her questionable choice of man.

'You managed to start again though and found love elsewhere?' She pointed at my treasured engagement ring and wedding band and I nodded, remembering the husband I had left at home, licking his wounds.

'Yes, I was very fortunate. I met a wonderful man, married him and we have two boys of our own. I say boys, but they're almost men now.'

'That's fabulous, and I'm so glad to hear it. I'd have liked more children, in different circumstances of course, but it wasn't to be.'

'You never met anyone else?'

'Oh yes, I've had relationships and was briefly married, but none of them lasted the course. After Bren and I split up, I thought I'd never be happy again but then I met the gorgeous Jake, a successful businessman with the looks and personality to match and we hit it off immediately. Charlie really took to him and everything was going swimmingly when – bam! The press ran with the story about Bren and his secret son and I found myself splashed all over the papers legging it to my car, looking like a startled gazelle. It was horrible. And worst of all, I hadn't told Jake who my son's father was – only that it was someone whose drug-taking and party lifestyle did not make for a suitable or responsible father. I was mortified and Jake was furious that I'd kept it from him. When the reporters turned up on *his* doorstep wanting his slant on the story, they sealed the fate of that relationship. We had a terrible row and he said some awful things about Bren and his substance abuse which really hurt, because I still loved Bren and I couldn't bear to hear him ripped apart like that. I said something like '…there by the grace of god go any one of us' and Jake yelled 'No Callie, not any one of us, just Bren because he's totally fucking stupid!''

'Jesus, what happened then?'

'I said I was done with him and went out and popped every one of the tyres on his poncy Porsche before heading home to cuddle my son and wonder if every future relationship was likely to disappear down the pan as a result of my involvement with Bren. I did go on to have another couple of boyfriends but they were nothing serious and the husband was a shocking mistake as a result of a mid-thirties meltdown about being left on the shelf – it turned out the guy was a real wanker and I left him on our first wedding anniversary.'

'Oh my, I think I've led quite a dull life then in comparison…'

'But you found love again and whilst I'm pleased for you, I'm also insanely jealous. Because there was no love to be had for me after Bren – I have never, ever experienced those same emotions with anyone else. I've never wanted another man the way I wanted him.'

Kim's heart bled for Callie and she wanted to hug her but the woman looked too brittle, too broken to squeeze, like she might just fall apart in her arms.

'Oh that's sad Callie. An attractive, intelligent woman like you could have anyone…'

'But you don't choose who you fall in love with…and ultimately I found it impossible to fall out of love with Bren.'

It really struck a chord with Kim. Looking into Callie's eyes Kim witnessed a glimpse of the woman she might have become. She had a vision of the life that could have been hers if she hadn't found the strength to move on - if there'd been no Adam. Or if she'd had Ritchie's baby – intentionally or by accident - and been tethered to him for all of her life.

Poor Callie had been trapped by the intensity of her feelings and the son they shared, whereas Kim had been freed by the love of Adam.

'Ah here he is…my life's work! Did you manage to park the car okay sweetheart?'

Kim had never seen this young man before but she immediately knew who he was. The shock of hair, the glint in his eye, the strong jawline and wiry physique – he couldn't be anyone other than Bren's son.

'Charlie, this is Kim. Kim – Charlie.'

'Not THE Kim? Of Kim and Ritchie fame?' Charlie gave her a cheeky wink – a lot like his dad. Wow, so everybody really DID know about her and Ritchie.

'The very same,' she replied, shaking the hand he'd held out. 'Unfortunately.'

'Sorry about my insolent son,' laughed Callie, ruffling up his mop of hair in an affectionate gesture. 'He's inherited his quick tongue from his father - not me!'

'It's okay. I can take it. Nice to meet you love. Do you think there'll be anyone else we might know here today Cal? I suppose I envisaged banks of familiar faces from the past…but you're the only one so far.'

'I take it you haven't seen your delightful mate Sally-Anne then because she was the first person I ran into when Charlie dropped me off…'

'Oh my god no! Sally-Anne's here? I can't believe she's still around…and believe me, she is most definitely not my mate.'

'Yeah, I heard she wasn't much of a friend to you when you needed it…but to be honest I never took to her anyway. Too loud, too brash, two-faced. Always slagging everyone off and always on the make, looking around for the next person to give her a leg up the *Show Me Yours* ladder. You were always too nice to be hanging around with the likes of her. Anyway, she's here with one of those Irish girls and a few others I haven't seen around before. Geraldine's here too – everyone remembers Geraldine. She's with her *husband* and he seems a real sweet, jovial kind of guy – definitely the ying to her yang. I can't believe that she has a husband and I don't, but it just goes to show that there is a lid for every pot. Oh and I take it you've said hello to Barry...'

'Barry! Now there's a blast from the past...although I did hear his voice the other day when he was being interviewed over Sky News. My, he was a character - a real grumpy old sod!'

'I used to think that too but underneath that bomber jacket of fury there was a heart of pure gold. He's always been kind to me and he went seriously above and beyond when it came to protecting all of the famous five – particularly Bren. I must admit though, I found him terrifying at first.'

'Aw, I will have to say hello...see if he recognises me. You say he's here already...if he's not already gone inside, whereabouts will I find him?' Kim's eyes started scanning around the gathering, trying to seek out good old Barry, but failing to see anyone who remotely resembled him.

'Seriously? He's right there behind you...on the doors like a bouncer but with slightly less flesh to pad out that overcoat.'

'NO WAY! That's not Barry!' Callie was pointing at one of the old boys Kim had noticed greeting mourners as they entered the church. She would never have recognised him, not in a million years.

'Callie, surely you don't mean that white-haired old chap on the left who looks more like he could be Barry's granddad?'

'That's the very fellow...and even now he's barring people from entering the building at band-related events, god love him. And don't forget, he was knocking on fifty's door when we first met him. He must be around seventy now.'

'And who's that other OAP next to him? Tell me that's not Gimpy Gav – universally despised and avoided at all costs...'

'Noooo...I think the other old fella may be Ritchie's uncle actually. Last I heard of Gav, he was moving home courtesy of HM Prison Service, if you know what I mean?'

'Oh my, really? No, don't tell me...PC World found some dodgy stuff on his computer and he got carted off, kicking and screaming and leaving a nasty slug trail behind him...'

'No, not quite. He was done for conning an old couple out of their life savings or something equally horrendous. Have to say, although I only met him once or twice, I didn't like what I saw.'

'No one did. Horrible git. And what about the other band members then? I wonder if they'll turn up…I know they didn't really see eye to eye with Ritchie much of the time…'

'Ady's still on Ibiza and is planning on staying there. He's sent a wreath but he already had dj-ing commitments lined up for the whole of this week and – between you and me – he honestly didn't want to be here. But Todd should be along soon…if only to ensure that Ritchie is actually really gone – you heard how they were at each other's throats towards the end?'

Nodding grimly, Kim replied, 'I witnessed a little disharmony myself but later read in the papers about the fights and artistic differences. My best friend told me Ritchie had spewed out some real bitchy stuff about Todd on a late-night chat show but I don't believe any of it for a minute. Todd was such a sound, kind-hearted guy - a real gentleman. Everything Ritchie wasn't I suppose. That's probably why they had nothing in common.'

'Mmm, I think you're right. Oh, Marty's going to be here though, with his lovely wife…although I think they're leaving their sixty squillion kids and grandkids at home on this occasion.'

'Bless him, he was always a real family man, even before he had a family of his own. So that only leaves Bren…?'

'Unfortunately he can't make it either so we're here to represent him. Bren…well he's quite poorly at the moment…not really in any fit state to attend…'

Callie's eyes shone a little brighter again and Kim could see the woman was struggling. Whatever state Bren was in, it didn't sound like a good place to be. Her son placed his hand on his mother's arm and gently urged 'Come on mum, let's go grab a pew.'

The two women did eventually hug before exchanging their goodbyes and Kim watched Callie gracefully walk away and fall into step with her son as they approached the church doors. She'd never appreciated before quite how lovely and loyal Callie was. Kim had never really seen past Callie's stunning looks and that was a shame, as she believed they could have been great friends. It had been amazing to see her after all of this time, although she couldn't imagine that they would ever meet again. She hoped Callie's inner strength would stand her in good stead in the future as it sounded like even more difficult days lay ahead. Despite Callie's unbreakable ties to Bren and the absence of any loving partner in her life, at least she had her son on side – the only part of Bren that was hers for the taking.

Kim's name wasn't on the list to enable her to walk into the church, but she hung around close to the entrance and the cluster of family members now gathered there greeting other relatives and friends, hoping she would blend in with the collection of mourners. Thankfully, she recognised no one and felt a sense of relief that there wasn't a soul present who'd known Young Kim. There could be no comparisons to who she was back then.

Her relative peace was shattered when she heard a familiar cackle that she couldn't pretend to ignore as it was quickly followed by a 'Fucking hell it's Kimberley Summers! Where have YOU been since the nineties?'

Forcing herself to swivel round, Kim was shocked by the appearance of her former friend. Where loads of people invariably gained a little weight over the years (guilty as charged), Sally-Anne had literally shed so much she looked painfully thin. Her jeans clung to her pencil-like legs and the black crop top she was sporting had no trouble holding anything in because she was almost completely flat up-top. The woman may have behaved appallingly towards Kim and she certainly had a real vicious streak…but, bloody hell, she hoped she wasn't seriously ill. Sal lit up a cigarette as she prepared to interrogate Kim, who noticed the tell-tale chain smoker's yellow fingers. She had a sneaking suspicion that Sal had replaced food with fags, particularly when she emitted a hacking cough prior to clearing her throat. Lovely.

'Hi Sally-Anne, it's been a long time.' Not long enough.

'Didn't think you'd have the balls to show your face here today…you've got some front I'll give you that.'

Resisting the urge to retort 'At least I've got a bloody front now you bitchy little bag of bones,' Kim merely replied, 'Not really. It felt like the right thing to do.'

'He was such a wonderful man, Ritchie,' Sally-Anne began to sniffle, making a show of supposedly wiping her eyes with the back of her hand. 'I can't believe I'll never see him again. We'd become incredibly close you know…'

'Really?'

Now why had she said that? She'd just given this devious little cow permission and positive encouragement to spew out a load of old crap because, although Kim hadn't known Ritchie at all really, one thing she was sure of was that he didn't particularly like Sally-Anne. He HADN'T particularly LIKED Sally-Anne – she must remember to refer to him in the past tense now. A genuine lump of something like grief formed in her throat…but she would never break down and cry in front of this odious woman who seemed to live to bring other women down.

'Oh yes, me and the girls were always backstage whenever he did any of his solo gigs and we often ended up in his hotel room sharing magnums of champagne and much more. He said I was beautiful – I only wished I hadn't had a fiancé at the time.'

Kim wondered which part of this bullshitting bitch Ritchie had supposedly thought was beautiful – her two inch dark roots contrasting against the rest of her custard-yellow long, lank hair or the nicotine stains on her uneven teeth. She was desperate to remind Sally-Anne that she had allegedly ceased to fancy Ritchie back when she realised which of the two of them he had a soft spot for and that she'd transferred her affections to Bren. Although perhaps as well that Bren was well shut of her – he had enough problems to deal with.

'You married then, Sal?' Kim refused to take the bait as far as the Ritchie stuff was concerned – Sally-Anne was only trying to wind her up and she knew it was pure shite anyway. And it didn't really matter because Kim honestly wasn't jealous anymore. Somehow, she didn't believe that Ritchie had turned over a new leaf after their affair had been outed in the press. As soon as the coast was clear again and the opportunity arose he would have had his pants down quicker than you can say 'Dirty, scummy bastard'. But the notion that he would ever have selected Sally-Anne for a quick shag – no, she wasn't having that. His celebrity pulling-power – although perhaps a little weakened throughout the latter part of his career – meant that he could still have done better than *that*.

'God, no. Three engagement rings though – been fighting them off! Got a daughter as well, just turned sixteen. But she mainly lives with her dad.'

No surprises there. A child would have interfered with Sally-Anne's galivanting and dubious activities. Kim couldn't help but think that the poor daughter was most definitely better off with her father.

A surge in the crowd and a flurry of excitement and it became apparent that one or more of the band had arrived, thankfully saving Kim from any more excruciating exchanges with Sally-Anne, who shot off to try and elbow her way into a more prominent position within the gathering. Kim heaved a huge sigh of relief. If she never saw Sal again, she would only be grateful.

As the photographers pushed forward to take pictures of a sombre Marty, dressed in a black tailored suit under an almost floor-length woollen overcoat, accompanied by an ever-beautiful and ageless Ebony in a navy blue and white striped trouser suit, looking extremely stylish for a funeral-attendee, Kim was roughly shoved further towards the church doors and came almost face to face with Barry. Now she knew it was him she could just about make out a resemblance to the angry manager he'd once been, but he no longer had the fear factor and she wanted to reintroduce herself. Kim remembered his kindness on the day she'd discovered she was Ritchie's mistress rather than girlfriend, but she didn't really expect the old man to recognise her after all of these years.

To her surprise, he bent forward, smiled weakly and said, 'Hello love. I wondered if we'd see you here. The years have been kind to you, I must say. Ritchie was a fool to let you go.'

Oh. Still kind. Spontaneously stepping forward to embrace him, he gently patted her on the back and she had to battle to curtail the river of tears that was threatening to burst its banks.

'Oh Barry, I was lucky to climb out of that mess relatively unscathed. But I hated him for a long time afterwards. With the exception of one more occasion when I ambushed Ritchie and tried to wring some truths out of him – unsuccessfully, I might add – I never saw him again. So I can't believe that I'm here today. I never dreamed that the next time I'd be near him would be at his funeral...this is some spectacular closure.'

'He was a little sod and he behaved badly...but he was like a son to me – along with the other boys – and this is a terrible, terrible day.'

'I know.' It was her turn to attempt to comfort him and she reached out to take his gnarled bony hand and squeeze it. 'I'm sorry Barry. For all his sins and shameful behaviour, I wouldn't have wished this on him and it's simply heart breaking for those, like you, who loved him unconditionally.'

Before she could add anything further, the other old guy gently shifted her to one side to allow Marty and Ebony to enter the church. As they did so Kim saw Marty's eyebrows raise as he recognised her face from the days when they were topping the charts and adored by millions.

'Hey,' he said softly, nodding in her direction. She was unsure if he remembered her name. She nodded back and responded with a 'Hi Marty,' before he was gone and she barely had time to collect her thoughts before there was a series of flashbulbs going off and a commotion in the crowd and Todd appeared by her side, clutching the hand of a cherublike little girl with chocolate brown curls and a tiny snub nose. She looked bewildered as all eyes were on her father and Kim noticed her tug at his sleeve for reassurance before she was immediately scooped up by a stunning brunette lady with the warmest of smiles.

'You go ahead with your mummy and I'll follow you in,' said Todd, kissing the cheek of the pretty little girl. Amidst her grief Kim's heart swelled with happiness for him, the sweetest and most genuine of men, who appeared to have found contentment with a gorgeous partner and child.

She briefly wondered if Todd would recognise her just as he whispered 'Kim' and pulled her into a bear hug, and she clung on to him for a moment, as more memories of another life flashed by inside her head. When they parted she noticed Sally-Anne scowling behind him and thought 'Wow, it's like we're back in the eighties again and she's still that sulky teenager who wanted what everyone else had.'

'It's good to see you Kim – you look fabulous.'

'You haven't changed at all Todd – you have the gift of eternal youth I think! And it's wonderful to see you again. Out of everyone from my former life, it's probably you and your kindness I missed the most. I just can't believe Ritchie's gone...it's been such a shock...'

Oh god, the tears, they were determined to break free.

'Ssshh,' Todd wiped her cheeks with his thumbs in the gentlest of gestures before Barry ordered him inside as apparently the arrival of the hearse was imminent.

'See you later,' said Todd, squeezing her hand, before he was guided inside and she stepped away from the entrance. This wasn't her place to be now.

The sight of the hearse rolling slowly up the road towards the church made her want to weep again. The floral tribute spelling out Ritchie's name and a second one in the shape of a guitar were so pretty and poignant…and when the coffin containing his body was removed and the pallbearers shifted into position she heard many others crying in the crowd. Kim recognised a couple of the pallbearers as Ritchie's friends and they looked utterly devastated…and it was honestly one of the saddest sights she'd ever witnessed. As the coffin passed her by she wanted to reach out and touch it – and she didn't even know why – but instead she lowered her head and closed her eyes, paying her respects even if Ritchie hadn't shown her one fleck of respect, ever.

Of course, leading the small group of family and friends following closely behind the coffin was Michelle, Ritchie's wife. For one awful moment Kim thought she saw a hint of recognition in Michelle's eyes - but as far as Kim was aware, she'd never known the true identity of Ritchie's long-term mistress, merely that Ritchie had been involved with a fan for quite some time but it had come to a swift conclusion once the papers had ran with the story.

Although still wary that Michelle might throw a punch on the way past, Kim strangely felt a weird longing to reach out to her, to tell her how sorry she was and that she truly hadn't known he was married. But of course that was highly inappropriate and would have involved blowing her cover for sure. Any hatred she had previously felt for *the wife* had completely vanished, to be replaced by a world of sympathy - Michelle had loved Ritchie for most of her life and had chosen to stay with him even after his numerous infidelities were exposed. Whatever Kim's thoughts on the matter, there had been love and now she had lost him and looked lost herself, her face devoid of any make-up, her eyes dark pools of shock and devastation, the bags underneath speaking of numerous nights without sleep. She looked like what she was – a grieving widow who didn't know how she could even begin to live without the only love she'd ever known.

Finally, they were all inside and Kim could breathe again, but as she prepared to go and find herself a quiet spot where she could disintegrate discreetly, Barry stepped out, took hold of her arm and quietly led her inside to the back row of seating.

'You should be here,' he insisted, before squeezing her shoulder and shuffling off to a bench near to the front, where he perched on the end, only a short distance away from Ritchie's coffin. He was there again – Barry – protecting one of his boys until the end.

Kim noticed for the first time the treble clefs that decorated the sides of the coffin and she thought to herself, Ritchie would have loved this – all the musical references, the crowds of tearful fans, the packs of photographers and journalists and not forgetting one or two minor celebrities who were dotted about the church, trying to make the day all about them.

The service was a blur. Afterwards she remembered his mum breaking down when Barry stood up to reminisce about the band's heyday and say how proud Ritchie had been to score number one hits and perform for the band's army of fans. And she recalled that there were only two hymns sung as the rest of the musical interludes were a mix of Ritchie's solo efforts and *Show Me Yours* tracks, all ballads but thankfully *Falling* wasn't one of them, because if she'd heard him sing that at his own funeral then it might just have been the undoing of her.

As it was, listening to his beautiful voice – because it *was* beautiful, there was no denying it – fill the whole of the church as he sang about true love never dying and 'always being by your side' made even the toughest of men shed a tear and Kim gave up even trying to remain stoic.

She knew with all her heart that she didn't love him anymore but she still wanted to run down to the front, rip open the coffin and see his face and his body one last time - for the sake of the love she'd once harboured for him, for the way he'd made her feel at a time when no one else in the world existed for her. To take one last glimpse of the man who'd been her very first love…but also the man who'd been the very first – and last – to break her heart.

She knew she had to leave before the end – she couldn't stand by and watch his coffin re-enter the hearse and be taken away to be lowered into the ground. That was too much.

She couldn't even say goodbye to any of them – Barry, Marty, Todd, Callie – and definitely NOT Sally-Anne. She needed to get the hell out of there and put as much distance as possible between her and that coffin. She wanted to remember Ritchie as the bright, bubbly poster-boy with the enchanting smile and the voice of an angel – not as the bastard who'd shattered her with his lies and deceit…and definitely not as the cold, lifeless body contained within the box.

As she took flight, through the church doors and down the path that would lead her to freedom, out of the corner of her eye she thought she saw a slimmed-down, solemn-faced Geraldine in the distance – was she actually wearing a fascinator? Even though it was unlikely she'd ever have the opportunity to speak to Gerry again, Kim kept on going. She wished her former acquaintance well but she had no desire to further dissect this dreadful day or prolong the agony. She was almost out of the church grounds when a grating voice from behind mockingly said, '*Kimmy...oh Kimmy...*' and she realised Sally-Anne was hot on her heels.

She wanted to throttle the woman who had no business even speaking to her after the way she'd used her and dumped her in the past.

Halting in her tracks, Kim swung round to see Sally-Anne's blazing eyes and the glare that could turn milk sour – clearly she was furious, presumably because Kim had been on the inside of the church rather than outside. Cue a flashback to a stage door in the late eighties when Kim had exited the building and found Sally-Anne sulking in the car park. Some things never changed.

'Thought you'd have stayed to the very end to say goodbye to *your* Ritchie...' she drawled, probably hoping to make Kim cry or perhaps intimidate her into divulging some insider information.

Kim viewed her through a different lens then. For a long time she'd accepted that Sally-Anne had a mean streak but it was far worse than that – she was basically a diabolical person, who had the potential to become downright evil given half the chance. She looked rough too – *really* rough and Kim wondered why that was. Sure, she had been brought up in a single parent family in a council house in a deprived area...but Kim knew plenty of others who'd had a similar start in life who hadn't let it define them. These people had gone on to break the cycle and fulfil their potential. And then there was *this*, standing there, smoking her roll-ups and spouting out tripe. Kim was done with even breathing the same air as this *girl* who'd never really grown up and who was clearly lacking in all departments.

'Fuck. Off. Sally-Anne. You're a sad, pathetic excuse for a human being and just so you know, Ritchie always hated you, so don't try and kid yourself otherwise.'

It felt good to finally deliver those words, and with meaning, before getting the hell out of there, leaving Sally-Anne gawping in her wake.

No idea where she was going. Left or right? She turned right, in the direction of the traffic, where there appeared to be a cluster of shops in the distance. As Kim headed purposely towards them, she began to pick up speed again – she couldn't risk the funeral procession catching her up.

She soon realised that (a) the shops were much further away than she'd reckoned and (b) she was embarrassingly unfit, but she had to keep on going.

'Kimberley! Hey, Kim...get in!' It was Todd – wonderful, wonderful Todd, at the wheel of a brand new 4 x 4 and minus his partner and daughter.

Kim stopped, panting. Hesitated. And then thought fuck it, and hopped in the back.

'Where you going Kim?'

'Anywhere but there,' she gestured behind her, where the old church stood proud, a place she never wanted to set foot in again. 'Probably for a hot drink somewhere...or maybe just back to the station to see if I can board an earlier train.'

'Well if you were hoping to buy a coffee at one of *these* places I think you'd have been sadly disappointed,' he replied, and Kim noticed on closer inspection that there was a grand total of four businesses comprising of a betting shop, opticians, estate agents and dog grooming parlour.

'Come on,' Todd added, performing a swift u-turn and carving up a pretty angry pensioner in her shiny red mini. 'We'll have to go back the way we came but there's a lush coffee shop two minutes away from St Jude's – you should have headed off in the other direction.'

'Story of my life Todd. One wrong mistake, you take the wrong path and you're screwed.' Kim winced as she said it – of course she didn't mean 'screwed' in the literal sense of the word but it didn't sound good, and her tone of voice made her sound like a bitter, twisted old crone.

Unfortunately they were passing St Jude's right as the churchgoers were spilling out into the grounds and Ritchie's carriage was being prepared to take him on his final journey. Kim sobbed all the way to Frothy's Coffee, where Todd deposited her at a table in the corner and grabbed a waitress so he could order a pot of tea, a mixed fruit juice for his little girl - 'Beth and Emma will be along in a minute' - plus 'a large cappuccino for this beautiful lady.'

It seemed odd to be sitting there with one of her former idols, conversing over their hot drinks, but without the smug, elated feeling she would have experienced in her youth. Once upon a time she would have almost fainted with excitement at the prospect of sharing the same table as a member of *Show Me Yours* but now she felt nothing other than relief that she was able to talk to a former colleague of Ritchie's on the day of his funeral, to allow him to comfort her and no doubt reminisce about the past.

'Hey, do you remember when Ritchie tripped up in those stupid heeled boots of his – the ones he insisted on wearing on stage every night for the *Dad Dancing* Tour - and nearly landed on those poor unsuspecting women in the front row? The look on his face as he clung on to the stage for dear life, desperately trying to look cool!'

Kim appreciated Todd's attempts at cheering her up and smiled as she recalled the gig in question.

'I remember him waiting for one of you to help him up but neither you nor Ady could do it because you were rolling about laughing, leaving good old Marty to save the day! And what about that time when that slightly unhinged girl from Brighton with the neon hair leapt on him when he came out of the stage door and he thought she had a gun but it was a plastic walking stick filled with sweets!'

'Ha-ha, god yes, I forgot about that. He nearly wet his pants when he thought it was loaded with bullets rather than smarties! Aah…those were the days eh Kim?'

'Yes, they were. I have to remind myself of the good times rather than the bad. Oh Todd…how did it all come to this? One minute you were five young guys - fabulous musicians with the looks and the ambition and you were riding high at the top of the charts and selling out huge venues and nothing could touch you…and it seems like only the next minute and the band is no more, Bren has more issues than you can shake a stick at, Ady's bogged off to Ibiza and Ritchie's dead and soon to be buried. I just can't believe how it's all turned out. And I don't think I'll ever get over the shock of Ritchie's passing…'

'Me neither Kim, me neither. I know we had our 'artistic' differences – namely I'm normal and he was a wanker – but I'm gutted he's gone. Still sad his life is already over. If someone had said two weeks ago that I would be at a funeral of a band member today, I would have put money on it being Bren's.' Even Todd, man of the perma-grin and the most positive of people, looked tearful as he considered the health and deterioration of his bandmate.

'He's that bad? I gathered from Callie earlier on that he isn't in a particularly good place.'

'He's on his way out Kim, not long for the world. He's been in and out of rehab so many bloody times and dodged a bullet more than once…but his body's shutting down and he's given up all hope. His demons have beaten him rather than the other way round and it's so distressing to see…oh god, I'm so sorry – I didn't mean to make you cry again…'

She hadn't realised she was. Dabbing at her face with one of the napkins from the table, she tried to take it all in. 'Poor, poor Bren. I always really liked him and of course he was so talented in his field…he could have had such a great future…'

'He was a top guy…brilliant drummer, brilliant ally, brilliant friend. But he's the textbook example of what drugs do to you – they should circulate his Before and After pictures in every school in every town and honestly, no one would touch the bloody stuff. He looks shocking now and he's penniless and would be homeless if Barry hadn't let him bunk down in his London studio flat – although he probably regrets that generous gesture because I think Bren sold everything in there that wasn't nailed down – and yet Callie is there for him and has never stopped loving him and will continue to do so long after he's left this earth…'

'If only they could have all settled down together and become a proper family…'

'He'd have been a great dad, you know, if he could have overcome his addictions. He does love Callie, although he hid it well by hooking up with some fairly dubious women while the band were away on tour.'

'He wasn't the only one though was he? Ritchie bedded half of Europe in his quest to become the next Hugh Heffner. I just feel sorry for his wife, finding out exactly what her so-called loving husband had been up to on the sly.'

'She knew Kim. About the one-night stands. It was agreed between them very early on that she would turn a blind eye to his fooling around while he was away on tour – seeing as he couldn't keep it in his pants. I think she realised she'd be on to a loser if she insisted he remain faithful and thought that giving him some leeway would be the only way to keep him.'

'NOoooo! How could she do that? How could she give her husband the green light to sleep with other women and then allow him to return to her bed afterwards?'

'She made him promise that he would always practise safe sex and that it would be meaningless. As long as there were no feelings involved and each liaison was a total one-off, well she accepted that Ritchie was Ritchie and she didn't want to risk losing him altogether. There was one condition though. If he ever started to develop feelings for anyone else then he'd better not sleep with them and he'd need to walk away – fast!'

'Has the woman no self-respect? I find that whole agreement abhorrent. Presumably she liked the money rolling in and the lifestyle that came with being hitched to someone famous.'

'There was probably an aspect of that...but she's a peculiar woman, in my humble opinion. And she's not really into all the partying and the glamour side of fame. She loved her huge house and her horses and she set up a riding school and invested in property...so I don't think she was too bothered about being seen on Ritchie's arm at any celebrity events. When all romantic relationships were banned, she was quite happy to remain in the background doing her own thing...'

'...and when the rules were relaxed and girlfriends and partners were finally accepted, she was content to continue as she was, which gave Ritchie the opportunity to shag around and lead me on, insistent he'd be fired if we went public, cleverly keeping me tucked away as his grubby little secret. What a naïve little numbty I was...'

'Kim, you were different. You were his downfall. There were plenty of willing women who were up for a session of steamy sex with a good-looking pop idol but none of them meant anything to him other than satisfying his needs for the night. When you came on the scene, everything changed and I genuinely believe he got in deeper than he ever intended to...'

'I just don't understand the man though. To begin with it was only flirting and the odd kiss and fumble – there *was* no sex between us and I started doubting whether he even liked me!'

'Oh he certainly did...and I'm not sure what all that was about...but I'd hazard a guess that he was aware he cared more than he should and was trying to keep his promise to his wife – no sex if any feelings were starting to come into play. Eventually he couldn't resist and had to have you. We were all warned to keep our mouths shut to swerve any scandal but to be honest, we presumed and *hoped* it would fizzle out as quickly as it had started – for your sake more than anything – and then no one would get hurt. But it went on and on and suddenly you were in deep and how could we tell you by then? We begged him to finish it...and he almost did on a couple of occasions, but then there you were again, sharing his dressing rooms and hotel suites. You were so lovely and genuine and I hated him for stringing you along and treating you like shit...and although I was never Kissy's biggest fan

337

and she'd kind of brought it upon herself with her stupid relaxed attitude to Ritchie's sordid sexual appetite, she didn't deserve this.'

'Hang on…who the heck is this 'Kissy' and what the hell kind of stupid name is that? I thought his wife was called Michelle?'

'Oh yeah, she is, but her maiden name before she married Dickhead was *Kisielewski* or something similar – I think it's Polish – and no one at school could say it so they called her 'Kissy' then and it stuck. Even Ritchie called her 'Kissy' rather than 'Michelle'. What? Oh no – what have I said? Please don't upset yourself again…'

'I'm such an idiot Todd! Ritchie's dedication on the band's last album: *'This is for K…for her patience and support and love…always Your Ritchie xx'*

'I thought it was for me Todd! I actually believed he'd dedicated his work on the album to me, saying things in that short message that he could never articulate when we were together. He never said I love you, you see…and *I* did, of course, so it was the nearest I got to having my feelings reciprocated. I'm just so fucking thick! All this time, I assumed he'd penned that message for me and it was the only solid thing I could take away from my on-off relationship with him. It was the only time he'd publicly acknowledged I existed…and all along it was intended for someone else. Those words weren't mine – they belonged to his wife!'

Kim felt sick and conned and she flushed crimson with embarrassment, remembering how her heart had soared when she'd first read those words. She cringed at her own stupidity, believing it was his way of saying that she was so much more to him than sex on tap.

'Listen Kim, I think those words *were* for you. But they were also meant for Kissy too. He thought he had it covered, keeping both of you happy, neither of you any the wiser. Don't feel silly for believing him – in his own weird way, I think he did have strong feelings for you but he could never admit that, no way. Because that would be another line crossed…'

'He thought he was so frigging smart and luck was on his side with the letter 'K'. Oh god, and now I'm crying again. How can I be so upset over someone I've barely allowed myself to think about over the last twenty years? I stopped loving him, I started loving someone else and I moved on! God damn you Ritchie Clarke for rendering me a snivelling mess again! Oh Todd, I don't love him anymore so why am I in bits?'

'Because all this is stirring up memories of how you *did* feel, how you *did* love him, how you *did* suffer. It's transporting you back to that period of your life whether you like it or not.'

Kim drained the last dregs of coffee out of her cup and then fiddled around with the spoon and individually wrapped biscuit, purely for something to keep her hands occupied in the absence of having Ritchie's neck to wring.

Todd was quiet for a moment, allowing her to take time to contemplate and digest this latest discovery.

'You know what it is, Todd? I think this finality is really getting to me because – and I know this will sound ridiculous, bearing in mind I hadn't set eyes on Ritchie for over twenty years and didn't intend ever seeing him again – he never said sorry. When he was finally busted and I was raging and breaking my heart right in front of him, it didn't occur to him to apologise. He didn't say sorry then and he didn't say sorry afterwards. You would think that with age comes maturity and at some point during the last two decades his conscience might have caught up with him and made him realise what a shit he had been to me, prompting an apology of sorts. But no – nothing. And now there never will be. And that really twists the knife again – that knife I thought I'd pulled out and discarded, enabling the wound to heal over. Do you see what I mean?'

'For what it's worth, I don't think I ever heard him say sorry in his life – he didn't seem to have it in him. He wasn't always such a bastard though. When I was first met him he was quieter, less sure of himself, and much kinder…but that was before the shiny shirts and the colossal ego took over. He became so self-obsessed, he really thought it was perfectly acceptable to walk all over people, you and me included.'

'The bloody wife gave him carte blanche though didn't she – ignoring all his indiscretions…'

'And the press hyped him up and the crowds of screaming women put him on a pedestal…and he thought he was invincible and could rip up the rule book. Even though he was smitten with you Kim, he wanted total control over you…expecting you to lie down and roll over every time he snapped his fingers, always keeping you just where he wanted you with his veiled threats that it would all be over if you spoke up or wanted more of him - even treating you like a complete stranger whenever Kissy was around…'

'Wait! Whoaaaah…rewind please! What do you mean when she was around? I never saw her at any gigs or personal appearances…'

'Granted, she didn't often grace us with her presence but occasionally she paid him a flying visit while we were on tour, probably to check up on him. She'd arrive at a gig with a friend of hers and they'd slip in front of house or backstage once the show had started, often leaving before the end or after the tour bus had departed. And occasionally she'd accompany Carmel, our backing singer – remember her? They'd become really pally over a bottle of wine after a gig in Germany. Nobody ever put two and two together and so Kissy was free to pop backstage to see Ritchie without any of the fans cottoning on.'

'Oh Christ, I remember that 'friend' of Carmel's – she nearly always wore sunglasses and seemed really shy – now I know why!'

'And now you know why he avoided you sometimes…'

'Of course! He couldn't talk to me when she was around and taking me backstage or checking us into a hotel room was completely out of the question. And not forgetting those times when he kicked off with me over absolutely nothing and stormed out of our hotel room – he was probably heading to a quiet place to place a phone call to his sodding wife! It's all making sense now. But at the time I thought I was going mad. I couldn't understand how he could be fawning all over me one day, making me feel like I was the only woman alive and then the next day I had ceased to exist for him. I used to think it was me you know – that I'd done something wrong. Was it because of anything I'd said? Had I gotten too fat? Was I too ugly? There were so many pretty girls surrounding him that it was possible he'd decided he fancied someone else more. Or, god forbid, was it because I was rubbish in bed? I tortured myself with these thoughts while all the while he was playing at being the loving husband, knowing he'd easily be able to pick up where he left off with gullible old Kim, as soon as the wife was out of the picture. And whenever I tried to take him to task about his appalling behaviour he invariably turned it around to make me sound like a nagging old shrew and fed me the same heap of bullshit about having to keep our relationship secret, constantly reminding me that he was under a mountain of pressure and insisting that I should be more sympathetic to his predicament. Fucking narcissist.'

'I'm sorry Kim but you were always too good for him. Okay, so he was a handsome guy and he was famous and successful and he could charm the knickers off a nun…but *you* were absolutely gorgeous – you still are, but don't tell the wife – and you knocked spots off all the other girls who hung around desperately trying to impress Ritchie.'

'You've got to be kidding me! Take those Irish girls for example…or those three vile bints that Sally-Anne went on to knock about with after she cut me off. As much as it pains me to say it, they were all absolutely stunning.'

'I'm not sure if I remember the Irish women but I do recall those girls who your ex-mate took up with – a couple of them were attractive but by god, they knew it, and that's a very *unattractive* quality. I can't believe I'm about to admit this, because it's going to make us all sound like real sexist pigs, but there were often polls circulating amongst the band and crew during the long hours we spent out on the road. You know the sort - Most Fanciable Fan, Most Shaggable Stalker, Most Rideable Rear…that kind of thing. Not our finest hour. When Beth found out she said we were all disgusting perverts and deserved to be horse whipped, but it was in an age before political correctness and it all helped keep the boredom at bay when we were couped up on that tour bus, bored out of our skulls. However, returning to my original point – on the few occasions I agreed to participate, you were always top of every single one of my lists.'

'Aw Todd that's so sweet. Perhaps I should have paid more attention to the loveliest guy in the band rather than swooping in on the typical bad boy…'

'Oh who are you kidding? You only ever had eyes for Ritchie!'

'Unfortunately, that's true. No one else ever got a look in because I was completely besotted with him…'

'Hey! You weren't talking about those bloody shameful lists you pervos used to make up on tour were you? You set of dirty drivelling deviants!' Todd's lady laughed as she approached the table with their daughter and Kim blushed again as she realised his *wife* (platinum wedding band proudly displayed alongside an elegant solitaire diamond engagement ring) had probably caught the latter part of the subject that was up for discussion. Fortunately, both Beth and Todd seemed completely unfazed, as she dropped a kiss onto the top of his head and wrestled their little girl onto a plastic seat, Todd's face positively lighting up at the sight of them both. He gave a rue smile and shook his head in mock shame.

'Sorry, but Ady and the female backing singers gave all males in the vicinity exactly the same treatment…not that it makes it right I would add, before my good lady here plants one on me!' She playfully swiped at him and it warmed Kim's heart to witness their love up close. What a delightful family unit.

'Anyway,' Beth continued, attempting to unbutton her daughter's coat as the pretty little imp wriggled like she had ants in her pants, 'Todd was just telling you how you were top of his lists...weren't you the lucky one?'

Smiling at this woman's generosity and benevolence towards a fellow female, Kim nodded and then forced herself to ask, 'Was I ever top of any of Ritchie's lists?' She felt bad for making this kind man uncomfortable and his momentary pause actually answered her question.

'I wasn't was I? For God's sake.'

'There's no doubt you were his number one Kim and that you meant more to him than any other fan ever could, but he probably wanted to deflect attention – to distance himself from his involvement with you. Plus, he probably couldn't resist playing the Big Man in front of the crew, pretending to fancy the more obvious choices who all the others were lusting after...'

Ritchie really had took the piss out of her, monumentally more than even she had ever suspected. It was only a stupid poll for Christ's sake...they were only fooling around and most of the backstage lads were aware of their clandestine relationship...and yet he still hadn't even afforded her any kind of credit. Wanker.

'I'm sorry he hurt you Kim. After you told him where to stick it that night – and kudos to you for doing so once you discovered the truth – he was really cut up that you were gone but received zero sympathy from anyone backstage. In fact, we were all furious about the way he'd treated you and dropped you like a stone to save his own skin. We all saw how devastated you were and something in me snapped. Remember the gouge above his eye and all the other bruising? Well I couldn't handle his lack of remorse and the way he'd simply cut you off...and after a couple of beers post-gig one night I flew at him and punched him in the face, determined to give him a real good hiding...'

'Oh god, that was *your* doing? Well, good on you because he bloody deserved it! I hope you beat him to a pulp?'

'Naw, he pasted me after I'd thrown the first punch, but it was worth it. We had to cancel those festivals as a result of the battling though. We could hardly perform up on stage to the best of our ability when we were all raging inside and half of us looked like we'd been in a tram smash. After that it all went downhill because we were barely speaking to Ritchie and no one's heart was in it. It was only a matter of time before we split.'

'Despite everything, I still thought it was a crying shame that the band disappeared from the scene so quietly and without any big send-off - that just didn't seem right.'

'I suppose not, but we were relieved when the ending came. And let's face it, we achieved more than most bands ever set out to – chart success, awards and accolades, a dedicated fan base and financial security – apart from Bren of course, who ended up without a pot to piss in. It was time to hand over to fresh talent - emerging bands and singers who would appeal to the youth of the day. Tastes change and I'm afraid we fell out of fashion. It happens.'

'Did you ever keep in touch with any of the boys?'

'Oh god, yes – I speak to Marty all of the time. He teaches music now to underprivileged kids and he's also ambassador for a few worthy charities. And I've caught up with Ady, both in London and on Ibiza. Who would have thought that introspective little soul would go on to be so successful in his own right? The DJ side of it really took off and he's doing something he loves.'

'And you see Bren from time to time?'

'Yes, I do. But his time's running out, so I try to drop by when I can but he's unrecognisable now from the man he once was and I'm not sure he wants to see any of us, the state he's in.'

'Oh god, I don't like to think of him like that. It's tragic. I don't suppose you kept in touch with Ritchie then?'

'Nope. We did once bump into each other at a charity event in Shropshire. He was on his best behaviour and we were civil to each other but there was no hope of us ever becoming the best of mates, even though by rights we should have been wiser, because we were older. Kissy was actually with him once, which might have been why he curtailed his wandering eye – who knows? He still looked the same though – skin tight jeans and flashy shirts. Groomed to perfection and not a hair out of place.'

That accurate description struck a chord with Kim. Only two years previously she'd been innocently watching a chunk of Friday night TV with her boys, while Adam had escaped for a pint with his dad, when Ritchie had popped up, without warning, as one of those floating heads on a 1980s flashback music segment, discussing a few of the band's biggest hits. Kim was shocked but switching over wasn't an option as Matty had commandeered the remote and both he and Will were seemingly enthralled.

After an initial 'Ey up, mother's teenage crush is here again,' the boys kept schtum while Kim's traitorous eyes remained glued to the screen, mesmerised by the image of the man she'd once loved. He hadn't changed at all. Same jet black hair (surely he must have a sprinkling of greys underneath that immaculately styled barnet). Same fetching green eyes, which sparkled under the studio lights. Same dress sense – black drainpipe jeans with expensive cream silk shirt hanging loosely over the top, unbuttoned to the waist of course. Same golden tan. Same megawatt smile. Same cheeky quips.

Same, same, same.

There was no denying he was looking good for his age and could still bring a grown woman to her knees.

Except her – not now, not ever again.

On closer inspection, absolutely everything about him was the same but how could that be? Why hadn't he changed at all since the days of the band? He actually looked like someone who was trying too hard to hold on to his youth - someone who desperately wanted to pretend he was still a young man in his twenties.

That was quite sad.

'Likes a bit of botox, old Ritchie,' laughed Will. Kim had instantly thought how Ritchie would have hated his appearance being criticised so viciously, particularly by a good-looking, younger lad who still had the rest of his life ahead of him. He'd probably still classed himself as a relatively young man rather than middle-aged. Ritchie was far too vain to grow old gracefully like his peers.

Shaking herself back into the present, Kim choked back a sob as it struck her that he would never grow old. Every so often she would be reminded that he was dead and it was as shocking each time as when she'd first heard the news.

'Oh Todd, even though he was a complete and utter bastard, I find it heartbreaking that he's gone. I shouldn't care one way or the other and yet I do because he's central to so many of my memories from that era of my life. No matter what happens, and though I don't often re-visit them, those memories will always be there – the music, the tours, the stage doors, the parties, the band, the laughter, the tears…the love.'

'We *did* have some good times Kim, didn't we? I know you viewed it from a different perspective, but in the beginning we had an absolute blast. When I was first introduced to Ritchie he was a pretty decent guy then and he welcomed me into the band along with Marty and Bren, and we picked up Ady along the way. Sometimes it seemed like we'd never be rewarded with that elusive recording contract and there were moments when we all questioned whether we were good enough to make it - whether luck would be on our side. We badgered anybody and everybody and worked like trojans, up and down the country, gigs in the worst shitty bars and clubs, until we mastered our craft and the word spread. Once we had the management they whipped up a storm about us and before we knew it, we'd been styled and preened and were on prime time television. The fan base swelled, the record sales went through the roof, and hey presto, we were on top of the world, on the cover of every magazine, on every radio station, sold out gigs throughout the UK and beyond. The first contract we signed was rubbish – the management basically fleeced us and we earned roughly enough to live on from week to week. But we learned fast, fired those greedy bastards, and found ourselves a fair and fresh record label…and soon we were raking it in and everyone wanted a piece of us. The sales were phenomenal and the gigs were mental and mobbed. We loved every second of it, even when we were knackered and ill and snappy with each other. Even when we missed our families and craved a normal life where we could nip into Marks and Spencer's for undies without being surrounded by hordes of chanting girls, escaping by the skin of our teeth. Even when the sales dipped and the crowds thinned a little, we still lapped up the success and admiration and wondered how we got to be such lucky devils when so many bands never even made it off the starting blocks.'

'It was insane wasn't it? I'll never forget those moments in the theatres when the lights dimmed and the hysteria was building, before you all burst onto the stage and we were deafened by the screaming. And the night I first saw you all – my heroes – off-stage and up close in the flesh in Croydon and I thought I would literally pass out with nerves and excitement. At first I loved swilling around in the pool of fans and seeing all the same old familiar faces at every gig. It felt like I was a member of an exclusive club and it was such a relief to mix with like-minded people who understood my passion for the band. I lived for *Show Me Yours* and in those days it all brought me so much joy…'

'They were brilliant times, amazing years…and *my* exclusive little club was the band itself. Only the other four guys knew how it really was for us – nobody else could ever understand how mad and wild and wonderful it was because nobody else was in our bubble and shared our experiences. And even though there were times when we cried and raged and forgot exactly what we were doing it all for – times when you yourself were no doubt pissed off for one reason or another, perhaps because of all the travelling and having to put up with the likes of that Sally-Anne day in day out - I still think if we were offered the opportunity to go back and do it all again, we would, in a heartbeat…wouldn't we?'

It was something she'd had years to reflect on. Kim sighed, deciding honesty was the best policy in this instance.

'To be completely truthful, no. I don't think I would go back and do it all again. Sure, the gigs were brilliant and meeting you guys was a dream come true…and I was always on such a high when there was a new single or album out to be purchased or I received a SMY gift for birthday or Christmas. I was obviously beside myself whenever you were all on TV or on the radio. I loved the music and the image…and of course the lead singer. In the early days when Ritchie was charming and charismatic and singled me out for attention, I was on Cloud 9, living my best life. And there was no feeling like it.

'But of course it was all just an illusion he had created…and there were more downs than ups for me. It seemed like I was always waiting - for the next gig…for the next single…for Ritchie to get in touch or throw me a lifeline in the form of a kiss or a smile. There was constant stress - scrambling around for money to pay for tickets and accommodation, desperately trying to wangle the time off work to actually be at the gigs, rising tensions within my family because of my apparently unhealthy obsession. It all cast a shadow over the thrill of seeing the band, getting to know you and becoming involved with Ritchie. I simply couldn't see it back then.'

Todd reached out to stroke his daughter's fine, silky hair and paused to consider his response.

'I did wonder from time to time how on earth you all managed to follow us as much as you did,' he replied. 'Please don't think it went unnoticed or unappreciated…but I suppose I could never have understood what it was like to be in your position.'

'Oh there were times when it was unbelievably fabulous, but there were also times when it was utterly miserable. Don't get me wrong, there were some nice people who followed the band around but the friendships I formed weren't real. I trusted all the wrong people and had no idea that I was being ridiculed and laughed at behind my back. I am of course referring to one little nightmare in particular.'

'Yes, she was a class act that Sally-Anne. I think she tried to bed every one of us at some point in the band's history – and she was bloody persistent as well. Marty once discovered her in his hotel suite after he'd stepped out of the bath. She nearly gave him a coronary.'

'*Marty!* Him of all people, when she knew he was married to the love of his life and never even so much as glanced at another woman.'

'She has no shame. I heard she also threw herself at every one of the crew, although there were few takers. She basically came on to anyone who was in any way tenuously connected to the band. I hate the name 'Groupie' but…'

'If the condom fits, wear it…'

'Mmm…quite. You're definitely better off without a friend like her.'

'That occurred to me on several occasions, when she took great pleasure in treating me with disdain and I was so unhappy in her company. So…away from home, no true friends, rapidly running out of money and Ritchie giving me the runaround. In addition, it was absolutely gutting to have hung around shivering in the cold for five or six hours only to have you all arrive and ushered in without stopping to even sign a single autograph…'

'Bloody hell, I feel terrible now. I mean, we often didn't have any say in it, but still…'

'Don't feel terrible, Todd. YOU were always smiley and kind and tried to make time for the fans when you could, whereas Ritchie's moods changed like the weather. I was constantly berating myself for not being good enough for him, for making him behave like that, for not being pretty enough, thin enough, exciting enough for him to want me and me alone, always.'

'He was a twat, god rest his soul,' soothed Beth, pushing another coffee towards Kim. She hadn't even noticed that a second round of drinks had been ordered. Thankfully their little girl was completely oblivious to the foul language and dubious subject matter, immersed as she was in a colouring book with pencils provided by the cheery waitress.

'He was, but I actually though he was MY twat for a while and consequently put up with all of his shit because I loved him, but ultimately that love made me miserable. It was a hard time and I put myself through a lot for the sake of him.'

Kim sipped the coffee, realised it needed sugar, and then added two sachets of demerara, stirring it in vigorously as she continued to reflect.

'It wasn't only the Ritchie fling. When I look back, I feel like I missed out on so much. The girls I knew from school were flying off to Benidorm or Majorca and partying their holidays away, whilst I was sitting on grotty trains or staking out stage doors, and even though I travelled all around the UK, from Blackpool to Brighton and everywhere in between, I never actually *saw* anywhere other than theatres and often substandard bed and breakfasts...'

'I totally get it. We often commented that although we'd travelled extensively all over Europe, we'd seen nothing of it - there'd been virtually no downtime to explore and see the sights...'

'After it went pear-shaped with Ritchie, I had a bloody good go at catching up with the clubbing and drinking, but it couldn't make up for the years I'd missed out on. Whilst all my friends had been getting pissed at each other's houses before heading off en masse to the local dives to dance the night away, I'd been stuck at home, lonely, miserable and skint. There were countless 18ths, 21sts, engagements and weddings when I wasn't around and my best friend actually binned me off from being her bridesmaid because I picked a *Show Me Yours* gig over her hen night. That was truly awful. I gave up so much to follow the band, Todd and it was both physically and emotionally exhausting.'

'Mum said something similar – that you had to be ridiculously dedicated to keep up with it all and have nothing much else in your life, because the drain on time and expenses was immense,' Beth chipped in. 'Her car packed up one year, meaning she missed most of the shows on the next tour and she was absolutely gutted.'

Kim frowned and mentally scratched her head. She was puzzled at Beth's comments and had no idea who she was referring to.

'You do know my mum by the way,' Beth added whilst deftly mopping up a pool of spilled blackcurrant juice with a collection of napkins and tissues.

'I don't think I do…'

'Trust me, you do. Mum was a fan as well, believe it or not! God knows how many gigs she went to but it was a hell of a lot. Her name's Hannah and the funny thing is that she was a massive Todd fan back in the good old days…'

'Shut the front door! *I* knew Hannah! Kindly curly haired lady who never went anywhere without her Todd t-shirt and…oh my god, you're her little girl aren't you?'

'Bet you didn't recognise me without my pigtails,' Beth smiled.

'I can't believe it! The gorgeous little thing who accompanied Hannah to every gig and who used to sing along and dance by the stage! I honestly had no idea Todd was even married because I've not really been following the lives of any of the band members since that final tour in the nineties. Of course! Elizabeth…*Beth*…you look exactly like your mum – minus the Todd t-shirt but with the real thing by your side instead! Oh this is brilliant!'

Turning to address Todd, she chuckled. 'I can't believe Hannah's your mother-in-law! And that you not only fell for her daughter but married her..,'

'Well, I only fell for her after she'd grown up and I hadn't seen her for years, let's make that clear before I end up sounding like some kind of twisted pervert! After the band split, I retreated from the limelight for a while, during which time I travelled around, pitching in with some charity work here and there. To be honest, it was bloody joyous to have a little privacy again. Eventually, I missed the music though and decided to dip my toe into the water again, writing new material for a couple of the boybands. I also agreed to a few personal appearances around the UK…and at one such gig when I was losing the will to live because of the rather lacklustre audience response, this stunning brunette babe approached the stage and our eyes met and I thought *Who the hell is that?* She was in conversation with Barry in the wings when I came off stage, although he made a hasty retreat after he'd introduced us…and from that moment on I was off the market. I knew from the second I saw Beth that I wanted to marry her. It was only after we'd been chatting for half an hour that I discovered who her mum was. Hannah was temporarily housebound as she'd recently had a knee operation, so we decided to surprise her. When Beth brought me home that evening we gave her poor mother the shock of her life!'

349

'Ha-ha, I would have loved to have seen her face when you walked in! Ah, lovely Hannah. I imagine she was overjoyed when you and Beth started to become serious and…oh my word…that means she's actually grandmother to your *daughter* as well – what a result!'

They laughed together, as one, and Kim secretly thought to herself: *I bet Sally-Anne was FURIOUS when she found out!* All her efforts to infiltrate the band's inner circle and Hannah had done it without even trying – REALLY done it – effortlessly blindsiding everyone.

'Mum still talks about those halcyon days when she used to follow the band and tells me how they rocked some of the best venues around the UK. She remembers you of course.'

Kim could feel the blush that stained her cheeks and coloured her chest too. The group of fans she'd been part of hadn't really had anything to do with Hannah and her daughter – like Geraldine, she'd always been on the outside, in her case almost invisible because of her commitment to her child and lack of fashion sense. She probably hadn't had the funds to splash out on new clothes and accessories, never mind all the latest make-up, hair products and girly crap they'd all deemed to be essential. She'd had a daughter to provide for, tickets to purchase and petrol to put in her car.

'Please say hi to your mum for me Beth. She was – and no doubt still is – a really lovely lady and was always very sweet to me. I'll be honest though – I didn't really know Hannah that well as amongst the many, many appalling decisions I made back then, I chose to be friends with people who I should have avoided at all costs. Sally-Anne may have been the same age as me but we were worlds apart when it came down to honesty, loyalty and morals…and the other girls we generally chatted to weren't much better. I'm embarrassed to say, I feel we could've have been much friendlier towards your mum and included her within our circle.'

'It's okay, mum knew exactly what was going down at the time. She said Sally-Anne in particular was very bad news and that there was a contingent who continually stabbed each other in the back and ran each other down…yet were all smiles to each other's faces. She actually liked you and thought you were a decent girl, but she worried about what you were getting yourself into...'

'She's too kind…and I should have been kinder. It made me selfish – worshipping the band, loving Ritchie. That life was my whole world. I hurt my parents, missed out on precious time with my beloved gran in her last weeks, alienated my brother for many years, let down decent employers and work colleagues, lost friendships I can never retrieve and I almost destroyed my relationship with my best mate. Worst of all...I twice broke the heart of the remarkable man who eventually became my husband. Thank god I finally came to my senses and we realised we couldn't live without each other...'

'I'm so relieved that your experience with Ritchie didn't damage you to the extent that you wouldn't allow yourself to fall in love again. What's he like then, Mr Kim? Do you have any children?'

Todd seemed genuinely interested so Kim dug out a crumpled family photograph from the inside of her purse and felt her chest puff out involuntarily as she identified the three grinning faces squashed in alongside her own.

'That's my eldest lad, Matty, he's at college now and all the girls love him. And that cheeky blighter is Will, who is planning on being a full-time beach bum when he leaves school.'

'And I take it this sexy beast is your husband?' enquired Beth, licking her lips lasciviously in mock lust – as if she would ever look at anyone other than Todd!

'Yes, that's Adam – the most patient, popular, perfect man I know. How I managed to entice a corker like him, I'll never know, but entice him I did.'

'What a beautiful family.' Todd covered Kim's hands with both of his and said, 'I'm glad you found love again Kim. After everything you went through, you of all people deserved to be happy...and it warms my heart to know that you have a good man by your side. You do have him by your side don't you? You are still married? Still together? Only you looked so despondent just then when I was talking about him...'

'We're still married but I'm not sure we're still together, Todd. He...he said I'd always chosen Ritchie over him in the past – even though that god damn relationship was twenty bloody years ago – and that this would amount to the same, if I came here today. I tried to explain to him that it was important to me and simply something I had to do to facilitate closure, but he wouldn't have it. So I received a totally out-of-character ultimatum – to stay away, for his sake, or come to the funeral and face the consequences when I return home. This is too much for him, you see, in view of what's gone before, when I broke his heart not once but twice, because I was still in love with Ritchie. He can't understand why I would need to be here and thinks it's pointless, because it's not as if I can actually say goodbye to Ritchie now or extract any kind of remorse from him.'

'This wonderfully wise husband of yours does have a point though, doesn't he? Don't get me wrong, it's been a real pleasure to see you again, even under these dreadful circumstances, but I can kind of understand where Adam's coming from. If Beth had loved and almost been destroyed by some dickhead and all the world had known about it…and she'd twice failed to even notice cute little old me because of this egotistical prick…would I be happy for her to go off and mourn at his funeral, being comforted by the very people who'd stood by and witnessed her downfall? Would it make any difference if it had been one year or twenty years since the last time she saw him? The fact this person that she'd once loved with every tiny slither of her heart was still making her cry, *feel* and no doubt remember all the times they spent together – including the many, many x-rated ones – wouldn't that bother me? Wouldn't I feel absolutely devastated if I'd specifically asked her to stay away, *for me* but she'd ignored my request and gone anyway? If the man truly loves you, Kim and has done for most of his life then this will be killing him. There's probably also a dollop of good old-fashioned male pride that needs factoring in too – when your wife's former lover is a famous idolised popstar and you're just Mr Average who lives for his family, I'm sure it must be difficult to feel that you measure up.'

'But I love my husband, it's as simple as that. Yes, I'm here, today, at Ritchie's funeral, but it doesn't mean that I have any regrets, because my life with Adam has been nothing short of amazing. I'll admit I lost my rag when he basically forbade me to come here today but on reflection I can see why my decision was so important to him. He surely must know by now though that no one could ever compare to him, especially not someone with fewer morals than a scummy pimp.'

'He probably knows, but I think he might need you to re-affirm his beliefs, Kim. Despite the fact that you married him and have probably proved your love time and time again, more than likely he still questions why somebody like you, who snapped up one of the most fanciable males on the planet – allegedly – would want a man like him…'

'Oh god, then he's bloody stupid because he's a billion times more gorgeous than Ritchie ever was – inside and out – and although, of course, for a time I loved Ritchie, Adam has always been the one…the love of my life…'

Kim heard her own voice trailing off and had to stop herself from clamping her hand to her mouth. Suddenly she had clarity.

'Christ, I shouldn't be here. I need to see Adam. There's something I've never said to him that I think he needs to hear.'

Digging a ten pound note out of her purse, she tried to pass it to first Todd and then Beth but they each refused to take it.

'Put that away,' insisted Todd. 'If I can't buy you coffee after the money you've poured into the band's bank accounts over the years then that really is a poor show.'

'Thanks Todd. And Beth. You're both incredible people and so well-matched. I can see you growing old together, settled and content with your gorgeous girl.' The little one smiled shyly back at Kim and she thought, this child couldn't wish for better parents. This absolute darling will want for nothing, neither materially nor emotionally and will grow and blossom into a fine young woman.

'Well, before you depart, we have a bit of a world exclusive for you. Can we share our news with Kim, love – is that alright?'

Todd cocked his head to one side, completely deferring to his wife, and she nodded, her face beaming, her body language screaming out her off-the-scale happiness.

'Back in the day any one of us would have craved an exclusive in connection with any single band member! Go on then – spill the beans, before I have to love you and leave you...'

'Well....the exciting news is...that baby number two is incubating in that there belly as we speak! We're expecting a little boy in December...I'm going to have a son!'

'Oh Todd that's just the best news to hear and I'm so pleased for you both.' Kim hugged the pair of them in turn – real meaningful, tender hugs that she hoped conveyed how much she adored Todd and how fabulous she thought Beth was. They were also goodbye hugs, not See-You-Soon hugs or Until-We-Catch-Up-Again hugs. There was a definite sense of finality about them - to Kim anyway. She knew she wouldn't ever see this genuinely awesome couple again but she was okay with that. She was only glad that she'd had this time with them - that she'd met Beth and seen for herself that Todd would lead the best of lives with this beautiful woman and their children.

Kim's eyes were misty with unshed tears as she hung her bag over her shoulder and fastened the button on her tailored jacket.

'Wait, I'll take you to the station – if that's where you're going...' Todd was already grabbing his keys, but she didn't want to drag him away from his wife and child and she especially didn't relish another goodbye. The knowledge that she was walking away from one of her idols and not hanging around to spend every last second in their company, soaking up everything they said and desperately trying to sneak their teaspoon/napkin/biscuit wrapper into her handbag as a souvenir of this unbelievable episode, made her realise how far she had come, and she was immensely proud of herself.

'No, Todd, honestly it's okay. I know it sounds odd and I realise that Ritchie will be gone from there now and is headed for the grounds of his home where there will be a private burial on his own land...but I think I would like to take a walk past St Jude's now, to have a quiet moment and maybe bid one last farewell to him – if only in my head. And then I'll be heading up the road to the municipal buildings where there's apparently a taxi rank and I will be at the station in no time. You stay here and amuse your daughter – I think Beth needs a break!'

The little girl had dropped her sweet packet, scattering the colourful contents all over the floor – she was not impressed and currently sobbing into a stuffed panda.

'Yes, I'm sure. It's fine,' she reassured him. 'Sit yourself back down.'

'It's been truly wonderful to see you again Todd and to meet you too Beth and I hope everything goes okay with the new baby. I can see Todd riffing with him as soon as he's old enough to hold a guitar!'

'Oh he already has Emma strumming along to one or two of the band's old tunes. When I watch the pair of them together I feel like I'm back down the front at the old gigs, singing along with my mum.'

'Give her my love please...and Todd...please pass on my regards to Marty, Ady and Bren. I'll never forget them – or you – never.'

'Of course I will,' smiled Todd. 'And you're pretty unforgettable yourself. Now go and patch things up with that diamond of a husband of yours...and Kim...'

'Yes?'

'Be happy. Live well and be happy. No regrets eh?'

'Well, maybe a few…but I can't alter my history so it's time I looked ahead to the future.'

She took one last look at him and felt a strange personal pride at having witnessed a little of the transition from enthusiastic, sensitive boy to mature and confident man.

'Goodbye Todd – or Craig - Hargreaves…you amazing, fabulous man.'

With that, she turned and snatched open the door and was outside before she could change her mind and linger for a few moments longer. She'd already started to feel those fiercely secured tears begin to break free and plop down her face. She'd never liked goodbyes.

It seemed quicker walking back to St Jude's and she soon found herself standing the other side of the old stone wall, staring at the remaining groups of fans, still hovering in the church grounds, one or two of them crying on shoulders, others swapping numbers and promising to keep in touch.

Everything had gone smoothly for Ritchie…but that had always been the way for him.

No matter what he'd done, he'd always gotten off practically scot-free and she'd baulked at the unfairness of it all. That charmed life was at an end now though and all that was left to do was leave flowers or light a candle. The public would never be able to access the site of his grave and his wife would finally have him all to herself.

Kim was relieved that she didn't have to mix with the fans. No doubt most of them who'd been there today were lovely – Sally-Anne of course being the exception – but she wasn't part of that world any more.

'Goodbye Ritchie,' she whispered. 'Whoever you were, you weren't mine, but you were in my life and I was in yours. And I'm sorry that you left this earth prematurely but I hope you're still making music up there. So long Ritchie Joe Clarke.'

She allowed the tears to leak out for a moment, before taking a deep breath and attempting to regain her composure. It was done. He was gone. She had a life to live and a husband and children to love and treasure.

Pulling herself together, she pushed back her shoulders and began to make her way to the taxi rank, to begin her journey home. She'd only taken a few steps when she was stopped in her tracks.

A familiar black Mercedes loomed into view – familiar because it had obvious scratches on the paintwork where Kim had scraped it along the gatepost as she'd been returning home in a hurry. Picking up a pace, she almost ran to where her husband was waiting – hopefully not in a car loaded with her belongings – and prayed everything was alright with the boys.

He didn't step out of the car and Kim merely opened the passenger door and slipped in, her first words seeking reassurance: 'Is everything okay? Are the lads alright?'

Since the day her first son was born she'd accepted that this would always be the case. It was a mother thing (and probably actually a parent thing in general), this immediate terror that some horrific injury or illness may have befallen one of her children – or worse. Scant regard for herself whilst conjuring up nightmare scenarios for her offspring. Conversations with other new mothers at parent and toddler groups had confirmed that this was indeed universal and quite normal and that she was not in fact going crazy.

'Matty and Will are fine,' he assured her, without looking her way. He was still staring ahead, agitated, his hands tightly gripping the steering wheel, his body stiff and uncomfortable.

'When I saw you I thought you were here because there was a problem at home and something terrible had occurred...'

She was babbling because she was nervous. Had he driven all this way to end their marriage?

Silence.

He was clearly struggling to form his words. She had to allow him a moment.

Eventually: 'I thought I might have missed you – stuck in bloody traffic. I fully expected you to be on the train by the time I arrived. And I didn't want that. I couldn't bear to think of you miserable and bone-tired using public transport...'

'Bringing my car wasn't an option Adam. My mind may have wandered whilst I was at the wheel and you know me – I hate driving somewhere for an occasion without first carrying out twelve reconnaissance missions...'

The corner of his mouth began to twitch, signifying the merest hint of a smile – it was progress.

'So I came for you...because I love you Kim. I was mad at you but I still love you and I don't want you to think that has changed, no matter what I said.'

He still loved her! There was a chance for them. There was hope.

'I never doubted your love for one minute, and I hope you didn't doubt mine. And this wasn't some kind of pilgrimage to declare my eternal love for Ritchie – because there isn't a dot of that left in my heart for him now. But I *did* love him once and he, unfortunately, represents a sizeable chunk of my history. You know me - I didn't have loads of boyfriends. There weren't raucous Club 18 to 30 holidays in the sun, shagging teams of drunken dickheads. Neither did I stagger from one relationship to the next in my teens and early twenties like most girls of my age – with many of those relationships overlapping. With the exception of one or two meaningless snogs, an innocent holiday romance, that idiot whose face you kindly re-arranged and a short-lived boyfriend when I was about seventeen, there's only been Ritchie and you. And I realise he turned out to be a prize shit and I'll never know if I meant anything to him at all, but I can't erase him from my history. He's always going to be there, whether you like it or not. I've often wished I could re-take the eighties and nineties like some people re-sit an exam, but I can't. I'm stuck with what I've done and who I fell for and I guess that's made me who I am today. But just in case you need me to clarify...it's YOU who I love and have loved for most of my life – not Ritchie. But I still needed to be here today. Ritchie's been out of my life for so long, but I'm still incredibly sad that he died so young. I'm still *allowed* to feel sad for him; there's no crime in mourning someone from my past.'

'I get that a little more now, I really do. Not only have I had Nicky constantly in my ear like a bloody worm, giving me grief for how I've been treating you – and *she* bloody HATED

357

Ritchie – but I've also had your mother pecking my head over the last couple of days, bollocking me for not listening to you properly, ringing me up when I'm at work to shout at me for hurting you, instead of trying to understand. Jesus, I've been such a fool…'

He started to sob noisily then, her Adam, and she instantly reached out to take his hand.

'…and you know I would never hurt you on purpose, Kim. I've spent my whole life trying to protect you and make you happy and I would never do anything to deliberately cause you pain…but…'

'…but you were hurting too. And you were probably right – maybe I shouldn't have come today. Perhaps it should have been enough for me to remain at home, listening to a few of the band's hits, raising a glass in Ritchie's memory.'

'No. On reflection I think you did the right thing Kim. The last time you saw him you were mad at him and I think you needed to make your peace before he left this earth. Even *I've* stopped hating him now. The funeral cortege passed me as I turned the corner by the park and it felt surreal that this man who had represented such a threat to our happiness for so long – this womaniser who you had loved like no other – was lying still inside, sleeping forever. Even I sensed a degree of calmness wash over me and muttered a quick 'Rest in Peace' as the funeral cars crept up the hill and away from the village. I see now why you were desperate to be here. I know what he meant to you.'

'But I don't actually think you do, Adam. You think I loved him more than anything and that's honestly not true. I really believe there's different kinds of love. My love for Ritchie was one-sided and destructive and it ran alongside an unhealthy addiction to him. Always dancing to his tune, forever waiting around for him, constantly seeking *his* love but being forced to accept dribs and drabs of affection instead. When he was in my life, I couldn't function properly, I wasn't happy, I was unfulfilled and lonely…and often people would say I had a crush on Ritchie or referred to me as a groupie and I seriously wanted to choke them. You were one of the few people who ever referred to me as his girlfriend, and although that doesn't sound like a major issue, it was important to me because it made it real and valid, rather than just some kind of fantasy that was taking place in my head. My god, I remember the fallout from it like it was yesterday…how much he hurt me. But it was still love, for my part anyway.'

'I accept that, and right from the off I always understood that it was far more than simply a childish crush. I would never have said or even insinuated that you weren't actually involved with him ...'

'No, because you *did* understand me and you *did* listen to me. You watched and waited...you saw everything – the anguish, the tears, the fury, the occasional exhilarations and numerous tribulations, and the unreciprocated love.'

'I wanted to kill him when he hurt you,' Adam said quietly but Kim could almost feel the heat from the rage burning inside of him as he remembered the tears and the torment she'd had to endure, sucked in to that celebrity world and Ritchie's conveniently erratic lifestyle but then spat out when she'd served her purpose...until the next time.

'But he wasn't worth it...and I'm so glad you didn't. When it was over, I'll always remember how you didn't judge and you sensitively cared and comforted, putting aside your own pain for the sake of love.'

'I wanted you to feel for me what you had felt for him...'

'I'm bloody glad I didn't! My feelings for you bear no resemblance whatsoever to those I had for Ritchie. My heart literally bursts with the love I have for you and it's honest and pure and perfect and our amazing sons are a product of that love. We've had our tricky moments - of course we have - but there's never been any real lows with you Adam – just a colossal amount of highs. So high that I feel I could reach up and pluck the stars right out of the sky when I'm with you...and your belief in me and the confidence you instil in me, well it makes me feel like I can do anything and be anyone. When we fell for each other it was the first time I'd realised that love doesn't have to hurt or be shameful or leave you with more doubts and questions than commitment and answers.'

'Thank god you came to realise that – that you were worthy of so much more. I love you so much Kim and I was so scared of losing you to that world again, even if all that's left in it is the memory of that first love...'

'You'll never lose me Adam. I love you more than I can ever say. But when I was chatting with Todd and his wife in the coffee shop just then I...'

'Hang on - you were casually hanging out with one of the band you worshipped from the age of thirteen and you're not hyperventilating or screaming about it from the rooftops...'

His tears had subsided and he was teasing her now, as he often did. She adored that mischievous side of him.

'I know, it's strange isn't it that it doesn't feel like a celebrity-fan relationship any more. He's one of the good ones is Todd. If you didn't know who he was and the two of you struck up a conversation in a bar, you would seriously hit it off like a house on fire because you have many of the same qualities - he too is kind, thoughtful and generous to a fault. Anyway, today I discovered that he has a stunning wife now, a gorgeous little girl and a baby boy on the way and that all makes me so happy, because he's happy. However, my teenage self would have worked herself into a frenzy if she'd been sitting having coffee with one of *Show Me Yours* and would probably have pilfered everything including the cup after he'd finished, to keep as mementoes forever.'

'I'll be checking your handbag later, you know, just to make sure there's no manky spoon or saucer in there.'

'Ah, you know me so well.'

She reached out to caress his face, still damp from the tears he had shed. Her fingers traced his familiar strong jawline, feeling the bristly stubble beneath her touch. As much as he looked the bomb when he was impeccably turned out, clean shaven and dressed in crisp white shirt, expensive silk tie and freshly pressed suit, this was the Adam that made her want to drag him upstairs and rip his clothes off. The stubble and the ruffled up hair made Kim flutter deep inside, in a place he knew so well.

She longed to take him home and ravish him but there was other stuff that needed to be said first. She knew he was in desperate need of reassurance…and she never wanted him to doubt her again.

'Adam…something Todd said – after he'd agreed what a wonderful man I was married to – well, it resulted in a lightbulb moment for me. I realised there's one thing I've never said and I wonder if that's contributed to your insecurities. I've never deliberately *not* said it – I just don't think it's ever come up and I can't remember ever uttering the words.'

He shifted in his seat, turning at an angle so he could clearly see the face of the woman who was everything to him and yet again Kim was overcome by the depth of emotion she felt for this man.

Her hand had dropped to his thigh now and she absentmindedly scratched the fabric of his jeans with her thumb nail as she prepared to spill the words that she hoped would stay with him if ever he had any further wobbles or if a tiny speck of doubt manifested itself at any point in the future.

'You...YOU are the love of my life Adam. Sitting in that coffee house, chatting with Todd and Beth, I had a flashback to being pissed in a stairwell in a shitty little nightclub and you were listening to me rant on about Ritchie, calling him every name under the sun - sobbing my heart out, howling that he was the Love of My Life. Fast forward to a Sunday drive out to the country where again I banged on incessantly about Ritchie before sinking my head into my hands and telling you again that he was the Love of My Life and I couldn't survive without him. And there were other occasion when I cried out those words that must have slashed you to the core...and you loved me and you had to hear that.'

Adam was fighting back the tears again and Kim hated that she'd been ignorant to all of this until now – that she hadn't appreciated it could have affected him so profoundly and was a situation she needed to face head on.

She had to continue. She had to make this better.

'You see, Ritchie was the only love I'd ever known at that point – I had nothing and no one to compare it to. Of course at that stage he was the Love of My Life because I'd only had the one love. When I fell in love with you everything changed and I realised that whilst I'd experienced love, it had been toxic, on-the-surface love at a very young age – when I still had most of my life ahead of me. Our love – me and you, Adam – couldn't be more different. I look at you and to this day I think, wow, how did I get so lucky? So handsome, so sexy, so funny...and such a hardworking, honest, decent family man too. You gave me the gifts of our boys and you showed me what true love really is – with friendship, companionship and red hot sex! When you're not with me I'm lost, I'm incomplete...I'm numb. I need you to hear this and know this Adam...YOU are the love of my life. You always have been and you always will be and nobody – especially not Ritchie - could ever come close.'

Who was the first of them to lurch forward, it was hard to tell, but suddenly they were in each other's arms, crying and holding on so tightly, they were almost squeezing the life out of each other. Kim never wanted to let him go.

She imagined a book slamming shut in her head, the credits of a film rolling up, the last notes of a song fading out...and she sensed Ritchie leave her be then and the peace that replaced the grief she had felt was all-consuming.

No more Ritchie. No more *Show Me Yours*. No more tears or regrets.

She felt liberated – free to live a life filled with love, truths and respect.

Learning to live with the past. Embracing the future with the love of her life.

It was time.

*****

Antonia K. Lewis is a writer of contemporary women's fiction who loves pop music, the beach, occasional nights out and chocolate, but not necessarily in that order.

She lives in the North West of England with her husband, children and delinquent dogs, Ronnie and Reggie*

*not their real names

ALSO BY ANTONIA K. LEWIS

I Called Him David

Your David My Dave

Summer on Loulouthia

ACKNOWLEDGEMENTS

I'll keep this brief, but I'm grateful to everyone who has supported me thus far on this journey, recommended my books and shouted out words of encouragement when I've been flagging!

Special thanks must go to my husband, son and daughter. I do it all for you.

The last couple of years have been difficult but I'm overjoyed (and relieved!) that this novel has finally surfaced and hope everyone enjoys it. My own experience of following a band around the country did of course provide the inspiration for this novel, and one or two elements of it are loosely based on my adventures, but otherwise I can assure everybody that Kim's story is pure, unadulterated fiction!

Book number 5 is currently in progress so do check out my socials and website for developments and updates.

Thanks, from my heart.

Antonia x

Keep in touch with Antonia

facebook.com/AntoniaKLewis

twitter.com/AntoniaKLewis2

instagram.com/antoniaklewis

www.antoniaklewis.com

Printed in Great Britain
by Amazon